PRAISE

THE HUSTONS: "A Masterpiece." –James A. Michener. "Extensive and fascinating."–*New York Times*. "The best book of the year."–J.P. Donleavy. "Reads like a romantic, exciting and compelling novel."–*The Atlanta Journal-Constitution*.

YOU SHOW ME YOURS: "Profoundly entertaining and extremely insane!"–Diane Keaton

CONVERSATIONS WITH CAPOTE: "A wonderfully outrageous read. The most entertaining glitz of the season."–*The Denver Post*

CONVERSATIONS WITH BRANDO: "You got me!"–Marlon Brando

AL PACINO In Conversation with Lawrence Grobel: "Journalist Grobel, who literally wrote the book on interviewing, puts his talents on full display…giving the reader as much insight into interviewing style as into the legendary actor…. Part of the book's draw is witnessing the two become closer as the years go by…making for increasingly engaging and illuminating reading."—*Publisher's Weekly* Starred Review

CLIMBING HIGHER (for Montel Williams): "An absolutely riveting read."–*N. Y. Post*

THE ART OF THE INTERVIEW: Lessons from a Master of the Craft: "Grobel gives readers the equivalent of a master class in this thoroughly entertaining treatise on one of the toughest tasks in journalism.... An invaluable resource for aspiring journalists, the book also satisfies the voyeuristic desires of a celebrity obsessed culture by raising the curtain on the idiosyncratic demands of stars and by putting the reader in the interviewer's chair...."
–Publisher's Weekly

ABOVE THE LINE: CONVERSATIONS ABOUT THE MOVIES: "This book satisfies on every level. I ate my copy and feel very full."–Steve Martin. "A diverse and lively collection, the highest art of the interview."–Joyce Carol Oates. "There are passages in this book that will leave you stunned." –Dylan McDermott. "In his quiet, conversational way, Larry gets people to talk about things they'd rather not talk about."–Elmore Leonard

ENDANGERED SPECIES: Writers Talk About Their Craft, Their Visions, Their Lives: "As an interviewer Larry's all the things Joyce Carol Oates has said he is: prepared, adaptable, and graced with the intelligence needed to shoot the breeze and elicit intriguing responses from uncommonly gifted and often uncommonly suspicious subjects."–Robert Towne

Also by Lawrence Grobel

Novels
Begin Again Finnegan
The Black Eyes of Akbah (novella)
Commando Ex (novella)

Memoir
You Show Me Yours

Nonfiction
Conversations with Ava Gardner
"I Want You in My Movie!" The Making of Al Pacino's Wilde Salome
Signing In: 50 Celebrity Profiles
Yoga? No! Shmoga!
Icons: 15 Celebrity Profiles
Marilyn & Me (for Lawrence Schiller)
Al Pacino: In Conversation with Lawrence Grobel
Conversations with Robert Evans
The Art of the Interview: Lessons from a Master of the Craft
Climbing Higher (with Montel Williams)
Endangered Species: Writers Talk About Their Craft, Their Vision, Their Lives
Above the Line: Conversations About the Movies
Conversations with Michener
The Hustons
Conversations with Brando
Conversations with Capote

Poetry
Madonna Paints a Mustache & Other Celebrity Encounters

Catch a Fallen Star

■ ■ ■

Dan — Happy Birthday

Lawrence Grobel

40!

Lawrence Grobel

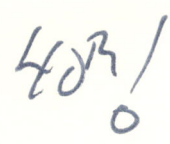

All rights reserved.

No part of this book may be reproduced in any form or by any electronic or mechanical means, including information storage and retrieval systems without written permission from the author except by a reviewer who may quote passages in a review.

This is a work of fiction. Names, characters, places and incidents are the products of the author's imagination or are used fictitiously. Any resemblance to actual events, locales, or persons, living or dead, is entirely coincidental.

Copyright 2014 by Lawrence Grobel

www.lawrencegrobel.com
Book cover design by Roberta Grobel Intrater
Back cover design: Paul Singer

ISBN-13: 9781500754617

1

The History Of Human Cannonballs

The 23-foot cannon lay on its truck bed at a 38-degree angle from its light gun carriage in the middle of the track as small clusters of young people began to gather. The cylinder was made of three-inch thick aluminum and measured three feet wide at its mouth. Inside the cannon was an eight-foot hollow piston, 16 inches in diameter–wide enough to stuff a full grown pig, a 100-pound lead ball, 130 sticks of dynamite, or a 6' 2" movie star.

The canned carnival music joined the giant rented Ferris wheel and the hustling of Mardi Gras barkers to attract passing motorists on Sunset Boulevard to this annual UCLA fundraiser. A camera crew from KTLA arrived to do a two-minute piece, with special focus on the cannon. By 1 P.M. two thousand people gathered on the track's inner grassy field to see if Layton Cross would really show. Two fraternities were giving even odds that he'd appear, but offering two-to-one that once he saw the cannon he wouldn't get into it, and three-to-one that if he did get in, he wouldn't allow himself to be shot out.

The reasoning was this: Cross was in need of a publicity boost, but getting himself blown out of a circus cannon was taking that need to an unnecessary extreme. The cannon worked like a slingshot and was fired by the same power that propelled a Polaris missile from a submarine. The piston gradually accelerated from 50 mph to 150 mph when it reached the mouth; this gradual propulsion was made possible by using compressed air at 225 pounds of pressure per square inch in order to propel a body 140 feet through the air. Once it was explained to him that there was an element of risk equivalent to being banged on the head with a sledgehammer, the frat men figured Layton would choose the public humiliation of backing down in front of a live crowd and a potential TV audience rather than put himself potentially in harm's way.

On the other hand, as TV reporter Mary White was prepared to tell her viewers, Layton Cross had done something each year to help raise money for UCLA causes over the last five years, and each time he succeeded in stepping further out on the edge of danger than the time before. Three years ago he had broken his leg jumping a motorcycle over a row of four parked buses. The following year he burned his feet walking over a bed of rocks heated to 130 degrees. Last year he had two ribs cracked when a six-ton truck rolled over his stomach. The cannon shot was Cross's own idea, as he tried to think of something that would bring in enough people to pay their $10 admission fee and witness this added attraction so that the Los Angeles chapter of Abused and Neglected

Children could benefit from his moment of courage and madness.

He had contacted two traveling circuses to find out if there were cannons wide enough to spit him out. After locating a member of the famed Zacchini family, he was assured that the truck-driven cannon could be at the field on the required day. Not to worry, he was told when he asked about the safety of the machine. In the whole history of human cannonballs, 32 had died because they didn't know what they were doing, but never a Zacchini. Reminding him that he was not a Zacchini, Cross was told that it didn't matter, he would be shot out of a Zacchini cannon. "You'll do fine, we will show you how, and when you are inside, just before you are sent into flight, you will do what all Zacchini's have done and you will succeed."

"What do you all do?" Layton had asked.

"You pray, of course."

When he arrived he was wearing an olive green suede jumpsuit and carried a UCLA football helmet complete with face guard. He smiled and nodded at those who had come to bear witness to his moment and thought of how many people might see him on the local news that evening. If he got hurt, he figured, he might even make the national news. If he got killed, well, it would certainly be one hell of an exit.

He walked slowly, stopping to sign autographs and reply good-naturedly to dimwitted remarks. An attractive coed stood on her toes to kiss his cheek. The girl she was with giggled and averted her eyes when Cross raised his eyebrows in her direction. The KTLA crew began its coverage as Mary White stuck a microphone in front of his face and asked him why he was doing this. Wouldn't it be easier to lend his name to a salad dressing or some popcorn like Paul Newman?

"Not really," Cross said seriously. "That involves a long-term commitment and an understanding of economics. This is a one-shot deal."

"No kidding," White said.

"Well, actually, I was sort of kidding," Layton said with a smile as broad as the hips of the fat lady who stood to one side listening. When he spotted her the fat lady swooned and said she was his biggest fan.

"I'm certain you are," Layton said, and to White he nodded, "She's not kidding."

When the crowd separated Layton approached the cannon and asked to speak to whoever was in charge. A thin-haired man with a mustache that covered his lips came forward and said he was the "trigger" who would fire the cannon. He walked the actor around the machine and showed him just how it worked, explaining that once he entered the inner piston it would be drawn deep into the cannon. Behind the piston was a small chamber into which air was forced by a compression pump. When he was ready, a remote-control button would be pushed and a small bomb would explode at the rear of the cannon sending smoke and flame out of the mouth as the piston lurched the length of the cannon, projecting him on his way. The bomb, Layton was told, was just for effect, it had nothing to do with the actual flight he would be taking towards the net, which stretched between two poles and measured 21 x 50 feet.

When Layton bent to whisper so that no one else might hear him, he asked the man very simply what might go wrong. He was reassured that all precautions had been taken and the worst that could happen was that the piston wouldn't work, in which case he could be stuck in there until they pulled him out. "What about missing the net?" Layton asked. True, that has happened, the man conceded, but only rarely. More likely was not doing the half-somersault to land on the back. If you don't land right you could get hurt. "How hurt?" Layton whispered. "Don't even think about it," the trigger said. "Just bones, ligaments. You'll heal." Then he told him that at the point of leaving the cannon the speed and the pressure would cause him to black out for a few seconds but that he would have plenty of time to recover before he hit the net. "Remember," the man said, "fear of failure is a hundred times stronger than the fear of death." Words Layton could easily relate to.

Confident the man with the walrus mustache knew what he was doing but less confident about himself, Layton waved his hand to the crowd, fit the asbestos mask the trigger had given him over his face, put on his helmet and got into the cannon.

"You sure you know what you're doing?" one fraternity member who had bet against Layton's going through with this asked.

"If I knew what I was doing," Cross replied, "I'd be making a movie right now instead of a fool of myself."

"Well, good luck."

Luck, Layton thought, had nothing to do with it. He thought of his three kids and two former wives and wondered what Amy would say if he wasn't there at three to take her to the airport. Even if he broke his back, her words wouldn't be kind.

2

Days Like This

"Jesus Christ!" was all Amy Cross said when she saw her former husband limp into her house. Before she could decide whether to rant or nurture, Andy came running into the living room looking for whatever Layton might have brought him. He, too, stopped short. Then he remembered.

"Was it the cannon? Didya get blown outta the cannon?"

"Oh," Amy remembered. "Mardi Gras."

"Whadya break this time, Dad?"

Layton wasn't sure. Everything on his right side was sore: his wrist hurt when he turned it, his hip ached, his leg was bruised purple, his shoulder was scraped raw. It had occurred to him, just before the trigger put him into motion, that he didn't quite get that part about doing a half somersault before hitting the net. And by the time he recovered from the temporary black-out, when enough of his early life passed before him to make him sorry he'd ever thought of this stunt, it was too late to do anything more than a half-twist, which thrust part of his body, the right part, against the edge of the netting. It couldn't have looked good, but he had managed to walk away from the field by himself, waving to the crowd with his left hand. Whether he was smiling or not he'd have to see on the evening news.

"Are you going to be okay to handle the kids?" Amy asked. Layton looked at her two packed Lark bags by the door and tried not to wince when he nodded. "Because I can change my flight. Wouldn't be convenient, but if you want me to...."

"Not necessary," Layton said. "The kids'll take care of me. Where's Leanne?"

"Next door playing with the baby. I'll call her."

"No, that's okay."

"She's got to come back anyway if you're taking me to the airport. Want me to call a taxi?"

"I can drive. I made it up this canyon. It's good to see you Amy."

"I'm surprised you can see anything out of that eye. It's pretty swollen."

"Like you got punched," Andy said. Layton tried to smile at his son. "What was it like, being shot out?"

Andy had wanted his mom to take him to see it, but Amy didn't think it was a good idea for a 7 year-old to witness what could be his father's demise. Besides, she had to pack and get things in order before her flight to Michigan to see her mother.

Layton put out his left arm and wiggled his fingers for Andy to come closer. He put his hand on the boy's head and said, "It was a blast."

Layton Cross was a movie star whose star had begun to fade the year after his picture appeared on the cover of *Newsweek* when he was 26. That was no small feat, as it was the year of De Niro, Duvall, and Peter O'Toole, who won acclaim for *Raging Bull, The Great Santini,* and *The Stunt Man.* His first four films had grossed over $200 million, which established him as a major box-office attraction, especially as they were not action adventure teenage fodder. His next four pictures didn't do quite as well, but they all made money, averaging $30 million each. Cross was seen to be a throwback to actors of another era. He was often likened to Humphrey Bogart, though he looked nothing like him. He was a good six inches taller than Bogie, had a strong square jaw which he wrongly covered with a beard, his dark hair was thick and curly and his eyes were a light gray. His once aquiline nose was slightly crooked where the bone broke when his first wife, Samantha Sanders, had struck him with a brass fire shovel. His teeth were nicely capped but he had a slight overbite that was never corrected. Critics seemed to feel it made him endearing.

He had acted with some of the best directors and had made three foreign films, one in Italy, one in France, and one in Australia. *Newsweek* called him a modern day Sisyphus, the existential Everyman who carried the burden of his generation on his shoulders. The description meant little to Layton, but he did buy a book on Greek myths. It didn't help.

Like many actors, he was victimized by his ignorance, allowing himself to become the creature the press had described. "Existential" was a label more associated with the sixties, coinciding, and not coincidentally, with America's involvement in Vietnam. But in the greed decade that was to become the eighties, it was not a common adjective. What happened to Layton was he lost his wink and became serious. He also dropped acid and became crazy. The combination was too much for him and it cost him his marriages, his rising career, his identity, even his tennis game. Now, with the Democrats in power, he was still trying to recover.

"I have an offer to do a film in Spain," Layton told Amy while she tossed cosmetics and toiletries into her carry-on bag.

"Wait until I get back before you leave," she warned, staring at him through the bathroom mirror. "If you leave them alone...."

"It's an interesting script," Layton said, his bruised body still throbbing but unable to resist. "About a guy who murders his former wife because she keeps trying to change him into her image of what he should be."

"I gave up long ago," Amy said. "How can you change someone who doesn't even know what he wants to be when he grows up?"

"Hey," Layton said. "You know I've never wanted to grow up." He forced a smile but his face lost its color as his body began to crumble.

When he came to he was on his back in Amy's bed. It was dark, he could hear the television in the living room, and he looked sheepish when Amy came in to check on him.

"I thought you were going to Michigan," he said.

"I got another flight tomorrow afternoon. Cost an extra six hundred dollars but I know you're good for it."

"I'm sorry Amy."

"You got a minute on the five o'clock news. It looked pretty good, too, except for the landing. But Andy's proud of you, so."

Layton closed his eyes and tried to forget.

Amy was eleven years younger than Layton but didn't look it. She liked to drink, smoke, get high, and had bags like small pouches under her hound-dog eyes. Still, she was roughly attractive.

She and Layton moved to the Hollywood Hills just after they legalized their relationship, when the booming real estate market kept prices jumping like popping corn. Had they bought the house three years earlier or four years later their mortgage would have been under $2,000 a month; instead she had a nut of nearly twice that to cover. But in the years she had lived there, both with Layton and without him, she had felt relatively safe: the children's bikes had only been stolen once, the mail twice, and there had been only one burglary inside the house when they weren't there. No one had been robbed at gunpoint, no tagger had spray-painted any logos on the side of the house, no arsonist had burned them down, no structural damage occurred after the 6.8 earthquake whose epicenter in Northridge was less than twenty miles away; all in all, a pretty good record for living in L.A.

After Layton walked out on her she learned to support herself and the kids by doing freelance film sound editing. It wasn't something she had been trained to do but she had two friends who did such work and they offered to teach her. Eventually she picked up a second-hand Movieola and collected sound scraps that were often discarded at the editing rooms where she apprenticed. Those scraps were carefully organized and she built up a virtual film library of sounds, neatly alphabetized in film reel boxes: A for Animal sounds, B for Breakage, C for Crashes, D and E for Dynamite and Explosions, F for Footsteps....In that way, she was able to work on putting the appropriate sound to match what was happening in the film right in her own home. Thus, she could be there when the children needed her and could work on a film whenever she had time, which often meant she worked early in the morning and into the night. She didn't make a working actor's kind of money but she managed to keep busy and not depend on Layton for support.

The sound of dogs barking through the canyon at a coyote hunting some rodent or rabbit awakened him. When he opened his eyes, Amy was asleep next to him. She was used to animal noises. It had been a long time, nearly four years, since he had shared her bed and though his body ached, his balls sent a different message to his brain.

He quietly lifted himself to a sitting position, looked at the clock, saw that it was four in the morning, and got up to pee. Then he walked down the hall to the children's rooms and stood over each as they slept. He entered Leanne's bathroom and brushed his teeth with her toothbrush. When he returned to Amy's room he took off all his clothes and lay down again, letting the toes of his right foot touch the toes of her left. She was sleeping on her back and he gently lifted his hand and placed it under her T-shirt. He felt the smoothness of her stomach and the softness of her breasts. Her nipples hardened into acorns as she slept and he let his fingers dance over their ridges. When he slid his hand below her belly she began to turn towards him.

"Layton, what are you doing?" she said, not quite awake.

"Remembering."

"I thought your bones ached."

"One bone still works."

"I don't think it's such a good idea," Amy said, her eyes beginning to open.

"You're leaving tomorrow," Layton said.

"So?"

"So it's been a long time Amy."

"Maybe for you, Layt."

He took his hand from her crotch and frowned. It was a cruel thing to say but she didn't know if she wanted to let him make love to her. He was the father of her kids and she once deeply loved him but he had hurt her in ways she preferred to forget. She had been over him for some time.

"You're saying no then?" Layton asked.

"I've got my period," she said, trying to let him down without rejecting him.

"So?"

"You don't mind? You always minded."

"I guess we've both held up on our own," Layton said.

It probably wasn't the smart thing to do, Amy thought, but he seemed so...humbled, so sad. He could have been killed being blown out of that cannon. "I'll get a towel," she whispered. "I just changed the sheets."

Layton made love like an actor. Sometimes he was Donald Sutherland in *Don't Look Now.* Sometimes, stoned, he was Brando in *Last Tango in Paris* or Nicholson in *The Postman Always Rings Twice*. He could be soft and caring or cold and ruthless. What he couldn't be was Layton Cross. Years of analysis didn't help. Every time he got in the sack it became a scene. Sometimes he played himself in a past film. Occasionally he couldn't make it at all and he was Warren Beatty's Clyde Barrow. It was very disturbing since he didn't like to consciously admit to thinking about other actors while making love. He had been a leading man and didn't want to follow other leading men. That was his biggest problem. Because of what he had once been he had a hard time accepting parts where he was second lead. And because of what he had become even that was rarely offered him in Hollywood. In

Spain he could still play the lead. But he'd be paid what an extra was paid in Hollywood. No matter how important a barometer money was, pride came first. What he couldn't quite overcome was the fact that it just didn't matter. Better to be second banana than no banana at all. Making movies in Spain wasn't even a raisin.

"He venido," Layton said when they had finished. "Tu?"

"Your mind's made up," Amy said, inserting a new tampon. "Is it a decent script?"

"I don't have it. Perce Dent told me about it, he's sending it tomorrow. In a couple of hours actually."

"You haven't even read it? Layt, you're as crazy as ever."

"Don't call me crazy," Layton said. "Call me Iron Man or Long Dong Silver or Thrusting Deeply, but don't call me crazy."

"How about I call you from my mother's to check on the kids?" Amy said as she turned to one side and went back to sleep.

"Daddy," Leanne said softly when Layton entered her room. "Look." She opened her small mouth and showed him the gap where her eye tooth was supposed to be. "It came out yesterday."

"Did you put it under your pillow for the Tooth Fairy?" Layton asked.

"I forgot."

"You haven't stopped believing have you?"

"I just don't like when she takes away my tooth. I like to keep them."

"So write and ask for it. You never know."

"I'll do it right now," Leanne said, getting out of bed to write her note. When she finished she showed it to him. It said she wanted the money but she also wanted her tooth and if she had to choose she'd keep the tooth but if she could have both then she'd like the money too. "I'll put it under my pillow tonight," she said.

She was an unusual kid, independent, creative, able to amuse herself. Since she was little she could spend hours alone finding things to keep her occupied. Never much interested in toys, she liked to find rocks and paint animals or flowers on them, or collect wildflowers and turn them into perfumes or potpourri. She made her own friendship bracelets, wove plastic strips into key chains, played the piano by ear.

Layton looked at her sparkling green eyes, caterpillar soft eyebrows, the slight budding of her chest. How big she was getting, how young and innocent she still was. Ten was on the border between fantasy and reality. The Tooth Fairy would go the way of Santa Claus and the ozone layer in a very short time but to believe in any kind of fairy at all...how exquisite.

"Dad, you're up, s'up?" Andy was still in his pajamas, his hair tousled, that mischievous gleam in his eye like one of the Dead End Kids of Layton's TV youth. The boy wanted to be friends but he was also concerned that with his mother gone things wouldn't be the same. He had grown accustomed to Amy's boyfriends, who always brought him something before laying his mom. His dad was more into discipline, mainly because he didn't have any patience, and that meant Andy would have a harder time getting away with things. Like not going to sleep until he conked out on the couch in front of the TV. Not cleaning up his share of the mess which had become a part of the lived-in look of the house. Eating whenever he felt like it and never vegetables. The list was long and he got away with it all because he had made a pact with his mom never to rat on her drinking habits to Layton whenever he came to take him and Leanne for the weekend.

Leanne was less concerned. She had gotten used to taking care of things around the house when her mother was too tired or spaced out to run the washing machine or pop a frozen dinner into the microwave. She was adept at getting herself and Andy ready for school, at sticking waffles in the toaster or writing down cold cereal lists when they got low. And when her mom went out late she didn't mind staying alone with her brother without a sitter.

Federal Express was at the door just as the kids were leaving for school. The package was for Layton, which impressed Andy but made Amy suspicious. "Must be that script," Layton said when she brought it to him.

He put the envelope with his name written on the label in black marker on top of the television. There was an importance in the way it was boldly printed. To acknowledge that importance he didn't rush to open it. Inside, he knew, were words of little substance. But when you live a freelance life and nothing's coming in he also knew what a Federal Express delivery meant: that he was not yet dead; that somebody was willing to cough up twenty or thirty bucks to get something to him. That somebody would take it off his paycheck if it ever got that far, or add it to his bill if it didn't, but that didn't matter. What mattered was that they spelled his name right. C.R.O.S.S. As in where Jesus gave up his earthly ghost.

When the taxi came for Amy, Layton feigned like he still wanted to take her to the airport, but his body was hurting and he was grateful not to drive. She kissed him on the forehead, yakked out warnings about what she'd do to him if he wasn't responsible, then smiled and told him he wasn't at all bad last night. Layton had no memory of it. He waved goodbye then clicked on the television to waste the morning watching Shelly Winters and Zsa Zsa Gabor arguing over who slept with more men. Winters made points when she said that Zsa Zsa's list not only topped her own, but that Zsa Zsa married everyone she slept with. Zsa Zsa threatened to walk. Layton knew the feeling. He had appeared on all the talk shows at different points in his career and had walked on more than a few. The questions seemed to get nastier as his career diminished. Talk show hosts felt they could take greater liberties with stars on their way down. Winters and Gabor were already relics, no longer fit for prime time or for afternoons with Oprah or Sally. Layton had at least another decade or two before it came to that.

Amy was gone for almost a week. Leanne and Andy weren't happy with the irregular hours their father kept. McDonald's on Sunset at nine was fun the first two nights, but it was knocking Andy out. "I'm supposed to be asleep before this," Andy said the third night out. "You used to be stricker."

"Take advantage of it then," Layton said. "Want to get some falafel sandwiches instead?"

"I don't like that stuff. And if I don't sleep then I'll stop growing."

"Nonsense, you'll grow no matter what. Even if you staple your eyelids open and walk around like a zombie, you'll still grow." They pulled into McDonald's and ordered their burgers and fries. "You might even learn something if you just look around and see what's going on when you're supposed to be sleeping."

"Big deal," Andy said, just as a Corvette smashed into a Hyundai Excel in the parking lot. "Wow, look at that!" Andy exclaimed.

"See, what'd I tell ya?"

"You're teaching him the wrong things," said Leanne. "He's going to grow up warped."

The owner of the Hyundai came running out of McDonald's screaming at the driver of the Corvette. When he leaned in to confront the kid who crumpled his car he got smacked in the face when the Corvette's door opened. The kid inside jumped out and swiftly kicked the stunned young man in his balls, sending him to the ground, where he kicked him in the head.

"Didya see that?" Andy shouted.

"Daddy!" Leanne snapped. She didn't like the violence and didn't think it was a very fair fight.

Layton went outside and stepped between the kicker and the kicked. "Well, now that that's settled, why don't you boys exchange insurance companies and chew on some fries?"

"Watch it, man," said the 'Vette owner. "Hey, aren't you Layton Cross?"

Layton smiled his recognition smile and nodded.

"I was a big fan of yours. What happened?"

Just what he needed. A teenage critic. "What happened is I got kicked in the balls, that's what happened."

"Hey man, this guy was coming to kill me just because I scratched his car, you know? Did I have a choice?"

"On that second kick, yeah." But maybe the kid was right, Layton thought. Maybe that's what he should have done all the years he was being kicked around. Attack first and survive. Layton was too nice. Marlon Brando sued his producers over their use of his image as Superman's father and hit the jackpot. James Garner sued Universal over *The Rockford Files* and did the same. Kim Basinger took it on her chin because she didn't act the asshole and close the door on a crazyass script about a woman who gets her limbs cut off and gets stuffed in a box. Can't be a movie star in this town and be too nice.

The other guy crawled up on his knees, bleeding from his nose. "You son of a bitch!" he shouted.

"Excuse me, Mr Cross." Layton took a step back and watched the Hyundai owner take a third boot, this one to the midsection.

"Daddy! Stop it!" Leanne screamed from inside.

"Okay," Layton said. "You're scaring my kids."

"Say, Mr Cross, I've always wanted to be an actor," the kid with the swift foot said. "Maybe you could give me some pointers."

"Maybe you should be a stunt man," said Layton.

"I'm serious. How about it?"

Layton looked at the kid and thought maybe he could learn something from him. "Sure," he said. "Come by tomorrow and we'll talk." He gave him his address and went back to Leanne and Andy.

"Hey," he said, "you guys ate all the fries."

When the kid showed up the next day Layton thought he was a messenger delivering another script. Andy and Leanne were in school and Layton was getting high watching *The Young and the Restless*.

"Here, want some?" he offered when he realized it was the kicker.

"Is it good?"

"What's your name?" Layton asked. No one had ever challenged his dope before. He didn't smoke as much as he used to, but when he did, he didn't need much.

"Barry Levine."

"Since when does a Jew learn to kick like that?"

"I've studied karate since I was eight." He took a hit from the joint.

"If it's not good enough I'll look for a needle," Layton said.

"Lot of dope now is mixed with other shit. My friends and I grow our own. It's safer."

"You got any on you?"

Barry opened his wallet, took out three slim joints, and gave them to Layton.

"I'll try one of yours," Layton said, lighting it. "So, what do you do to pay for that car of yours?"

"The car was a deal. I park cars at The Palm. How come I never see you there? They got your face drawn on the wall."

"That's why. Never eat where you have to look at a caricature of yourself."

"I just do that at night. I'm studying acting whenever I can."

"You take courses?"

"Nah, just watch the tube."

"Yeah," Layton said. "I know what you mean."

They finished the three joints and the one Layton had been smoking earlier and the best Layton could make out was that Barry did some guys some favors and they got him the 'Vette for the price of a Toyota Corolla. When Leanne and Andy came home they found their father getting his first karate lesson. Layton had a kitchen knife in his right hand and was charging. Barry crossed his fists and took Layton's downward thrust, grabbed his wrist and flipped the knife to the floor. Then he came up with his foot and gave Layton a shot in the chest. Leanne screamed and Andy went running head first into Levine's groin. As he bent over in pain, Andy struck with his head again, jumping under Barry's chin and causing him to bite his tongue. Layton was impressed. "I've been getting lessons from the wrong kid," he said.

"I think I bit my tongue off," Levine said, dripping blood onto his shirt. Leanne took him to the bathroom.

Before he left Layton gave Barry the envelope with the script inside. "Read this," he instructed, "let me know what you think."

"Daddy," Leanne said, "you haven't even opened it."

"Let's see how he reads," Layton said. "That's the true test of a warrior."

■ ■ ■

When Amy called from the airport Layton was practicing leg kicks in the backyard, switching radio channels between Howard Stern, who was promoting himself as usual, and KCRW's reports of local fires set by arsonists and the attempted assassination of the mayor. Why anyone would want to shoot the mayor of Los Angeles was beyond him; there never was a mayor worth the effort. You want to knock off someone of significance, hit Michael Ovitz, or the head of city planning, or the chief of the DMV. When he passed gas as Stern did one of his on-air belches Layton felt strangely in tune with things.

"Get the phone, Andy," Layton yelled. "I left it inside."

"I can't, I'm playing Genesis."

"You're supposed to be getting ready for school."

"It's not even seven, dad. We're cool."

Layton leaned through the open window to answer the phone. Amy was on the other end, slushed.

"Come get me," she said.

"Morning traffic, take a taxi."

"I don't have money."

"I'll pay when you get here."

"I forgot the address."

"You don't know where you live? What's wrong with you?"

"How're the kids?"

"Why didn't you call them?"

"Forgot the number."

"Get a cab and take it to Ralph's on Sunset. I'll meet you there in an hour."

"I'm going to be sick."

"Don't forget your luggage."

"O God."

"What?"

"I don't have it."

"You're still at the airport, go get it."

"I left it in Michigan."

He had been gone long enough to forget most of the things about Amy which drove him away. For a woman who was not an actress and had dropped out of college to work at a drycleaner's she was more self-centered and irresponsible than she had any right to be. At least he had *earned* his selfishness. What he forgot was that Amy had learned a trade and never asked him for anything–but that was after they split up and he didn't know that Amy. Now she was coming back in such bad shape, how could he leave her with his kids? She needed more taking care of than they did. His problem was that he could barely care for himself, let alone a family. He had tried twice and failed both times. But the week had gone quickly and he liked being with Leanne and Andy. If Amy wouldn't object–and was she in any condition to object?–perhaps he'd stay on. For a while, anyway.

■ ■ ■

"Why don't you like mommy?" Leanne asked.

"Do you like tequila?"

"I don't want to kill her."

"Why'd you come back?" asked Andy.

"Who's your father?"

"You are."

"Next question."

Andy was game. "Why does mommy have other boyfriends?"

"How do you know she does?"

"I've seen them."

"Me too," Leanne said. "They sometimes make her scream."

"You hear her?"

"Only at night when we're supposed to be sleeping."

"You ever make her scream?" Andy asked.

"This isn't the kind of conversation we should be having before you go to school. Now get ready and get out of here."

"She doesn't scream with daddy because she was married to him," Leanne explained to her brother as they went to the kitchen. Layton followed them. It was bad enough he had to deal with lousy reviews but now he was getting panned by his kids for being a lousy lover.

"So tell me Leanne," he said as she poured syrup on her Eggo, "you going to be a critic when you grow up?"

"Critics are assholes with legs," Leanne said.

"Who told you that?"

"That's what you always say."

"Never. I say critics have assholes for heads."

Instead of laughing Leanne started to cry. Layton told her to stop or she'd ruin her mascara. That made her laugh.

"How can you ruin a massacre?" Andy wondered.

"I'm going to Ralph's to get your mother."

"I thought she was in Michigan," Andy said.

"She's back."

"Do we have to go to school?" Leanne asked. "Can we stay home and see her?"

"I don't think that's a good idea."

"Maybe he wants her all to himself so he can make her scream," Andy said.

"Why on earth would I want to do that?" Layton said.

"Because mommy's happiest after she's screamed."

■ ■ ■

"I'm irresponsible! Me!"

"And you stink from whiskey."

"You're the one who did the leaving. You taught me how to walk."

"You're a sick woman, Amy, you know that? You don't think the kids are onto you?"

"What are you trying to say?"

"They see everything. They hear everything."

"They didn't seem to notice that you were gone for three years."

"Maybe because they were too busy counting the men sleeping in your bed."

"Well at least I didn't hide anything from them."

"Not even your screams. The neighbors keep track of time by the sound of your orgasms."

"You want me to leave? Take me back to the airport. The kids are all yours."

"Fine. I'll take them to Spain with me."

"You're not taking them to Spain, it'll be good for them."

"Having a father during their Freudian years would have been good for them, you creep."

That night as Amy bathed Layton sat on the toilet and wondered whether to return to his apartment or stay a few more days. Amy left it up to him. If he stayed, he could sleep in her editing room.

"I don't know why I find that amusing," Layton said. He also found it appealing. Erotic nights sneaking into Amy's bed, having her come into his. She might look a bit worn but she was still an attractive woman with shapely legs and a great ass. And she had the same appreciation for low-risk, non-addictive drugs as he did. It was just the alcohol where they differed. He'd been through that one and made it to the other side. She seemed to have little desire to cross over.

Layton looked at her with the wash cloth covering her face and her coin-size brown nipples breaking the water's line. He took off his clothes and slipped in beside her.

"What are you doing?" she demanded, peeling the cloth from one eye.

"If I'm going to stay, we might as well start clean together."

■ ■ ■

Barry Levine appeared the next morning saying he didn't understand the script. Layton said too bad, he had high hopes for him. "I just never learned Spanish," Levine said. Layton looked at him, then thumbed through the pages. Spanish? Was this a joke or did they send him the wrong version? He knew his star had been sinking but it hadn't vanished altogether. He lit one of Levine's joints and called his agent, who was as astounded as Layton was annoyed.

"Why would I do something like that?" Perce Dent asked.

"That's why I'm calling, Perce. I thought you read the script."

"Layton, c'mon, who has time to read? A hundred scripts come into this office every day. When they have a specific actor in mind I pass it on if I know the actor needs work. You need work. It sounded like a good idea. And Spain. Could be fun."

Dent's name was almost appropriate, Layton thought. Damaged. Dense would have been perfect. Perce Dent was once to agenting what Cross was to acting, a formidable force, a risen star, but when his clients began to decline, so did Dent's power. He left William Morris the same month Jimmy Carter left the White House for that B actor and started his own management company when managers ruled the roost. But he wasn't one of them and returned to agenting a few years later. He found clients at acting schools like the Strasberg Institute, Milton Katselas, or Howard Fine's classes, and was good at getting them commercial work, but the big stuff–the features, the movies-of-the-week and miniseries–passed him by. He remained loyal to Layton, however, because he believed in his talent, especially his first four films when Charlie Greenbloom had represented him. He had known Layton for twenty years, became his agent as the offers diminished, and knew that he had nowhere to go.

"You have every right to be angry on this one."

"Angry? Me, Perce? Why should I be angry? I'll give the script to your maid, you can cast her."

"That's funny. Hold on a minisec, I'm being buzzed."

Layton hung up. If he was Tom Hanks would he be put on hold? Let him call me back, Layton thought as he went to the refrigerator to polish off the kids' Haagen-Dazs. Barry Levine was sitting at the table finishing it for him.

"This is the best," Levine said. "Ben & Jerry's don't even come close. I like to microwave a whole pint and drink it like a shake."

"That'll keep your cholesterol on a par with Barry Bonds' batting average," Layton said as he grabbed his keys.

Levine gave him his goofball teenage stoned smile, repeating "Barry Bonds" like Homer Simpson. Layton's sarcasm transferred to Levine as a compliment.

"Should I hang around or what?" Levine shouted as Layton left.

"Do what you want," Layton mumbled. "There's celery and cream cheese when you finish the ice cream."

■ ■ ■

Theo Soris was gently running a comb through his hair when Layton walked in. "Layton, my man, is that you? I'm in the bathroom."

Layton looked at the wall-to-wall books. His agent didn't have time to read and his best friend decorated his house with books, not one of which was legally purchased.

"You know Spanish?" Layton asked, looking at Theo's reflection.

"Si, habla Espanol un poco, por que?"

"How many of those books you read?"

"It's not the reading, it's the aesthetics, you know that Layton. Besides, most of them are first editions, you don't read first editions. There's a lot of knowledge in that living room. If you just sit a while you begin to absorb it."

"Your hair coming in?"

"Look at it–there was nothing in the front three months ago. I'm a new person. Forty bucks a plug, two hundred plugs: instant hair. I'm ten years younger for what, six grand? Why'd I wait so long?"

"It almost looks real."

"Fuck you, almost. It's my hair. They just move it from the back to the front."

"They should take it from your ass and leave your head alone."

"Bald guys probably do that. So what's with the Spanish?"

"Forget it. What have you been stealing lately?"

"Borrowing, Layt. Stealing is not part of my vocab."

For as long as he'd known Theo he marveled at his quick hands and thief's perception of right and wrong. To Theo, police harassment of hookers was wrong. Starving children, government corruption, not legalizing drugs, and nuclear bases were wrong. Taking–or borrowing, as he preferred–from a Have to enrich your mind or feed your stomach was all right with him. And he prided himself in that every book he ever snuck between his pants or under his arm he, at the very least, browsed through. There was just so much to learn, who could afford to pay for it? Certainly not a mostly out-of-work actor like himself. His reasoning broke down as soon as the words *public library* were mentioned but Theo only shuddered at the thought of browsing through used books that had a deadline attached to them. Truth was, if a certain book wasn't available to 'borrow' from a bookstore, Theo wasn't beyond sneaking it past the scrutinizing eyes of a librarian. Layton had seen him do it.

Their friendship began in a New York acting class. They had agreed to work together on Edward Albee's *Zoo Story* and had rehearsed every day for weeks, during which time Layton observed how Theo lived: 'borrowing' meats from supermarkets, watches from jewelry stores, colognes from department counters. Life was a lark then and Theo was just playing the city like a giant island candy store where everything was there for the taking. One didn't need money to live extravagantly. Just guts.

But it wasn't Theo's world view or deft hands which attracted Layton as much as his talent for talking his way out of trouble. Once, when caught picking up a pack of cigarettes, he told the newsstand owner that he was practicing for a role as a petty thief who gets caught and he was so convincing that the owner let him keep the pack. When it happened again, over a Colibri lighter from an electronics store, Theo became very upset with himself.

Not for taking something but for getting caught, which was a sign of failure. He'd stand before a mirror for hours practicing his sleight of hand.

Layton never took anything himself nor encouraged Theo. His friend was just this crazy character who was making up life as he lived it and Layton was curious enough to observe him the way one did a character in a novel. As the years passed and the books piled high Theo became part of Layton's own story. They had shared enough experiences, inhaled enough dope, snorted enough powders, rehearsed enough plays to be like family. Actors often felt competitive but Layton and Theo were more like cousins. They were supportive when others were critical, they brought each other up and they understood the struggle. When Layton married Samantha Sanders, Theo was at the wedding and he didn't borrow so much as a fork. When Layton got some breaks and became a star, Theo beamed like a proud relative, bragging to acquaintances that Layton Cross was his best friend and not giving a shit when he wasn't believed. And when Layton was able to throw a small part his way Theo was grateful.

"You plan on giving back all those books one day?"

"When I die. It's in my will. Every bookstore will get its share. They don't want them, they're to be given away to the homeless downtown and along Santa Monica Boulevard. Want a hit?"

"What's it cut with?"

"Not enough to make your teeth clench. It's pretty clean."

It was Theo who introduced Layton to cocaine. Until then it was grass or the occasional acid, but coke was so smooth, so alive, that Theo couldn't wait to share the discovery. It was just after Layton's first starring role and it gave him the sensation of clarity and supreme confidence. Over the years he never took enough to become dependant, but it added to his troubles as he mixed drugs with increasing doubts, making his personality far more complex than he could comfortably maintain. It wound up giving him a reputation as being 'difficult.' Which was another way of saying he was, at times, incomprehensible, and at others, confused. It also brought him closer to the few people who knew him and who stuck by him.

"Listen to this," Theo said. "My manager got me a Tennessee Williams' play at the Coronet on La Cienega. The lead."

"That's major," Layton said.

"Tennessee fucking Williams! I didn't even know he wrote this, it's his last play. It's fucking Marlon Brando time."

"It should only happen to you."

"That fat slob, shit, give me the glory, not the gory. You got anything?"

"Looking at things. In Spanish. This fucking town. There any money in the play?"

"Fuck the money. Exposure. People will come see Tennessee Williams. Theater in this town sucks, you know that."

"How'd you land it."

"My manager, fucking guy knows people. Spider Ray."

"He was Samantha's agent after Greenbloom went to Fox."

"Right. Of course. Samantha–boy, did she move fast. Like that cocksucker Greenbloom. Bastard's head of a studio and you can't get near him. I remember when he had us all–you, me, Samantha. You still with Perce Dent?"

"Yeah. He sends me scripts in Spanish."

"Get rid of him. Didn't he make the switch to managing and couldn't hack it? Ray jumped over and he's still floating. Agents don't do jack one for you, they just wait for you to bring them an offer and skim off their ten per cent. You're an artist, Layton, you don't know fuck about business. Agents just close deals you make yourself. That's why you're not working. What's Dent done for you in the last six months? What'd you do, one television walk-on?"

"Plus offers to play a genetically altered freak in a horror movie, a sand scavenger in a beach movie, and this Spanish thing."

"None of which increases your visibility or strengthens your reputation. You're a big name, Layton, and he isn't capitalizing. At the very least you could be doing commercials in Japan for a million bucks a pop. Cut and run. Spider Ray is a bigger crook than Perce Dent. He's hungrier. Go talk to him. He owes you."

"Nobody owes me squat."

"You're right. So how's being a family man again?"

"The kids're great. Amy's driving me nuts."

"Who the fuck are you?" Amy asked when she walked into the kitchen, drying her hair with a towel.

"Don't you use a blow dryer?" Barry Levine asked, sliding some cream cheese along a stick of celery.

"Deadens your hair. So who'd you say you were?"

"A friend of Layton's."

"The friendly dope dealer."

"I know what's available."

"I bet you do."

Levine introduced himself and Amy put up some coffee and offered him a shot of tequila. Before Leanne and Andy came home from school they managed to knock off the bottle. Amy wanted him to fuck her but Barry worried that Layton might come home at any time, so she settled for a hand job right there in the kitchen. It wasn't her coming that surprised him, but her screaming. "The neighbors think I'm practicing singing," she told him when she was able to talk.

"Jesus, I never heard anyone do that before. That was really something."

"You got fast fingers, Barry."

"You should feel my tongue."

"Keep visiting your friend here and I'm sure I will."

Andy was surprised to see Barry in his kitchen and told his mother all about him as soon as he left. Amy didn't like violence but there was something exciting about that boy.

Back in his car, on his way to fire Perce Dent, Layton stopped at a light and smiled at two teenage girls in a Miata convertible. They were giggling in recognition and one of them asked, "Weren't you in *The Man, the Cat, and the Wild*?"

Layton nodded and said, "And the question is, was I the cat or the wild?"

"Wow, I really liked that picture."

The other girl, behind the wheel, shouted, "Where are you going?"

"I'm following you," Layton said.

"Far out." She cut in front of him when the light changed.

The girls were roommates who lived in an apartment in Westwood. They shared a single bedroom and neither minded who went first with Layton, who suggested they all get into bed together.

"Nobody's gonna believe this!" the girl named Linda said.

"Of course they will," the other girl, Sally, said. "Warren Beatty used to sleep with strange girls all the time."

"Not after Madonna and his marriage," Linda said.

"Warren's a friend of mine," Layton said, "and I happen to know he doesn't actually sleep with all the women who claim they have slept with him."

"He may not sleep with them, but he does fuck them," Sally said. "I've got three girlfriends who did him."
"Before or after Annette?" Layton asked. "And did he spend the night?"

"Actually, he didn't. But still."

Layton was practicing his profession. Beatty was no friend of his. If he was, why didn't he ever give him a call? Why didn't he cast him in one of his movies? Fuck Warren.

"Do you know Tom Cruise?" Linda asked.

Layton ignored the question. He lifted her onto the bed, pulled off her top, unzipped his fly, and said, "Here, suck on this." His head was still coked up and a blowjob was as far as he'd go.

"I don't like to give head," Linda said.

"But you like to get it, right?"

"That's different. Let Sally suck you off. I'll just watch."

"You girls will never get on Howard Stern this way. What do you think, Sally?"

"I think we should try this," Sally said, taking out a small liquid canister of GHB. "This is really good."

Layton had never tried gamma-hydroxy-butyrate before but if it got these girls going he'd give it a shot. Linda suggested capping that with a joint she had soaked with Ecstasy in the microwave. Layton was still game. But after mixing these designer drugs no one wanted sex. The girls wanted to just hug and snuggle and talk about other movie stars. Layton wanted some fresh air.

He put his dick back inside his pants. "We'll do this another time real soon."

The girls smiled weakly as he walked out their door. A few years back girls like these were yanking out his joint in parking lots, letting him come in their mouths in broad daylight.

That's how he met Amy.

She was nineteen. A student at Santa Monica City College, she had arrived by herself from Michigan determined to experience "life," which showed up in the person of a movie star. And not just any star but one of Hollywood's most famous, who was coming off a marriage to another of Tinseltown's high risers, Samantha Sanders.

Amy was living in a studio apartment in West L.A. Layton had a house in Bel Air, a hotel suite at the Beverly Wilshire, a condo in Santa Monica, and an apartment along Central Park West in New York. Their paths crossed in the vegetable aisle at Ralph's where Layton had stopped to pick up some cantaloupes and Amy was buying tofu floating in water, asparagus spears, and bean sprouts. Layton made a silly comment having to do with the contents of Amy's basket and Amy recognized him immediately, having seen him on the cover of *Newsweek* just that week. That cover managed to sneak in during the slight calm between the anti-draft and pro-ERA demonstrations, the year when the Soviet Union invaded Afghanistan, America pulled out of the Olympics in Moscow, *Nightline* was counting the number of days the hostages were being held in Teheran, and Roman Polanski gave the American legal system the finger when he fled to France the day before a judge was to sentence him for fucking a minor.

With the exception of the hostages, Layton couldn't have cared less. He'd gotten his shrink to help him beat the draft, so that weight had been lifted. Polanski had talked with him about working together but Layton wasn't impressed with his fixation on teenage girls. Not that Layton wasn't cut from the same hangdog stock, but Amy at least was over the legal limit. By the time they passed through the checkout counter they were flirting openly. When Amy saw Layton's Jaguar she knew she was about to do something she'd never done before in the back seat of a car she'd only seen in ads.

Layton had truly loved Samantha but when she decided they weren't right for each other he went into a deep depression and found relief through brief encounters at supermarkets, restaurants, friend's houses, gas stations, back lots, anywhere he went. Such moments were usually exciting while they were happening and very flat and empty afterwards. But with Amy it was different. She was so young, so fresh, so naive, so good with her mouth. He asked for her phone number and four years later she gave birth to Leanne. They were married soon after, had split up three times before Andy came along three years later, and Amy had lost every ounce of that naiveté that Layton had found so attractive. What she found was the bottle, which she took to like the Irish Republican Army took to bombing and kidnapping. Two years after Andy's birth in 1986 Layton was out of her life. They had been together eight years, married four, twice what Jeanne Dixon had predicted in the *Enquirer* and seven and a half years longer than Samantha Sanders thought possible. Even Layton, who had never gotten over his first wife, wouldn't have touched the odds of their staying together through most of the decade.

■ ■ ■

"What are you talking, fired?" Perce Dent asked, picking up the phone when his secretary buzzed.

"You're too fucking busy for me, Perce."

"Hold it a mome," Perce whispered, "I've got Dusty's agent on the line."

"Fuck this, Perce, I don't care if you've got Dusty himself on the goddamn line. Or Jeff Katzenberg or Charles Greenbloom. You're not putting me on hold while I'm in your fucking office, you putz!"

Layton yanked the phone off Dent's desk and flung it against a wall. Dent, remembering how violent Richard Pryor used to get in similar situations, tried to remain calm. "Are you on something Layton? You're being awfully unreasonable. I'm doing all I can."

"Not enough. Spanish movies in Spanish is not enough. Take your ten percent of my nothing and use it to pay the phone bills you won't be making to me any more."

"What are you going to do, Layt? You're not really in a position to pick and choose."

"I'll find someone who knows the business and can read scripts before sending them out. You're just not the guy I want to go down with Perce."

"We've been together a long time, Layt. Let's do lunch next week and talk about it."

"I don't do lunch, Perce, I eat it."
"I'm talking as a friend."
"I'd rather you acted like an agent."
"No hard feelings then, Layt?"
"Fuck you Perce."
"Right."

That felt good. Got to preserve whatever pieces were left after living in Los Angeles the second half of your life. Came out here after Broadway and was treated with respect. Samantha had nothing to do with it. Well, some, but still–it was a city opened like a hooker's thighs. Take what you want. Part after part. Scripts by the box load. Six-figure offers at a time when money was worth a lot more, when Pacino got just $35,000 for the first *Godfather*. Limos to take us to screenings. Realtors in Mercedes showing us how stars live. Names in the social column of the *Times* whenever we went anywhere. Reserved tables at Chasen's, La Famiglia, Imperial Gardens without making reservations. Parties where guests actually applauded our entrance. Perks, stock options, percents of the gross. Antique shopping. Twenty fucking six years old.

When he thought of the antiques he and Samantha used to buy he drove by The Antique Guild to browse, maybe pick up a spittoon to celebrate the day. But the place made him dizzy. All that money, the real estate, the cars, pissed away by his greed-driven accountants, careless management, and his own negligence. He could no longer afford to be extravagant. Amy would never stoop to cleaning a spittoon.

A small, hand-printed sign by the Stone Canyon entrance to Bel Air said "Garage Sale." Layton turned off Sunset and followed the arrows. Bel Air liquidations were always worth a look. One more poor slob drowning in the dream. Manicured putting green lawns. Sprawling, like the homes, which truly made one feel like royalty. Fairyland. Cars parked for the sale were mostly neighbors, like vultures, looking to pick up the goods at bargain prices. Mercedes', BMWs, Rolls', Range Rovers, and a sprinkling of American luxury cars. In the driveway a Daimler with the name SAM on the license plate. He should have guessed. His ex had a nose for these things. In spite of all her millions she could never pass up the opportunity for a deal. She believed storeowners and workmen overcharged her by thirty percent because of who she was, which made her automatically subtract that percentage from anything that she wanted to purchase. Which, of course, made the sellers jack up their merchandise or services by forty percent. Even these garage sales took stamina. When you lived in Bel Air it wasn't considered dignified to haggle like an Arab. You named your price, the buyer named hers, and you settled quietly. Samantha never settled. She was too used to getting her way. If Hollywood had unofficially crowned her, then she would play out her role to the hilt. It was the way it was.

"I've been thinking about Mark," Layton said when he saw her. Their son was the only thing they still had in common though she had full custody and he saw him rarely.

"Don't start," Samantha whispered. "You know I don't like scenes." She was wearing gray silk pants with matching silk sweatshirt, a red AIDS ribbon pinned above her left breast. She had on Armani black sunglasses, a gold necklace, red suede Cole Haan sneakers and a red baseball cap.

"No, that's not what I know," Layton said.

"Am I going to have to leave or are you going to leave me alone?"

Her skin was shining under the cap; so smooth you could snort cocaine off her cheek. It wasn't always that way but even enlarged pores have a way of receding when money's no object and the world's most advanced skin care artists are available to you.

He couldn't see her green eyes because of the Armani's which balanced delicately on her small, straight nose, her pinched nostrils the result of endless teenaged nights of sleeping on her back with a clothespin clamped over them. She had a sensual, enticing mouth with a hint of a crooked, knowing smile. Like Garbo, whose face could be divided evenly into quarters, Samantha Sanders had that rare balance to her features that the camera seemed to caress. Her legs were long and muscled from exercise, her body well conditioned. She had the tenacious look of an athlete at the top of her form ready to spring forward at the blow of a whistle. Knowing no matter how stiff the competition, she was in a class by herself.

"I want to come over and see Mark's room. He told me you fixed it up."

"I don't want you in my house."

"He needs me. He doesn't play sports. He's turning into a girl."

"Because he's refined you can't understand him. He's got culture. He plays the saxophone. He's even composing."

"He's fifteen, he should be sliding into bases."

"Sorry, he's not living your dreams."

"What colors did you give him, pink and mauve?"

"It's all mahogany if you must know."

"I must." He was feeling an adrenaline rush, his heart pumping abnormally, his brain swirling from the mixture of cocaine, grass, Ecstasy, and GHB. He was doing all he could to suppress what he knew was a full-blown anxiety attack.

"He'll take Polaroids and bring them his next visit."

"Why are you like this? You can afford to be generous, lift the lid, let the sun shine in."

"I can't stand the way you talk. It's the same old stoned gibberish."

"You mean you can't *understand*. That's because you never listen. You only hear yes."

People in the driveway were discretely hanging on their words. This was the kind of talk that made the lead paragraph in Robert Osborne's or Army Archerd's columns. If there was a photographer around he could live nicely for three months off one picture here. Samantha hated photographers. Layton welcomed them. But there wasn't a camera to be seen. Just a lot of wealthy people acting interested in lamps and chairs, trying to hear what the former married couple were saying.

Samantha walked away from Layton but he followed behind her. Just like the old days. A deja vu feeling of nausea rose like a wave over him. That's what she did to him: made him feel small and unworthy.

"Mark's my kid too!" he shouted at her.

He saw the muscles in her neck tighten. He didn't have to see her face to know that her lips were pursed and her eyes narrow. But he never expected her to whip around and hiss, "That's the one regret I have: that you're his father."

"And how do you think he feels having a cunt for a mother?"

Huge mistake.

"At least he doesn't have a failure for a mother. He doesn't have to make excuses to his friends about *me*!"

"He doesn't have any friends," Layton shot back. "That's part of his problem. No one's good enough for him."

"Certainly not his father," Samantha said. That's when Layton put his left hand on her shoulder and swung his right fist across her chin, knocking her sunglasses off her face. Samantha would have fallen if he hadn't held her shoulder. Her driver and three other men jumped to her aid, grabbing Layton and pulling him away.

"You'll regret that," she snarled like some wicked Disney witch.

"You've had that coming for thirteen years."

"My lawyers will be in touch." She turned her snake eyes slowly at the crowd watching and then disappeared inside the Daimler. Layton rubbed the knuckles of his right hand and smiled as he stepped on her glasses. It was a good audience. The only thing missing was their applause.

■ ■ ■

He couldn't go back to Amy's now. It was too big a moment. News would travel fast and he'd be back in the papers again. Like the old days. Samantha and Layton battling it out. Only this time it would be uglier. If only she had hit him. That was always his problem; he never got to play the sympathetic character. How existential was his Everyman? This punch was almost inevitable. Especially with the drugs in his system. If only she could be reasoned with. But you'd have to be on equal footing with her, and no one was. She decreed; you obeyed. He had wanted to get custody over Mark, but no judge would side with him. Even if she wasn't who she was. Layton was just not stable enough. He had a history of walking out on his kids. He put work above family. Even more when he wasn't working. He worried too much. He feared dying before he had made a comeback. George Segal, Rod Steiger, Elliott Gould...all had shrunk from the public's consciousness; but Jimmy Caan came back, he had a second act. Layton was a generation behind them. He didn't want to get lost like those Brat Packers who followed him and had their fifteen minutes. Rob Lowe. Judd Nelson. Molly Ringwald. He wasn't ready to be forgotten like Margot Kidder, Valerie Perrine. He had too much to prove and not enough opportunities. It was a merciless business. A lot of people would be secretly glad when they heard about the punch. Spider Ray most of all. She really screwed him.

He turned down the Avenue of the Stars in Century City and pulled into an underground lot. Took the elevator to the 34th floor. Told the receptionist he wanted to see her boss. She asked which one, Ray, Methusa, or Mahoney?

"The first," Layton said.

She asked his name and he flinched. "You work in this place and you don't recognize people?"

"Should I know you? Are you a client?"

He told her he was once Samantha Sanders' husband and that got a rise. He wondered if he was starting to hate women.

Spider Ray was a busy man but he made time for Layton. They shared being screwed royal by Samantha, so there was a bond.

"You're looking good," Ray said. "A little heavy, but otherwise."

"Don't get up," Layton said. Ray was fat and rarely left his chair when someone came into his office. You had to really rate for Spider Ray to stand and shake your hand.

"So, how's the family?" Ray asked.

"A catastrophe, like all families. Theo Soris says you got him a good play, he's grateful."

"It's not much. Tennessee hadn't written anything for years, but it's something. I took Theo on because of his mother. I used to date her. What can I do for you?"

"I punched Samantha in the mouth this afternoon."

"Good for you, she deserves it."

"There were people around."

"Not so good."

"Thought you'd like to know before you read about it."

"Did you do any damage?"

"Doubt it. She's got an iron jaw. She says she'll sue."

"You need a lawyer?"

"What for? They cost money and I don't have any. What can she get besides bad publicity? She won't go through with it."

"She's beyond bad publicity. She might. Depends on how hard you hit her pride."

"Knocked it right to the ground."

Spider Ray cradled his chin between his thumb and forefinger and looked at Layton for a minute. Layton stuck a stick of cinnamon Trident in his mouth and pocketed the wrapper. "You know," Ray said, "it could work for you."

Layton hadn't considered any positive repercussions. He didn't regret throwing the punch but he certainly never thought of capitalizing on it. His heartbeat had slowed to normal, his anxiety had begun to subside. He wasn't sorry he had come to see the Spider man.

"Who handles your publicity?" Ray asked.

"Al Low. I haven't talked to him in months."

"You paying him?"

"I owe."

"Al's a good man. Got a nice viciousness about him. Can be a good buffer for something like this."

"I don't want to pay for this to be publicized. It'll get out without me."

"But then you won't control it. Doesn't matter so much if the press is bad or good as long as you've got a handle on it. Low can give your side, make you available or unavailable, put things on or off the record. Punching Sam makes you a viable story. Low can pick the press he lets in. You can give a few exclusives. People forget too easily, this is one way of reminding them."

"That I was once married to the bitch? That's not how I want to be remembered."

"That you're still alive. You got any projects coming up?"

"I'm taking Andy to the Dodger game next week."

"Perce Dent still your agent?"

"Not for the past two-and-a-half hours."

"You were with him a long time."

"Look where it got me."

"So what are you going to do?"

"Theo thought I should talk to you."

"You want me? I'm not right for you, I got too many clients already. Theo was a favor."

The look on Spider Ray's face told Layton something else. That Layton wasn't big enough any more. He'd be too much work for too little return.

"How much you take, twenty percent?" Layton asked.

Ray nodded, joking that was why he got out of agenting. Layton finessed the moment. "That's too much for me anyway."

"I'm sorry, Layton. Nothing personal. You understand. I'm just too busy. Wouldn't be fair."

"Business is business. When I'm hot you'll come running, right?"

"I'll flood you with faxes," Ray said, reaching for the phone now that their meeting was over. "Enjoy the game. Haven't seen the Dodgers since they left Brooklyn. Go see Al Low, it's worth it."

Ray was punching buttons as Layton closed the door behind him. They didn't shake hands and it didn't matter.

Layton crossed the walkway connecting the office building to the mall on the other side, stopping to listen to the singing flower vendor. It was Harry Sales, who used to be a small-time character actor until his ulcer forced him to come to his senses. The few shoppers passing ignored his performance but it didn't bother Harry, who was used to it.

"How you doing, Harry?" Layton said.

"Layton Cross, is that you? Hey!"

"Keep singing, Harry, I like it."

"It's something to do, you know? Longest running gig in L.A.," he laughed.

"You got nice flowers."

"Fresh, daily. I go down to the flower mart every morning. Sushi makers pick fish, I choose flowers. Nobody hassles me. So, you working?"

The actor's question.

"Here and there."

"That's what drove me to milk," Harry said. "Now I'm singing every day. The kids love me." He pressed the button on his tape recorder and sang "*O My Poppa,*" which made Layton think of his father, who always predicted acting was a bum's life. His mother was the one who pushed.

In the men's department of Bullock's Layton bought a blue and white striped rugby polo shirt and had it gift wrapped. The saleslady smiled and he winked back. She didn't say anything but she knew who he was. He didn't say anything but he knew she knew. If he never made another picture that lady would always know. The small receipt of fame.

From Century City he drove east on Santa Monica Boulevard to Melrose, turned right on Robertson, left on Third, and parked at a meter in front of Cedars-Sinai Hospital. He took the north wing elevator to the seventh floor and knocked at the closed door of room 7118. Judith Lee opened the door and smiled when she saw him. "We were just talking about you," she lied. "Farrell was just asking about you."

"You're sweet," Layton said, kissing her cheek. Judith was a good, determined woman. Half her famous husband's age, she had a faded model's looks, a face not yet in need of lifting, a sincerity that immediately struck one as genuine. No one ever accused her of being a gold digger but that didn't mean friends of her husband, and his first three wives, didn't think it. She wasn't ready for Farrell Lee to die. Not yet. He was too precious, too important, to leave her all alone. He might not be able to act again but they could surely count on his name to meet their needs. Respectable advertisers, like banks and electronic firms, wanted his endorsement. Film schools wrote wanting to honor him with retrospective festivals. Politicians sought him because they knew he was capable of making believers out of skeptical voters. And there was always the lucrative lecture circuit, if he could just get well.

Layton looked down at the old actor, flat on his back, with tubes in his nose, and didn't bother to ask how he was. Too weak to raise his hand, Farrell stuck up a finger and Layton acknowledged it. "Brought you something, tiger," he said, giving Judith the box. "For when you're up and about."

Farrell blinked and Layton took it for a thank you. Judith took out the shirt and held it up for her husband to see. It puzzled him; but then, from Layton Cross that was to be expected. He never could understand Layton. Too temperamental, too many drugs, too unprofessional. An actor should be like a carpenter, always sawing away at his craft. Farrell was from the old school of acting where you worked all the time and didn't question the parts you were given. There was nothing more depressing than an out-of-work actor. Now the town was full of them. Waiting on tables, parking cars, working as bank clerks, gardeners, insurance salesmen, realtors, lifeguards; standing in unemployment lines, collecting welfare checks, sticking needles into their arms, sniffing powders and vapors, staying high and miserable.

Layton didn't have to say anything. Farrell could tell by the way he looked that things weren't going well. Judith did all his talking for him, asking Layton about his family, his upcoming TV movie, praising some of his old films. Unlike her husband, she was good at that sort of small talk. To Farrell, you talked when you had something to say, otherwise, shut up and listen. Learn more about acting from watching and listening than from opening your mouth all the time. But in a social business someone like Judith was necessary and he never once complained, to her or to anyone else.

When Judith finally excused herself to check with a nurse about Farrell's medication Layton moved his chair closer to the old man and asked him if he was going to die. "You've still got a lot to give," Layton said. "We need you."

The old man was about to say, 'What for?' but it was too much effort. His career was already history and if Layton thought differently the man was a bigger fool than he assumed. Still, it was the first time anyone had mentioned death in his presence. It was what everyone thought but it was unspoken, like bad breath or a string of mucous hanging from one nostril.

"Judith's terrific," Layton said. "You're lucky." Farrell nodded slightly. "They got you on a lot of pills?" Farrell's eyes moved to the nightstand. "No pain, huh? All those pills. Zombie time, right? No concept of night and day, no energy, no desire to get out of here." Layton leaned close to Farrell. "Cut the pills in half."

Farrell's quizzical look remained but his mind was thinking about what he just heard. It was true, he was taking too many pills, he didn't have any energy, he didn't care if he got better or just stayed this way, flat on his back, tubes coming in and going out.

The old actor motioned with his eyes for Layton to lean in again. Layton put his ear to Farrell's mouth and heard the word "work" whispered with great effort. It was Farrell's way of reciprocating advice. It was the only message that made any sense.

■ ■ ■

Al Low's office was in the 9255 building on the western end of Sunset Strip. He worked for Sawyers and Roberts, one of the three big PR films, who charged their clients $1,500 a month to keep their names in or out of the media's hungry eye. They also acted as go-between for the press who sought interviews or comments and the stars who preferred to pick and choose the people they had to talk with. Only the very biggest stars paid to keep a low profile. Marlon Brando didn't use a PR firm. Or an agent. But he was Brando.

Layton Cross owed six months to Sawyers and Roberts but for the little they did for him he felt he deserved a discount. For nine grand the public shouldn't have to wonder what happened to him. Al Low should have thought up some campaign, some stunt, to get him in the news. It shouldn't have been left to Layton to do it. First the cannon, now his fist. But done was done; Spider Ray was right, he should see Low and discuss ways of turning what happened to his benefit.

Low was a slender eel of a man, gay, who could be as offensive and abusive as anyone in the business when he chose to be. In that respect he was unlike most of the people in publicity who, as a group, attempted to put on a friendly front to the press. Low never hid his disdain. He saw himself as a future producer or studio head and cultivated that image rather than that of a flak.

His eyes ignited when Layton told him what had happened in the driveway of a Bel Air garage sale. This was prime material.

"Might be the smartest move you've made in years," he said. "You'll probably get smeared but you will get out there. Hello Idaho, come in Kansas. Have we got news for you!"

Layton sunk into the antique leather chair and pursed his lips. He felt himself beginning to crash. "You got anything to smoke?" he asked. Low threw him a pack of Gaulois cigarettes. Layton's eyes rolled to the ceiling. "I don't do cigarettes."

"I don't like the smell of dope in my office," Low said, passing him a vial of cocaine.

"I'll get you a clean air machine next time I come," Layton said, dipping a small spoon into the vial.

"You know what I think? Before this gets too out of hand you should go see Samantha and apologize. Just between you and her, doesn't matter if you mean it. It'll sound better when the raccoons start getting nasty." Low referred to journalists as raccoons.

"A lot of them hate Samantha, I don't think they'll attack me."

"You're right. Which will only infuriate her more. That's why you should go see her. So it won't look like you planned it."

"Using her, huh?"

"Exactly."

Low was right. If the press had a field day at her expense she'd want Layton's balls the way a mosquito sought blood. And she was powerful enough to make sure that anyone who ever harbored hopes of doing something with her would have nothing to do with him. Ever.

"This is a shitty business," Layton said.

"Name me one that isn't? But this is the cream shit. That's why you're here and not out selling personal copiers and cellular phones."

"Give me first base for the Yankees," Layton said.

"Same business as this. You gotta perform, bring in a paying crowd, or you're back on the farm."

"I'll go, but she won't see me, I can tell you that right now."

"Doesn't matter. You'll have made the effort. Then drop her a note. Or buy one of those cards that apologizes for you. I'll make a few calls and find out if the story's floating. If it is I'll arrange for some rags to send raccoons, they'll eat this up. I bet *Entertainment Tonight* or *Inside Edition* would bite if we want that kind of exposure. This may not have the legs of an intern blowing the president in the Oval Office but it's still prime. If no one's heard about it, they will after I call."

"This is going to bring me back?"

"If we milk it right it might even make you money. There are a lot of parts out there for wife beaters. You've just got to be seen, that's all. Right now you're invisible."

"I don't beat my wife. I'm an ex-wife beater." Layton liked that. Like an eggs-white beater.

Going home Layton thought about the first time he met Samantha. Charlie Greenbloom suggested they get together. He liked his clients knowing each other and these two were young and hot. Greenbloom was an established agent who had dreams of backstage stardom himself. He would often punctuate his remarks with exclamations about the ripeness of Hollywood, just waiting to be plucked, sucked, and fucked dry. Since Greenbloom ran his business out of Brooklyn Layton thought he was just another marginal player. But Greenbloom had a master plan that, with the help of some of his clients, would one day make him one of the true Industry powerhouses. His biggest club was Samantha Sanders, whose talent Greenbloom recognized early. She was a young woman of enormous presence, and she could act. Greenbloom used to compare her to Ted Williams. He knew with the right parts and the best directors there'd be no stopping her.

As for Layton, he wasn't a natural but he had a certain spark, an energy that needed nurturing. Like Floyd Patterson.

From the morning they first met–at breakfast at the Carnegie Deli in Manhattan–Layton and Samantha recognized that each had something the other could use: Samantha's strength and directness; Layton's vulnerability and lopsided view of things. They were rarely apart after that.

Greenbloom was pleased to have played Cupid, but as Samantha's star began to illuminate his office he began having doubts about their relationship. Although married with three children, Greenbloom was also infatuated with Samantha. Wisely channeling her career he furthered his own–he went on to develop projects at Fox, then became a vice-president of creative development at Universal, and finally realizing his dream, head of Quickstart Studios.

Samantha made pictures for him wherever he was, as did Layton, until they split up. Then Charlie Greenbloom became a very busy man whenever Layton came calling. And when Layton did manage to see his former agent it seemed the only subject of conversation was Mark. They never talked about Samantha.

Layton thought about how, when Mark was born, the world seemed a different place. It was as if the birth of his son gave him new eyes. Both he and Samantha were already celebrities and their every move in public was subject to video lights and shouts of 'Look over here, this way, this way!' He never minded. Photographers and TV cameramen had their jobs to do, they too had kids and families to provide for. He often mugged for them and they responded by snapping more and more pictures or taping more coverage than they needed. It used to annoy the hell out of Samantha, who always moved quickly whenever they went anywhere. She never smiled. The media dubbed them Happy and Grumpy, which made Layton happy and Samantha grumpy. But when Mark was born Layton didn't want him to grow up under the glare of hot or flashing lights and he asked the photographers to lay off the kid. Which was like saying, the kid won't be as easy as I am to shoot, so he'll be worth more when you get him. Sometimes it got bad. Crowds would gather, people would be pushed, Samantha once was knocked to the ground while holding Mark. Layton nearly went crazy, swinging wildly at those near him. They needed a police escort to get away and their lives changed after that. Sam never wanted to go anywhere without protection and Layton thought it made them prisoners.

    Mark was undoubtedly affected. He didn't start talking until he was two. He was a nervous, clumsy child who always seemed worried. Layton thought he was as fragile as an egg and tried to toughen him up by throwing him around, but the boy cried when he went up in a swing. He cried when his parents argued, and since they were often shouting at each other, he was often crying. As he got older he developed an ethereal, withdrawn look. When Layton and Samantha finally split at the beginning of 1980 Mark didn't cry at all. It was as if he never believed they were his real parents. He was four at the time and Layton couldn't remember the boy ever laughing. Samantha always said there was nothing wrong with him, he was just high-strung, like her. And, like her, would grow up neurotic, protected, estranged.

Andy was climbing a tree when Layton pulled up. "Hi," he called out.

"Hey, a talking tree," Layton said.

"It's me, Andy."

"You're kidding. I've got a son inside named Andy. What a coincidence." Andy slid along a branch until he was above his father and then let go with a squeal. "You're in a good mood."

"I made it to the Kingdom of the giant Jumungas. A new record!"

"Ter-*rif*-ic," Layton said. He wondered how he ever made it through childhood without video games. "Did you go to school too?"

"That guy with the Corvette was here today. Why don't we get a car like that?"

"What's wrong with my car?"

"It's not a car, it's a Jeep. It doesn't go fast."

"When the Big One hits and this becomes a desert you'll be glad I've got a Jeep."

"How come you always have a silly answer whenever I ask you something? How can we end up in a desert where we live?"

"Remember the last earthquake when you told me the whole house shook like a giant was trying to lift it? Well if a stronger one comes and California falls into the ocean, what's left will be a desert. That's something to think about isn't it?"

"You're just trying to scare me."

"Nah. I've got the Jeep."

Leanne was doing her math homework at the kitchen table. She looked up at Layton when he walked in and shot him a smile. "Dad drove 470 kilometers from St. Louis to Chicago," she read. "Then mom drove 670 kilometers from Chicago to Toronto. How far did they drive together?"

"470 kilometers," Layton said.

"How can that be right? You have to add it."

"You said together, right? After they drove to Chicago, the mother left the dad sleeping in the motel and she drove by herself to Toronto."

"It doesn't say that," Leanne protested.

"Doesn't have to. Happens all the time."

"The answer is 1,140 kilometers. It's an addition problem."

"I thought it was a family problem."

"It's not about us, dad. It's just math."

He always admired his daughter's ability to rationalize. When she was four and he was still living with them he taught her poker, which she picked up immediately. Instead of reading to her before sleep they'd play Texas Hold 'em. She rarely lost. He'd mumble about beginner's luck and she'd point out that after a hundred hands she was no longer a beginner. Her friends were beginners, and stayed that way because they refused to learn how to play. Their fathers weren't actors.

"So where's your mother?"

"Sleeping."

"At dinner time?"

"She said you should make us food."

Layton glanced at the plastic garbage bag in the corner and saw the empty bottle of tequila. He walked into the bedroom where Amy was sprawled on her back, her right leg dangling off the bed.

"Well," he said to his kids, "where shall we go to eat?"

"The beach," Leanne suggested.

"Pretty far away," Layton said, but he liked the idea. There was still plenty of light, it would take maybe forty minutes to go down Sunset until they reached Gladstone's. Driving down the canyon Layton spotted a young buck deer, its antlers reaching out about two feet. He had never seen a deer on this road before. Once they had seen two deer on Mulholland Drive, staring into the headlights of passing cars, but the canyon was a much narrower and twisting road. The deer seemed to be looking for a place to hide, or for a lost friend. Leanne and Andy wanted to stop but there was no place to pull over, and what would they do if there was? It was encouraging to know there was still some wildlife left in the canyons and that the coyotes and bobcats hadn't chased away all the deer.

"Do people eat deer?" Leanne asked.

"Sure," Layton said. "Deer, cow, buffalo, horse, rabbit, frog. It's all meat."

"I could never eat a deer," she said.

"Me neither," Andy agreed. "I don't even like fish."

"Too bad," Layton said, "because we're going to a fish restaurant. You ever try shark?"

Andy didn't know sharks could be eaten. He'd like to try it, he said. Layton reminded Leanne that she always liked fish and that when she was four her favorite thing in the whole world was to go to the ocean when the grunion were running and chase them.

"You always remember things Leanne did, you never remember anything about me," Andy pouted.

"That's not true, you little shit," Layton said. "It's just that I was around Leanne a few years longer than you."

"What do you remember about me?" Andy asked.

"I remember the sound of your running all the time. I remember when I put on any of Beethoven's symphonies in the car you would conduct with your finger while sitting in your car seat. You were about a year old then. When you were two you used to like when I put on Caruso because you thought he was crying."

"Who's Cruzo?"

"Only the greatest tenor who ever lived."

"I don't even know what a tenor means. Is that all you remember?"

"I used to laugh the way you hopped around doing the 'Uh-uh Pigeon' to your Burt record. And the way you liked to fake sleep and ask me to poke-poke-poke you so you could say to me, 'Ernie, why'd you wake me up?' Only you never said it right, you'd say, 'Ernie, why'd you make up?' And then you'd laugh and laugh and say 'Oh my Jesus.'"

"I remember that," Andy said.

"Do you remember the monsters in your tushie? And poo-poo milk and pee-pee juice?"

"And ca-ca and doo-doo pies!"

"Oh, gross," Leanne said.

"You're the one who told him about the monsters," Layton said to her. "You had them too, only yours were men with tails."

"Daddy! That's not true."

"Sure is."

"Me," Andy said. "What about me?"

"Remember when he almost electrocuted himself?" Leanne said.

"How can I forget? You stuck a wire in an outlet and I had to pull you away. Boy, did you cry then."

"Like he always cried when you and mommy left us with a sitter," Leanne said.

"I did not," Andy said.

At Gladstone's Andy didn't like the shark, Leanne wasn't happy with her sand dabs, and Layton tasted better filet of sole, but it was a fun dinner in spite of the food. Afterwards they went for a walk on the beach where they saw a dead dolphin and studied it for some meaning.

Andy poked at its eyes. Leanne yelled at him to leave it alone. Layton asked them what they thought death was.

"Death," Andy answered, "is a dolphin."

It was a remark that would stay with Layton for the rest of his life.

■ ■ ■

With the kids and Amy asleep Layton turned on the TV to watch a movie on cable. *Reservoir Dogs* was playing but he didn't feel like seeing it again. He'd had enough violence for one day. He pressed the remote buttons aimlessly, switching from sit-com to family drama, from CNN to home shopping, public access to E! Even with all the new channels choices were still limited and dull. Springsteen was right, fifty-seven channels and nothing to choose. How could there be such a glut of programs and still be nothing worth watching?

He shut off the box and sat in the dark. He'd go see Samantha in the morning but he didn't look forward to that. If they could only be friends. He loved her of course. If she wanted him back he'd be there in a minute. Amy wasn't someone to return to. If only she had something that had meaning for her. Nothing held her interest for long. Not the kids, not books, not television, movies, friends; certainly not him. Just drinking. And he wondered if she really enjoyed that or just forced it down in order to lift herself to a place where she could tolerate things. She liked sex, but how long did that take? How many orgasms did she need to make it through a day? She could still turn him on but not like she used to. He couldn't say the dirt she liked to hear. He wasn't into tying her or licking sherry off her thighs. It didn't even bother him to think of her with other men. How was he going to get through these times? What else could he do with his life? He had no other training. He had lived a freelance life, going from one role to another, but the offers had stopped coming, the money wasn't there, he was reduced to taking whatever bit part was thrown his way, whatever commercial work that leaned on whatever fame was left. He was a recognizable face and that was still worth something. With all those TV channels there would always be something for him to do. But even there he had to hustle. There were hundreds of other actors who came up when he did and who were also struggling. Only a handful maintained their stardom. For the most part actors were like models. They bloomed young and then faded into the background. His kids were growing fast. He could see parts of himself in both of them. And in Mark. Brooding, troubled Mark.

He thought about parts he'd like to play if he was in Samantha's position. He'd like to remake *Dr Jekyll and Mr Hyde*. He'd be good at that. And *Dracula*. Not the way Francis Coppola monstered it or the way George Hamilton goofed it, but like Bela Lugosi. The world's greatest, most terrifying lover.

He felt like crying. Who could he call? Kevin Costner? Oliver Stone? Gary Oldman? Denzel Washington? He had their numbers but what would he say to them? Wanna play some ball? Go fuck women? Be friends? They had their own problems, didn't need him. And he didn't want to be anybody's problem. Why did it have to be so lonely being an actor? A movie star. Former star. Current failure. *The Invisible Man*. That's what he should revive. Wouldn't have to see him at all.

"Layton? You in here?" Amy walked groggily into the dark room. "You scared me," she said when she saw his outline. "What are you doing in the dark?"

"Thinking dark thoughts."

"Where'd you take the kids?"

"What if I didn't come here tonight?"

"They know where the food is, they can feed themselves."

"I'm going to have you committed."

"Swell, I could use a vacation."

"You just had one."

"My mother's no vacation. She makes me very nervous."

"Don't turn on the light."

"I want to see you."

"I haven't changed."

"This gives me the creeps."

"Go back to bed."

"I've got a headache."

"I wonder why."

"Will you massage my neck?"

"No."

"What do you want, Layton?"

"A life."

"You've got that."

"Is that what you call this?"

"What about me? What have I got? You were no prize."

"I don't care about you. You better start caring about yourself."

"I make out."

"That's not what I mean."

"I'll survive. You're the one who's got to worry."

Layton sighed. If he could snap his fingers and make her disappear forever he'd do it. Was this the burden he was meant to carry like Sisyphus? Is Amy what *existential* meant? Could he kill her and put her out of her misery? Oh my Jesus.

"There's no aspirin in the house," Amy said.

"Take a vitamin."

"Could you go get some?"

"It's two-and-a-half miles down the canyon. I don't want to go out anymore. I've been out."

"Then I'll go."

"Go."

"Please. My head. My eyes, just behind my eyes. I can't drive like this."

"Christ, Amy, I should punch you too."

"Too? Did you hit the children?"

Layton stood up, glared at her in the dark, and walked out. She asked where he was going and he answered he'd be back.

Half a mile down the canyon he caught a glimpse of a coyote running towards him, then cutting away behind a house. Further down his lights picked up something in the road, an overturned garbage can perhaps. When he got closer he saw it was the deer, laying across half the road, bleeding from his nose. His eyes were opened and Layton could see the struggle for breath. He stopped the car and approached the dying animal. There were teeth marks where his face had been partially chewed. The deer was too big for a coyote to take on alone. What must have happened was a car hit the buck, and then the coyote came to finish him off. He was being eaten alive.

There was nothing Layton could do to save the animal and he didn't want him to suffer any more than he already had. So he got back into his Jeep and drove forward, then put the car in reverse and attempted to back up over the deer. But the deer was too bulky to run over. Layton thought of trying just the head, only the antlers could cause damage to the Jeep. Frustrated and wanting to help put the deer out of his misery Layton got out of his car and walked back to where the deer lay, his eyes seeming to plead for protection from the coyote who had returned and was watching Layton from the other side of the road. Layton didn't sense the coyote but he could see the look of terror in the deer's eyes. He remembered watching a documentary about lions and how they often defeated a larger animal like a water buffalo by getting their mouths around its mouth and nose, closing off the air supply and suffocating it. Layton went to his Jeep and took the duffel bag he kept in the back seat, emptied out the gym clothes in it, and returned to the deer. He placed the bag over the deer's bloody face and held it tightly. The deer at first didn't move, then his body jerked in quick spasms. Layton felt the hot rush of tears well up in his own eyes, overwhelmed with sadness by what he was doing. Like the character George in Steinbeck's *Of Mice and Men*, he was mercifully killing one of God's creatures. The deer's hind legs fluttered but it was obvious that he was too far gone to fight the death that was running through his body. It only took a few minutes until his life was stilled.

The duffel bag was too wet with blood to keep and Layton used it to grab the deer by his antlers and move him to the side of the road. When he looked up he saw the coyote–a hungry, bony animal whose body had been ravaged by other animals, perhaps dogs or raccoons or possums. Its body was mangy, the fur spotted and uneven with patches of raw skin showing. Driven out of its natural habitat and forced to scrounge among garbage cans, picking off rats and the occasional loose cats and small dogs, the deer was too big a feast for the coyote to back away. Layton raised his bag in the air to threaten the scavenger but the coyote stood its ground. There was nothing Layton could do. The deer was dead. The coyote was hungry. Layton got back into his Jeep and drove down the canyon into the city. He didn't return to Amy's until morning. She never asked what had happened.

3

Just Tell Me When To Stop

Samantha Sanders couldn't decide what color tile to choose for the pool. She'd narrowed it down to three shades: charcoal, smoky gray, and misty black, but they were so close she just knew whichever she selected would not satisfy her once it was installed. The problem was trying to imagine what it would look like under water. She tried looking at each of them in a bucket of chlorine water but it wasn't the same. The tile man was coming this afternoon but how could she decide under such pressure? He'd just have to make another appointment. After all, this wasn't a small decision. She'd have to live with this for a long time. Unless she found it totally unbearable, in which case she'd have the pool drained to replace the tile again. That meant no swimming pool for weeks, more workmen, more noise. She'd been through that one. Who said rich people have no problems?

She was convinced the world was out to cheat her because of who she was. And she was determined to fight. For every hundred letters of praise and adulation she received from fans there were always a couple of snotty ones. Her secretary attempted to shield her from those but Samantha saw enough to know that she wasn't loved by everyone. Which bothered her. She knew it was irrational: no one was totally accepted, not even Dolly Parton. But knowing that didn't make it any easier. She gave so much when she acted she wanted that much in return. And it wasn't just from fans—she wanted the tile man and the roofer, the gardener and her personal trainer to love her too. She was paying for it, she expected it. If it wasn't there, she'd make them miserable.

Her swollen jaw ached. The doctor said it wasn't broken but she didn't believe him. He said the swelling would go down in a few days. She couldn't look in a mirror without feeling an intense hatred and need for revenge. Her face was her life, how dare he disfigure it. She had to cancel all her meetings, including one with QVC's Barry Diller, and that made her restless. So she concentrated on her house. The game room needed work, the pool was empty, the screening room should be redecorated. There wasn't a room in the 12,000 square foot house which couldn't be changed.

Mark was upstairs in his room reading *The Castle,* which didn't make sense to him. He had read and liked Kafka's story "The Hunger Artist," but this one was too much, he couldn't relate. His mother said she couldn't see him for a few days and he knew when she was angry to stay clear of her. The house was big enough for them to easily keep apart. When she called him on his phone to tell him she needed to be alone he had asked if he should go stay with his father. When she hung up on him he figured it had something to do with Layton and didn't press.

He liked his father but thought him strange. He didn't know why Layton was an actor. Mark had seen six of Layton's films and wasn't impressed. He always seemed like he was trying too hard, like he was acting. For Samantha, acting seemed effortless; what you saw was who she was, except for her nasty, violent side, which she rarely showed on screen. Her public, she once told him, wouldn't understand.

He didn't talk about movies much. It was boring watching them being made. So little got done in a day. Even as a small boy he never enjoyed being on a movie set. There was never anything to do. Just a lot of waiting around, listening to his mother rant about how lousy the script was, how the writer should be fired, how the lighting wasn't flattering. He used to get embarrassed when she'd call in the director and start complaining about his direction. Nobody was ever good enough for her. Making a movie was a constant battle. He never once saw her happy on a set. The only time she laughed was when she had to. Or when she was able to change directors.

His mother had a lot of men friends but none were good enough to live with. On that he happened to agree. The only man who ever talked back to her was his father and he wasn't allowed to see her. So when he heard the Rottweilers barking outside he assumed it was anyone but Layton.

The dogs kept Layton in his Jeep, honking his horn. Normally the electronic gate at the bottom of the driveway would have stopped him but because Samantha was expecting a delivery of some palm trees the gate was open and he just drove up. When no one came out to call the dogs off he decided to out-psych them. He knew their names and started to talk softly to them. Their ears perked and their barking stopped. But as soon as Layton stuck his foot onto the pavement they bit him.

Mark heard the commotion from his room and looked out the window. His father was pinned against his Jeep screaming at the dogs as they growled and chewed at him. His left leg was bleeding and had Mark not yelled from above they might have turned him into a soprano. They were very mean, high-strung, viciously trained attack Rottweilers.

Mark came running. Samantha was dipping tiles under water and missed what had happened. The dogs backed off but kept wary eyes on Layton, ready to jump at him on signal. Mark smacked their noses as he passed them. Tears came to his eyes when he saw his father's torn, bloody leg and his genuine pain.

"They're foaming," Layton said. "Don't you feed them?"

"I'll call mom," Mark said, then remembered that she didn't want to see him and went inside to call a doctor instead. Layton limped behind him, dripping blood on the hall tiles. When he saw how much blood he was losing he hopped to the living room so he could ruin the white carpet.

"Mom's going to go nuts when she sees that," Mark said, awed that even his father dared such a defiant act.

"Where is she?"

"Out back. I didn't tell her."

Layton looked at his son and saw clearly the kind of tension he lived with. He hobbled to a bathroom, rolled up his pants and stuck his leg into the toilet. Mark handed him the soap and he washed the deep puncture wounds. Layton could have stuck his little finger in four of them. He wrapped a towel around his leg and removed it from the bowl.

"I called a doctor," Mark said.

"Is he coming?"

"No. He said he'd treat you in his office. It's not far, it's in Beverly Hills."

"Would he come for your mother?"

"Probably."

"How do you expect me to get there? Go get Samantha."

"I can't."

"Why not?"

"She said she doesn't want to see me."

What kind of pitiful life was this boy living, Layton wondered. He stood up, blood still running down his leg, and made it to the garden door before he fainted. Mark screwed up his courage and yelled for his mother.

"How'd he get in?" Samantha asked Mark.

"The dogs attacked him. He's bleeding."

"I can see that." She asked about Manuel, her sharp-shooting security guard. Mark reminded her she had given him the day off. "Your father's lucky. Manuel would have shot him."

"He doesn't look too lucky," Mark said, bending over Layton. "What should we do?"

"Throw some water on his face. If he'd made it out the door I'd turn the hose on him."

"Why are you like this to him?" Mark asked.

"Your father is a jerk," Samantha said. "If he had any brains he wouldn't get himself in trouble all the time."

Mark looked up at his mother and saw her swollen jaw for the first time. He was about to say something but the way her teeth were clenched warned him against it. He didn't dare argue with her. She might sic the dogs on him. He ran to the kitchen and brought back a glass of water that he splashed on Layton's face. Layton opened his eyes and saw Mark's concerned look. And behind him, the knit brow and dagger eyes of his ex-wife.

"I think you might call this even," he said.

"You call it whatever you like, I've already called Sol."

"I came to apologize."

Samantha just stared at him as if he had three eyes. "I want you out of here," she said. She walked into the house and saw the ruined carpet. "Goddamn you!" she shrieked. "You're going to pay for that!"

Mark gave his father an 'I-told-you-so' shrug, then helped him up. Together they made it out of the house and back to his Jeep. "You drive," Layton said.

"Me? I don't have a license."

"Fuck a license, this is an emergency. Get me to that doctor before I faint again."

"Dad, I don't know how a Jeep works."

"Same as any car. Get in, I'll show you."

From a window Samantha saw Mark get behind the wheel and came running out the front door. "You get out of that car," she demanded.

"Ignore her," Layton said.

"Did you hear me!"

Mark was confused. "Dad, what should I do? I have to live with her."

"You'll stay with me, just drive."

Samantha stood in front of the Jeep with her hands on her hips. Superwoman, Layton thought. If we went forward she'd probably dent the car.

"Step on the gas," Layton said to his scared son as he shifted into reverse. The Jeep jerked backwards. "Don't worry about anything, we'll make it."

Mark didn't say a word until they reached the doctor's office. Then, in the elevator, he said, "I'm in a lot of trouble."

"You're in trouble? I might have to have my leg amputated and you're worried about yourself? What's wrong with you?"

"Why'd you come to the house?" Mark asked. "Why didn't you call?"

"I wasn't coming to see you."

"You know mom doesn't want you to come there."

"You're beginning to sound like her. I hate that whining."

"What happened to mom's face?"

"She ran into a traveling fist."

"You're not making my life any easier," Mark sighed.

"I'm your father not your psychiatrist. Nobody said life was supposed to be easy."

The doctor treated his leg in half an hour. Nasty bites but no punctured arteries or veins. Mark skimmed *Architectural Digest* and *Town & Country* in the waiting room, wondering if he should call his mother, who probably called the police to report his kidnapping.

"The doc said I can drive, so let's go, partner," Layton said when he came out.

"I'd better go back," Mark said.

"Tomorrow. Let's do something together."

"Like what?"

"How about flying to Catalina for lunch?"

"That's crazy."

"Then it's settled. Terrific."

■ ■ ■

Samantha was on the phone. To her lawyer, her manager, her agent, her only friend Alicia, her mother, and the tile man. Her lawyer, Sol, warned her any legal action against Layton would generate publicity and did she really want that? Especially for Mark? Her manager thought she was overreacting but didn't tell her that; he listened sympathetically and offered to take her for lunch, but she couldn't think of eating until "that schmuck" brought her son back. Her agent agreed with every foul thing she had to say about Layton and thought she should sue the shit out of him for all the physical and psychological abuse he had given her. Alicia said she knew someone who knew someone who once hired a hit man and if Layton continued to be a pain in her psyche maybe she should consider having him eliminated. Samantha took her seriously and said she'd think about it. Her mother told her what she always told her: find another man already, get married, try living a normal life; but even she wouldn't dare suggest that Samantha give Layton another chance. "He still loves you, that's why he does these things," was as far as she'd go, always adding, "If only he wasn't so crazy in the head. What you ever saw in him in the first place I'll never know." The tile man told her he wouldn't be able to come for four days if she cancelled him today; he didn't offer her any personal advice, even though she used her son's kidnapping as the reason for the postponement. When she asked him, "So what do you think I should do?" he replied, "I'd go with the smoky gray."

How could this be happening to her? Her life was just too important for a nobody like Layton Cross to so upset it. Even when he was box-office he was still a lousy actor. And a lousy lover. A lousy husband. A lousy human being. There wasn't a single elegant thing about him. The tile man had more class. Whenever Mark spent a weekend with him it took her the rest of the week to undo his influence. She didn't even put smoking dope beyond him. In fact, she was sure if Mark ever tried it, it would be Layton who turned him on. The lousy creep.

■ ■ ■

"Have you ever smoked grass?" Layton asked Mark as they drove to San Pedro.

"Come on, Dad."

"You have, haven't you? Every kid in America has smoked a joint by your age."

"I tried it," Mark said. "Didn't do much."

"Did it do anything?"

"I don't remember."

"How about sex?"

"What about it?"

"Am I embarrassing you?"

"A little."

"Just tell me when to stop."

"I will."

"If you don't tell me, I won't know."

"I know."

"So."

"So?"

"Don't want to talk about it, huh?"

Mark didn't answer. Layton figured there was nothing to discuss. "We don't have to go to Catalina, it was just an idea."

"That's okay."

"Okay you want to go or okay let's not bother?"

"Whatever you want to do."

"I want to ask you something. You don't have to answer, but I want to ask. Are you ashamed of me?"

"What do you mean?"

"Don't answer me with a question, just answer me straight."

"I don't know. Maybe. Sometimes. Not all the time. You're my father."

"I know what I am. When?"

"When what?"

"When sometimes?"

"Like when I read things about you."

"Do you believe everything you read?"

"Not everything."

"What things then?"

"I don't remember."

"You remember."

"Like when you pee'd in Amanda Rash's hat."

"Where'd you read that?"

"Someone told me."

"Your mother?"

"A kid at school."

"How come you never asked me about it?"

"I don't know."

"It's true. I did. Want to know why?"

"Yeah."

"Because she deserved it."

Layton laughed at the memory. Amanda Rash was his costar in *Rainy Day in L.A.* She was never on time, she didn't know her lines, she complained about the director, the crew, her hemorrhoids. Nobody could stand her. Layton was the only person on the set she liked but he agreed with all the others, she was a giant pain in the ass. Nobody cared about the film because of her; the production was going into the toilet. So, before a scene that called for her to wear a large hat, Layton and the crew waited a half hour for her to emerge from her dressing room. The hat was on her chair on the set. Layton pulled down his zipper and did what he felt was needed to bring some life to the film. The entire crew knew about it within five minutes. Spirits were revived. The rest of the shoot was a breeze. Amanda Rash was disgusted and outraged and threatened to quit but she was never late again.

"What else?" Layton asked.

"Why'd she deserve it?"

"Movies are a strange business. It's teamwork. When an actor refuses to play along everyone suffers. She just forgot she was part of a team. I reminded her."

Mark was quiet. Layton took a joint from the glove compartment and lit it. He passed it to his son, who was scared. "Go ahead," Layton encouraged. "Trust me."

Mark took a puff but didn't inhale. Layton showed him how. He took another puff and coughed out smoke. He was so worried what his mother would do to him if she found out that he couldn't relax. Layton was determined to break through. There were other joints in the glove compartment.

Even though traffic was tied up on the freeway, they were flying. Mark was telling him stories about Samantha Layton had never heard before. How she once dropped a soufflé on the floor, picked it up and served it to her guests anyway. Or when Mel Gibson dropped by unexpectedly and she refused to let Mark or anyone else answer the door because she had a pimple on her chin. Then there was the time she fell into the toilet bowl because Mark had left the seat up; her thighs were bruised and she wouldn't go swimming until the marks went away.

Layton added stories of his own. When he and Samantha were being driven to the Oscars and she was so nervous she pee'd on the floor of the limo, making him swear he would never tell as long as he lived. And in New York once they were eating in Chinatown when a cockroach crawled out of the lo mein; Samantha jumped and kicked over the table, then slipped on the noodles and landed on the mushu pork.

By the time they reached San Pedro they had forgotten why they had driven there. Layton saw a sign by the harbor that read WHALE WATCH and Mark thought it was a good idea, so they pulled into the parking lot and climbed aboard a boat filled mostly with third and fourth graders from a private school. Mark became paranoid about getting seasick but Layton told him that grass was better than Dramamines.

"Are you making that up?" Mark asked.

"Me? Your father? Trust me, you won't get sick."

Mark didn't. Layton did.

As soon as the boat left the harbor the rolling of the waves brought on a hint of nausea. Layton went below and bought a box of Saltine crackers. Two miles out the first whale was spotted. Mark was as excited as the school children, standing transfixed at the awesome sight. First a spout of water from its blowhole; then the large round head covered with crusty coral-like barnacles, sticking straight out of the sea. Then what seemed like a back flip as the whale dove down, its huge tailfin flapping in the air before disappearing.

"Hey Dad, did you see that?" Mark turned to look for Layton, who was sitting below on the floor.

"Dad? You all right?"

"I'm fine. What'd I tell you, you're not sick, are you?"

"Jesus, you don't look good."

"Something I ate."

"Your face is green."

"Go watch the whales."

"You should come up, it's amazing."

"You'll tell me about it in the car."

The boat stayed out for two-and-a-half hours. Mark counted seventeen whales, the official count was twenty-nine. Layton saw none. Mark had no idea you could see so many whales so close to shore. Layton didn't feel they were close at all. To him close was when he could jump over and swim back.

■ ■ ■

Andy and Leanne were happy to see Mark, although both showed disappointment that they hadn't been included on the whale expedition. Andy asked Layton if he'd take them on the weekend but Layton ignored him. When Andy persisted Layton told him to get Amy to take them, he'd never step foot on a boat again. Mark described Layton's seasickness and the children teased him for the rest of the evening.

Samantha's secretary Faye called, Amy told Layton. "She made a big fuss about bringing Mark home."

"He's staying here with us."

"For how long?"

"Long as he likes."

"What are you going to do about her?"

"Fuck her."

"Then you answer the next call," Amy said.

When it came Layton told Faye Collabella that if Samantha had something to say let her get on the phone.

"She's not going to talk to you," Collabella said.

"And I'm not going to talk to you," Layton said, hanging up.

Five minutes later the phone rang again. "You goddamn son-of-a-bitch," Samantha shouted, "if you don't bring Mark back here in the next half hour I'll have the fucking police at your door."

"And I'll have those dogs of yours shot," Layton yelled back.

"You were trespassing."

"I was coming to apologize, you stupid cunt."

"Don't you dare call me that."

"Mark's staying for dinner. He's visiting with Leanne and Andy. When he's ready to go home he'll go. And if he wants to spend the night he'll stay."

"I don't want him spending the night with you. Since when did you move back there anyway?"

"None of your fucking business and why don't we let him decide."

"Because he's under your influence. You manipulate him."

"I manipulate him?! You're the one he lives with. You're the one who won't let Mel Gibson into your house because you don't want him to see a pimple on your chin."

"Did Mark tell you that?"

"No, I ran into Mel at the Self-Realization Center, putting flowers by Gandhi's ashes."

"You get sicker by the hour," Samantha said. "I can't talk to you."

"Then why'd you call?"

"Let me speak to Mark."

"He's playing Genesis with Andy."

"PUT HIM ON THE PHONE!"

"They're in the middle of a game."

"I'm hanging up now and calling back in five minutes. Make sure Mark answers, you creep."

Layton kept the phone off the hook until Mark finished his game, then suggested he call his mother. Mark looked at him sheepishly and said maybe he'd better just go home instead. Layton told him to develop some spine, to stand up to her. "What do you want to do?"

"Stay, I guess."

"Then tell her that."

"She'll only punish me."

"What's the worst she can do?"

"Ground me."

"That's how you live anyway, isn't it?"

Mark looked like he was about to cry. Layton realized he was pressing him too hard. "Look, just call her and say you'd like to stay overnight. I'll bring you back in the morning."

Mark nodded and made the call. When he hung up he said he had to leave now and would take a taxi.

"Can't you even stay for dinner?" Amy asked.

"Yeah, stay," Andy added.

Layton looked at Mark's sad, angst-ridden face and told him to get in the car.

"I had a great time," Mark said when they approached Samantha's automated gate. "Really."

"Don't let her intimidate you so much," Layton said. "And don't be afraid to call when you want to talk."

"You gonna be there for a while?"

"For a while. Until Amy kicks me out."

"Mom's all right," Mark said. "She just has to get her way, that's all."

"Nobody always gets his way," Layton said.

"She does," Mark responded weakly.

Layton pressed the intercom button and was told not to drive onto the premises. Mark got out before Layton could make an issue out of it and said he'd be okay.

"Call me tonight," Layton said.

Mark said he would, but he didn't. Part of his punishment was losing his phone. And his big-screen TV, use of the game room, screening room, Jacuzzi, steam room, trampoline, and tickets to the Luciano Pavarotti private concert and Yo-Yo Ma cello recital at the Music Center which he had been looking forward to.

He'd learn to obey his mother from now on. Or write a book about her when he was no longer dependant on her.

■ ■ ■

Al Low had left several messages but Layton didn't check his service until after dinner. He hadn't told Amy or the children about the punch which would surely be in the news soon and decided to wait until hearing what Low had to say.

"Everybody's got the story," Low said. "It's going over the wires. Every paper in the country will probably carry a blurb. Liz Smith may pass because she didn't get it first but I doubt it. It's too juicy."

"Maybe this will get me out of storage at the Hollywood Wax Museum," Layton said.

Low had talked to the editors of the news and gossip weeklies and most felt they could get what they needed over the phone but Low didn't like that approach. Layton had a way of saying things over the phone—like getting back into the wax museum—which could be misinterpreted. *Rolling Stone* said they'd send a photographer and put the picture with a few quotes in their Random Notes section, which Low thought was a good idea. But Layton balked, remembering when he was on the cover of *Rolling Stone*. Low convinced him by pointing out that Bobby De Niro, Michael Bolton, Clint Eastwood, and Michael Jackson were often featured in Random Notes. *The Star* might go with a split cover of the two of them but Low warned Layton that it would most likely be a full-page shot of Samantha and a small insert of him. Still, cover stories like that put his puss on the counter of convenience stores and supermarkets across the country; and since Samantha would never talk to them the article would, by default, be dominated by Layton's comments. *Time* said they'd stick a mention in the People page but felt they didn't need any quotes unless there was a picture of the event to accompany it; fortunately or unfortunately, there was none. *Newsweek* passed. *People* would stick it in the Chatter page at the end of their book. *Entertainment Weekly* would mention it up front in their News & Notes. The Los Angeles *Times* would run it in their second page Newsmakers column. *Variety* and the *Hollywood Reporter* would make sure the Industry knew about it. *Movieline* and *Premiere* would have some fun with it but since they were monthlies it would be old news by the time it appeared. All in all Layton's pop to Samantha's chin was worth about four to six lines of newsprint in the more respectable publications and whatever could be squeezed out in the rags. As for the TV tabloids, they'd have it on the air by tomorrow.

"So where does *Rolling Stone* want to take the picture?" Layton asked.

"You choose it," Low said.

"How about in front of Gandhi's sarcophagus at the Self-Realization Lake Shrine?"

"There's a place I'd never have thought of," Low said.

"I wonder whether the Mahatma could have held back if he was once married to a woman like Samantha," Layton said.

"There is no other woman like Samantha," Low said. "That's why this is happening."

"Maybe I'll call Mel Gibson to come pose with me."

Al Low laughed that unsure go-along Hollywood laugh which he used so often he mistook it himself for sincerity. He promised to get back to him first thing in the morning with a schedule. Layton said he'd be sure to wear his Free Mike Tyson T-shirt, which Low took seriously.

"Maybe you'd better hold off on that."

"Just bring boxing gloves, huh?"

It was all so silly, the way the media rushed to make something like this into news. Had he split her head open with an axe, had he cut out her liver and fed it to her dogs, had he injected her with AIDS-contaminated blood, there'd be reason to make him a feature. But then, he wasn't the object of this attention. It was only his fist. Samantha's precious jaw was the focus. Her jaw, her pride, her response. Would this goad her into the open? Would she take her former husband to court where she would have to appear, to the endless delight of photographers and video camera crews? Who could forget the sensational shot of Anna Kashfi belting her ex, Marlon Brando, with her handbag outside the courtroom, where they were battling for custody of their son Christian? Or, when Christian grew up to shoot his sister's boyfriend and Brando made those public appearances in his defense? What a field day the media would have if Layton could publicly provoke Samantha Sanders to strike out at him! That's what this was all about. Showtime.

Layton spent the night playing Monopoly with Leanne and Amy, thinking about Samantha. They hadn't been linked for many years and even at their worst he had never struck her. When Leanne accused him of not concentrating after he passed up a chance to buy Marvin Gardens and prevent Amy from a monopoly Layton told them what he had done.

"Does that mean you will go to jail?" Leanne asked.

"He should be so lucky," Amy said. "What it means is he'll soon be living in a one-room motel in Culver City."

"It'll die down in a week, then be forgotten," Layton said. "I'm not worried."

"She doesn't forget," Amy reminded him. "She remembers every picture ever taken of her. She knows exactly who cheated her since she was seven. You've really done it this time, my dear."

"Does Mark know?" Leanne asked.

"Probably."

"No wonder she was so crazed," Amy said.

Leanne excused herself to go to the bathroom and when she returned she was smiling. "You won't have to go to jail," she said. Her parents looked at her. "I just talked to Samantha. She said she was only going to sue daddy, not send him away."

"You called her?" Layton asked.

"Good for you," Amy said.

"You called her?"

"What else did she say?" Amy wanted to know.

"She said that what daddy did was very wrong and he should be punished otherwise he would never learn."

"What did you say?" Amy asked.

"I told her daddy was very upset about it and couldn't concentrate on our Monopoly game."

"You called her?"

"Stop it Layton."

"I don't want you to call her."

"It's too late, she already did."

"Who the fuck does she think she is?"

"Layton, you're talking about your daughter."

"I'm talking about Samantha. What does she mean I should be punished. I should have knocked her out, that's what I should have done."

"You shouldn't hit women," Leanne said.

"You shouldn't hit anyone," Amy corrected.

"I can't believe you called her."

"Believe it Layt. She did."
"Now can we finish the game?" Leanne asked.

■ ■ ■

Amy came running into his room in the middle of the night. "You were screaming," she said.

Layton looked ghostly. "What a nightmare I had."

"Samantha?"

"No, Francis Coppola. He wanted to remake *Apocalypse Now!* in Vietnam. He wanted me to play Martin Sheen's part. He said he had asked every actor in town and they all said he was crazy, including Sheen, who had had a heart attack the first time. Finally he came to me because he felt I would never turn him down."

"And did you?"

"Of course not. The first week there the fighting started all over again, for real, and I was captured by the Vietcong and put in a small room with bugs and leeches crawling all over only I couldn't see because they had burned out my eyes."

"My God, how awful."

"It was a relief after Coppola! Only then I heard the whirring of a camera and it dawned on me: he had started the war himself to make the film as authentic as possible. He was filming me. There was no script, it was all really happening."

Layton got up to wash his face and tripped over the bed sheet landing on his nose. Amy asked if he wanted to come to her room. He told her to throw the comforter over him, he didn't want to move again. He spent the rest of the night curled up on the floor, wondering if there was a Col. Kurtz at the end of his dream. He had a feeling there wasn't.

■ ■ ■

It was a cloudy, overcast morning as Layton drove Sunset Boulevard to the Palisades. The luster was off Los Angeles as the seasons of riots, fires, storms, mudslides, and the earthquake had all taken their toll. People in Reseda and Northridge were abandoning their homes to foreclosure rather than choose to rebuild above a fault line where the ground might open up beneath them. The Lakers no longer played to capacity crowds after the loss of Magic Johnson, when the team began to crumble. The Dodgers were no longer pennant contenders, the Clippers barely qualified for the playoffs, the Kings couldn't bring home a trophy, the Rams and the Raiders had futures in other cities. Only the UCLA Bruins seemed to show some spark of what it was once like when winning teams made celebrities of athletes and made L.A. a place where entertainment expanded to include sports as well as music, TV and films. Now the focus had shifted to the on-going glut of disasters, to the decline of the tourist industry and the departure of big businesses, to the televised trials of overzealous cops, Oedipally murderous children, and multimillion-dollar hush money payments to keep superstars from burning out. But though the city was basically falling apart nothing had really changed over the years on this drive west. The Strip was still the Strip with its rock clubs, exotic car dealerships, Tower Records, Book Soup, Geffen's place, Paul Kohner's agency (though old Paul had died), Gil's liquor store, and the two office buildings facing each other where many of the agents and publicists hatched their deals and schemes. The Beverly Hills homes that lined Sunset had been enlarged, remodeled, rebuilt but they remained hidden behind walls of shrubs or concrete or set back by sweeping, carefully manicured lawns. The graffiti which marked up the walls of other neighborhoods didn't appear in Beverly Hills or Holmby Hills or Bel Air or Brentwood, mainly because these communities hired patrols to make sure their land wasn't besmirched by such foul signs of decadence and decay, and when a tagger managed to spray his personal hieroglyphics onto some blank space the paint police were out in force covering the dirty deed.

The drive west was a reminder of what people with money could have and even though one never, ever saw these people, the assumption was that there were living bodies (and sometimes dead, when sons raised shotguns to their parents' heads and blew their brains onto the sofa and carpet) who occupied these stately homes because the caretakers were constantly out there grooming, pruning, planting, and painting. The open bed trucks with their gardening tools and fire-lit roofing tar were parked along Beverly and Canon and Rodeo just off Sunset. Without these workers the tour buses would be driving visiting tourists through what some might consider the Twilight Zone, a few square miles of pared lawns and oversized houses that were really just movie set fronts with no one behind them. Californians who actually ventured outside were being held up at Readyteller bank machines in Studio City, stabbed to death in Woodland Hills, carjacked in West Hollywood, shot at along the San Diego and Ventura Freeways, wounded at Fairfax High, raped in Beechwood Canyon, robbed in Laurel, dealt bad drugs on Hollywood Boulevard, but along Sunset west of the Strip and all the way out to the Self-Realization Lake Shrine just a few miles from the Pacific, you'd never know that despite the weather L.A. was a really shitty place to live.

The shrine, built on property once owned by an oil company until the Indian Swami Paramahanca Yogananda had a dream that this was the place to merge one's consciousness with the infinite, was a tranquil oasis where visitors could buy a stick of incense and walk around the man-made lake, watch black and white swans float gracefully, meditate in the small chapel, contemplate a statue of an open-armed Jesus, daydream by a waterfall or river wheel houseboat. It had been a place to trip on peace, meditation, and taking marriage vows since 1950, a good movie year (*The Third Man, All About Eve, Born Yesterday, The Asphalt Jungle*, and, interestingly, *Sunset Boulevard*) but not exactly a time of tranquility, with Senator Joseph McCarthy sniffing out Communists in the film industry, the Soviet Union playing atom bomb catch-up with the U.S.,

Catch a Fallen Star

while the U.S. took the next step towards the apocalypse with the development of the hydrogen bomb. The swami preferred his dreams to the world's cold realities and after his friend Gandhi was assassinated in 1948 he had some of his ashes brought to the new shrine. And that's where Layton waited for the photographer from *Rolling Stone*.

She was fifteen minutes late and came with a young, nervous, balding reporter who said he was assigned to get a few quotes from the actor who punched out his ex-wife.

"Didn't lay a hand on her," Layton said. "Well, not exactly true. I was holding her by the shoulder and when she turned she walked into my elbow."

The young writer thought Layton had punched her, that's what this was all about.

"I may have liked to have punched her at times," Layton said, "but this was purely an accident."

The photographer, who was more professional than the young man, played with her cameras and joked, "Most punches are." She glanced quickly at Layton, who raised his eyebrows at her. When she suggested he sit on top of the sarcophagus, Layton said, "Why don't I just open my fly?"

She shot him in front of the memorial as he posed with his hands extended, palms to the sky. A goof.

"There were eyewitnesses," the reporter said.

"A lot of people see spaceships, too," Layton said.

"It's in the *Times* today."

"Write whatever you want. I'm sticking with an elbow."

"Are you making any movies?"

"I'm talking with Jean Claude Van Damme," Layton said with a wink.

The photographer laughed as she caught his expression and the writer had his quote.

A half hour later another writer showed up from *The Star*. When Layton told him what he thought about that piece of trash, Alex Briar, who only occasionally freelanced for them, agreed. "But they're paying me a thousand bucks to turn this into a story," he said. "Beats working for a living."

"What if I give you eleven hundred not to write it?" Layton asked.

"You're making this a better story," Briar said. "You know, I've always felt you've been dealt a raw deal. You're better than your last four movies and you're rarely used to your potential.

"You a director too?"

"Just an observer. I think you've lacked direction, if you want to know the truth."

"I'm a big fan of truth. Where'd you find yours, writing for *The Star* or reading the *Enquirer*?

"Take *Rainy Day in L.A.* That could have been a classic L.A. picture, but it was shot like a play. Amanda Rash walked through it like she had a rod up her ass. You acted like you couldn't take her emotions seriously."

"Considering the circumstances, she did an admirable job."

Catch a Fallen Star

"What were they?"
"She had a rod up her ass."
"She has that reputation."
"That's amore."
"Like Samantha Sanders."

Briar was good at this but Layton could see these things coming two questions away. *The Star* was going to screw him no matter what he said so better to read compiled quotes than say anything that he wouldn't later be able to deny.

"How come you don't use a tape recorder?"
"Gets in the way," Briar said.
"Of accuracy?"
"Of conversation."
"Oh, is this what we're having? I thought this was an interview."
"I've got a good memory."
"I'll let you know."

Briar asked Layton if he smoked grass, but Layton declined. Then he asked him if he ever considered writing his memoirs.

"I haven't lived long enough."
"You've got a good story."
"How do you know?"
"Your life isn't exactly private. There's a large file on you at the Academy library."
"You read it?"
"Looked through it. There're lots of unanswered questions."

"Which you want to ask?"
"Not for this story but I wouldn't mind."
"Let's see what you do with this one."
"So, how hard did you hit her?"

Alex Briar could have gone all day with him but Layton cut it short when Briar started asking about the rumor that a picture Layton was doing called *Helix* was abruptly cancelled because of his bizarre behavior, which culminated when he took a swing at Charlie Greenbloom when he visited the troubled set. It was a sensitive subject, one that Layton felt he couldn't address because he still couldn't piece together what had happened. All he could remember was eating breakfast in his trailer, then feeling very strange, as if he were in a German expressionist movie of the twenties, where buildings tilted at strange angles and actors faces turned to skulls. He hadn't taken any drugs but felt like he was hallucinating anyway, which scared certain members of the cast. Work was halted mid-day and Greenbloom was summoned. Layton's memory was also foggy about what had happened then but witnesses said that when Greenbloom threatened to close down the production Layton threw the punch that killed the film and made Layton Cross a pariah in the business. No one would insure him for a feature after that and his career just seemed to splatter like pudding dropped on a floor. The worst part for Layton was that he couldn't remember what made him act the way he did.

While he was living with Samantha it had occurred to him that his life might make a good book but he hadn't

Catch a Fallen Star

thought about it again until it was suggested. Might not be a bad idea if the money was right. He stopped at a gas station to call Spider Ray.

"You want to write a book? What for?" Ray asked.

"Money," Layton said. "What's it worth?"

"All depends. Everybody writes books. Hepburn's was a bestseller, James Earl Jones' fizzled. How much you willing to say about Samantha?"

"As little as possible."

"Then that's what it's worth."

Layton picked up the L.A. *Times* and read the short paragraph telling Southern Californians how he struck Hollywood's biggest female star and was heard shouting like a lunatic that he had no regrets. With his TV movie coming out in a few weeks he wondered if this would help the ratings.

■ ■ ■

In his second grade class that morning Andy found himself defending his father. He was the only one in the family who hadn't been told. Now two other seven-year-olds were saying that his father was a bully and why didn't he pick on men instead of women? Andy responded by saying their mothers suck the mailman's dick. Eventually this led to blows.

Amy had to go to the school to pick him up early. She had already put back a quarter of a bottle and wasn't in the mood to apologize to anyone. If Andy got into a fight he must have been provoked.

"I was," Andy said in the car. "What's provote?"

"Was it about your father?"

"I don't want to talk about it," Andy said. "Why'd he do it?"

"Do what?"

"Hit you."

"He didn't hit me."

"That's what I said."

"He hit Samantha."

"He did! Boy!" Andy seemed happy and Amy wondered why.

"Because I don't like her," he said. "She never lets Mark stay with us."

"Is that the only reason?"

"She doesn't like us to visit Mark."

"She's a big star," Amy said. "She protects her privacy."

"So's dad and he doesn't care who comes to see him."

"Your dad's not as big a star as she is."

"So what? Who cares? I like him better. She's a dick."

"Where'd you learn to say that?"

"She is."

"How can she be what she doesn't even have?"

"I only said that because you don't allow me to say the C word."

"Goddamn right."

"So what else should I call her?"

"Just keep it to yourself."
"Then how will you know how I feel?"
"I know. Believe me, I know."

Leanne also had a rough day because of the story but she handled herself nonviolently. When her friends came to ask her in whispers if it was true she said it probably was but added that Samantha often swung at her father and he never said anything to the press about it. A lot of the fifth graders were very interested in what Samantha Sanders was like, mainly because their parents wanted to know. Leanne always said nice things but this time she hinted that her father was justified to have hit her. When asked to explain how a man was ever justified to hit a woman she would only say that Samantha wasn't considerate of other people. "We know that," one of her friends said, "but she's such a big star." "That doesn't always make her right," Leanne said. Sure it does, they all thought, but no one said it. When your folks were in the business, no matter how peripheral, the biggest stars swung the pendulum the others all rode on.

Mark would never admit to it but he secretly wished that his father had laid her out. As she raved about the item in the *Times* he found her anger amusing. He thought of how he could act as a middleman between them. His father didn't deserve all her rage but he was going to get it, unless some project came up which diverted her attention. Samantha was very one-directional. Now that she was in-between films and hadn't found a script she liked her frustrations would be aimed at Layton, who also, desperately, needed a project. While one employed two readers to sift through the scripts delivered to her in boxes, the other had to enroll in a Berlitz language course to read the material coming to him. Still, ironically, they were in a similar position. What they had was each other to keep their adrenaline bubbling.

4

Bring Me A Dream

"Hey dad, Rupie's here, can we go for a bike ride?"

Rupie was a neighborhood kid, two years older than Andy. He had a large collection of baseball cards all in unopened boxes and he liked to hang around the younger kids because he learned early that it's a charge to be looked up to.

"How long you been riding a bike pardner?" Layton asked. The last time he visited Andy hadn't learned.

"Rupie taught me."

"Your mother usually go with you?"

"Or Leanne. They've both got bikes."

"Rupie," Layton said, "where's your bike?"

"I didn't bring it," Rupie said. "But it's okay, I can use Leanne's."

Layton followed the boys into the garage and helped them lift the bikes off the wall hooks. Andy's bike was small and had no gears. Leanne's was a three-speed Schwinn. Amy had a ten-speed which was about eighteen inches too short for Layton, who hadn't ridden a bike for years and was a bit shaky. Andy pedaled down the driveway but Rupie had some trouble getting on Leanne's bike and Layton suggested they walk the bikes to a side street where there were fewer cars.

"Ah c'mon, dad," Andy said. "Don't be chicken." He rode into the street and called to Rupie. Rupie got on the Schwinn and followed Andy into the road. But the pedals were a bit hard for him to reach and he soon stopped trying, extending his feet out, coasting as he picked up speed on the decline.

"Hey, stop!" Layton shouted, seeing Rupie swerve from one side of the road to the other.

"I don't know how," Rupie shouted, trying to find the pedals. Layton realized that Rupie had never ridden a gear-shifting bike and didn't know that the brakes were on the handlebars. Jesus, he thought, the kid is out of control.

He jumped on Amy's bike and went after Rupie. When he got alongside he saw the look of terror on the boy's face. He was doing a remarkable job of balancing himself as they sped down the street and when they came to the corner curve he managed to stay on the bike as he whizzed past Andy.

"Look out, look out!" Layton shouted at Andy. "Stop, just stop!" he ordered as they caught up with his son. Andy pedaled backwards and stopped his bike as Layton and Rupie went around the curve.

"I'm going to try and stop you," Layton said as they rode side by side.

"I'm scared Mr. Cross. I'm gonna get killed." The wind blew Rupie's hair back and his face had whitened considerably. In the distance Layton saw a pickup truck coming in their direction. There were also cars parked on both sides of the street. Rupie was steering but his legs were swaying as the bike continued to pick up speed. Layton reached out with his right hand and grabbed Rupie's shoulder. He held the boy for an instant when he felt himself losing control of his bike. He let go of Rupie and flew over the handlebars, the bike crashing on top of him, twisted out of shape. He felt pain in both knees and a fire along his left arm. Rupie continued down the street, unaware of what had happened to Layton.

Layton looked up from the ground and saw the pickup truck approaching, with Rupie headed straight for it. It was a gardener's truck, probably Mexicans or Koreans inside. The kid's gonna die, Layton thought, and I'm gonna get blamed for it. Though his knees were throbbing and his arm bleeding, Layton didn't feel the pain. He jumped up, lifted the bike, and stepped down so hard on the right pedal it snapped into pieces. He had to allow for the crooked handlebar, the creak of the gears, and now for the missing pedal but he got the bike in motion as he went after Rupie, knowing he might go down again, might break a leg or a wrist or suffer a concussion. It didn't matter. He'd give up a few bones to save the kid.

"Stop! Stop!" he shouted at the pickup truck, waving one arm. Rupie thought Layton was yelling at him and started screaming "I can't! I don't know how!" He caught up to Rupie once again. Oh shit now what? If I pull him he's gonna fall and will get hurt. If I brake myself I'm gonna lose him. If I don't stop him now he's going to get killed.

Layton reached out his right arm for a second time and grabbed Rupie by the shoulder. He felt his own bike going out from under him again but this time he didn't fly forward. By some miracle he managed to force Rupie straight down and once the boy's feet hit the ground he was able to come to a stop, about six feet from the slowed truck. Layton was off his seat and landed hard on the ground, his left leg caught between the spokes of the front wheel as he skidded right up to the pickup truck. He rebruised the bruises he had suffered from the cannon as he lay there thinking how close Rupie had come to biting it, how close he had come, how fucking *insane* it all was. It never should have happened. Didn't the kid know what kind of bike he was getting on? Why didn't they listen to him when he said to walk the bikes? What would Rupie's parents have said if Rupie had gotten hurt?

"You saved my life!" Rupie said as he stood holding Leanne's bike looking down at Layton.

"What happened?" Andy asked as he finally caught up with them. "Dad? Are you okay?"

Layton now felt the pain in his knees and arm and knew he wasn't that okay, but nothing felt broken and he was thankful, he would have given a few broken bones to have saved Rupie. He didn't muffle his anger however. "What did I tell you?" he yelled at the boys. "Didn't I say..." Then he caught himself. Rupie had just been through a terrifying few moments and Andy hadn't even seen what had happened. What was the point of yelling at them?

"Just walk the bikes home," he said. "Everything's all right."

"You're bleeding Dad," Andy said.

"I'm really sorry," Rupie said.

Layton looked at his scraped arm, then lifted his trousers to see his two bloody knees. The bike was a mess but he was able to turn the handlebars and limp alongside the boys as they walked in silence back to the house.

"We're very lucky," he whispered more to himself than to them. "We're all very lucky."

Later, after his heart slowed down and he had some time to relive the incident, Layton found himself thinking about John Ford's *Stagecoach*, how that stuntman Yakima Canutt galloped along on his horse to stop the runaway stagecoach, leaping onto one of the coach's horses, then under them to get into the coach and rescue the passengers. What a great moment captured on film! And here was Layton, on a sunny Sunday in the Hollywood Hills, involved in a chase and a rescue, saving the kid from a serious accident, becoming a hero–only no one saw it. There were no witnesses. No applause. His own kid was too far away. Rupie had no idea that Layton had fallen and gotten back on the bike. Only the pickup driver saw what had happened and who the hell was he? He probably didn't even speak English. Had no idea who Layton was. And how much of a hero could Layton be if no one could acknowledge it? He could feel good about himself, that he acted responsibly in a moment of crisis, but was that enough? For some people it would be. But for Layton Cross, if nobody saw it, it never even happened.

At two that morning Layton was awakened from the fifth rerun of the day's events—each dream turning up a different ending involving Rupie's death, his death, Andy's death, the pickup driver's death—by an annoying non-stop knocking on the door. It was Barry Levine, just off from his work at The Palm and higher than the hills he had just driven up.

"Do you fucking know what time it is?" Layton asked.

"Hey man, if it wasn't important I wouldn't be here." He would have liked to be there to see Amy, but Layton was too important for him to get caught fucking her.

"You can't come in, everyone's asleep."

"Come out to my car, we can talk there," Levine said.

"I don't want to come out. Go home. Or wherever it is you go at night."

"Hey, I thought we were friends."

"What are you talking about? Because I smoked a joint with you? We're not friends. Not at two o'clock in the morning."

Levine looked crushed. He had important news, something that would help Layton's career, and he was blowing it. When you're nineteen you don't think about what it's like when you're forty-four with a former wife and two kids, living in a quiet canyon home with a rooftop view of the ocean on a very clear day.

"It's a beautiful night, man. Let's take a ride."

"You've taken too many drugs," Layton said. "Are you hallucinating?"

"Just some super sinsemilla. Come and smoke some."

Layton was sympathetic to the stoned state of mind. He didn't want to smoke with Barry but he didn't want to send him out to get killed driving wildly along Mulholland either. First Rupie, now Barry. He was feeling very much the adult.

"Let's sit on the steps," he said, putting on a jacket over his pajamas.

"Thanks, man. You won't regret it. Just hear me out."

Levine had made a lot of contacts working at The Palm. He had parked the cars of the very rich, the famous, the hustlers, the whores, and those who had everything but were still looking for something. It was the drugged and the restless that he had come to know on a more intimate level. Mainly because he scored such high quality dope. If he wasn't getting some for these people he was getting it from them, to deliver to lesser dealers for a small share of the goods. Some of these guys were making so much money they didn't know what to do with it. They were searching for sources of investment and thought the easiest way to buy legitimacy was the movie business. Everybody wanted to make a movie. These guys could actually come up with the dough.

Layton had heard this rap so many times he could only shake his head at Levine's naiveté. This was just bullshit talking. It never got anywhere. Drug dealers were drug dealers, not producers. When the time came to put the money in the hands of competent people, suddenly, the money disappeared. Layton was annoyed at being awakened to have to listen to this.

"Paranoids make lousy movies," he said.

"I can set up a meeting," Levine said. "These guys I know, they like you."

"Sleep in your car," Layton said. "You can join us for breakfast."

"Let me just bring these guys over, it's not what you think. They got limos. They wear hand-tailored shirts and ostrich leather boots. They snort what this house probably costs every month.

"I don't want you bringing anybody here, you understand?"

"Okay then come to the restaurant. I'll set something up there, okay? Okay man? I'll never bug you again if I'm bullshitting you. They can make your movies. You won't have to go to Spain and learn fucking Spanish."

"What's in it for you?"

"Hey man I'm nineteen. It's pretty exciting already. I ain't gonna park cars all my fucking life."

"I don't want to go to no fucking restaurant to meet with pushers."

"Listen, they're not pushers. Don't think of them as pushers. Some don't even deal, they just buy. They hang out together because they got all this money and don't do nothing but spend it. How about it?"

Layton saw that he wasn't going to get rid of Levine until he agreed so he said he'd think it over and would talk to him in a few days. Levine said he'd come back later that morning but Layton put him off. "I'll stop by your business," he said. "You can park my car."

● ● ●

The kids were amused when a man-sized chicken knocked at their door before they left for school. Andy came running to wake his father. "There's a chicken at the door," he yelped.

"Shoo it away," Layton muttered.

"It's too big! It's Big Bird," he laughed.

"Then kill it and we'll have it for dinner."

"It's a talking chicken. He wants to see you."

Layton moved the pillow from his face and lumbered to the door where the chicken was throwing feathers in the air and singing chicken songs to Leanne and Amy. When he spotted Layton he sang:

"I've got a special delivery for you.
It's nothing like a cheese fondue.
It's a script, not a knish,
and it's not in Span-ish;
this very special English
delivery for you."

Layton looked at his name sprawled in black marker and signed for the package. This time he opened it and read the few lines of apology from Perce Dent, who had stapled a small tin foil of coke to the note. Apparently the movie was still going to be made in Spanish but Layton's part would be dubbed; if it was successful they'd make an English version, dubbing all the others and leaving Layton's voice alone.

Layton thought Perce Dent was either nuts to send him this again or he was admitting that he couldn't find him anything better. He read through the first twenty pages as he ate a bowl of puffed wheat and sliced banana. It was a ludicrous story of a blind American whose one dream was to flight a bull in Madrid.

"You going to do it?" Amy asked when she returned from driving the children.

"I'm going to enroll in an electrician school," Layton said.

"Just make sure you're here this afternoon. It's Leanne's birthday and we're having a party."

"You're beginning to like having me around."

"I could care less."

"Any night now you'll be knocking at my door."

He liked being back, playing husband and father again. Those years shuffling between boring and lonely Hollywood hotels, sleeping with boring and lonely actresses who didn't stand a chance of finding a break, had lost any rogue appeal they once had.

"Layt, I don't need to go knocking to get laid."

"So what do you want me to do?"

"Buy her a present. And get one for Andy too, since you forgot his."

Andy's was easy: Mortal Kombat for Genesis. Another cartridge to keep him bug-eyed before the TV. For Leanne he decided on a pet tortoise and dinner at Spago's, topped off with a pair of tickets to a Bette Midler concert.

Layton came to the party as a *Star Wars* bar monster, which was a big hit with Leanne's friends, none of whom had seen the movie in a theater but a few had seen it on tape. He grabbed and hugged them as they squealed and ran from him. He put a chain around his neck and Andy led him around like a pet. He dished out large scoops of Ben & Jerry's into bowls of strawberries, pineapple cubes, kiwi and papaya slices and covered it with chocolate syrup. He put on a tape of Marilyn Monroe singing "Happy Birthday" to Jack Kennedy and led the kids as they sang to Leanne. He stuck a cushion down his pants and bent over, encouraging them to play pin-the-tail-on-the-monster. When he began to run out of ideas but saw that the sugar the kids had ingested was still kicking in he announced a poker tournament. Only two boys and another girl besides Leanne knew how to play poker but Layton thought it was time for them to learn. "Any child who's reached double digits should know when to hold 'em and when to fold' em," he said. They didn't know what he was talking about.

He found three decks, gave each child four dollars in colored chips, and introduced them to twin beds, tic-tac-toe, and the cross, three games where the last card turned is wild, games that took good players half a night to understand. But these were Leanne's favorites and she knew that four-of-a-kind didn't often win, royal flushes were not uncommon, and five high cards were worth raising. As he had yet to tell Leanne about the Bette Midler tickets he decided to offer them up as the prize to whoever won all the chips. Layton had full confidence that Leanne would win and this was a fun way of giving her the present. It only took her an hour.

The only kink in the entire party was when an angry woman came to the door and demanded to speak to Layton. It was Rupie's mother, who wanted to know how Layton could have allowed Rupie on a bike he didn't know how to ride. "He said you almost got him killed!" the woman yelled.

"He said he knew what he was doing," Layton said.

"And you believed him? What kind of a nut are you, listening to a nine-year old?"

"I listen to my kids when they tell me something."

"Listen to Mr Big Shot Movie Star. Let me tell you something, you're not so big and you're not much of a star if you want to know what I think."

"Thank you for that," Layton said. "I really want to know what you think. Want to know what I think?"

"I couldn't give a shit what you think because I think you came damn fucking close to a lawsuit if Rupie got injured because of you."

"I think your son's a swell kid," Layton said. "Now if you'll excuse me I've got to get back to my daughter's party."

"Well I just wanted you to know that some parents don't let the near death of their child slide by when they hear about it."

"Ma'am, I saved your boy's life yesterday. What happened scared the crap out of me. I've got the cuts and bruises to show for it. Now if you want to come back tomorrow to thank me, I'll be happy to let you in. If you want to insult me, I'm afraid you won't be welcome."

"You want my gratitude for your being a smartass you've got to be out of your fucking mind."

"Maybe I am but Rupie's got it far worse than me."

"Oh yeah, watch what you say smartass."

"He's got you for a mother."

Layton smiled when he said it to show there were no hard feelings. He didn't blame the woman for being distraught. Rupie could have been killed. So could Layton. But it was over, like Leanne's party, and Layton had to deal with that. He didn't want that woman to spoil what had been a good afternoon so he offered to drive the kids home, saving their parents the trip. Leanne was very proud of him and so was Andy. Amy was nearly in shock, knowing that some of the children lived in the Valley and others in the city. Best of all, not a single kid brought up the Samantha incident.

"I love you Daddy," Leanne told him that night as she unwrapped her presents.

"Me too," said Andy. "When are you going to leave us again?"

"Is that what you want?" Layton asked.

"As long as you keep coming back with presents," Andy said.

"I don't want you to leave," Leanne said.

Layton felt very good about himself. He had saved Rupie. He never showed his face at Leanne's party. He didn't fuck up. The mask and costume worked. "Let's look at the loot," he said.

It was the usual assortment of gifts: designer labeled clothes, CD's, Bath & Body Works skin cleansers, weird shaped pillows, a T-shirt stencil and paint kit, and a book called *Mr Sand Man*.

"Let's see that," Andy said, pulling it away from his sister. "Who's this Sand Man guy? Where are the pictures? What a yucky book."

"It's not for little boys," Leanne said, "is it Daddy?"

Layton shrugged. "I don't know. What's it about?"

"Read it to us," Andy said.

"It's Leanne's book."

"I don't mind. You can read it to us before bed."

It was ninety-six pages. "Let's make a deal," Layton said. "You guys clean up this room and do the dishes and I'll read the first chapter to you. If we still like it, I'll read some more tomorrow night."

It had been years since Layton had read to his children. He used to read to Mark when he was a baby and enjoyed when the boy started to recognize characters and story lines. Leanne also loved to be read to as a little girl— until she learned to play poker. He had never read to Andy and didn't know whether he had an interest in stories or not. Amy was always too restless to read to them.

Mr Sand Man was about a twelve-year-old girl whose family was very poor. They couldn't afford new clothes, they didn't celebrate birthdays or Christmas, and they ate a lot of potatoes and starchy white bread. She had four younger brothers and sisters and her father died when she was ten. Her mother worked in a factory; her aunt, who lived with them, was a clerk in a shoe store; and her grandmother stayed with them, filling their heads with tales of how hard and cruel the world can be.

Whenever she went to sleep her grandmother would whisper to her that if she fell asleep straight off and didn't wake up all night Mr Sand Man might visit her in her dreams and take her away to a better world, where children are always laughing and having fun and there's always plenty to eat.

The girl often humored her old grandma and told her how Mr Sand Man came to her in her dreams and what a wonderful time she had with him, but it was never true. There was no Mr Sand Man. Her dreams were just like her life: grim, dreary thoughts of longing, of wanting but never having, of her father when he was alive, coming home so tired he could hardly stand up, never having the time to play with her.

But then one night Mr Sand Man actually came to her. He was nothing like what she had imagined. He looked just like her father, only he was smiling and happy and was there to show her what it was like in other places. He could take her anywhere she wanted to go. At first her requests were simple: a movie, a circus, an amusement park. But after a few weeks Mr Sand Man promised new dimensions and took her to places she never knew existed, where animals talked, gardens bloomed, and people were loving and friendly. Each night Mr Sand Man showed her something she never could have imagined. They traveled through time in mere seconds. It was as if she had stepped through the Looking Glass, followed the Yellow Brick Road, was sprinkled with fairy dust, and hopped into cartoon drawings to a world of fantasy and magic.

When she'd awake her head was filled with what she had seen with Mr Sand Man and she would tell her grandmother and her brothers and sisters all about it. Soon her enchantment caught on and the family would gather around her as she told about adventures she had had, about distant lands she had traveled to, flowers she had smelled. No one else was able to have such vivid dreams but she was able to share all that she dreamt with them and so they were never poor again, for they now had the great wealth that imagination can bring.

Andy and Leanne loved the story. So did Layton, who finished it in one sitting. "Why don't you make a movie like that?" Andy asked.

"Wouldn't that be great!" Leanne added.

"This is better than a movie," Layton said. "You can dream this every night, all night long, and it can always be different. Let Mr Sand Man come into your head, take you to the moon, to Mars, to the inside of the Earth.

"Will he look the same to everybody?" Andy asked.

"He looks different to everyone," Layton said. "He might look like a dog to you and your grandmother to Leanne. Just keep your mind open and let him in."

"Will you look for him too?" Leanne asked.

"Are you kidding? I've been looking for him all my life. And when he comes you guys will be the first to know."

* * *

The Star piece was a surprise. True, they sensationalized the punch but after the first two paragraphs Alex Briar treated Layton sympathetically, calling him a victim of a Hollywood system that crushes what they cannot understand. Overall it was a shallow article but it didn't make either Layton or Samantha ogres and was actually pretty fair. Most of the pictures were of earlier times when they were married and Layton could remember exactly where they were taken, what they were doing, and the mood they were in at the time. There was a mention of his upcoming TV movie and a hint of more work to come.

Layton read the piece twice, eliminating the lead two paragraphs the second time. When Alex Briar called to ask what he thought Layton told him there were a few mistakes but his quotes were accurate and there would be no suit. Briar said it was the best he could do under the circumstances and suggested they get together to discuss a more substantial article which Alex would like to write about him. He didn't have a specific magazine in mind but thought that perhaps *Vanity Fair, Esquire*, or *Playboy* might be interested. Or maybe the *Village Voice*, even though they didn't pay enough to make any extensive reporting worth a writer's while.

"Is that why you were nice to me?" Layton asked.

"I'm a fan," Briar said. "I also think you could benefit from an analytical look at your career and who you are."

"You think you can tell me who I am?"

"I can try."

"My wives couldn't tell me that. My shrink couldn't do it for six years. You got a license to analyze?"

"I'm a writer, that's what I do."

"I'm an actor, which I'm not doing."

"Sure you are," Briar said. "You're doing it right now."

"I thought you were trying to get on my good side?"

"You can't help it, you're always on."

"So what is it you want to discuss?"

Briar said he'd like to just hang out for a while, do whatever it was Layton does in a day. They could talk or Layton could ignore him and he'd just observe. He'd write the piece on spec, without an assignment, and if it came out the way he thought it might he'd have no problem selling it. The risk, Briar said, was all on his side.

"What about my time?" Layton asked. "That doesn't count?"

"Sure it counts. That's why I'm calling. Without your permission I'll go on to somebody else."

"Man's gotta live."

"You got it."

"Call me tomorrow and I'll let you know."

The phone rang again. It was Samantha's lawyer Sol. An old friend. "Layton, could you come see me today?"

"This business or you just want a signed picture for your wall?"

"She's hocking me to sue you."

"That's what she told me."

"I don't like it."

"We're in agreement there."

"So what are you going to do about it?"

"Hey Sol, I made my peace offering and almost lost a leg."

"Come this afternoon, we'll talk. See if we can't work something out."

Amy was in a rush. Her hair was unbrushed, her sandals unstrapped, and if she was wearing a bra it looked like one of her breasts was uncupped. She said she had things to do and then had to get Andy and take him to the dentist and then to a dance class she had enrolled him in against his will. Leanne was staying after school to work on the school play and since Amy was going to be tied up with Andy, Layton should pick up Leanne at four and take her for dinner.

"Sol Gordon wants to see me this afternoon," Layton said.

"So go early. I can't talk, I'm running."

"You look like shit."

"I love you too sweetheart. Have a wonderful day."

When the phone rang for the third time it was Theo Soris. He had been arrested for shoplifting and wanted Layton to come bail him out. His play was opening tomorrow night and he didn't think it would be lucky to spend the day in jail.

"I thought you only borrowed books," Layton said after writing out a thousand dollar check to get Theo out.

"I had this premonition," Theo said. "If I had the right look the play would be a success. I kept trying to put clothes together but it wasn't working; then I remembered the snakeskin jacket Brando wore in *The Fugitive Kind*. That hit me, you know? Williams wrote that one too. So I went over to Gucci's and found the perfect thing: a patchwork hipline jacket made out of the softest glove leather you've ever touched. Cost $2,600. It's the only one on the rack and it's my size. I noticed it didn't have one of those plastic clip detectors on it so I put it on when I thought no one was looking and ripped off the price tag. Then I walked up to the counter and asked if there was another jacket like the one I'm wearing, which someone had given to me a few days back. I said I wanted to buy one for a friend. This guy tells me I'm in luck, there's one left, and we walked to the rack. It's not there, obviously, and he said they must have sold it in the morning, so I said I'd come back in a week and walked out. I didn't get five feet when another guy came up besides me and asked to see me. I go into how I'm in a rush but he'd seen me take the jacket. I offered him five hundred bucks if he'd forget what he saw but the bastard must have been Gucci's son. I couldn't believe they'd call the police over a jacket; that freaked me. I thought, there goes the play."

"You're a fuck up," Layton said. He wasn't big on giving advice. No one had ever said anything to him during his self-destructive years but perhaps if someone had he could have caught himself. Theo had come close a number of times but he never caught on. Now, with a new chance a night away, he winds up at the police station. "I'm talking as a friend. I know what you're doing. If you couldn't get bail you'd be out of the show before it opened. What better excuse than to be imprisoned against your will? Only it was what you wanted, you dope. If this play's a success you'll find some other way to crap out."

"Hey, Layt, don't come down so hard. It isn't that."

"Sure it is. You can't hear me, can you? I've been there. I know what you're doing. Step outside and look at yourself. You're keeping yourself down. No one else is doing it."

"Look, I owe you for bailing me out but don't lay this heavy psycho shit on me, okay? I've got this part down; I'm not running away from it. Just wanted that jacket, that's all. That extra touch."

No sense talking, Layton figured. Every man for himself. Let Ann Landers dish out the advice.

Theo suggested they go for a drink but Layton had to go see Samantha's lawyer, then go to CBS for some last-minute looping of his TV movie. Theo's trouble had altered his schedule and he'd never make it in time to pick up Leanne so he asked Theo to do it, giving him twenty bucks to take her for dinner.

"I don't need the money," Theo said, "I like your kid."

"I'll pick her up at your place around eight, that okay? If it's later I'll call. You sure you got the part down?"

"I can handle it. We're through rehearsing. She'll be fine."

"Don't offer her any coke, she just turned ten."

"Only from the can," Theo said as Layton dropped him off. "And thanks buddy, I owe you."

Sol Gordon was the kind of lawyer other lawyers hired when they needed the best. His clientele included Arab sheiks, U.S. Senators, the presidents and chairmen of the boards of multi-national corporations, and the Hollywood heavyweights: the studio chiefs, producers, directors, and stars who brought product and talent to the local theaters and TV screens, and who were constantly involved in lawsuits over broken contracts and hidden clauses, defamation of character, delinquent payments, and pests who wouldn't go away.

Samantha was a loyal, lovable, oft-harassed star who called upon Gordon like she would a trusted uncle. When she wanted to take action it wasn't easy to gently dissuade her. She thought of Sol Gordon as a steamroller with her in the driver's seat. What she and all his clients liked most about him was that he didn't often lose. Soft and lenient in appearance he could be like a razor when it was appropriate.

Layton knew him well. If Sol Gordon was going to sue him Layton would sooner or later lose. Knowing this made it easier on him because he wouldn't have to spend a small fortune trying to defend himself. He'd throw himself on the mercy of the court.

"You'd really do that?" Gordon asked when Layton said he wouldn't hire a lawyer if it came down to that.

"What do you think Sol? I thought of hiring you but that's a conflict of interest. So I don't hire anybody and the jury sees it's someone like you against no one like me–it's a long shot but if I'm gonna go down, put me on the side of the people. Yes."

"I don't want to go to court over this any more than you don't. Why'd you have to pop her in front of people?"

"You mean I should have waited until I was alone? It wasn't that kind of punch."

"What if you agree not to take Mark on weekends?"

"Come on, I can't do that to him, I only get him once a month. Have you seen him lately? He needs a father. He's fifteen and he doesn't know how to hold a hardball. He flinches when you pass him a basketball. Then he closes his eyes before he shoots. I'm fighting for his life Sol, I can't give that up."

"Just for a cool-down period. We won't talk specifics. It's an offering."

"No."

"We don't have much to bargain with."

"Not Mark."

"He's all there is, you don't have anything else she wants."

"What about me? Why not make some agreement that she never has to deal directly with me for a year or two? I won't call her or talk to her about Mark, there'll be no physical or any other communication between us. I'll leave her alone. That should be worth something."

"Won't be enough."

"I don't like this Sol. I keep wanting to say fuck her and walk out of here."

"Look at it this way: Samantha can do more for you than anyone else in this town if she's so inclined. Every studio head would do her a favor if she so much as hinted–and getting you some parts in movies is the kind of favor you need right now. You know she's got guys like Charlie Greenbloom wrapped around her ankles. She can help you Layton. Why offend her like this? Why not give yourself a break?"

"What break's she given me all these years Sol? I don't want her favors. Shove her favors, her power, her golden ankles. What if I reverse this? Make a play for more of Mark's time? Hang around her more?"

"It's an idea," Gordon admitted. "You'd be giving yourself more to exchange."

"But it won't work?"

"I'm afraid not."

"Have you ever punched someone?"

"More than once."

"Felt pretty good, didn't it?"
"You don't ever forget it."
"You know," Layton said, "no matter what happens..."
"...it was worth it?"
"You got it."
"We'll talk some more."

■ ■ ■

Fairfax Avenue between Wilshire and Melrose was a tourist attraction for visitors to Los Angeles who liked to look at the freshest produce money could buy at the Farmer's Market, buy hand-rolled cigars at a pipe and tobacco shop across the street, eat large, high cholesterol triple decker sandwiches and bowls of oily matzo ball soup at Canter's, which was open all night, walk along the few blocks from Beverly to Rose, which gave one the feeling of being in downtown Tel Aviv, and stand in line at the CBS building to see how a TV show was shot.

Layton found a space in the far corner of the CBS lot where Fairfax and Beverly met. Standing on that corner was a strange-looking ragman. Patches of hair were missing from his head and what was left hadn't been washed in months; the mangy tufts stood stiffly but what struck Layton was that he was clean-shaven. So he did care. He was wearing a torn oil-stained shirt, a ratty vest, a buttonless jacket, dark wool pants, moccasins missing laces, and colored handkerchiefs tied in a bow around each ankle. He wheeled a shopping cart overflowing with boxes, packages and newspapers tied with twine.

"Howdy," Layton said, nodding.

The man eyed him suspiciously, gripping the shopping cart handle with both hands. Layton noticed the man's knuckles whiten.

"I'm a friend," Layton continued. "Need some money?"

The man didn't respond but kept his eyes focused on Layton.

"Hey, if I'm invading your turf just tell me, I'll back off."

Again the man narrowed his eyes, increasing his grip on the handle.

"What's it like living out of a shopping cart like that? All your possessions right there with you. Do you feel free? Or trapped?"

A purring sound started to come from deep within the rag man, turning into something more like a growl as his lips parted.

"I just wanted to know," Layton said, his hands held up. "Here's a five for your time." He put the bill on the ground. The man didn't go for it. "Sorry to have bothered you. I know what it's like."

Layton's words triggered an angry, emotional, deep response from the rag man, whose growl became a roar as he said, as if in an echo chamber, "YOU. DO. NOT!"

It wasn't expected, but dealing with such a character there could be no expectations. The homeless were everywhere; you couldn't avoid them. They slept on benches, in doorways, above and below freeway overpasses; they panhandled at busy street intersections, holding signs or their babies; they were all ages; they each had a story to tell; they deserved better. The country had let them down, Layton believed. These were the people who slipped through the cracks, and the cracks were widening into caverns. He often wondered about their lives. People who had surrendered, dropped out, lost their edge. Who didn't know from Sol Gordon or Perce Dent or Spider Ray. Were they better off?

Than what? Layton wondered, waving at the tourists in line to see a taping. Someone called out for a picture and he stopped, mugged, was applauded. The rag man stood on the corner staring at Layton as he disappeared into the building.

The movie he had done for television, his first, was a ghost story; not very original but they often did well when a big name was attached. When the networks asked for names they meant television stars. Most TV watchers didn't go to the movies anymore, didn't relate to the Pacinos and De Niros and Hoffmans, and felt more comfortable with Tim Allen or Tom Selleck or Ted Danson. When none of the TV names were available the network agreed to Layton Cross on the assumption that people might tune in out of curiosity: So that's what happened to him. Remember when we used to go to the movies, he was a big star. Now he's on TV. See, you don't have to go out and spend money...they all come to you.

He met the director in the editing room working with the editor, splicing bits of film together, cutting scenes to make the action flow more effectively, pacing the show with the commercials in mind. Because there would be nine breaks in the movie the director wanted to make sure she ended each segment on a note of suspense so the channel changers wouldn't push their remotes during the hard sell. That's why she asked Layton to come down. Two of the segment breaks ended on him. The first, he looks at his two kids and says, "What's going on here?" The second, he says to his wife, "We're not being forced out of our home by ghosts, for pete's sake. I don't even believe in ghosts!" Since these now became dramatic points the director wanted Layton to lip synch the words more emphatically than he had originally.

One would think mouthing a few sentences was a few minutes work but Layton was there for three hours. He emphasized "What's going on here?" four ways, stressing a different word each time; then he tried stressing the first two words, the second two, the last two. As the film was already shot he had to make sure the way he spoke corresponded to the way his lips moved on film.

He had more trouble with the second sentence because of "for pete's sake." He'd never say that nor, he argued, would his character. "Goddamnit," was the proper expression, but though they got away with "schmuck" and "asshole" on shows like *N.Y.P.D.*, this was a more family-oriented TV movie and the producers didn't want God damned. Layton tried other expressions but nothing sounded like "for pete's sake" except "for pete's sake."

The director was patient, considering she was on a deadline, and they did it again and again and again until it didn't seem to matter anymore. "Layton," she said to him during a break, "it's only television. It won't be remembered the day after it airs."

"Yeah, I know," Layton said. But he also knew it was all he had at the moment. What's going on here? he thought. "Let's do it," he said.

■ ■ ■

Theo Soris thought it remarkable that Leanne was also rehearsing a play. His enthusiasm far exceeded her parents' and he wanted to know everything: how she was feeling, how she learned her lines, did she have any anxiety? was it her first play? how big was her part? had she gone to many plays?

Leanne told him it wasn't much of a part and she wasn't nervous about it because she memorized her lines more than a week ago. A lot of her friends were in it so it was fun.

"Fun!" Theo exclaimed. "I know. Isn't it though! That's the actor's secret–that acting is a lot of fun. Especially play acting, where you do the whole thing from the beginning to the end without stopping for anything."

"I don't know how my dad stands doing movies," Leanne said. "They take so long to do so little."

"And there's no continuity," Theo added.

"Yeah," Leanne said, not sure what he meant.

Theo asked her about school and what she liked most, about her favorite movies and TV programs, about books. When she said she didn't read all that much but liked things like Nancy Drew mysteries Theo said he had a library full of interesting books and he'd give her a tour, even let her choose any she'd like to borrow.

"Are we going to your house?" she asked.

"Your dad said he was going to be late so I thought we could have dinner together and then we'd meet him back at my place, if that's all right with you. You've never seen where I live, have you?"

Leanne hadn't. Theo said he had lived in apartments all over L.A.: in Westwood, West L.A., Culver City, Venice, Santa Monica, downtown. Each place had its own personality and for an actor taking on the persona of an area only broadened his abilities. For instance, he said, you don't see as many homeless lying in doorways in Westwood Village as you do in Venice or downtown so you tend to walk, dress, and think differently when you're strolling leisurely through Westwood than when you're hunched over, walking fast, talking to yourself in wino areas.

"My mom got her wallet stolen in Westwood," Leanne said.

"That's another thing," Theo said. "The unexpected! Because you let your guard down in a place like Westwood, bam! you get robbed. So you use it as a learning experience. If you're an actor, you try to act your way out of it. Unless the thief's got a weapon and looks crazy. You can tell by the eyes. If they're opened wide and he's not blinking much just make peace with the fellow and hand over your money. But if he seems unsure and nervous then maybe you can try to talk him out of it. Say you're a bit out of luck yourself, or try acting confused, like you don't know what he wants. Look at your watch and tell him the time. Or better yet, say you left your watch at home and ask him for the time. You might even try crying, that often works."

"My mom told the robber to go fuck himself."

"That might work."

"He just grabbed her bag and walked off with it. Then he threw it in the street after he got her wallet."

"These are tough times," Theo said.

"My dad's learning karate."

"That helps. How about you, what are you learning?"

"Math, history, science, about biomes."

Theo smiled and stroked her hair. He didn't know what a biome was. He doubted he could do the math she was learning. And history? Forget about it, he still couldn't figure out the grievances between the Czechs and the Slovaks and that was current; he shuddered at the thought of having to explain the difference between the Truman and the Monroe doctrines.

After eating at Taco Bell they went to his apartment where he showed her his books. Leanne never saw so many books in a person's house before. He had more books than her school's library.

After a careful search he came up with *The Little Prince, The Hunting of the Snark*, the short stories of Poe,

T.S. Eliot's *Old Possum's Book of Cats*, illustrated, and the Marquis de Sade's *Bedroom Philosophy*, which he said he wouldn't lend her but she could read it whenever she visited.

He gave her a Pepsi, some seven-layer chocolate cake, and asked if she wouldn't mind helping him prepare for his opening night the next day by reading with him.

"I can do that," Leanne said.

"Sure you can," Theo said. "I wouldn't have asked if I didn't think you could. Now that you're doing plays yourself you're grown up enough."

"What's it about?"

Theo went to his desk and took out a folder with some loose pages. "It just happens to be about a young girl about your age and an older guy like me. The girl is very pretty and very smart and the guy is really in love with her, like the way Lewis Carroll was with Alice. Did you know that's how *Alice in Wonderland* was written? Anyway, it's very hard for the guy because the girl is so young and so he tries to express himself and even though she isn't sure what he's doing she goes along with it because she kind of likes him and she feels she can trust him and she knows that whatever they do it will be a secret that they will never tell to anyone. Can you understand that?"

"Sure. I can keep a secret."

"You think you want to do this now? We don't have to."

"I don't care."

"I mean, it would help me a lot but it's okay if you don't think you're old enough."

"I'm ten," Leanne said.

"I know. That's how old this girl in the play is."

"Is this the play you're doing tomorrow?"

"Almost," Theo said. "I'm superstitious. Do you know what that means?"

"Don't walk under a ladder or let a black cat cross in front of you."

"Right. Before I do a play for the first time I like to rehearse another play that's similar but different. It loosens me up, gets rid of some of my tension and allows me to think about other things. That way I feel fresh for the other play the next day. Does that make sense to you?"

"I don't know."

"Well, shall we try this?"

"Okay. When's my dad coming?"

"He said he'd be here around eight or else call. It's six now, we've got plenty of time."

He handed Leanne six pages and took a copy for himself. Theo had written the pages himself and it wasn't the first time he had asked a young girl to read with him. He sat down and told her to stand a few feet from him. "Now, read your lines. Your part is Mary, I'm Dan."

Leanne looked at the page and read, "'Oh Dan, I'm all confused.'"

"That's good," Theo said. "But try it again, this time with emotion. Like you really are confused."

"This is my first time," Leanne said. "I never read this before."

"Of course. You're right. I just thought that if you get into it right away you'll be able to go with the flow of it easier, that's all." A thin line of perspiration appeared along Theo's plugged hairline. Leanne noticed this as she read again.

Theo, as Dan, responded, "'What's the matter?'"

"'I was at school today and the boy who sat next to me said he wanted to kiss me.'"

"'What's wrong with that, you're a very pretty girl.'"

"'I don't like him.'"

"'You don't like him or you're not sure what to do if he tries to kiss you?'"

"'I've never kissed a boy before.'"

"'It's not hard. You've kissed your father haven't you?'"

"'That's different.'"

"'What about your dog? You've kissed your dog haven't you?'"

"'Not like that.'"

"'Are you afraid of the boy?'"

"'I don't know.'"

"'Has anyone ever shown you how to kiss the right way?'"

"'No.'"

"'Come here Mary and I'll show you.'"

"'Oh Dan, you're too big, you're a grownup.'"

"'That's why you can trust me, because I am a grownup.'"

"'Oh all right. She goes to him.'"

"No," Theo stopped her, his nostrils beginning to quiver, "you're not supposed to read that, that's a stage instruction. See, it's in capital letters and off to the side. It tells you what you're supposed to do. Now you come closer, right next to him. That's it." Theo returned to his character Dan.

"'Okay Mary, now close your eyes and lean forward.'"

"Do I have to?" Leanne asked. His anxiety confused her. She had been warned about strangers and about the dangers of drugs–those topics were covered in school. But no one ever told her what to do when her dad's best friend started acting strange. But then she realized that actors *were* strange. They talked differently than other people; they often confused real life with make-believe.

"We're just acting," Theo tried to reassure her. "It's not really you and me doing this, we're characters in a play. That's what acting is, we become other people so we can do things we don't normally do ourselves."

"I've never done this before."

"That's perfect, then you're just like this girl. All you have to do is close your eyes and I'll do what my part says." Theo had crossed a narrow line. This was Layton's daughter. He had known her since she was a baby. He knew he shouldn't be doing this but he also knew that he couldn't stop. Not now. Not with the play opening the next day. He needed to do this, just as he needed to swipe the jacket. It was his high-wire act. He was balancing high above a deep canyon now, his whole body was alert.

Leanne looked at him for a moment and then bent over, her eyes closed. Theo kissed her gently on the lips. She backed away and wiped her face.

"No, no," Theo said. "You're supposed to like it. See, you say: 'Oh, is that what it feels like?' Go ahead, say it."

"'Oh is that what it feels like?'"

"'It feels even different than that. There're all kinds of kisses.'"

"'Really? Like how?'"

"'There are kisses with your mouth closed and ones with your mouth open. There are kisses when I put my tongue in your mouth and kisses when you put your tongue in mine. And there are kisses when we touch tongues too. And that's just some of the kinds of kisses there are.'"

"'How does someone learn how to kiss?'"

"'That's what I'm showing you. You need to learn from a teacher, just like in school. Otherwise you'll never really know how until you're all grown up because your friends don't know how either, unless they have a teacher.'"

"'Will you teach me?'"

"'If you want me to I will.'"

"'Okay.'"

But Leanne backed away when she said 'Okay.' She didn't want to learn how to kiss from Theo. He was her father's friend. She didn't know him all that well and this wasn't the kind of play she wanted to do. Besides, he smelled bad. Theo sensed her fear and suggested they stop for a few minutes because he had to make a phone call. He brought her another piece of cake and went into his bedroom where he quickly took off his jeans to change underwear. He had been wearing white briefs that were yellow stained. He went into the bathroom and washed his penis, then put on dark blue bikini briefs.

Leanne was looking at the *Snark* book, finishing her cake, when he returned.

"Well, what do you think?" Theo said. "Shall we continue for good luck or stop?"

"I'd like to stop," Leanne said.

"Fine, no problem. Superstitions are silly things anyway." He would control himself. He would not push her. He would not self-destruct. "Want to watch TV?" He turned on the tube to a *Roseanne* rerun and they sat in separate chairs, watching.

At seven o'clock *Free Willy* was on HBO and Leanne said she had seen it twice but would like to see it again. Theo, who was struggling to contain his willy, watched it for the first time. By 8:15 he wondered about Layton, who called a half hour later to say he was running late and wanted to stop off and see some people at The Palm for about an hour, would Theo mind entertaining Leanne until around ten? Theo said it would be no problem and put Leanne on to talk to her father.

"Why can't you come now?" she asked.

"Is everything all right honey?"

"Yes. We just watched *Free Willy*."

"Great. Look, baby, I've just got one more thing to do and I'll be there as soon as I can, okay sweetheart?"

"I've got school tomorrow Daddy."

"I know. Maybe you can take a nap on Theo's bed and I'll pick you up and take you home when I get there and you won't even know it."

"That's all right Daddy, I'll wait up for you."

"Goodbye darling. See you soon."

"Bye Daddy."

When the movie ended Theo went into his bedroom to go over the Williams play. Leanne went back to reading Lewis Carroll. Theo came out in a half hour and said he was starting to feel nervous about the play. His demons were getting the best of him. Leanne said her father always got nervous before he acted, too.

"But this is a play not a movie, it's different. You can't make any mistakes. There's no stopping to reshoot in a play," Theo said.

"Is there anything I can do?" Leanne asked, regretting it as soon as the words came out of her mouth. She knew what he would say.

"Well, if you want to know the truth, if we could just finish those pages we started that would take my mind off this."

"Why don't we do something else? Do you know Hangman?"

"It's bad luck to start something and not finish it, don't you know that? Do you want me to have bad luck?" Layton said he'd be here at eight, Theo thought, this is his fault.

"I'm only ten," Leanne said.

"So's the girl you're supposed to be playing. And how old do you think Alice was? Ten's old enough."

There was a desperation in Theo's voice which was beginning to scare Leanne. His eyes were wide open and he wasn't blinking.

"Okay I'll do it," she said.

"No, forget it, you don't have to, I don't want to make you."

"Okay."

Theo ignored her. "But it's got to be between us. Otherwise it will ruin my career tomorrow. That's part of the luck."

Leanne was getting nervous. Theo was going ahead, getting those pages from the folder again. He handed them to her and said they should start from the beginning.

Even though Theo kept telling her it was just a part and that the Mary character was not her own character Leanne couldn't stop her head from aching as Theo told her to open her mouth and then put his tongue inside and slid it around her teeth. She didn't know what he was doing when he pulled down his zipper, as the character Dan was instructed to do, and asked her, as Mary, to put her hand inside. By the sixth page Mary is taught that there are other kinds of kisses that aren't done on the mouth and after she did it Theo jumped up and ran into the bathroom, then came back and told her she must keep her promise of silence.

"You're a wonderful actress," he said. "Especially since you've never done anything like this. A lot of girls wouldn't have been able to do what you did. I'm very proud of you."

He saw her tears and looked at his watch. It was 9:30. He had time to calm her before Layton arrived.

■ ■ ■

Barry Levine wasn't sure Layton was going to show. He had told Arno and Macky, the ones who wore the ostrich leather boots and had money to burn, that everything was cool; Layton would be pulling into the lot sometime that evening. Arno, who was in his early thirties, said they'd be inside the restaurant at nine. Macky said they'd reserve a table for three. When Levine questioned the number Macky reminded him that he was still parking cars. "When something goes through you'll be eating inside and not the leftovers you sneak out of the kitchen," Macky said.

"Things are going to happen," Levine said. "Some other schmuck will soon be eating off my plate."

Arno and Macky liked Levine's balls. He talked big, bluffed well, had the makings of becoming one of them. Or he could fuck up and wind up a liability. They were watching him.

Arno grew up on a farm in New Jersey. His boyhood memories were of picking prickled berries in the berry patch, of walking barefoot through puddles in the dirt road after rain, of holding baby yellow chicks for inoculation by his father, of growing marijuana at fifteen, a hundred acres away from the family house and being caught by his father a week before harvesting. His dad really laid into him for that, worried that had anyone else discovered the nearly half acre of weed Arno had cultivated it could have meant the end of the farm. His most vivid memory was of his father cutting down the nearly thousand stalks, all more than six feet high, then burning the beautiful weed as Arno cried and protested. Not even Arno's offer to give him the sixty or seventy thousand dollars such a harvest would have fetched stopped his father from destroying it all. The lesson it taught the boy was that his father was a fool, doomed to suffer as a farmer his whole life because he had a peasant's morality. The incident was never a matter of right or wrong, just one of incredible waste and stupidity.

His friend Macky, who lived in the same township and was partners with Arno, also couldn't believe what had happened. Macky played tackle on the school football team and had a tackle's mentality. Arno preferred baseball but had he played football he would have been the quarterback. The two grew up as neighbors and complemented each other. Arno came up with the outrageous schemes; Macky provided the backbone. Lucky for them that they had another half acre growing on Macky's dad's land that they immediately harvested before it too was discovered. The money they earned from that sale bought them into the fast-paced world of cocaine. And the money they earned from that made them the richest boys to grow up in Freehold, New Jersey. By the time they were eighteen they could afford the Porches they wanted to drive to California. Fourteen years later they probably could have bought Freehold if they had wanted to return. Instead they thought they'd try their hands at the movies.

Layton pulled into The Palm a half hour after Arno and Macky. Barry Levine breathed a heavy sigh of relief. "You're going to like these guys," he said. "They're inside waiting for you."

"I don't want to go inside," Layton said. "I don't want to be seen with anybody I don't know I want to be seen with."

"Hey they're not gangsters or anything. How'm I gonna bring them out when they're inside eating?"

"I'll watch the cars for you."

"You're going to park cars?"

"I've got a license."

"I don't believe this."

Layton sat on an old orange crate thumbing through the *L.A. Weekly* Levine had been reading. Inside The Palm Levine got past the maitre d' by saying he had a message for Arno.

"What do you mean he won't come in? Who does he think he is?"

"Layton Cross, man. I told you I'd deliver. He just wants to talk outside is all."

"We just got our lobsters," Macky said. "Tell him to wait."

"He's not going to wait, he's famous, he'll get mobbed out there and then what?"

"Who's out there to mob him, James Caan maybe? Liza Minnelli?" Arno asked.

"Look, I'll get the waiter to bring your lobsters out. You can eat in your limo. We'll order an extra for Cross, he'll like that."

"What's wrong with eating in the restaurant? At a table. Where we can be served."

"Mack, c'mon, don't break my chops like this. If it was me I'd eat with you. He'll eat with you too, once he gets to know you. Just got to get this going, know what I mean? Once you're in, ain't no fucking star going to meet you in a parking lot."

"Tell him to forget it," Arno said. "Just a mistake."

"Arno, for Christ's fucking sake, you know what I had to do to get him here? I was at his house at three in the freaking morning. I got pulled over for speeding, almost got busted. Give me a break will you?"

"If you weren't my cousin, kid, I'd tell you to take a hike. But we're blood, so okay, this time I'll eat my food in your parking lot."

"You won't regret it Arno. I'm telling ya."

"Is that what you told your buddy Cross?"

"Natch. He won't. You guys are gonna bring him back and make a bundle and be smack in the middle of this business. Believe me, I got it all figured."

"And you, Barry boy, what's your bid?"

"A break. You make a deal, I want to be in the picture."

"Up there on the big screen," Arno said. "You and Jason Priestly and Will Smith, that it?"

"You got it. We'll show 'em."

"You're a laugh, kid. A real laugh."

Layton had retrieved two cars and collected fifty cents from one of them by the time Levine appeared with Arno and Macky. Levine rushed to his key box and got the keys to Arno's Cadillac limo. Layton got in the back with Arno.

"Barry here says you don't like the restaurant," Arno said.

"Any place that has my picture on the wall can't be that tasty," Layton said.

"We're bringing the food out," Levine said. "I ordered you a lobster."

"Listen fellows, it's been a long day for me. I'm not exactly sure why I'm here, but I am. I'm tired. I don't want lobster."

"What do you want Mr Cross?" Arno asked.

"Same thing you and Rodney Dangerfield do."

"And you figure we can get that making movies?" Arno said. "We already got that without the movies."

"Then how about legitimacy?"

"What kind you talking about?" Macky asked.

"The kind that comes from making bucks in a legal way."

A waiter tapped the window. Levine jumped out, got the food and passed it around. Layton gave his back to Levine.

"I don't know what Barry here has told you Mr Cross but we do quite well for ourselves in a number of legitimate businesses. Our meeting here with you is exploratory. It might not be right for either of us."

Layton looked at these two new faces. Clear clean skin on both of them. No traces of childhood blemishes. No scars or broken noses. Well-groomed hair and fingernails. Rattlesnake eyes. Cosmetic teeth.

"Look, I'm glad you've got legitimate businesses," he said. "I assume you make what it takes to keep them up by less than legitimate but probably far more exciting means. I don't need to know details. I more than likely have done business with you without ever knowing it and as long as the stuff that goes inside my body is clean and makes me feel good I'm the last guy to question how you choose to make or to cover up how you make a living. I'm interested in one thing only and that's my career. And I'm interested in who I work with and who wants to screw me. I've found there are more of the latter than I care to recall. If you've got a movie you want to make and a decent script and you want me to consider it I'll do that without hesitation. If you don't, I'm not sure why we're talking."

"I don't have a script," Arno said, cracking open a claw and sucking in the red meat. "Do you?" he asked Macky, who shook his head no. "Do you?" he asked Levine.

"I got a million of 'em," Levine answered.

"What about you Mr Cross? Maybe you have something you want to do that might interest us? That would be more logical, wouldn't it? You being in this business after all."

Layton looked at Arno and at Macky and thought they were no better or worse than most of the people in Hollywood who called themselves producers. He didn't have a script in mind but he thought he should mention something to see how they reacted. After some thought he said, "Yeah, I've got something. A book. A children's book actually, but it's a hell of a story. *Mr Sand Man*. You know it?"

No one did, which wasn't surprising.

"Well now, why don't you look into that?" Layton suggested. "See what you think. If you like it and the rights are available maybe you can get it and you'll own a property. Then get a writer to write the script and you're in business."

"You want to do that movie?" Macky asked, dribbling lemon sauce on his shirt.

"Let's say I'd seriously consider it if I liked the script."

"Let's take it a step further," Arno said. "I'm new to this but the way I see it you want us to take all the risks and leave you an out in the end. Is that it?"

"That's the way it works," Layton said.

"Maybe if you're Tom Cruise," Arno said. "But you haven't exactly been in demand lately. Isn't that why you're sitting here now?"

"Hey," Barry Levine interrupted, "listen, how can we talk deals when we don't even know if the story's available?"

"Let's say it is," Arno said, taking a swallow of beer. "How much would you want to do it if you liked the script?"

"That's agent talk," Layton said. "I stay out of that."

"Let's talk straight," Arno said. "We land the book, we expect you to follow if the money's right."

"A lot depends on the money being right," Layton said.

"One other thing. Barry here wants a crack at this business. He's part of our deal."

"If the lad can act that's fine," Layton said, picking a thick white piece of meat off Arno's plate.

"I hope we're not wasting our time," Macky said. "I've always liked you as an actor."

"Gentlemen, it's been interesting. I wish you luck."

"We'll be in touch," Arno said.

In his Jeep Layton fumbled for a roach in the ashtray. Those guys weren't so bad, he thought. Must be smart or they'd have numbers on striped pajamas by now. And Levine. One more Sammy Glick in town. Wait till they see *Mr Sand Man*, he laughed, nearly burning his lip with the car lighter. They'd need Judy Garland in pigtails to pull that off. "Oh there's no business like show business there's no business I knoooooow," he sang. He was half-way up the canyon when he remembered Leanne. His sweet wonderful innocent beautiful Leanne. Diamond of her daddy's eye. God, he loved her.

5

No Magic Mirror, No Paid Assassins

Theo Soris was in his underwear when he heard Layton's footsteps. He wrapped a terrycloth robe around him and opened the door, raising his eyebrows and nodding toward the beanbag chair in the corner where Leanne was sleeping.

"Just in time for a nightcap toot," Theo said. "Leanne was getting worried but I managed to calm her. 'An actor's day is never done' and all. She's some kid."

"You ready for tomorrow?" Layton asked.

"In two days I'll be."

"I know the feeling. Thanks for tonight; I owe you one. S'been one of those days."

"Hey, no trouble, leave her here any time. But in three more years I won't be held accountable," Theo joked. "She's turning into some beauty."

"Maybe she'll be the actor in the family."

"Wouldn't surprise me. She says she's already in a play."

"Play's the thing," Layton said. "Know your lines?"

"Only when I'm snorting them. You're coming aren't you?"

"Wouldn't miss it. Tennessee Williams' last play, that's one for the resume."

"You look beat," Theo said.

"I am."

"Get some sleep so you can party after the show tomorrow."

"Rock till the reviews are thrown, the old Broadway tradition." He went over to Leanne, who had been listening the whole time, and stroked her hair. "I'll take that toot and then carry her into the night."

Theo tapped out two lines of blow onto a pocket mirror and passed it to his friend. Layton sniffed them into each nostril and smiled. Leanne thought of what she had learned in her D.A.R.E school program about the dangers of drugs and how Layton had helped her with the poster she made, spelling out Drugs Are Really Evil. He was so serious about it. Now he was doing drugs with Theo, she was sure of it. Theo was a really bad person, making her do what she did to him and then making her daddy take drugs. But Theo was her dad's best friend. How could he be?

"Until tomorrow then," Layton said as he lifted Leanne.

"You're gonna be surprised, amigo. Even without that snakeskin."

"Just remember," Layton said. "If you get stuck, mumble. It works with Williams."

"Either that or start yelling for Stella," Theo said.

Once safely in the Jeep Leanne opened her eyes and said, "You're so late."

"Sorry baby, I just couldn't help it."

"I have school tomorrow."

"I know. You'll get there."

"I don't want to go."

"Let's see how you feel in the morning, okay?"

Leanne's lips began to tremble, then her body. Layton, coked, thinking about the TV movie, about Barry Levine and his two wanna-be friends, about Theo's shot at something real, didn't notice.

"Daddy?"

"Sweetheart?"

"How important is friendship?"

"Very. It's rare."

"Do you have a lot of friends?"

"I know a lot of people but I wouldn't call very many friends. A lot of those who I thought were once friends have turned out to be not very friendly. How about you?"

"Is Theo Soris your friend?"

"I've known him a long time."

"Is he your friend?"

"I'd count him among the lucky few, yes."

Leanne still trembled. Layton looked at her and put the heater on. "We'll be home in fifteen minutes," he said. "Why don't you try to sleep."

"Daddy?"

"Sweetheart?"

Leanne paused. She was wrestling with her thoughts. Why had he left her with Theo? Why had he praised her D.A.R.E. poster when he didn't believe it? Why did Theo do what he did? She wanted to tell him what had happened but she was ashamed. She didn't want her father to get mad at her. She knew what had happened was wrong but somehow she thought it was her fault. She closed her eyes to hold back tears.

"Nevermind."

Amy was out the door, fire in her eyes, as they pulled in. "I'd like to kill you!" she shouted.

"Let's get her inside first," Layton said, struggling with his sleeping daughter.

"You must be really crazy, you know that? How dare you keep her out to this hour and not even call."

"Everything's fine. We're all tired."

"I'm not tired! I just want to punch."

"Fair enough."

"I'd like to kick your balls."

"Let's keep it at arm level."

She was so angry she picked up one of Andy's small bats and started swinging. Layton shot her a sharp, fierce look. Amy hit him in the thigh.

"You want me to drop her?" Layton hissed.

"I want to drop you."

"Put it down Amy."

"You don't scare me you big baboon."

Most men, Layton thought, after a long day at work, came home to a hot cup of coffee, perhaps a sleepy wife happy to see her man return, ready to snuggle. What had he done to merit a woman like Amy? Her passion, that he had once loved, was now so out of whack that she was as unpredictable as a fighting bull. He just didn't want to play the matador any more.

"Amy, if I'm going to stay I need a peaceful home life."

She swung the bat again, missing his other leg by inches.

"Stop that before you regret it."

"Regret? I regret ever letting you back. I regret ever letting you into me in the first place. Don't tell me about regrets you bastard."

Somehow Layton managed to get Leanne into the house. "Can we beat each other up tomorrow? I've had enough for today."

"I'm not satisfied."

"What will make you happy Amy?"

"Violence."

"Then let's go in the backyard and have it out, once and for all."

"You're a very sick man, Layton."

"Sick," Layton said, "and tired. Make me healthy tomorrow, okay? I'm sorry I'm so late. She was with Theo Soris all night; nothing happened to her, she's fine."

Amy lifted the bat over her head and burst into tears. Layton approached carefully and put his arms around her. "Let's try, baby. I should have called, you're right. I'm sorry."

"I really hate you," she sobbed.

"I know you do."

"More than you know."

"I don't doubt it."

"Why do you make me like this?"

"You've always been this way. It's your nature."

"It is not, fuckhead. You made me like this."

"I love my kids," Layton said.

"You're an impossible man."

Slowly her crying ceased and Layton lifted her and carried her to the bedroom. "Things will get better," he whispered. "I can feel it."

"How much worse can they get?"

"Look, I've got an erection. Want to use it?"

The sight of his straightened member softened her. A stiff cock was like a Valium for her. She spread her legs and let him enter. Making peace.

■ ■ ■

Leanne's scream brought Amy running. It was 4:30 A.M. and Layton remained soundly, deeply asleep. Leanne was sitting up, shaking her head, crying. "I don't want to kiss it, I don't. Please." Amy picked her up and tried to calm her but Leanne appeared terrified.

"It's just a nightmare," Amy said. "Wake up honey, I'm right here. Everything's all right."

"It's not! It's not!" Leanne cried, coming out of it.

"What's not, baby?"

Leanne opened wide eyes and looked strangely at her mother. She frightened Amy.

"What were you dreaming?"

"I can't tell. It's so horrible mommy. Why did it happen?"

"I don't know what happened unless you tell me."

But Leanne withdrew. She had been holding tightly to Amy, now she dropped her arms. Her body went lax and she curled into herself. "I'm so tired now," she said.

"Just go back to sleep honey. We'll talk about it in the morning."

"No we won't," Leanne said softly. Amy sat on the bed stroking the child's hair, wiping off the tears on her cheek with her finger.

"Mommy!" Andy shouted from his room. "What's wrong with Leanne?"

"She just had a dream, go back to sleep."

"What was it about?" Andy asked.

"Sleep, Andy. Just go to sleep."

"I'm thirsty, I want some pop."

"I'll pop you," Amy said, getting up. She went to the bathroom and brought him a cup of water.

"Hi mom."

"Drink."

"I need some sugar in this."

"You want to go to the dentist and get drilled?"

"Will you sleep with me?"

"No."
"Can I sleep with you?"
"It's almost morning Andy. Give us a break."
"I can't sleep, Leanne woke me."
"All right, move over. But if you kick I'm leaving."
"I won't mom. You just get comfortable."

In the morning Leanne had a fever and didn't go to school. Amy cancelled her tennis game and stayed home with her. "You really had some nightmare last night," she said. When Leanne didn't respond Amy told her of the time when she was pregnant with Andy. Leanne woke up screaming as she had last night, asking over and over, 'Do I have to go back inside mommy's stomach?' Amy hadn't thought about that in a long time. Leanne didn't remember. After a while she asked her mother about getting pregnant.

"You or me?" Amy asked.
"I mean how does it happen?"
"Didn't I tell you seven years ago when Andy was born?"
"I mean how old do you have to be?"
"What's the matter Leanne? You can tell me."
"I..."
"Do you think you're pregnant, is that it?"
"How many ways can you get pregnant?"
"Just one as far as I know. This is a very strange conversation. What happened yesterday?"
"Nothing."

"Why were you screaming last night? Do you know what you were saying?"

"No."

"Something about not wanting to kiss it. Kiss what?"

Leanne turned towards the wall. "I...can't...don't know."

Amy knew it was more than Leanne's imagination that was disturbed. She tried to control herself and not get angry. She didn't want to frighten the poor child any more than she already was. "You try to sleep now," she said, patting her back. "We can talk later if you want to."

If she didn't Amy was going to find out anyway.

When Barry Levine called to get details of *Mr Sand Man* Amy spoke with him. Layton was out jogging. Levine was cautiously friendly with her. He knew she would be part of his future in some clandestine way but he didn't want to blow it with Layton. First things first.

Amy was in no mood to flirt. Leanne had disturbed her and she was thinking about all the things that might have given her nightmares. The thought even occurred that Layton might have tried something with her but that was too sick. He was irresponsible, unreliable, selfish, and not the world's greatest lover, but he wasn't perverted. He had a certain charm, he was lovable, and he really did love his children. So if he left her at Theo's apartment, what could have happened there? Theo? No, he was too screwed up himself to screw up anybody else. And with the anxiety of the play he must have been focused on that. Still.

No. "What?" Amy asked Barry, who was shouting into the phone to get her attention.

"I was wondering if–say, is everything all right? Can you talk? You being robbed? Just grunt something and I can be right over."

"What are you talking about?"

"I don't know. I thought...I mean, I'm talking to you and you're not hearing, I thought maybe, you know, there was something going on. Never mind. Look, what I wanted to know was who wrote *Mr Sand Man*?"

"I don't know, who?"

"I'm asking you."

"Who's Mr Sand Man?"

"I don't know. Layton told us about it."

"Who's us?"

"Some producer friends of mine. Layton suggested it."

"I never heard of it."

"He said it was a children's book."

"You want to produce a children's book?"

"I'd like to read it, anyway."

"How old are you again?"

"Please, it's important to me."

"Why don't you go to a bookstore?"

"I should have."

"Good idea."

Amy hung up first. Levine chalked it up to the nuttiness of show business. Actors' ex-wives are nutty people he figured. It goes with the territory.

Amy went to check on Leanne, who was asleep all curled up holding a large stuffed panda. The thought of someone violating her sent Amy to the living room for a drink. It was early in the morning but she felt she needed one.

Leanne's fever continued throughout the day and Amy decided not to go to Theo's opening. When Layton came back from wherever he was all day Amy told him of her concern. He went into Leanne's room and bent to kiss her. She recoiled and turned away. He tried talking with her but she was unreceptive, withdrawn. He asked if she wanted something to eat. She shook her head no. Ice cream? No. Nothing.

"How about if I read you a book?"

No.

"Tell you a story?"

No.

"Make shadows on the wall?" He held his hands together and made a duck, a dog, an eagle, an anteater. She wasn't amused. She wasn't being stubborn, just distanced, as if she wasn't there.

"Do you mind if mommy and I go to the play tonight?" She didn't answer, just looked at the wall. "Mom says she'll stay home with you if you like. Or I can ask Enid to babysit for a few hours and we'll come right home, early. What do you say, your choice?"

"I don't care. Go."

"You sure it's okay?"

"I'm just going to stay here, it doesn't matter."

"Are you mad at me honey? About yesterday?"

"No Daddy."

"I get the feeling you are. I'm feeling really bad about leaving you for so long."

"You can go to the play Daddy. Really."

"It's not tonight I'm thinking about, it's you. You're not yourself. Do you think you caught a cold being out so late?"

"Maybe. I don't know."

"How about one hug before I go? Just a little one."

"I don't want to."

"Okay you don't have to; I'll survive a broken heart."

Leanne wasn't amused. Layton was sure she was punishing him for keeping her out so late and because Amy was so angry at him as well. He convinced Amy that it would be all right if they both went to the play as long as they came right home. Enid was like family, she could take care of the children.

In the Jeep on the way to the Coronet Theatre Amy kept saying she should have stayed home.

"Look, it's been three years since we've been out together," Layton said. "There's going to be a lot of people we know there tonight, won't they be surprised."

"Is that why you wanted me to come? Leanne's a zombie and all you care about is how it will look if you show up alone after you punched out Samantha?"

"That's not exactly the case but now that you bring it up it's not a bad idea to have you along."

"You're not going to revive your career, what there is of it, by having me holding your arm."

"At least it will quell rumors that I have chopped you up and buried you in the freezer."

"If I wasn't so worried about Leanne I'd join this volley, but I'm scared about her Layt."

"It's me she's upset with. I never should have left her for so long. She got worried that I wouldn't come back. She told me last night in the car that she didn't want to go to school today, so when she wakes up, she's got a fever. It was in her mind. She'll come around in a day or two, you know how sensitive she is."

They had to park three blocks from La Cienega. Amy held Layton's hand. Maybe he was right. She shouldn't worry so much. Leanne and Andy were rarely sick; she'd just forgotten what a sick child was like.

"What about us Layton? What's happening between us?"

"I don't know. I like being back but I'm not sure we're right for each other."

Amy tried to think of what had once made Layton so attractive. He was fun then—he'd gone through the tragedy of his first marriage and managed to reach stardom on his own. His movies were wonderfully iconoclastic and he actually enjoyed being an actor. He wasn't hung-up on finding the "right" roles, he didn't brood over his characters the way Sean Penn or John Malkovich or Gary Oldman seemed to. He just liked to work, he liked the attention, and he liked being a father. They shared a lot of good times, until the drugs, when their lives got out of control. They thought that they could get away with anything but found that their behavior was intolerable. He developed a reputation of being unreliable and she once, accidentally, almost drowned their baby. He made a show of being linked with other well-known women and she countered with affairs of her own. Their relationship took on the drama of a soap opera played out in the tabloids. Her mother in Michigan read the stories and flew in to see for herself. Layton told her not to interfere, then moved out until she left. It got to be too much. They had exhausted their feelings for each other. They both had wanted out.

Layton's problem was that he acted like the star he once was. He didn't return calls, he didn't know the price of things, he stood mesmerized before mirrors whenever he passed them. Only now there were fewer calls to not return, less money to spend on things he could no longer afford. As for mirrors, like the one that told the evil Queen that Snow White was fairer than she, he didn't believe what they had to show him.

He had bought into the adulation and had convinced himself he was worthy of it. When his career came to an abrupt halt, he didn't understand–stars were stars; it didn't suddenly stop. When Amy told him he wasn't the same man she had fallen in love with she too was telling him he was no longer the valuable commodity he once was. She had learned to adjust, he never had. How could he? Why should he? There was no other way he could be, even though his time had past.

Now he was back in her house, being a father. They were sleeping together, going out, having a relationship and child problems like a couple again. Her feelings were very mixed. She had other boyfriends but no one interested her enough to become regular. She was older than Christ when he was crucified and was getting tired of raising the kids by herself. If Layton had changed over the last three years then perhaps they could rekindle whatever spark there once was between them. She wasn't sure but there was nothing else at this time. And the poor guy was living like some student in an apartment. What kind of life was that?

But he didn't seem to be any more responsible now than he was when they had split up. Keeping Leanne out so late, not calling, not thinking of her. Was she wrong? Was she too selfish? Was that just the nature of men? Was she expecting too much? What would her mother say when she found out Layton was still there?

"Do we have time for a drink?" Amy asked.

"Maybe once we're there. How about this for the walk?" He took out a joint and they shared it. When he saw the crowd outside the theater he was glad they did.

"Isn't that Amanda Rash?" Amy asked, looking at a woman so made up it was a wonder her head didn't tilt.

Layton smiled and thought of Mark when he saw her. "Think I should say hello?"

"Maybe after the show. She might remember you."

"I don't think she'll ever forget."

"Hey, look at the beauty with the famous man. Since when do you go out with such terrific looking women?"

Perce Dent was so effervescent it was close to stomach curdling.

"Hello Perce," Amy said, "you're looking chipper."

"Amy, I thought you left this lug to give the rest of us a chance."

"Since when did you return to the closet?" Layton asked.

"Now, now Layton, just because you stopped being a client doesn't give you a license to be cruel."

"You mean I have to be paying you ten percent before I can slap you around?"

"From the commissions you earned me this past year you aren't even allowed a gentle pinch."

"I like you better when you're not working for me," Layton said. "Or maybe it's just the night air."

"Listen Layton," Dent said in his confidential tone, "I got a call the other day from this guy in Palm Springs looking for a name actor to work with some people there. Doesn't pay much but you can pick up pocket money if you're interested. I gave him Amy's number, hope that's okay. Nothing in it for me, just thought, you know, you could use it."

"Layton," Al Low interrupted, holding a program of the evening's play. "Did you catch yourself on *Entertainment Tonight* last night? They had a thing about the incident, then reran an old interview they did with you. Gave you about four minutes."

"*Entertainment Tonight* huh? No wonder my phone's not ringing."

"You're back in the picture," Low said.

"Is that anything like being back in the saddle?" Layton saw Sol Gordon arriving in a limo and Spider Ray going to meet him. There was a time when those two used to sit in his and Samantha's living room talking figures so high Layton used to lose his wind and have to go to the bathroom to gulp air. Samantha was always like ice when it came to big dollars but Layton could never get used to it.

Ray noticed Layton and waved. Gordon nodded. Layton figured he'd wait until the party afterwards to say hello.

"Hello," Alex Briar said, smiling at Layton like some old friend.

"I'm supposed to know you right?"

"Has it been that long?" Briar asked.

"Oh right, the shrink posing as writer."

Briar nodded to Amy and waited to be introduced but Layton didn't. He was looking around seeing who else was there. Briar felt uncomfortable and backed off, saying "Enjoy the show." But Layton didn't hear him, he was walking towards Judith Lee, who came with Farrell's nephew from a previous marriage.

"It's good to see you out," Layton said.

"It's nice to get out," she said.

"You remember Amy don't you?"

"Yes, where is she?"

Layton turned and wondered where she went. He saw her talking to Amanda Rash of all people. "You know Amanda?"

"I've never met her."

"Lucky you. I did a picture with her once."

"I believe I read about it."

"Nobody ever read about that picture."

"You're right, it had to do with what happened during the filming."

"You're being tactful. How's Farrell doing?"

"No better. It's been difficult. The doctors say different things. One is optimistic, another is not. Some days he's able to sit up by himself, read, watch TV. Other days he just lays there, those damn tubes running in and out of him, his eyes hardly blinking. I'm thinking of taking him out of the hospital and bringing in a private nurse. He hates it there. He says if he's going to die let it be in his own bed."

"He's a very dear man."

"I know," Judith said, her neck muscles tightening. Her husband's illness had taken its toll. That she left his side to attend a play meant that she was beginning to face the reality that she would soon be alone. To be forever known as Mrs Farrell Lee.

The lights in the lounge flickered. The excitement of this opening was all for Tennessee Williams, whose last play was discovered after his death. No one expected it to be any good—Williams' powers had been on the decline long before he choked on a bottle cap—but that it was his last, written under his perpetual haze of pills and booze, made it a curiosity. What message was Williams going to bring from the grave? Was he going to go out with humor or cynicism? With crackling wit or ponderous dialogue?

Did he still have the power to elevate his often bizarre ideas to poetry? Would his women dominate?

Theo Soris was on his knees in his dressing room bathroom driving the porcelain bus. He was convinced that he wasn't prepared for this night. Try as he did he couldn't recall his opening lines. He called for his understudy an hour before and told him to be ready to go on but his understudy was a 22-year-old student still enrolled at the Strasberg Institute who began puking at the possibility he'd be opening the play. The director had come backstage and tried to calm them both. Butterflies were normal, even the greats tossed their cookies on opening night. Now it was almost show time and Theo was alone, his head in the toilet, joining the greats in an old theater tradition.

Layton was looking for Samantha. With so many people from the industry in the audience it wouldn't have surprised him if she made a quiet entrance just before the curtain went up. Theo was an old friend of hers as well, only she turned it into a passing acquaintance years ago. Whereas Layton held dearly to those who were friends during the early lean years, Samantha removed herself from them. Success bred success. She didn't want anyone's failures to rub off on her.

If she was there he didn't see her. Nor was there a rush of whispers that usually accompanied her presence. The lights dimmed on time and the play began. Theo Soris made it on stage but would remember nothing of the performance.

During the intermission Amy called Enid to check on Leanne. Enid said she had never seen the child so despondent. She didn't want to watch TV, she wouldn't let her read any of her favorite stories, she just stayed in her room looking so sad. Amy returned to her seat and told Layton she wanted to go home.

"How can you do that? It's not that bad."

"It's Leanne. I shouldn't have left her tonight."

"Did something happen?"

"No, she's just like we left her."

"So sit another hour and we'll go."

"You sit. Give me the keys, I'll go myself."

Layton didn't want her to go but he couldn't stop her. She had been uncomfortable watching Theo perform. Something about him was making her anxious. Layton gave her the keys and wondered how he'd get back. Amy suggested a taxi. It hadn't occurred to him. Not in L.A.

"If you go now I'll stay for the party. If you stay I'll go back with you when it's over."

"Do what you want, I'm going now. Enjoy yourself."

"You're not mad at me are you?"

"Not yet."

Spider Ray watched Amy leave and thought Layton wasn't capable of keeping his women. Alex Briar noticed the empty seat next to Layton and made a mental note. An hour later when the play was over Briar approached Layton and asked him if he needed a ride home.

"What'd you think of the play?" Layton asked.

"It needs work."

"That's stalling, not answering."

"It's too obscure. The actors aren't strong enough. It seemed almost tired."

Layton looked at Briar and wondered why writers hated other writers. Just like actors. Or jocks. It was human nature to be competitive he thought. What the hell does that mean, tired?

"I'm not going home," he said.

"You going over to the Beverly Connection for the party?" Briar asked.

"You invited?"

"No, but I'll walk over there with you if that's all right."

"Pass."

Briar smiled and walked away.

The Beverly Connection was only a block away from the Coronet. The producers of the play had closed the Daily Grill for a private party. Most of the audience had been invited.

Layton waited until everyone had left the theater then went backstage to congratulate Theo. He found him in the toilet.

"It's over man, you can come out now."

"Oh Christ," Theo said. "I can't believe it. That was the worst experience of my life."

"You got through, it's behind you."

"Was I shitty?"

"You were terrific."

"Wish you were writing the reviews."

"They'll be fine. The play's got some problems but that's Williams' fault not yours. This is a new beginning Theo, I'm happy for you."

"You think that jacket would have helped?"

"Come on, snap out of it, there's a party waiting to applaud you across the street."

"Let's party here first."

They snorted a few lines, then Theo took off his makeup and Layton phoned Amy. Theo watched his friend in the mirror, catching Layton's concern as he asked her questions.

"What happened to Amy?" he asked after Layton hung up.

"She was here for the first act but Leanne's not feeling well so she had to leave." Layton looked into the mirror. "Did anything happen with Leanne last night when she was with you?"

"What do you mean?"

"She's been acting strange."

"No. She helped me read some lines. She was looking at some of my books. Maybe something upset her?"

"I'm sure it's nothing. Kid stuff, you know? They withdraw into a world of their own."

"Maybe she's got a boyfriend," Theo suggested.

"She's only ten."

"These days that's old enough."

Layton watched him blot off the rest of his makeup and soak his head under the faucet. "Christ, I was nervous tonight."

"It's good for you. Keeps you on edge. It'll be the same every night."

"Can't be. I knew half the people who were out there."

"Doesn't matter. Tomorrow you won't know anyone and you'll still be on the crapper with five minutes to go."

The lights were off as Layton and Theo walked through the lobby, stopping outside to look at the poster behind glass. His name, Theo thought, could have been set in larger type.

The Grill at the Beverly Connection was smoky, noisy and crowded when they arrived. Theo was applauded, which gave everyone in the room a theatrical moment. He raised a fist like a fighter then changed it to crossed fingers. Snatches of praise filtered by him like a soft breeze. Spider Ray patted his back. Al Low shook his hand. Judith Lee nodded. Women with extraordinary cleavage and long shiny hair smiled. Certain well-groomed men winked. It all went straight to his head. He felt as if he was floating, like one of those dreamlike characters in a Marc Chagall painting. All those years living in lousy cramped rooms waiting for some break. Now this. The morning papers might slap him harshly but tonight he could bask in his stardom.

"So this is what it's like," he said.

"You've never been down until you've been up," Layton said.

"Doesn't always have to be canned tuna."

They swiped a few sushi hor d'oeuvres from a passing plate and went to the bar for champagne. Theo got lost among the congratulators, most of whom had politically correct red ribbons pinned to their clothing, as Layton sidled up to Sol Gordon.

"Sam would have hated it," he said.

"She never cared for Tennessee," the lawyer said. "You remember when they met?"

"Remember? I was in shock for three days after."

"He was pretty far gone."

"Just because he told her she'd be better playing some of his male parts than his women? He was right, you know. The man saw into her instantly."

"He was a very strange man."

"Genius."

"That too. Still, had Samantha done one of his plays it would have brought him back."

"He never left."

"He certainly could have used a hit."

"That's not what it was about for him," Layton said, sipping champagne. "He was an artist."

"He catered shamelessly to the press."

"We all need love."

"Sam wants me to file papers."

"You gotta do what you do."

"It might get ugly."

"Most definitely will."

"She wants to teach you a lesson."

"Fuck her, Sol. She never even went to college."

"Have you thought about letting Mark go?"

"What would you do Sol? If you were me?"

"I'd have saved the punch for a more private moment."

"There are no more private moments with her."

Amanda Rash stopped in front of them and smiled sweetly. "Layton, you old cocksucker, it's been years since I've seen your face. Have you retired?"

"Do I know you?" Layton said, gaining the advantage.

"Oh dear, lost your memory, now I understand."

Layton smiled and put his arm around her, whispering, "Something stiff, between your legs, later tonight. You look lovely."

Amanda kept the smile and whispered back, "Your little worm couldn't reach between my legs, but charmingly thoughtful, you cockroach."

"Great seeing you," Layton said, backing away.

"So tell me Sol, any juicy lawsuits lately?" she asked Gordon.

Layton walked over to a young soap opera actress and told her she was a favorite of his. The woman smiled engagingly and returned the compliment. Layton lingered, making small talk. Scoring in such social situations was almost too easy but he had to weigh it against the soap opera,

which he actually watched on occasion. Her character would indelibly change for him if they commingled. Plus, she wasn't wearing one of those red ribbons. He opted to keep the fantasy intact.

"Did you really do what the papers say you did?" the actress asked.

"What do you think?"

"I guess it's possible. Samantha Sanders has a reputation as difficult. But you should know better than anyone."

"She's a regular moose."

"What does that mean?"

"They're very peculiar."

"So are some people," she said with a slight giggle.

"Are you referring to moi? Peculiar? Why, next to Sanders I'm a pussycat."

"A moose and a pussycat, what a strange marriage that must have been."

"Why we split. I'd lick, she'd buck with her antlers."

Judy Jacobs, the *Times* people and party observer, couldn't hear the rest of their conversation because someone approached her and started yakking away with unimportant tidbits. She had been all ears concerning Layton, slyly following him around the room, working on her column. The stuff about Tennessee and Samantha was insider's gold, and this bit about the moose and the pussycat was quality icing. She quickly excused herself and headed for the ladies' room to jot down her notes.

As the evening turned to early morning Layton had enough schmoozing. He thought of asking the soap opera actress for a lift but didn't feel quite up for any extracurricular athletics that might spontaneously occur. He hadn't the slightest idea how to find a cab and wouldn't think of asking Gordon or Spider Ray for a ride. But when he saw Al Low going for his coat he made an approach.

"Gee, Layton, those hills are a lot further than my house. I'm in Beverly Hills you know, just below Wilshire. The Sofitel is just across the street, you can grab a taxi from there."

Judith Lee overheard them and offered Layton a ride if he didn't mind stopping at the hospital first. Layton asked about Farrell's nephew but he had met an old flame and had left a half hour before. So Layton thanked Al Low for nothing and went to the parking lot with Judith.

"I forgot how tiring these things are," she said, as she unlocked her baby blue Mercedes 450SL. "It's been so long since I've been in so much company."

"Caring for the sick is almost like being sick," Layton said.

Judith couldn't agree more. She unlocked Layton's door from the inside then asked if he'd like to drive. He preferred being driven.

They were at Cedars in two minutes. Visiting hours were over long ago but the staff knew Judith and made an exception. Layton said he'd wait outside but she insisted he come in. "He'll be sleeping anyway."

Farrell was having a bad dream, calling for his first wife Alicia. Judith wiped his brow as he opened his eyes and said, "Alicia, you've finally come. What the hell took you so damn long?"

"I'm Judith honey. Alicia died a long time ago. I'm your wife now. Judith."

Farrell looked at her, trying to make out what she was telling him. He thought Judith was his daughter. Alicia was his wife. Where was Alicia? Why was Judith saying these things?

"Look who's here again—it's Layton Cross. He's come to see how you're doing." She motioned Layton to come close. Farrell squinted to get him in focus.

"I'm gonna help you move back home," Layton said.

"You taking me outta here now?"

"Soon as they give the word."

"Not just now," Judith said. "But soon. We'll take you home soon."

"Let me die in peace."

"You're not going to die," Judith whispered.

"Of course I'm going to die. So're you. So is everybody. Make sense girl. I'm just going sooner."

"You've got a lot of years left."

"Bull. Couple days maybe."

"Are you afraid?" Layton asked.

"I'm afraid they'll keep me alive in this place too long. I'm not afraid of leaving. My time's up."

"You're talking like a cowboy," Judith said.

"Don't be an idiot girl."

Judith turned from the bed and went to the sink. She didn't like his grandstanding. Death wasn't a comfortable subject for her.

"I know I should face it but I just can't," she cried in the car. "Farrell's been my whole life for fifteen years;

I don't even know anybody who doesn't know him. My friends are all his friends. I don't have a life of my own."

"Sure you do, you just don't know it."

"I know what I have," Judith said, tears dripping down her face. "And I know what I'm losing."

Layton felt uncomfortable trying to console her before Farrell had actually died. There was no doubt the old actor was going. Perhaps he was lingering on so she could get used to the idea. He wondered how long it was since she had sex.

"These are hard times but you'll get through them. You've got to start facing life. Farrell's right, we're all going to vanish sooner or later. You've had some pretty good years with him, that's a lot more than a lot of miserable people have."

"I know I should be thankful for what I have, but what I have now is a sick old man who thinks I'm his daughter and who I love very much. I don't know what to do for him. I feel so utterly helpless."

"You're there for him, that's enough. He knows that. Once you get him home you've done all you can. That's what he wants, that's all you can do."

Layton wanted to take her, right in the car. Give her what she hadn't had in years probably. She was still an attractive, sturdy woman.

"You've been good to talk to," she said. "I'm sorry I go on about it. I just feel that when I'm alone no one will bother with me."

"That's nonsense. The same people you know now will be there for you when you need them. Hollywood's callous but not shallow."

Well, he thought, maybe both. But instead of saying any more he leaned over and took her hand, then kissed her on the mouth. For a moment she responded with a quick purse of her lips, a quiver. He felt her body shudder. He put his hand lightly on her breast and squeezed, then backed away, thanking her for the ride and telling her she could always count on him. He left her with a bewildered look on her face; as if he had awakened some long smoldering desire which she felt must be immediately suppressed.

Leanne was sleeping in her mother's bed, her fingers holding Amy's ear. Layton checked Andy, who was hugging his Elmo doll, then went to sleep in Leanne's room. Her bed was several inches too short and his feet hung over the edge but he managed to put himself to sleep by reading the first two chapters of *Mr Sand Man* that had been on her night table.

He dreamt of being the Sand Man, coming into his daughter's head to take her away from her nightmares and bad thoughts. He whisked her to a Hollywood studio where a new production of *Alice in Wonderland* meets *Snow White and the Seven Dwarfs* was underway. Then he took her to a magical ice skating rink where the ice floated like an island in a deep blue lake. You could only get there by rowboat and though the sun shone brightly above, the ice never melted. They danced and slid and skated figure 8's, laughing at the animated characters who acted in cartoonish ways on the ice. When they tired Layton-as-Sand-Man took Leanne to the World's Greatest Amusement Park, filled with exotic and thrilling rides, mirrored hologram fun-houses, virtual reality interactive stations, and delicious shakes to drink. She loved it all, going from roller-coaster to whirling tea cups, from loop-de-loops to rocket launches. But at the cackling Fun House she hesitated, then turned away in fright. Layton looked up at the ticket seller who wore a snakeskin jacket and large funny ears. It was Theo Soris.

He woke up.

His daughter's room was sending him messages. She had suffered terribly and it was his fault. He knew that he had to find out what had happened at Theo's apartment.

When he couldn't fall back to sleep he went into the living room and tried the couch. He no longer wanted to feel like a guest on the pull-out sofa in Amy's editing room.

■ ■ ■

Andy jumped on him in the morning, excited to see his father in a new place. Al Low, who called, was also excited. The morning paper not only favorably reviewed Williams' play but there was a picture of Layton talking with Judith Lee in Judy Jacobs' column. The paragraph about what he said to Sol Gordon was the lead and it gave him a headache when Low read it to him.

She had caught all the details: what Tennessee Williams had said to Samantha, what Layton called her, how she was suing Layton.

"I'll tell you, for a guy who hasn't been heard from for a while you sure are getting coverage," Low said.

"Goodbye Al, we'll talk again after I shoot somebody."

He went to the door to get the paper. Amy was in the kitchen pouring Mueslix into bowls. Andy was running after the cat as Leanne sat quietly.

"Going to school today?" Layton asked.

She nodded.

"Think we could talk later?"

She shrugged.

"Maybe you could drive them," Amy said. "I'm still feeling tired."

"I slept on the couch," Layton said. "I need some bed."

"You take us, you take us," Andy said.

"Give me a break. Look at this," Layton said to Amy, opening the paper to his picture with Judith Lee. Innocent enough, only he had wanted to lay her last night.

"You look happy. It's a good picture."

"Read it."

Amy took the paper and read as she poured the milk into the bowls. "Oh my God...this is very funny."

"For who?"

"The moose and the pussycat. That's hysterical."

"Now the suit's public. It's going to force her into a corner."

"Where's the moose and the cat?" Andy asked, grabbing at the paper.

"Take it easy," Amy said. "It's just words, no pictures."

"Look, it's Daddy. What's that woman?"

"It's Mrs Lee, Farrell Lee's wife."

"Do I know her?" Andy asked.

"Does it matter?" Layton looked at Leanne, who was usually as curious as her brother. She just sat there chewing cereal. "Want to see?" he asked, taking the paper from Andy and showing Leanne. She looked but it didn't seem to register. He took the paper back and turned to the Calendar section review of the play. He looked again at Leanne and started to read aloud. When he mentioned Theo's name her body stiffened and her head shuddered. He stopped reading and left the room. "You take them," he said to Amy.

■ ■ ■

Samantha Sanders was sitting at her breakfast table, across from Mark, being served Eggs Benedict by her cook. She had a pimple on her chin that put her in a foul mood. When she opened the morning paper and saw Layton's picture she scowled. Then she read what he said and grew furious.

"The man's a bigger moron than I've given him credit for," she said with a hiss.

"Who?" Mark asked, suspecting the answer.

"Your father, that's who! Look at this."

Mark put down his fork and read the paragraph. He found it amusing.

"You think it's funny?"

"He's just saying you two are different, that's all."

"We're different all right."

"See."

"He's got a screw loose, that's where we differ."

"He's not so bad."

"He's not clever enough to be bad."

"Why can't you get along with him?"

"Because moose and cats are different breeds. Natural enemies."

"He's not your enemy. He loves you."

Samantha eyed Mark. She knew Layton never stopped loving her but she didn't know Mark did. The boy was sensitive and perceptive. Like her. But she stopped loving Layton years ago and wished he would simply disappear. If she had real powers she would like to make all those she no longer cared to see or know vanish. But lucky for Layton and hundreds of others, she had no magic mirror, no paid assassins.

"He's a pussy," she said, "at least he got that right."

"He's my father; I wish you'd treat him with some respect."

"Respect's got to be earned. Punching women and calling them names in public is no way to earn it."

"Maybe you could do something for him."

"I will," she said, picking up the phone to call her lawyer.

Who then called Layton.

"Not still sleeping are you?" Sol Gordon asked.

"I was just running out to buy more papers," Layton said.

"Better save your money. She's pissed."

"It's her natural state."

"She'd like to break some bones."

"She can get in line behind Amy. We provide the bats."

"Just warning you to be prepared."

"I was once a Boy Scout. We never forget." There was a beep on the line; someone else was calling.

"Goodbye Layton."

"Ciao Sol."

Layton clicked the other caller on. It was a man named Harlan Finder, a talent coordinator for the Desert Hot Springs Spa Hotel near Palm Springs. Perce Dent was the contact and Layton listened to the pitch: the guests who came to sit in the various mineral pools were often from the east and mid-west, usually over fifty, and had money to spend for a memorable experience. Finder had come up with the idea of bringing down movie stars to act out a few scenes from any of their films with one of the hotel's guests. For this privilege the guest would pay $500 for a half hour's reading and the hotel would split it with the star. All expenses and use of the hotel's facilities would, of course, be covered.

"You want me to come to the desert for $250?" Layton asked.

"Per client," Finder said. "If we have ten clients spread over two days, that's $2,500 plus a free vacation."

"And for this Grandma Jones gets to act with a real movie star to tell all her friends back in Minneapolis?"

"Not just tell, show. We'll videotape the scene after you've rehearsed it."

"Five hundred's too cheap," Layton said. "People pay six for a Shaq signed basketball."

"You're probably right," Finder said, "but we've never done anything like this, it's a new idea. Mr Dent thought you might be willing to give it a try. Then if it's popular we can raise the price."

The idea was ludicrous but Layton didn't say that. He knew that his luck had taken a turn for the worse but he didn't think he had sunk so quickly to the bottom of the movie barrel, actually considering playing one of his characters in some yokel's home video. "Give me your number and let me think about it," he said.

Leanne's P.E. teacher saw Amy in the school's parking lot and asked her if anything at home had disturbed Leanne. "I've never seen her so down before."

In the car Amy knew she had to get to the bottom of this. Her daughter had dramatically changed overnight, it was affecting her behavior and it had to be stopped. With Andy bouncing around in the back seat full of his usual energy it was impossible to talk to Leanne. So she told Andy that he and Layton would go for a tennis lesson when they got home.

"I can't play tennis," Andy said.

"That's why you'll take a lesson. You'll learn."

"I'd rather go to the arcade."

"Ask your father."

"How do you know he's home?"

"He's probably still sleeping."

"That's funny," Andy said. "It's three o'clock in the afternoon, nobody sleeps now."

Layton was on the patio asleep in a lounge chair, the cordless phone on his bare chest. Andy squirted him with his atomic water blaster and laughed when he opened his eyes. "Mommy wants you to take me somewhere so she can talk to Leanne."

"Did she tell you that?"

"Sure she did. Leanne's turned into the Creep From the Deep and mommy wants to find out why."

"Do you know?"

"She's not Leanne."

"Who is she?"

"I told you. She's been replaced."

"Then why are you so cheery?"

"I like living with a zombie. It's fun."

"Your sister's not a zombie. She's upset."

"Why?"

"You're the one with all the answers."

"All right. See, when she went to school there was this fire drill and everybody had to run outside, only Leanne didn't run, she stayed in her classroom and this creature came and no one saw it because they were all outside and then he found Leanne and ate her so he could change into her. And that's why."

Amy came outside and suggested Layton take Andy away for a few hours. Layton offered the weekend.

"Where will you go?" Amy asked.

"The desert," Layton said. "I've been offered a job, maybe we'll take a drive and I'll check it out."

"An acting job?"

"You could call it that."

"Just make sure you're back early Sunday night so he won't be tired for school."

"We're outta here," Layton said. "Soon's I make one call."

Amy's efforts with Leanne were getting nowhere.

"I'm tired now Mom, can I just go to my room?" Leanne asked.

"Leanne, I'm worried about you. Something has happened and I know you're scared and feel you can't talk about it but I can help. You don't have to be alone in this."

"I just can't. It's bad luck."

"What is?"

Leanne looked at her mother and began to cry. The shame and guilt was too much for her. Theo's play had opened to good reviews and if she told, something would probably happen to him. Her father was an actor and she knew, even at ten, what it meant to be in something successful. She understood superstition. She was there to help bring Theo good luck. She hated him for it and she worried that she might get some disease and she wanted so badly to tell her mother. But she was afraid.

Amy took her to her room and hugged her closely. "Honey, I promise it won't hurt you to tell me. Trust me, baby."

Leanne wanted to. The struggle within herself began to lean towards revelation. She looked again at Amy. "Promise not to tell Daddy?"

"Promise."

And then Leanne tried to tell, in a halting, choking way, what had happened in Theo Soris' apartment.

Amy's anger rose with each detail. She managed to restrain herself from pressing or interrupting as she listened to her daughter's horrible tale of manipulation and seduction. Leanne didn't elaborate and it only took a few difficult minutes to relate how Theo made her read those filthy pages, how he kissed her with his tongue, and how he got her to kiss and fondle his cock. When she finished she was crying, holding onto Amy, asking her what's going to happen now, saying, "I don't want to get AIDS and die. I didn't want to do it."

Amy tried to comfort Leanne but found herself feeling such enormous rage that she had to leave the room. "I just got to go to the bathroom," she said, squeezing out words. "I'll be right back."

She went to throw up. This was so sick, so evil, how dare that fucker do something like that to her daughter? And Layton was as much to blame for leaving her there.

She had promised Leanne not to tell Layton but it was a promise impossible to keep. Layton would hear about it all right, as soon as he called from wherever the hell he went with Andy. He hadn't told her where he was going, just to the desert. He'd better call, she thought. Because she wasn't going to wait and do nothing through the weekend.

■ ■ ■

Harlan Finder welcomed Layton as if he was Clint Eastwood or Kevin Costner, neither of whom would have considered visiting Desert Hot Springs to act with some middle aged woman for anything less than mid-five figures. $250 was as low as it could possibly get for an actor who was once as big as either of those stars. But it was the timing more than the need that brought Layton and Andy to the hotel. And Finder was able to get two clients on just two hour's notice.

"Wow, look at all the pools," Andy said as they walked outside.

"Some of them may be too hot for you," Finder cautioned, "but the bigger ones should be okay."

"I'm gonna go in all of 'em," Andy said.

"Wanna bet?" Layton asked.

"Why can't I?"

"I'm not stopping you, it's just that they're not what you think they are."

Finder brought them to their room that was on the ground floor and had a sliding glass door as an entrance. It wasn't elaborate but it was convenient for late night soaking. Andy wanted to go swimming immediately. Layton told him to knock himself out as he and Finder went over whatever business details Layton needed to know before meeting with the two amateur thespians.

"It's amazing," Finder told him, "that when they heard you were coming both of them chose the same film, *Canvases*, the scene between you and Cleo Warner on the beach, wearing masks. I've rented the video and we're having that scene transcribed for tomorrow. You'll work with Martha Loesser in the afternoon for two hours and with Kate Moesk on Sunday. What I thought we'd do is meet for lunch, then you can rehearse for an hour and we'd shoot the scene the next hour."

"That's a sexy scene," Layton said. "You sure there isn't some other that might be more appropriate?"

"You'd have thought but that's the one they wanted. *C'est la vie* I guess. We're making this a dream come true. It could be very big you know. Word-of-mouth is how we get most of our visitors."

Canvases was not what Layton had thought about when he agreed to do this. The story was about the conflict between a rebellious performance artist (Layton) and his businessman father. The woman Cleo Warner played was older than Layton's character and younger than his father. Attracted to both men, she first buys into a performance piece in which Layton auctions himself to the highest bidder in an art gallery, and then later convinces the father that the way to reach Layton is through her. Literally.

This is going to be some weekend, Layton thought. The food better be good.

■ ■ ■

That evening, when Layton still hadn't called, Amy decided she wasn't going to wait any longer. She asked Enid to stay with Leanne and drove her Mazda MPV to the secluded, patrolled, electronically sealed home of Samantha Sanders. When she announced herself at the gate the guard's voice came back through the intercom saying Ms Sanders couldn't be disturbed.

"Disturb her," Amy shouted into the metal box.

"Who is this again?" asked the voice.

"Amy Cross. Just tell her that."

"I'm sorry..."

Samantha, who was watching an old movie of hers on one of the cable stations, heard the squawking and turned to her closed-circuit TV monitor. She recognized Amy and wondered what she could possibly want. Layton must have sent her, she figured. He would stoop to that. Unless Layton himself was stooping so low that he couldn't be seen by the camera. If he was hiding then it could be a kidnap attempt. But he couldn't be that dumb, he knew she had armed guards at the house. And biting dogs.

She flipped the intercom by her bed and told the guard to let her in. The gate opened slowly and Amy sped through, her fury in tact.

"Ms Sanders will be down shortly," the guard said icily, informing Amy that it was not his job to open doors and greet guests but the maid and butler had retired since they were not expecting anyone and she could make herself comfortable in the living room.

Amy, who had never been inside Samantha's home, didn't take the opportunity to look around. She was perfectly focused on a plan of action and had come to seek Samantha Sanders' help. Other than some Mafia don she believed Sanders was probably the only person in America who could get done whatever she wanted done.

When Samantha came down, wearing a flaming red silk kimono with a fiery dragon on the back, Amy apologized for bursting in like this and then quickly told what had happened to Leanne. Samantha, who knew Theo, didn't seem surprised but she appeared sympathetic. "I don't know why you've come to tell me this," she said.

"Because you can do something."

"What?"

"I want something done to him."

"What can I do?"

"You must know the right people. A phone call can do it. I'll pay whatever it costs."

"You want to hire some goons to beat him up?"

"To kill him. Or cut off his cock."

"That's not going to undo what's been done," Samantha said. "Look what happened to that Bobbitt slimeball, he turned into the victim. Shouldn't you be talking to the police?"

"What will they do? There's no proof. Just a ten year-old child who's gone blank upstairs."

"Does Layton know you've come here?"

"He's somewhere in the desert with Andy, I don't know where and he hasn't called, the bastard. He's as much to blame as Theo."

Samantha smiled at the woman who had taken Layton in after she had discarded him. With her blurry eyes and blotched face Amy looked older than Samantha though she was ten years younger. Mark had mentioned that she drank too much, especially in the years since she and Layton had split up. Now she was asking her to put out a contract on an actor who performed some kind of sex act with Leanne Cross. The woman was acting out of an insane rage.

"You look like you need a drink," Samantha said, getting up to find a bottle of whiskey. She poured half a glass of Jack Daniel's and gave it to Amy straight without ice. Amy drank it like water.

"You won't help me will you?"

"I'm not sure how I can. In spite of what you may think I don't know the kind of people you're referring to."

"But you know people who know people. Half the fucking producers and executives in the industry are gangsters."

"You're very upset," Samantha said. "In a few days you'll be embarrassed by tonight. If you'd like to spend the night there's a guest room. Tomorrow you can call a lawyer to discuss this. Let Layton handle Theo, he's perfectly capable."

Amy remembered Samantha's swollen jaw and felt like an idiot being there. How could she have expected this woman to do anything for her? She stood up to leave. "Here, take this," Samantha said sticking the bottle of Jack Daniel's under her arm. Amy left without saying another word. She got back into her MPV, unscrewed the cap, and slugged the whiskey all the way to Westwood.

■ ■ ■

The heated pools had knocked Andy out early and Layton wasn't sure he could last two more days in Desert Hot Springs, so he called Harlan Finder and suggested he meet with one of the women that evening, get it over with. Martha Loesser, who had been coming to the spa every year since her husband retired in 1989, was even more excited to work with Layton Cross at night. The pages they would act together had been prepared and they met in the empty breakfast dining room.

Martha, who weighed 180 pounds and wore a size 16 dress with a flower print, brought her husband to meet the movie star. Mr Loesser was also heavy, smoked a cigar, and looked at Layton as another item on his wife's shopping list. She wanted to act with a movie star, he'd pay for it. Only the best for his Martha in the twilight of their lives. That's why he worked so goddamned hard in the insurance business all his life, so they could enjoy the fruits of his labor in the end. "Just don't fuck 'im," was the only thing he said to her before leaving them alone.

"Not to worry about that," Layton, who could only go through with this stoned, said.

"This is all very hard to believe," Martha said as they sat opposite each other at a table in the middle of the room. "I acted in high school and in Hadassah plays we put on but never with a real actor like you."

"If you acted in plays that makes you an actor," Layton said. "Anybody can do it. And if you can't then you can go into politics."

She giggled with nervousness and Layton thought of offering her a joint but let it pass. That's all he needed: to connect with this woman and wind up fucking her on camera. Mr Husband would not be pleased.

They read through their lines half a dozen times and each time Layton found himself wondering how he got into situations like this. Martha Loesser was a decent, perhaps foolish woman, not unlike his mother. She was buying into a new experience and tried very hard to please which was the problem. The scene called for her to be the aggressor, to sit on the beach under a pier with the waves roaring behind them, getting Layton to drop his guard, put on a mask, and become the incarnation of Eros. They couldn't actually kiss because of the masks but they embrace, and in that moment the audience senses the power and sensuality of their joining. In the film Layton ran his hands along Cleo Warner's body as she did his. How Mr Loesser agreed to pay for this scene was not something Layton could understand after meeting him. He probably never saw the movie and she probably never told him what it was about. It would be the first time Layton ever felt up a senior citizen.

■ ■ ■

Theo Soris left the Coronet an hour after the final curtain. He was hungry and drove to Katsu's on Third. The sushi didn't look fresh so he ordered tempura and two bottles of saki. He had appeared in three performances now and was beginning to feel he could reward himself. The applause wasn't deafening but it stayed with him for hours. He liked being an actor acting.

Amy was waiting for him outside his apartment building. By the time he pulled into his space she had knocked off the Jack Daniel's and had mentally murdered him in a dozen ways. She fingered the Swiss Army knife attached to her key ring. The long blade in the heart first. The ice pick in each eye. The Philips screwdriver up his pisshole. The corkscrew in his ear. The small blade under each fingernail. The saw up his ass. The scissor to cut the tip of his tongue.

She could barely get out of the minivan when she saw him. But she was determined to do this by herself. Fuck Layton and his superstar first wife. Fuck the doctors, lawyers and police. Theo Soris pulled his dick on her daughter and she wasn't going to let a judge and jury stand between her and revenge.

Theo was whistling when he got out of his car. Warmed by the saki, proud of his performances, he bounced on the balls of his feet as he jumped up each step to the entrance of his building.

"Theo."

He turned when he heard his name. Amy was two steps away, swaying. He recognized her and felt a twinge of danger. Still, he walked down to greet her and felt the knife enter just below the left shoulder.

"You sonuvabitch!" Amy blurted as she tried to pull the blade out so she could stab him again. Theo wrestled with her and took hold of the knife. They fell to the ground. Theo hit his head on the curb and was dazed. Amy withdrew the knife and ran back to her MPV. She got in, started it, and floored the accelerator. Theo tried to roll out of the way but he wasn't fast enough. He felt the weight of the minivan as it ran over his legs. She heard his scream as she drove down the empty street. It wasn't enough she thought but she was too nauseous to turn around for a second pass at him. She pulled over so that she could puke out the window then put the car back into gear and drove home hoping that he lay in the street bleeding to death.

6

Paying The Piper

"I don't understand, we just got here, why do we have to go back?"

"You'll understand when you get older," Layton said. "Play with your Game Boy."

"Why did that man hit you?"

"He was crazy."

"Did you know him?"

"Just his wife."

"He was really angry."

"Yeah, he was."

Layton had got carried away with Martha Loesser and had pressed his palm against her mound. She was wearing her dress but it so flushed the woman that when she returned to her room Mr Loesser just lost it. He wasn't paying out good money for his wife to be raped by some punk movie actor. Poor Martha couldn't stop him from storming out to Layton's room and pounding on the door. When Layton opened it Mr Loesser took a swing and hit him on the side of the head. Layton stumbled back with

Mr Loesser coming at him. Andy woke up and started yelling. Harlan Finder came into the room and grabbed Mr Loesser from behind. Martha was also there, flushed now from embarrassment.

"I ain't paying a dime to this guy," Mr Loesser was saying. "You hear that? Not a dime."

"Nothing happened," Martha Loesser finally said, "you're being ridiculous."

"Yeah, well you got the tape? I wanna see what's on the tape. He touched you anywhere he shouldn't have, I ain't paying."

"I'm sure it was all very professional," Harlan Finder said. "Wasn't it Mr Cross?"

"She chose the scene," Layton said. "I gave her her money's worth."

"It's not her money it's mine," Mr Loesser exclaimed, "and I ain't giving you any of it."

"I believe my agreement was with Mr Finder," Layton said.

Layton got his share but the next day's scene was cancelled and after soaking in the waters early Saturday morning there didn't seem to be any reason to stay, so he told Andy they were going back. He had no idea what he was going back to but he had a premonition that Amy had got to the bottom of Leanne's troubles. Whether that was good or bad he'd have to wait and see.

He heard the news on the radio just as they crossed the county line: Actor Theo Soris, currently appearing at the Coronet Theater in Tennessee Williams' final play, was in serious condition at UCLA's Medical Center. It appeared that Soris had been mugged, then run over.

Layton turned off at the first freeway exit and drove to a pay phone at an Arco station. He didn't have enough change to call the hospital so he gave Andy a five and told him to go inside and get quarters. While he waited he dialed Amy's number collect.

She answered on the third ring. Her voice sounded as if she was underwater. "Something happened to Theo," Layton said. "He's in the hospital."

"Is he dead?"

"They say serious condition. Maybe you should go there, he's at UCLA."

"Where are you?"

"I don't know, near Pomona I think. We're on our way back; I just heard on the radio."

"I've got a terrible headache."

"How's Leanne?"

"He should be dead. I wanted him dead. I just got sick."

"What are you talking about?"

"Your friend. What he did to Leanne he doesn't deserve serious, he deserves critical, he deserves dead."

"Amy..."

"What are you going to do about it?"

"Do about what?"

"What he did to her?"

"What did he do?"

"You come back and I'll tell you. She doesn't want you to know but I'm going to tell you. You did it to her. You brought her there. You did it."

"Amy, did you run over Theo?"

"After I stabbed the fuck."

"Amy listen to me, don't do anything, don't go anywhere, don't answer any more calls. Just take some aspirin and go back to sleep. I'll be there in a few hours."

He heard the phone go dead. Amy had hung up.

"I got the quarters," Andy said, holding them with both hands.

"Never mind, I don't need them now. C'mon let's get back in the car."

"Here, don't ya want 'em?"

"Keep them."

"Wow, thanks dad."

Andy's thoughts were of arcades and video games. Layton's were of Theo. How could he, his oldest, closest friend, who had shared with him all the actor's humiliations and upsets, who was there during the acid highs, the mushroom and peyote trips, the years of marriages and separations, the birth of his three kids goddamn him, how could he have done something to Leanne that would make Amy want to kill him? What was it he did? How sick was he? What did Amy do to him?

It was a long, agonizing drive and when he reached the bottom of the canyon he was still asking himself questions. His mind was racing though his temper was kept in check only so that he wouldn't scare Andy or get into an accident. He had muffled a huge roar for at least fifty miles.

No one was home when they arrived. No note, no phone messages. Leanne had straightened her bed, Amy's was a mess. Andy went looking for them next door as Layton picked up the phone when it rang.

"Amy?"

"Not quite," said the unmistakable voice.

"Sam?"

"Amy was here last night. She told me what happened and wanted me to use my connections to castrate your friend."

"Jesus," Layton sighed, still unsure exactly what had happened.

"She was very disturbed. Is what she said true?"

"I don't know what she told you."

"I guess it comes back to you."

"What are you talking about?"

"Violence breeds violence."

Layton felt his fingernails dig into his palm, his knuckles trying to break through his skin. He was breathing heavily. Samantha could sense his anger and realized she had gone too far. Leanne was a lovely child. She felt sorry for her.

"That was wrong of me," she said, getting as close to an apology as she was capable of.

Layton relaxed his hand and controlled his mouth. He didn't want to say anything nasty. Deep within him

Samantha had touched a nerve. Was this the way you paid for your mistakes? Through your children? All that karma crap. More cynical, wiser now, was this the way it was, paying the piper with your own flesh and blood? Mark-the-Timid. Leanne-the-Violated. All he ever wanted was to be a good actor; to deserve his fame; to be loved. Now the woman he still loved was calling to tell him his behavior had caused a chain reaction that hurt his daughter and snapped her mother. If he could take it all back–all his own craziness–to reverse the events of the last few days, he'd pay with his soul. But there were no bargains to strike with the past. Only in the movies could Lois Lane be brought back to life, Daniel Webster outwit the Devil. The goddamn movies.

But what was happening was no movie. His best friend had done something to his daughter that had turned Amy into a potential killer. Samantha wanted to sue him for whatever he had left. The media had found him a relic of minor interest. He was only 44 but he felt like Methuselah.

"So what are you going to do?" Samantha asked. Her voice brought him back...to the days before Amy. When they used to talk about their personal problems over the phone when she was shooting in Hollywood and he was working in New York. They were close then. Sharing their joys and frustrations. Their secrets. They weren't always there for each other but there was love between them. She had some highly publicized indiscretions. His were more private. They were never the ideal couple but they had loved each other. Until she outgrew him. Now, for the first time in a decade, she was on the phone with him discussing his problem. What was he going to do?

When Amy pulled into the driveway alone Layton rushed out to meet her. "Where were you? I told you not to go anywhere."

"Fuck you, telling me what to do. Since when? You've never known what to do, how do you come off telling me or anybody else?" She was still in an alcoholic stupor. If he lit a match near her vicious mouth flames would spew.

"Where's Leanne?"

"At Jeannine's."

"So she's all right?"

"Not in her head she isn't. But she wanted to see her friend."

"Tell me what happened."

"I already did."

"No, you told me what you did, not what he did. Samantha called here to tell me you went to see her. What's going on?"

"Can't you figure it out? He molested her."

The words shot through Layton like electricity. He knew it but he didn't want it to be true. "Can we go inside?"

"What would you have done?"

"I don't know. Did he...have sex with her?"

"Depends on what you call a blowjob."

"Jesus."

"I tried to kill him."

"Did anybody see you?"

"He did."

"Who else knows besides Samantha?"

"How should I know?"

"Amy, this is important. You could be in a lot of trouble."

"Don't worry about me."

"The kids don't need this now. We have to deal with it but we don't need charges brought against you."

"What jury would convict me against that bastard? Who knows how many other kids he's done that to."

"We don't want a trial, think what that means. Leanne's too young to be so exposed."

"So Theo recovers and goes about his business?"

"Theo will pay. You got to him. I'll get to him. But Leanne...we should take her to a doctor. Then we'll talk to a shrink." His mind was racing. He still couldn't figure out why she had dragged Samantha into this. He had to ask.

"Because I thought she was different," Amy answered.

"Different than what?"

"Than you. I thought she had balls. But you're all the same. Big stars and fallen stars. Just look out for yourself. There's nobody else. Right, Layt? Nobody but Mr Uno. There's no Leanne, no Andy, no wife, no nothin'. Just you. And anything that upsets your universe isn't dealt with. Just forget it. Well you can't forget this one Cross. I made sure you can't."

Layton wanted to slap her but it would do no good. She was wrong, he did care, he cared deeply. It pained him when Amy called him useless and said she didn't want him in the house anymore.

"Now's not the time," Layton said. "The kids need to see us together."

"You left us before, you're going to leave us again, we don't need you."

"You do, they do. I'm here."

"Why aren't you angry?"

"I am."

"Why don't you want to kill him?"

"I do."

"So?"

"I'm going to go to the hospital."

"Take a bigger knife, mine was too small."

Layton got back into his Jeep and drove Sunset to UCLA. He needed to know Theo's condition, how serious were his injuries? What did Amy do to him? He needed to look him in the face and see how he had missed knowing who he was. He'd known him nearly twenty-five years and never once suspected something like this. An actor was supposed to be in touch with how other people behave; an actor is an observer of human nature. What kind of observer was Layton to have so missed Theo? What kind of an actor?

He began making deep guttural noises. Angry: at himself for leaving Leanne; at Theo; at Amy for complicating everything; at Samantha for saying what she said. Scenes were unraveling like bad playwriting; subtleties were out the window. He wanted Leanne whole. He wanted a normal family life. He wanted someone to offer him a good script, in English. He wanted what he couldn't have.

Jeannine was Leanne's closest friend. They were in the same class, they knew each other since pre-school. Jeannine's parents were in the travel business and Leanne often went away with them on trips to San Diego or Lake Tahoe. Jeannine was the only person in the world other than Amy that Leanne would talk to about what had happened. And when she did, even though Jeannine had promised not to tell anyone, her secret was out. Jeannine would tell her parents.

* * *

Theo had spent the night under emergency care and was moved to a private room in the morning. His legs were crushed and he'd need multiple operations before any prognosis could be given. The femur bones were both broken, his kneecaps were badly cracked, his shins were splintered, the nerves in his right calf flattened. He had also lost a lot of blood from the stab wound and the doctors were concerned about infection that could lead to blood poisoning. At best he'd be in the hospital for weeks. At worst he might never walk again. Returning to the stage was out of the question.

He was conscious when Layton walked in but he wished he wasn't. He hadn't expected visitors. Especially Layton.

"Layt, she was drunk. I don't know what happened."

"I do," Layton said.

Theo forced a pathetic smile. His eyes were watery. Despite the morphine he was still suffering.

"In pain?"

"Only when I laugh."

"Not too much to laugh about is there?"

"Layton, I'm sorry. I know that doesn't mean anything. I'm just fucked."

Layton felt his skin tingle as he tried not to lose it. Trying to figure out what makes a man do what he did. He fought the urge to take the pathetic cripple by his throat and choke the life out of him.

"I didn't give Amy's name," Theo said. "They had me fill out forms, I said I didn't see who attacked me. I couldn't believe it."

"You couldn't believe it! What the fuck do you think's going through my head?"

Theo started to cry. "I didn't hurt her. I swear I didn't."

"How do you know what hurts a ten-year-old girl? Amy was trying to kill you."

"I wish she would have."

"Don't go actor on me Theo, I'll fucking punch you out right now if you do that."

"What do you want me to say? I'm sorry. I really am. I did a stupid, unforgivable thing. What am I supposed to do now? You want to punch me, go ahead. You want to stick a knife in me, do it. I can't fight you. You're my goddamn friend."

"Was, Theo. Not any more." Layton felt drained. He had lost some of his anger because Theo was no longer a man to him. He was some creature. The poor bastard. "Why, Theo? Why'd you do it?"

"I can't help myself," Theo sobbed. "I can't explain it. It's not the first time." As he tried to talk his eyes went wild. It hit him quickly, that someone, maybe the police, might somehow search his house. If they did they'd find the pictures. He'd go to prison for sure. He looked at Layton. About to ask an incredible favor.

"Can I talk to you?"

"I'm listening."

"Layton, I'm a sick man. I need help. But I don't want to go to prison. I'll commit to a shrink. I'll take tests. But if the police find the pictures I'm in deep trouble."

"Of Leanne?" Layton couldn't believe this conversation was happening.

"No. There've been others. I've taken pictures of them. They're all in a shoebox in my closet. I should have put them in a vault but I look at them Layt. I can't help myself. I look at the pictures."

Layton didn't want to hear Theo's confession. Let him tell it to a priest. He was only concerned about Leanne. And Amy. Theo had done damage to them both and now was talking about others. Layton didn't want to know.

But Theo wasn't confessing to get it off his chest. He wanted Layton to go to his apartment and get that box. He didn't want Layton to look inside. He didn't want the pictures destroyed. What harm were the pictures now? He'd go into therapy, but the pictures might help him through. After all, he had taken each one. He knew every detail. They transported him back to the events. They were his pictures.

"You must be out of your mind," Layton said.

"Look, the play's yours, I'm out of it. Just do me this favor."

"Now what the hell are you talking about?"

"I'm up shit's creek. If this thing gets out I'm ruined. I'm not able to go back to the play now. You do it. Your name will attract. It's a good part. You know that."

"Theo, that's why there are understudies. The show will go on without you. Or me. That has nothing to do with what you're talking about."

"The kid under me's not going to hold it together. He's still in school. He'll last maybe a week, then it's over. Closed. You could keep it open. I'll talk to the producers. They'll jump to get you."

"I don't want to do your fucking play. Your brain must be fried. You've got a lot more troubles than the play."

"What's more important than a career? You know that. Give me a chance. I can get another shot after this if this other stuff doesn't come out. Those pictures will hang me."

"You deserve it."

"Then you do it. Go to my apartment, get the box and take it to the cops yourself."

"I don't want to go near your box of pictures." What was going on? He had come to see if Theo was going to live, and if he was then to pummel him for what he had

Leanne do to him. Now Theo had him talking about his box of child porn, wanting him to participate in a cover-up. Theo was trying to make him a partner to his crimes.

"I'm begging now, Layton. You have every right to hate me, to want me locked up. But it's a sickness. I'm a sick man. I'm saying so. I know so. I don't want to be locked up. Give me a chance to be cured. Just do this for me, I'll go out of your life for good."

"You'll never go out of my life, you've already seen to that."

"Layton, just give me this chance. Why drag this out any further? Why bring Amy into it? Leanne. If they go after Amy it's all going to come out. Who's going to benefit? We don't need this Layton."

"Who's going to go after Amy if you never told she did this to you? Are you making some threat here? You think we're not going to report you ourselves?"

"You can't do that, then I'll have to say Amy did this. I don't want any more trouble. I just want a chance. The key's in my pants. Take it. It's a Bally shoebox in my bedroom closet on the shelf. Put it in a bag and keep it in your garage. You don't have to look inside; you don't have to know. It's just a shoebox to you, that's all. In a week you can put it back. That's all I'm asking. If you can't do it, okay, I understand. Take the key and think about it. Make up your mind later. Please Layton, please, just take it."

Layton had played out different scenarios on his way to the hospital but no imagined scene could have led him to this bizarre twist. The man was the worst kind of criminal. Now he was asking the father of one of his victims to help him hide the evidence of his misdeeds.

Why did he take the key? Why didn't he just walk out? It had something to do with Theo being an actor. A fellow descendant of thieves and gypsies. It wasn't something Amy could ever understand. But the man was down. Way down. Amy helped put him there. Layton just couldn't kick him. He still wanted to get even, but that would come.

"Thanks man," Theo whispered as Layton walked out.

"We're not finished," Layton said.

■ ■ ■

Amy told Leanne what she had done to Theo on the drive back from Jeannine's. "I just want you to hear it from me, not read about it later. He did something to you no one has a right to do and I wanted him to know that. I wanted to fix him."

Leanne didn't understand. Stabbing someone with a knife and running him over was what the bad guys did on TV. Mothers didn't do that. "Are you going to get in trouble?" she asked.

"I don't know. Maybe."

"Isn't it wrong, what you did?"

"Wasn't it wrong what he did?"

"I thought two wrongs don't make a right."

"Nothing will ever make what he did right, honey. But he needed to be punished."

"But who's going to punish you."

"Leanne, baby, I've been punished. What happened to you is punishment enough. But no sonuvabitch is going to get away with what he did. Do you understand?"

"I'm not sure," Leanne said. "Now daddy's going to know."

"He already knows."

"You promised not to tell."

"He found out. Look, something like this can't be hidden from your father, he's got to know. He never should have left you there."

"It's not daddy's fault," Leanne said, beginning to cry.

"I didn't say it was. But you and Andy are our children. We love you very much. We don't want anything to happen to you. When something like this happens, we have to know. So we can do something."

"Mommy you're scaring me."

"You're upset," Amy said. "I understand that. I'm upset too. Your father went to see Theo."

"Where?"

"The hospital."

"Is he going to stab him too?"

Layton left the hospital fingering the key. Two pretty coeds smiled at him in the parking lot. Two jocks were tossing a Frisbee between the aisles. A dog, locked in an Infiniti, was barking. A tossed copy of the *Daily Bruin* lay on the ground by his Jeep. The headline told of a petition to ban genetic testing on animals. The story below that was about the increase of rapes on campus.

He drove into Westwood, remembering the time he accompanied Samantha to one of her openings. Crowds had lined the streets for a glimpse of her. Girls threw flowers. Amateur and professional photographers called her name. Her grip was tight on his arm. He was invisible.

When he got to Theo's apartment building he parked in a red zone. The key felt slimy in his hand. He bound up the steps, noticed the row of mailboxes, and dropped the key in Theo's slot. Fuck the pictures. He didn't want to know.

Driving back to the Hollywood Hills Layton wondered whether Amy was right in her action and in wanting him out. He wasn't the kind of person who could pull a knife on anyone–yet Amy's behavior was that of a mother protecting her young. It hadn't been easy for her when he left and she had obviously become a tougher, self-reliant woman. She had managed to earn a living on her own and not depend on his often-delinquent payments. She never called him for a favor until she brought him back when she went to see her mother, and now that return seemed to end in disaster. She had every right to feel that she was better off without him. Except that now was no time for him to leave. The kids, especially Leanne, needed a father figure in the house. And Amy was too out of her mind to leave them alone with her. No, he definitely could not leave now.

When he returned home he saw the glum faces of Amy and Leanne. "He'll live," Layton said. Amy waited for him to say more.

"Any messages?" he asked.

"Is that all?" Amy said.

"WHAT DO YOU WANT ME TO SAY!?" His shout startled him as much as it did them. The frustration had turned into this roar and he didn't know where to go with it. Leanne quivered and began to cry. "DON'T CRY," Layton yelled. "IT'S NOT YOUR FAULT!"

"Stop it!" Amy screamed at him. "Just stop it!"

Layton wanted to punch, to pound, to do something physical. He didn't want to scare Leanne. He really wasn't angry with Amy. He decided to go for a run.

"Barry Levine called Daddy," Leanne said. "I wrote the number."

In the business twenty-four years, Layton fumed as he jogged through the canyon, and the only call he gets is from a nineteen-year-old karate pimp who wants to use him to get into the movies.

Levine was excited. Not only was *Mr Sand Man* available but no one had ever called about the film rights before. Layton wasn't surprised. Levine had picked up a copy and saw the potential, though he thought they'd have to make some changes.

"Couldn't find a part you liked?" Layton asked.

"That, among other things. But the news is that they gave it to us for five grand. We're in business."

"You're in option," Layton corrected. "Business is a script away."

"The point is, you're in. Arno and Macky are setting up a production company. This'll be their first movie and you'll star. It's all in motion now, just like I told you. These guys move fast."

Layton, who needed some relief, was amused. *Mr Sand Man* was no more a movie than Levine was an actor. It was a children's story, a fantasy; it could only be done in animation. But these people had taken him seriously; the least he could do is appear interested. For a while.

"You have a writer?" Layton asked.

"We just got the book this morning, but I'm calling agents all day today. We'll find out who's available and see whom we can interest. That's why it's important to have your name attached."

"That and seven-and-a-half bucks will get you into any movie theater in town." Layton knew he had to be careful when it came to using his name. No one in the movies could afford to forget what happened to Kim Basinger and *Boxing Helena*.

"They want to meet with you again. This is serious Layton. They've got money."

"I don't talk money, my agent does that."

"Okay, okay, so who's your agent? We'll take a meeting with him."

Good question. Layton had no agent. He wasn't going back to Perce, especially about something as absurd as this. No, this one was best done alone. An agent would laugh him out of his office if he brought these characters in.

"Tell 'em I'll meet them at the paddle tennis courts in Venice tomorrow at nine."

"Be serious," Levine said. "These guys want to do business in an office not at the beach. Christ, I thought you wanted to do this movie."

"That's where I'll be. Don't worry about paddles, you can rent them."

"I don't know if they play."

"It's easy."

"Will your agent be there?"

"Don't worry about that, you just come, I'll be listening."

When they hung up Layton went to Leanne's room to find the book. He took it into the living room and spent the rest of the afternoon reading it. When he finished he shook his head. They'll have to pay me a million bucks to get my name onto this he thought.

Spider Ray's call was unexpected. Sick news travels fast Layton knew but he couldn't believe what Ray was asking him to consider.

"Out of the question."

"I know he's your friend, that's why you should give this some thought. You've got an opportunity to capitalize on a mean incident. Theo's mugging is box-office if you take over. It will sell tickets. It's his idea."

Layton realized that Ray had no idea what Theo had done or who had put him in the hospital. The news hadn't yet traveled. "Theo is a sick man, Spider."

"Obviously. But the show has opened, it's booked for six weeks, it's got another five-and-a-half weeks to run. It's not a large chunk of time for what it can do for you."

"I never knew you were so concerned about my career."

"Circumstances, Layton. This is a business of filling cracks that open unexpectedly."

"Now I'm spackling paste in your hands."

"It's an opportunity. There may be a film in it. You can rehearse for two weeks while the understudy goes on. By then the audience will have dwindled and you would revive it. It'll go out over the wires and the whole country will pay attention to you."

"What's in this for you Spider? You don't represent me."

"I feel responsible. I got Theo the part. I owe it to the theater to find a replacement."

"Call Jon Voight, he likes Williams."

"If you won't consider it I might. Just don't be firm. Give it a few days. I'll messenger a copy of the play. Read it."

Two crazy offers in one day, Layton thought. A ridiculous children's story and a replacement for the guy who molested Leanne. No wonder this business is unreal.

The phone rang again but Layton didn't answer. He just counted the rings. He had enough to think about for one day.

■ ■ ■

It would be a most difficult conversation but Layton knew if he didn't talk with Leanne about this he couldn't make a decision. She was still morose and distanced but he managed to get her to go with him to Swenson's in Studio City. Andy stayed home because he never missed *Family Ties*.

"I know you've been through a rough time," Layton said as they drove. "Mommy's upset and overreacted. I'm upset and am trying to understand how Theo could do what he did. This is not easy for any of us. But I want you to know that it's not your fault. In any way." He paused, groping for words. Leanne was silent. "Is there anything you want to talk about?"

She shook her head no.

"You know how much we love you, don't you?"

She nodded yes.

"I didn't think we'd have this kind of conversation for a few more years but I'm going to talk to you about sex. We shouldn't be embarrassed about it. Are you embarrassed?"

"A little."

"Me too. Maybe we should talk about ice cream."

Leanne smiled. It was easier being silly than serious.

"Your mother and I have considered your seeing a kind of doctor, the kind who just talks and listens to you."

"I saw *Ordinary People* on video," Leanne said.

"Right. Didn't that guy from *Taxi* play the psychiatrist?"

"Judd Hirsch," Leanne said. "Will he be the one I will see?"

"No, he's an actor like me. We're not doctors. But it will be something like that. I'm not sure yet if you will go to one, I'm just telling you that we're thinking about it. You might want to try it and see what you think. Sometimes it's easier to talk to a doctor than to your parents. Parents can get too emotional. Doctors never do. They just listen and nod their heads and tell you when your hour's up. Then they thank you for giving them money for listening to you. But that's something we both can decide in a few days. After we've talked about sex. So you can have things to think about. Okay?"

"I'll listen to you Daddy."

"Who do you think you are, a psychiatrist or something?"

Leanne giggled and he felt he was getting through.

"Sex is usually a lot of fun," Layton started. This was unexplored territory for him. He didn't know how much he should tell her but she had been through such a negative sexual experience he wanted her to understand that it wasn't always sordid. It wasn't even sex. It was, but it wasn't. "When two people are in love they feel attracted to each other. That's when sex is fun. They touch each other, kiss, laugh, feel their hearts beating faster. They get excited being together. When they're old enough they make love with each other. I don't have to tell you about that, do I?"

Leanne blushed, which was enough of an answer.

"You don't have to be married to have sex. When grandma and grandpa were young they were told you had to be married, but you really don't. It's nice if you can find the right person to both marry and have sex with but I'll tell you the truth, I'd rather you didn't marry for sex. Because marriage is more than that. Sex is only a part. If you're careful about it you can have it without having to worry. Well, you have to worry because of AIDS that is why you must know about contraception. Besides getting pregnant you have to worry about getting diseases. It's not easy to talk about this Leanne. I'm trying to tell you that sex is nothing to be ashamed about but something to give a lot of thought to before you try it. I know you're only ten and you may not have to worry about this for another seven years but somehow the time has come to talk about these things. Now, what Theo did was not really sex. Because sex is something that two people do willingly. And knowingly. You didn't know what he was doing. And if you did you wouldn't have been willing. So it's different. I've known Theo a long time and I never knew he could do what he did. It's not something he wants to do but it's something he can't control. It's a sickness. Only he's hurting other people, children, and that makes it a crime as well. What he did to you was a crime. It's against the law. But that doesn't make it any easier for you, I know. And what's really sad is that there are hundreds of men like Theo who do what he did. I'm not trying to scare you honey. You know how we always have told you to stay away from strangers? One of the reasons is that we don't want any sick stranger to do what Theo did to you. These people are called perverts. There's something wrong with them, so they can't have sex naturally. They get excited by manipulating children to do things. In your case even though what he did was very wrong and very sick on his part it could have been worse. When a man who is perverted gets sexually excited he can lose control of himself. Thank God nothing worse happened to you. It was bad enough. But it's over now and you're safe and we only have to deal with how you feel inside your head. That's why we thought a psychiatrist might be helpful. Just give you a chance to think about these things and sort it out. It won't necessarily make sense because it's not a rational thing what happened. Am I making any sense to you?"

"Why did Theo do that to me?"

"He couldn't help himself, I guess."

"But I didn't do anything to make him."

"I know that. And it may just have been your very innocence that provoked him. It's hard to say. I really don't know much about these things myself. I just know that when I went to see him he was very sorry about what he did. He was crying and asking for forgiveness."

"Did you?"

"Did I what?"

"Forgive him?"

"Not really."

"Maybe you should have. Maybe it would help him get better."

"You're a bigger person than I was then, to say that."

"Would mommy really have killed him?"

"She wanted to."

"What would have happened if she did?"

"Let's not talk about 'what if.' Mommy was very angry. You're her child, she was trying to protect you and that's what she did. It was too late but she didn't know what else to do. Sometimes you don't know how you're going to react to something unexpected. This is a learning experience for all of us."

They had been sitting in the parking lot outside Swenson's for a while now. Layton thought it was time for a break and they went inside and ordered two gooey sundaes. While they ate he brought up the Williams' play. Leanne said she didn't mind if he replaced Theo, why should she? Layton asked her if she would like to see him in a play. She said she would. So Layton decided to go for it.

7

No Sense Falling Apart Now

The paddle tennis courts at the beach were empty when Barry Levine arrived with Arno and Macky exactly at nine. Levine was wearing shorts and sneakers. Arno and Macky had not come to play and when they saw that Layton wasn't there they told Levine to hang around to let Layton know any deal they might have made was now halved.

"I'm not going to tell him that," Levine protested. "We're just early."

"My watch disagrees," Arno said.

"Hollywood time is like Mexican time," Levine rationalized. "You know that."

"We're not in Hollywood, we're in Venice," Macky rasped.

"You don't think Venice isn't Hollywood? This is where Hollywood comes for its ideas."

"This is where I get sand in my shoes," Arno said.

"So rub your toes together and make a pearl," Levine joked.

"Watch yourself," Arno warned. "You're still parking cars."

"Look, here he comes. See, and you guys were ready to blow it over a few minutes."

"Sometimes that's a lifetime," Macky mumbled.

Layton came to play. "This is a great game," he volunteered, "take off your pants, you'll be more comfortable."

"We'd prefer taking care of business first," Arno said.

"What do you think this is?"

"We thought we were doing movie business," Macky sneered.

"How do you think movie business gets done? This isn't an insurance deal, we're not out playing golf."

"I'll play with you," Levine said. "It's like tennis, right? I brought my tennis racquet."

"It's played with wooden paddles," Layton said. "Go rent three." He looked at Arno and Macky and shook his head. "Gonna be tough playing in shoes like that. Where'd Barry tell you we were meeting?"

"Here."

"Well, we'll play a soft doubles so you won't have to run much."

Macky looked at Arno, who shrugged. They took off their shirts and pants. Levine returned with the paddles and the four of them began to hit a half-dead tennis ball back and forth. Macky's boxer shorts didn't stand out as much as Arno's silk plaid bikini briefs but since no one was around they were spared any embarrassment.

After they scuffed up the court with their shoes for a while Layton called it quits and suggested they walk down the beach to an outdoor cafe for breakfast.

"You play this often?" Macky asked.

"Only when I want to check out my opponents."

"So what do you think?" Levine asked.

"I think you'd all play better in sneakers."

Over croissants and coffee they discussed turning *Mr Sand Man* into a movie. Neither Arno nor Macky had read the book through but that didn't stop them from talking as if they had. They owned the option, it was now their book, and if Layton was willing to sign a letter of intent they'd proceed to the next level: getting a script written. Arno wasn't surprised when Layton said for a guaranteed million he'd sign. A million dollars wasn't that high for a top name star—Pacino was offered nine for *Noriega*, which never got made, and Costner and Cruise more than that for their films; even Kurt Russell was getting seven to play macho cowboys. But Arno knew Layton wasn't a seven-figure actor any longer. He was prepared to offer $50,000 and settle at a hundred. For that Layton said he'd want to see a script first.

They were both playing blind poker. $100,000 was twice what Layton received for his TV movie and far more than he was being offered by anyone else. Arno suspected as much but also knew that Layton Cross was a highly temperamental actor who didn't necessarily act out of his own best interests. Arno had been advised by some friends never to give an actor final script approval so what he offered Layton was $25,000 up front "good faith" money, $25,000 on the first day of shooting, and the other half on the last. He threw in writer approval but that was as far as he was willing to go. When Layton brought up points and perks Arno said their lawyers could dot the i's and cross the t's.

Layton was interested but had a small problem: Samantha's threatened lawsuit. Once word got out that Layton had signed to make a film Sol Gordon could attempt to tie up that money in legal maneuvers. And if it really came down to Samantha going through with it Layton was better off filing a Chapter Seven, which would give her whatever he had, which wasn't much, but which wouldn't touch future earnings. He learned that one from Kim Basinger.

"Yeah, I read what you called her in the paper," Macky rattled. "What was it like being married to her? She seems like a lady with a big dick between her legs."

"Her dick has tentacles that can wind around your body and squeeze you dry," Layton allowed.

"So how serious is she about suing you?" Arno asked.

"She's a serious lady."

"What if we take care of it for you?"

"Now you're talking like a gangster."

"There are legitimate ways of getting her to change her mind," Arno said.

"Yeah, well, she doesn't stable any prize horses to bloody her bed sheets."

"Does she live in fear of being a target?"

"What star doesn't?"

"So what if we exacerbate her fears and turn you into some kind of hero in her eyes, think that might do it?"

"Keep talking," said Layton, "we might come up with a better plot than *Mr Sand Man*."

It was simple, Arno suggested. All that was necessary was to hire a goon willing to take a rap, have him fire some shots into Samantha's compound at a time when Layton was there. Layton catches the guy, the cops are called, Samantha is impressed and the lawsuit is dropped.

"How many guys you know willing to spend time in jail?" Layton asked.

"Let me worry about that," Arno said. "You interested?"

"I like it better than beheading horses."

"Good. I'll make some calls; you give me a date, and let's get on with the business of making a movie."

"You're serious aren't you?"

"I told you he's a man who moves fast," Barry Levine twittered, impressed with his cousin's solution.

"Maybe too fast," Layton said. "Let's take it a step at a time. Anything backfires I could really be up shit's creek."

"I'm as cautious as you are," Arno said. "We'll plan it carefully when the time comes. Don't worry about it."

Don't worry about it? This guy's proposing taking potshots at Samantha at her home where his son lives, where there are armed guards, attack dogs, and police in helicopters at the push of a security button, and he's saying it's simple, not to worry. Hoo, Layton thought, perhaps he had underestimated these guys. Getting a little dangeroso here.

Remembering his promise to meet with the producers of the Williams' play at the Coronet at noon Layton thanked them for an interesting morning and said they should talk more the next day.

"What's to talk about?" Arno asked. "We settle this legal matter for you, you in or out of our project?"

"When your first check's cashed you'll have your answer," Layton said smiling. "I've got to run."

"Barry will call you tomorrow."

Layton winked at Levine as he got up. "You think you're ready for stardom?"

"It should do until something better comes along," Levine answered.

At the Coronet Layton listened to another proposition and thought that for an actor on the decline he sure seemed popular. A $100,000 offer in the morning, a Tennessee Williams play in the afternoon.

It was just as Theo had proposed: a four week run, to begin a week to ten days from now. The money wasn't much—a thousand a week with an extra grand bonus at the end of the month—and the work was grueling, but actors, if they were really actors, didn't always work for money or shortcuts to fame. Layton still had the motivation of an actor and the anticipation of applause was incentive enough to want to get back on stage and act in something from beginning to end without directors and technicians yelling "Cut" and treating you like baggage.

"It's a delicate situation," one of the producers, Kevin McCollough, said.

"Most likely it's distorted," the other, Malk Armen, added.

"Which won't make it easy for you," McCollough continued.

"However," said Armen...

"What are you talking about?" Layton asked.

"Haven't you seen the trades this morning?"

"Gee, we thought you knew," Armen said.

"What have I got to look forward to this time?"

Neither man wanted to be the one to tell Layton that in both *Variety* and *The Reporter* Army Archerd and Hank Grant reported in their columns that Theo Soris would be missing from the play because he was recuperating from wounds inflicted upon him by Layton's angry ex-wife in what was being conjectured as a possible lover's quarrel. Rumors were that Layton was living with Amy and was being asked to replace Theo in the play.

"Maybe you'd better read them yourself," McCollough said, passing him copies.

"Those assholes," Layton said after reading them. "This is almost funny."

"It's none of our business," Armen said.

"It's not about fucking," Layton said.

"What do you suggest we do?" McCollough asked.

"We should release a statement," Armen said.

"Sure, quote me as saying I'm only sorry the play's not *School for Scandal*."

"That's good," a relieved McCollough said.

"As long as they keep my kids out of it I don't give a peacock's fart what they say. It'll just sell more tickets."

"We think so too," Armen said.

Layton gave him a four-letter look and got up to leave.

"You'll do it then?" McCollough asked.

"What time should I be here?"

The arctic chill that was predicted to pass through Southern California never arrived, which was what Layton listened to over the radio as he waited to hear more about Amy and Theo. Layton was convinced that since most people who lived here were displaced Easterners they needed to hear about weather even if it didn't quite exist where they now lived. Haze and smog alerts weren't as thrilling as tornadoes and hailstorms but freeway snipers and celebrity warfare made up for all the boring sunshine.

When he arrived home three reporters were waiting for him in Amy's driveway wanting to know if it was true. When Layton asked them to define truth they looked at each other and smirked, as if they had made bets on how Layton would respond and he came through predictably.

"What's your story?" Layton asked. "Where's your angle?"

"Your wife stabbed, then ran over, your friend," one said.

"Rumor has it they were also friends," said another.

"We just want to set the record straight," said the third.

"Records are round," Layton said, "like the Earth. There are no edges, there is no truth. And besides, records are obsolete."

"What do you suppose happened?"

"Suppose? I suppose if Castro shaved he'd be a convertible."

"What does that mean?"

"About as much as what passes for news."

"Did Amy stab Theo Soris?"

"I don't know; I wasn't there."

"Have you talked with her?"

"Since when do former husbands talk to ex-wives? Have there been any charges?"

"Not from Soris."

"So what's your story, gentlemen?"

"Are you denying it happened?"

"What happened?"

"The innuendoes make for embarrassing reading," one of the reporters said. "It's all probably a lot simpler than it sounds at the moment. If you cooperate we'll be fair with you."

"Have I issued any no-comments? You're asking the questions, I just don't have the answers."

"Was Amy having an affair with Theo Soris?"

"Wouldn't I be the last to know?"

"Why do you suppose she attacked him?"

"I don't suppose."

"Why did she then?"

"Did she?"

"For a twice-divorced guy your ex's seem to keep you in the news. You may think nothing of such violence but there are three newspaper editors who believe there's a story of public interest coming out of your house. How about giving us a little time?"

"Time?" Layton asked. "How about giving me a little *Newsweek*? How about a little *U.S. News & World Report*?"

"Mr Cross, we're under the gun. We've got to file a story whether or not you give us a straight answer."

"So shoot, fellas. We categorically deny everything you insinuate. So does Burt Reynolds, Mickey Rourke, and the ghost of River Phoenix. How's that?"

It was obvious that Layton Cross wasn't about to bare his soul so they scratched some notes and left without bothering to thank him for his series of non-sequiturs.

Inside, Amy had washed down a Valium with a tall glass of tequila and was laid out flat on her bed with a cold towel over her face. Leanne was sitting next to her changing the towel every few minutes.

"What do those men want?" she asked Layton.

"They want to know why your mother attacked Theo."

Leanne looked scared and Layton went to hug her. "Don't worry," he said, "they don't know what happened and we won't tell them. It'll soon pass."

"I told Jeannine," Leanne confessed. Layton tried to shrug it off but figured her friend's parents might be the source of the leak. Either they or Samantha who might have told Sol Gordon who would have told his wife who might have told her hairdresser. There were no secrets in Hollywood, just huge distortions. Right now the story was a love triangle. That was juicy enough.

"Is it going to be in the newspapers?" Leanne asked.

"Who knows? Something will but it won't be what really happened. They'll make up a story to fit in with their facts and the papers will be used to line rabbit cages the next day and that will be that. How long has she been like that?"

"Since we came home."

"Was she conscious?"

"No."

"It hasn't been easy for her."

"It's my fault, isn't it?"

"How could it be your fault? You're the victim, you didn't do anything."

"But I did."

"Against your will. What happened happened but don't start taking the blame when there isn't any blame to take. Your mother overreacted and now we've got to deal with the press and that's the kind of life we live. It's all a lot of bullshit and you are in a unique position to see that."

"It's going to be all over school tomorrow," Leanne said.

"So you won't go to school for a few days and it'll blow over."

"Daddy?"

"What?"
"Why did this have to happen?"
"I don't know."
"What's going to happen next?"
"I don't know that either."

Amy stirred. Andy came running into the bedroom wanting to know what all the commotion was outside. Leanne was crying. Layton looked at his crumbling family and wished them strength. Life would go on, with or without them. No sense falling apart now.

After hearing about Amy over KFWB Mark called his father to find out if she was in a lot of trouble.

"It's all rumor and conjecture at this point, nobody's saying anything other than 'alleged'," Layton said.
"But is she?"
"Only with herself."
"Mom said it's about Leanne."
"She tell you the details?"
"No."
"You sure you want to know?"
"Is she all right?"
"I don't know. She was molested."
"By Theo?"
"That's what this is about."
"Is there anything I can do?"
"I don't know." Layton didn't know a lot, he realized. If he had a dollar for every 'I don't know' he said in the last two days he probably wouldn't have to be in

negotiation with drug dealers about making a children's movie.

"How about if I take Andy off your hands for a few days? He can stay with me."

"You'd better ask your mother about that."

"She's cool. She said she'd like to see Leanne."

"Think that's a good idea?"

"Leanne likes Mom."

"That's because she doesn't know her."

"I think Mom regrets never having a girl."

"Sam has no regrets."

"You're wrong there Dad."

"Maybe one day you'll tell me about them."

"How did it happen?"

"What?"

"Theo."

"I left her there while I finished dubbing my movie at CBS. I don't know how it happened, I only know it did. He didn't rape her but he messed up her mind pretty badly. She has nightmares. Amy tried to get your mother to have Theo killed; when she refused, Amy tried to do it herself. The papers have it all mixed up but it's better that way."

"Dad, Leanne is so young."

"Not any longer. Theo took that away from her as well."

"Will he go to jail?"

"We want to keep the police out of this."

"So what's going to happen?"

"We're all going to try and forget."

"Come on Dad."

"That's a good idea about Andy. Ask your mom. I can bring him later."

As he drove Andy to his half-brother's house the repetitiveness of the questions played like a tape loop in his head. Why did it happen? How? What are you going to do about it? Only Andy had an answer: Leanne had become the Creep-From-the-Deep. Today it made the trades and the radio. Tomorrow the newspapers and television. Years ago actors planted stories about themselves to keep in the public eye. *Confidential* magazine was full of them. Now Layton couldn't pay to keep his profile low.

"How'm I gonna get to school tomorrow?" Andy asked, unbuckling and rebuckling his seat belt.

"Samantha's got drivers."

"Yeah but what if she's using them?"

"Since when did you become a worrier?"

"I'm not worried, you're the one who's worried."

"Oh yeah? What am I worried about?"

"About me finding out too much."

"About what?"

"About Leanne and mommy."

"What makes you think that?"

"I've never stayed overnight with Mark before."

"Maybe he'd just like to get to know you better."

"I'm seven Dad, remember? Mark's fifteen."

"So?"

"All I know is something's going on."

"Is that all you know? Surely you must know more than that. You know who Superman is. You know that movies aren't real. You know Haagen-Dazs is better than Baskin-Robbins."

"I know that you aren't going to tell me why I'm going to Mark's tonight."

"Don't you want to go?"

"Sure I do."

"So?"

"So you think you can handle it?"

"Handle what?"

"Leanne and mommy?"

"Andy, one of these years we'll sit down and have a long talk about this. But not now."

"When you think I can handle it?"

"No, when I think I can."

Mark was waiting for them when they arrived. Andy was excited to play the latest video games and look at Mark's collection of *Playboy's* and *Hustler's*.

Samantha was in the screening room discussing a possible film project with a director she had wanted to work with, whose reputation for insisting on control over his productions equaled her own.

"You want to come in Dad?"

"Thanks," Layton said. "But once bitten, twice crazy."

"You can come up to my room, it'll be okay."

Layton looked at his two sons and shrugged. What the hell. If Mark wasn't afraid why should he be?

Andy had never been in Mark's room before and couldn't believe the size of it. "You could get our whole house in here," he said. "We could play football if we wanted to."

Layton thought that was a good idea and soon they were passing, running, and tackling each other, bumping into chairs, falling on the floor. Mark and Andy ganged up on their father and it turned into a wrestling free-for-all. The boys laughed and shouted as Layton grunted macho pro wrestler threats, hurling Andy onto the bed, twirling Mark on his shoulders. He stopped mid-twirl when Samantha's voice cracked through the room over the intercom.

"What's going on up there Mark?"

Layton put Mark down and signaled that he shouldn't let on that he was there. Mark pushed the intercom and told her that Andy had come and they were just fooling around.

"It sounds like you're more than just two," Samantha complained. "Is Layton in the house?"

"No, he left."

"You know I don't want him in this house."

"We'll keep it down."

"I'd appreciate it."

"I'd appreciate a beer," Layton whispered.

"I'll get you one," Mark said, turning off the intercom. "I'm sorry about that."

"Why do you keep that thing on so she can listen to you?"

"She likes to know what I'm doing."

"She can't do that, you have no privacy."

"It's her house."

"And what are you, her prisoner?"

"I'll have a 7-Up," Andy said.

"It's in the refrigerator under my desk," Mark said as he went down to the kitchen to get Layton a beer.

"Boy, Dad," Andy said, "being a superstar ain't bad if you can live in a house like this."

"Yeah, but it can also be like a jail. Can you dig that?"

"Not really. Wow, look at all the pop he's got!"

Layton walked around the room looking at the posters of the Red Hot Chili Peppers and of Samantha on one wall, at the electronic gadgets and mechanical gizmos on Mark's shelves. It was a room filled with the most expensive items from Brookstone and Sharper Image catalogs. There was a 4-in-1 game table combining a mini-pool table with hockey, Ping-Pong, chess and backgammon. He had a golf nylon practice net and a plastic grass mat so he could drive balls right in his room. He had signed baseballs from Mickey Mantle, Joe Dimaggio, and Barry Bonds; signed basketballs from Shaquille O'Neal and Charles Barkley; signed footballs from Joe Montana and John Elway; and a signed hockey stick from Wayne Gretzky. A large, sophisticated robot stood in a corner next to a vibrating reclining shiatsu leather massage lounger. Layton sat down in the chair and turned it on.

"When did your mom get you this?" Layton asked when Mark returned with the beer.

"She didn't, it was from Uncle Charlie," Mark said.

"Charlie Greenbloom may be the head of a studio but he's not your uncle," Layton said.

"I've always called him that. He got me that laptop computer, and the robot."

"Why's Charlie so good to you?"

"I dunno, he likes me I guess."

"You mean he likes having your mother working for him." Layton wondered how much Greenbloom spent on gifts for his stars' kids each year, and was it out of his pocket or the studio's? The last time Greenbloom sent Layton a gift was just after he and Samantha finalized their divorce. It was a black leather bound address book with a tasteless note attached.

"You sure it's okay for me to stay here?" Andy wondered one last time.

"Think there's enough room for you?" Layton asked. He noticed a framed picture of a girl on Mark's desk. "Pretty," he commented. "Someone special?"

"Kind of," Mark said, his face flushing slightly. "Her name's Reya."

They drank their drinks and Layton instructed Andy to listen to Mark and Mark not to let Andy manipulate him. "You're a good kid," he said, hugging Mark. "Both of you," he added, opening his arm for Andy.

"You take care of yourself," Mark said.

"And mom and Leanne too," Andy added.

"I'm a pretty lucky man to have two guys like you."

"I better sneak you out," Mark said.

"You think she'd sic the dogs on me?"

"I doubt it."

"So?"

"She's been taking target practice. She's a pretty good shot now."

"You go first," Layton said. "Signal when the coast is clear."

■ ■ ■

Leanne dropped the phone and began to shake once she recognized Theo's voice. He was calling to speak to her dad and was saying through the receiver on the floor, "Is that you Leanne? Leanne? Hello?"

Her mom was still knocked out and Leanne felt very alone and very scared. Inside her head she saw Theo's hand pulling down his zipper and taking out his penis. "Come and kiss it," he was saying, the words echoing inside her, words she had suppressed until now, when his voice brought it all back, making her feel sick and shivery. She felt his invisible hand applying pressure to the back of her head, pushing her down, telling her to open her mouth and kiss it with her tongue. Then she thought of her mother passed out and her father saying how sorry Theo was and how much bigger she was to be willing to forgive. Only it wasn't true, she didn't want to forgive, she couldn't even pick up the phone. Her mother was right in wanting to kill him. She should have. She should have!

"Leanne," Theo's voice said, filling the room, his presence there with her, just him and her. "Please, if you're listening honey, please say something. I just wanted to talk to your dad. I'm...sorry...Leanne. Can you hear me? How...sorry...I...."

"Stop it!" Leanne shouted. "Stop it, stop it, STOP IT!" She kicked at the receiver, screamed, but couldn't touch it, couldn't pick it up to hang up on him. "Leave me alone!" she shouted and ran from the room back to her mother.

She stood in front of Amy's bed, moaning and rocking back and forth. Amy never opened her eyes. Theo had returned. He was inside her and there was no one to help her.

She looked at her mother's puffy face, lips apart, snoring, makeup uneven and splotchy on her cheeks, and whispered, over and over, "I hate you. I hate you. I hate you."

Layton found her standing there, her anger spent, when he returned. She was staring blankly at Amy and his initial thought was that Amy was dead. He looked at Leanne and saw her face so blanched it frightened him. She moved her eyes towards him and said with a great deal of disappointment, "Where were you? He called. Where...were...you?"

"I took Andy to Mark's. Who called? What happened? Don't look at me like that. Turn your whole face to me."

When Leanne said "Theo," Layton's body tightened. How dare he! How fucking crazy could this get?

"Did you speak to him? What did he say?"

"I couldn't. But he was here, I felt it."

"If he was on the phone then he wasn't here. Listen to me now. You were shocked. You got scared. Theo is in the hospital. He wasn't here. He can't walk. Do you understand?"

"He was. He was. I felt him. He was pushing my head. He wanted me to do it again. And you weren't here. No one was. I was all alone and he was here and he was talking to me and I kicked him and ran away but there was nobody. Mommy didn't wake up. She just...didn't...."

He knew she needed to be calmed and tried to hold her but her body was rigid and unresponsive. He saw the vial of Valiums on the night table, took one, bit it in half and told her to take it. She swallowed it with some water and he swallowed the other half. Then he sat on the edge of the bed and just looked into his baby's eyes. She was in shock. He picked her up and carried her to her room.

"I'll stay right here with you," he said. "I want you to rest. Just close your eyes now and don't think about anything. I'm not going anywhere. Everything will be okay."

But everything wasn't going to be okay. Leanne wasn't coming out of it. Amy was in a stupor and also in need of help. He had come back into their lives and made a terrible mess of things. He thought his children had needed him. Now he was beginning to feel he was the last thing they needed.

He slept in Leanne's room keeping his promise not to leave her alone. When Amy awoke the next morning she felt as if she had been diced through a Cuisinart. Her throat was dry, her tongue felt swollen and small men with jackhammers were drilling behind her eyeballs. She had to look around the room to get her bearings. Somehow she managed to lift herself and make it to the bathroom where she turned on the shower and then sat on the tiled floor letting the cold water shoot down on her as she peed through her clothes into the drain.

Layton heard the shower running and got up to see how she was doing. Amy was sitting in water up to her hip and flowing onto the bathroom floor, her body acting as a stopper over the drain. He turned off the water, lifted this soaked and sorrowful woman out of the stall and undressed her. Then he wrapped a large towel around her, carried her back to bed, and went into the kitchen to put up some fresh coffee.

The phone rang.

It was Al Low. "Didja see the papers?"

He hung up. It rang again. It was one of the reporters who had been there the day before. He hung up.

It rang a third time. Perce Dent wanted to know if there was anything he could do. He didn't know, he hadn't seen the papers. He hung up and went outside to bring whatever dreaded news there was this time back into his home. The phone rang again. He let it ring.

The stories were elaborations of those in the trades the day before, only this time he was quoted, sounding irrational and confused. The banter with the reporters came out all dizzy in cold print. There were pictures of him and

Amy, him with Samantha (the same ones, always the same ones), family shots, studio stills, photos of Theo Soris. The Serbs hadn't destroyed any towns in Bosnia, no radical PLO members had blown up an Israeli bus, no Arkansas security cops were proving Clinton had mistresses after his election but before the Inauguration, no photos of Michael Jackson's mottled penis had surfaced. It was just his luck to be caught on a slow news day. What should have been no more than a mention had turned into a feature. Still, Layton couldn't help but be impressed with how much fabrication could be built around a single 'alleged' fact. Amy stabbed Theo. That they got right. All the rest was entertainment.

The phone rang again. And again. A tireless reminder of the world outside. A world of curious, sadistic people who hungered for news about the ill-fated Crosses. Like a punched-out pugilist who refused to go down, refueling between rounds, the phone paused only between callers who refused to take the hint that Layton wasn't answering because he didn't want to talk.

When Amy dragged herself into the kitchen asking for aspirin and complaining about the goddamn phone Layton, for a change, agreed with her. During one interval between calls he dialed the operator and requested an immediate number change. The operator told him he'd have to call the business office.

"I want it now!" Layton demanded. "I don't care what the cost."

She repeated that he was calling the wrong number but she would connect him to the business office. A recorded voice came on giving him four choices to choose from. Layton chose number two for a change in service. Another recorded message came on asking which of four options he wanted, Call Waiting, Call Forwarding...he couldn't listen to recordings any longer. He just wanted a human voice to make a simple change. But everything was computerized now; you had to know what numbers to choose from the electronic menu. He slammed down the phone and disconnected it from the jack. Then he went into the bedroom and living room and did the same. He'd be damned if he was going to let some fucking machine get the best of him.

"I want to take the kids and get away from here," Amy said, dipping a Milano Pepperidge Farm cookie until it crumbled into her coffee.

"You can't run from reality," Layton said.

"Who says you can't?"

"Because it stays with you."

"Not if you stay here."

"I didn't stab anyone."

"But you're the movie star."

"I don't want to be a point in some phony triangle."

"Isn't it too late for that?"

"Meaning?"

"You're involved Layt. You're the one who can't hide. I can go to Michigan with the kids and stay with my mother."

"You're crazy enough already, you don't need that."

"You got a better idea?"

"I want you to see Dr Lugow."

"When I come back."

"No, you need help now. If he says you should go I won't stop you."

"Call him then."

Dr Lugow was a busy Beverly Hills shrink who practiced in Malibu where most of his clientele had homes. What he knew about the private lives of famous people the *National Enquirer* would pay in signed blank checks to publish. When Layton called, the good doctor himself answered.

"Why so long?" he asked.

"Since when do you read newspapers?" Layton said.

"With all the commotion you've been stirring up I figured sooner or sooner you'd call."

"I want you to see Amy," Layton said.

"How is Amy?"

"That's what I want you to tell me."

"Amy's not so good I suspect."

"And then I want to know if my daughter is too young for you."

"I'm already married."

"To talk to doctor. She's had a traumatic experience."

"She is how old?"

"Ten."

"When do you want miracles?"

"Amy today if you can squeeze her in. After you listen to her you tell us when you want to see Leanne."

"And you? Don't you want the family special?"

"This family is beginning to crumble."

"So? Amy then, at four o'clock."

"You still skip rope?"

"Jogging is for youngsters. Skipping rope is for when you get smart."

"I'll unknot the noose then and start jumping."

"Sometimes the noose is the better way to go."

"I knew I could count on you for uplifting advice."

"You want advice, read Ann Landers. You want to talk, call Dr Lugow. Tell Amy I'll see her at four. As for you, make good pictures."

Layton unplugged the phone again and told Amy she had the rest of the morning to get rid of her hangover and half of the afternoon to get herself together for the drive to Malibu. Then he went into Leanne's room, saw his daughter curled up in the corner of her bed and kissed her gently on the head. The longer she slept the better. He went to Amy's editing room and fell onto the couch. If he could find some free time he would get a massage. His body would like that.

Barry Levine got a busy signal whenever he called Layton and finally asked the operator to have the number checked. Informed that it must be temporarily out of order he wondered if he should drive up to see Layton. Arno wanted them to talk today, to push *Mr Sand Man* forward, but Levine didn't want to push too far too fast. If Layton wanted some space he'd give him the day. But like his cousin Arno, he had a thing about time. He was too young and too new to the movie business to understand that nothing gets done today that can be put off indefinitely.

Alex Briar was also trying to reach Layton. With Layton getting so much media attention CBS had decided to push his movie forward and release it in four weeks. *TV Guide* agreed to do a cover story on Layton and gave the assignment to Briar. With only a week to write the story Briar called Al Low to help him reach Layton. Low was excited by the cover. Layton hadn't been on the cover of anything for years and *TV Guide* was perfect because it wouldn't focus on his personal life—or, at the very least, it would balance that with the movie. But by noon, when Low realized that Layton had disconnected his phone, he told Briar to just drive into the canyon and see if he could find him. At Briar's suggestion Low agreed to send a messenger first to let Layton know that Briar was coming.

Briar arrived at two-thirty. Layton spoke with him in the driveway. Yes, now that it was an assignment he'd talk to him, but only about the movie. No, he couldn't talk now because he had to take Amy somewhere. No, Briar could not tag along. They'd meet later in the evening and go for a drive.

It was a clear, pleasant afternoon as Layton, Amy, and Leanne drove out to Malibu. As Dr Lugow's office was located along Pacific Coast Highway, Layton and Leanne would walk on the beach for the hour Amy would be with him. Both Amy and Leanne were subdued and Layton, not wanting to stir things up, mentioned that *TV Guide* wanted to put his mug on its cover.

"Pure exploitation," Amy said.

"It's concerning the movie," Layton protested.

"Bullshit."

"You think it's bullwhacky Leanne?"

"What?"

"That *TV Guide* wants to write about me and the movie I made for television."

"Is it a good movie?"

"How do I know, for Pete's sake."

"They're just using you," Amy said.

"That's the nature of the media."

"So how can you allow yourself to be manipulated like that?"

"You think it's going to hurt my soaring career to be on the cover of the largest mass-circulated magazine in the country? Why don't you ask Dr Lugow what he thinks?"

"Why don't you ask him yourself? You need to see him just as much as I do."

"Well at least we agree that you do."

"We don't agree on anything."

"It's a pretty nice day isn't it?

"So?"

"So there, we agree again."

"Just remember that we also agreed to split again."

"Why?" Leanne asked.

"Very bright," Layton said to Amy.

"I've given you something to talk about while I'm gone," Amy said.

"Your mother feels it might be best for you and her and Andy if you went to stay with your grandmother for a while," Layton said, feeling the cool sand along the ocean's edge between his toes.

"What about you?" Leanne asked.

"I've got the play to do, remember?"

"Do you want us to go?"

"No I don't."

"Do you think it's better that we do?"

"What do you think?"

"Mommy's not very stable."

"That's right, she's not."

"And grandma's a lot like her."

"You've noticed."

"That means I'll have to take care of everybody."

"You might but that's your choice. You're only responsible for yourself. And your brother."

"Yesterday I hated mommy."

"I can understand that."

"I used to hate you when you were gone."

"What about now?"

"Now I love you."

"I love you too. Very very much."

"Are you and mommy going to stay together again?"

"I don't think so."

"You're not sure?"

"I'm not sure the sun will rise tomorrow. It's hard to predict the future. Right now we're not even talking about it. We're only trying to get through this time and living in Los Angeles is not the best place to be when you want to avoid reporters and TV cameras and nosy people who try to turn private lives public."

"What about school?"

"It's not settled you're going yet–that's why Amy's talking to Dr Lugow. But if you do there are schools in Michigan."

"Why is life so complicated?" Leanne asked.

"Do you remember the first time you saw your own blood? You were about three-and-a-half and your foot started bleeding. You panicked and started crying and I took you into the bathroom and wiped the blood away and there was a little hole on the top of your foot where the blood kept coming out and you said, 'I can't be bleeding because my teacher said blood is blue.' You tried to be very brave as I put on a Band-Aid and you looked up at me and said, 'I'm going to die, aren't I?' Well, you're still here, life hasn't gotten any easier, and it's only just beginning...for all of us."

"I don't ever want to have sex," Leanne said abruptly.

"That's what nuns say when they decide to take their vows."

"What's so great about it?"

"At your age? Nothing."

"Do you like it?"

"It beats being whipped with a stick."

"I'm never going to get married."

"You're full of never's today aren't you? What do you want to do with the rest of your life?"

"I don't want to grow up. I think maybe I'll probably kill myself."

"I don't think I'd like that," Layton said, disturbed by the turn of the conversation but not wanting her to sense his concern.

"You don't always do what I'd like."

"What would you like me to do?"

"Not leave us."

"I'm not going to leave you."

"Promise?"

"Your visiting your grandmother is not my leaving you is it?"

"Not if we come back."

"Then I promise. If you promise not to kill yourself."

"Okay, I won't."

"You mean it?"

"Did you believe me?"

"Should I have?"

"Don't worry Daddy, I won't kill myself."

That night after checking with Mark and Andy and putting Leanne to sleep Amy told Layton she wanted him to leave.

"Is that what you and Lugow talked about?"

"It came up."

"I thought you were going to ask him about a short visit to your mother's."

"That too."

"Must have been some session."

"It's just not working between us," Amy said. "I was better off without you. We all were."

"You've polled the kids?"

"Look at us Layton. Andy isn't even here right now. And Leanne's certainly not the same girl she was when you weren't here."

"And you're an alcoholic," Layton added.

"You've played a part in that as well."

"Don't lay your weaknesses off on me."

"I don't want to get into any more arguments."

"What makes you think you're a responsible mother?"

"I think I've proved that while you were gone for three years."

"No court in the country would give you custody if I challenged you."

"That's fine with me. You want the kids, they're yours. I just want out."

Layton didn't expect that. How could he possibly raise the children himself? "I can't leave now."

"Why not?"

"I promised Leanne."

"We're not good for each other Layton."

"Let's get Leanne through this time in one piece, okay? Then we'll discuss each other."

"Dr Lugow thinks I may be having a nervous breakdown."

"May be? I think you're smack in the middle of one."

"I can't take it any longer. I just can't."

"He didn't think it a good idea to go to Michigan did he?"

"He doesn't know what I'm going through."

"What did he think?"

"That I should see him three times a week."

"That's a lot."

"He thinks I'm a sick woman."

"Is he so far off?"

"I wish I could love you."

"I wish you could love yourself."

"I'm tired."

There was a knock at the door. Alex Briar had arrived to go for their drive. Layton had forgotten about it.

"You're moving up in the world," Layton said as they drove up to Mulholland towards the scenic view overlooking the Hollywood Bowl.

"The editor knew I knew you," Briar said.

"Do you?"

"Does anyone?"

"I'm experiencing deja vu. Didn't we have this conversation already?"

"Must be all the writers you've talked guardedly with over the years. It must all become rote."

They could hear a Chopin nocturne drift through the night air from the Bowl. With the moon full they could silently reflect upon the couples making out in the cars on each side of them.

"This is some place for an interview," Layton said.

Briar was impressed with Layton's relaxed appearance. For a man whose personal life was obviously in turmoil he acted as if he hadn't a care in the world.

"Want to talk about the movie?" he asked.

"Sure. What do you want to know?"

"Not much." Briar looked at Layton and the two men held eye contact, then smiled.

"I didn't think you did."

Briar shrugged uncomfortably. "Theo Soris was a good friend of yours, wasn't he?"

"You're getting your publications mixed up," Layton said. "Leave *The Star* behind you, you'll be a better person for it."

"It just seems to me that the papers have it wrong—they're painting a picture of you that's untrue."

"And this is my chance to correct it?"

"If you like."

"Let's just say I prefer to let it die and go on living."

"We can go off-the-record."

"For what purpose? I'm not looking for a confidant at the moment."

"Want to know what I think?"

"Not particularly."

"Theo Soris has a drug problem. It's fairly common knowledge...."

Layton turned his head and got straight with Briar. "Listen to me. Whatever you're about to conjecture is going to be off-base so don't say anything more about it. The subject is closed, understand? I have no comment and I won't be coy about it, whatever happened is history and it's not going to help anybody, not Theo, not my family, and not me, by going into it. You've tried and I'm saying we pass."

"Can I quote your discomfort?" Briar asked.

"You want discomfort, keep pushing me."

Briar backed down. He was going to come back with something to the effect that *TV Guide* was family-oriented and he just wanted to straighten out the facts about Layton's family but his instincts told him if he said that Layton would walk, leaving him with too many holes to fill. So having made the journalistic mistake of not warming up his subject he retreated to the less controversial grounds of the movie he was there to write about.

When Layton returned there was a message from Dr Lugow asking him to call back. Layton did and Lugow told him that he was under a professional and legal obligation to report what Amy told him regarding what Theo did to Leanne to the police. "If you do that," Layton said, "you're jeopardizing your patient. I don't care about Theo, but what happens to Amy when it becomes more than conjecture that she was the one who hit-and-ran? And to Leanne if this becomes public?"

"I know, I know," Dr Lugow said. "I've got the law on one side and my personal ethics on the other."

"So what choice is that?"

"None, I guess. But Leanne shouldn't mention any names to me. If I don't hear it I can't report it."

"Thanks doctor."

"I know your friend. I even went to his play. This surprised me."

"Me too."

"He also needs help."

"He's not my problem."

■ ■ ■

While Mark did his homework Andy decided to venture out past Mark's room and stroll through the enormous house. It was after nine and he should have been sleeping but he was restless. Mark had been great, letting him play with all his games and look at his magazines, and Samantha let them screen some of his favorite sci-fi and space movies in her private screening room. She was a pretty good person, Andy thought. Moody as hell but so were his father and mother; so was every adult, in fact. But she wasn't the witch that people who didn't know her said she was. She was interested in what he had to say, she liked the same flavors of ice cream he did, and she even had some kind words about his father, whom he always thought she hated. When he told her this she laughed and assured him that was not so, they just had differences of opinions on most subjects because they saw things from very different points of view. Andy could accept that, whatever it meant, since he and his dad didn't agree about certain movies and baseball teams and sugarless bubblegum, which Andy felt was a waste since it lost its taste after ten chews.

Samantha was a very busy woman, always meeting with someone or talking on the phone or reading or exercising in her bedroom. Andy wasn't surprised, when he walked quietly past her room, to hear her grunting. When he noticed she had left her door slightly ajar he stopped to peek inside.

She was lifting hand weights, working up a sweat as she did various exercises with them. When she had finished she went to a corner of the room and adjusted a video camera. She then peeled off her leotard and stood dripping sweat before the mirror looking at her body. Andy was embarrassed but riveted. Samantha then buckled metal gravity boots to her ankles and got onto a gravity-guiding contraption, stretching out her arms to slowly lean backwards, putting her arms back to her sides to go forward. She did this a number of times and then she went upside down, swinging and gyrating freely. Andy watched her boobs, which looked strange upside down, like papayas. When Mark tapped him on the top of his head he jumped nervously.

"What are you doing here?" he at least had the good sense to whisper.

"Look," Andy whispered back.

Mark moved his head slowly to see his naked mother hanging upside down holding a vibrator in her hand and getting ready to insert it into her vagina. Andy, gazing below Mark, asked him what she was doing.

"None of your business," Mark said, but neither boy could take his eyes away.

Samantha now had the vibrator deep inside her as she swung her free arm over her head and back, rocking gently up and down, her eyes closed, as her body shuddered in delightful orgasm.

"Is she hurting herself?" Andy asked.

"Shut up," Mark whispered.

After ten minutes Samantha withdrew the vibrator, got off the gravity contraption, unbuckled the boots and stopped the video recorder. Mark and Andy hastily retreated to Mark's room.

"I want you to swear on your life that you'll never tell anyone what you saw," Mark asserted.

"I will," Andy said, "if you tell me what she was doing."

"Exercising."

"Why'd she put that thing inside her?"

"To keep her from having a baby."

"How does it work?" Andy asked.

"I'm not sure."

"You're not telling me the truth, are you?"

"She did it to make her feel good, okay? My mom's not married so she's got to do those things."

When Samantha played back the tape she saw the two pair of eyes staring through the crack in the door that the camera had picked up. Oh Christ. Angry and humiliated she paced the room like a panther thinking of what her son must think of her...and of what little Andy might tell his parents...friends...the whole fucking world!

The next morning Samantha joined them for breakfast. "Well what are we having today? Pancakes, French toast, Eggs Benedict?"

"We asked for white fish, smoked salmon, and pizza bagels," Mark responded, not looking at her.

"I usually eat cold cereal at home," Andy said. "You guys really know how to eat."

Samantha smiled civilly. "Mark, what would you think if I decided to make an erotic movie?"

"I don't know," Mark blushed. "Is it a good script?"

"I'm not sure. There are all kinds of strange scenes in it...masturbation, personal abuse, bondage. But it's not pornographic...just different. Unusual."

"Do you want to do it?"

"I've been thinking about it. Probably not very smart for my image, whatever that is. I've tried rehearsing certain scenes to see how they'd play but I just don't know. My instincts tell me no."

"I agree," Mark said quickly.

"What's bondage?" Andy asked.

"Shut up," Mark blurted.

"It's like being tied up," Samantha said, "...turned upside down...that kind of thing."

"Oh," said Andy, his face turning beet red.

"Well," Samantha said, having successfully solved last night's potentially embarrassing affair, "I think I'll have some cold cereal and say no to that script."

"Good idea," Mark said. "You don't need it."

"Yeah," Andy agreed. "It's good you rehearsed it to find that out."

• • •

Alex Briar was waiting for Layton when he arrived at the Coronet for his first rehearsal. Layton had agreed to let Briar observe as long as there were no questions or interruptions. They'd talk one last time over lunch and that would be it, Briar would go write his article and Layton would concentrate on replacing Theo's understudy.

He had read the play only once and during the morning's reading he enunciated every syllable clearly and missed all the nuances. The other actors rolled their eyes upwards, McCollough and Armen clapped encouragement, and it was like starting from scratch, only this time it was only Layton who had to find his character.

"Good, fine, it only goes up from here," McCollough said when they broke for lunch.

"I've got a long way to go," Layton conceded. "My heart's not there yet."

"You'll get there," Armen said. "It's always like this with Williams."

"You've been away from the theater too long," McCollough said. "It's not the movies. Here it's bup bup bup."

"Maybe that's why he's been away," Armen joked.

"Nah, he loves it. Don't you Layton? You love this right?"

Layton smiled. "You two are some routine. Too bad vaudeville's dead."

"Those were some days," Armen said.

Had McCollough broken into a tap dance Layton would have hugged them right there but Tennessee Williams wasn't a joking matter and he was made aware of that this morning. He would have to sweat in order not to appear foolish. It would require a concentration that meant he'd have to stop thinking about Amy, Leanne, Theo, Samantha, his sons, his TV movie, his next feature, and the reporters who wanted to catch him off guard.

"That was a very rough rehearsal," Alex Briar sympathized over burgers at Ed Debevic's.

"You ever do any acting?" Layton asked.

"In high school I played a number in Elmer Rice's *The Adding Machine*."

"What was the number?"

"Four. Mr Four."

"Not much of a future in numbers unless you're running them."

"The guy who played Zero forgot his lines halfway through. Since he was in every scene it proved a fiasco. He's now a character actor, been in over a hundred pictures. Nobody remembers his name; he never forgets his lines. Lives in Bel Air.

"And you're talking to me."

That evening as Layton paced in the kitchen struggling to memorize his lines Leanne finished washing the dishes and asked him if she was going to talk to Dr Lugow.

"Is that what you want?" Layton asked.

"Mommy talked to him."

"That's right. And he said he'd like to talk with you, or listen to you if you felt like talking to him. It's no problem, we can arrange it tomorrow if you like."

"Do you think I should?"

"Are you still thinking about it a lot?"

"Yes," she said lowering her eyes.

Layton walked over to his daughter and hugged her. "First thing tomorrow morning I'll call," he whispered. "We'll go as soon as you get back from school."

"I can go with mommy."

"That's right, you can. I think she has an appointment with him. That's perfect."

"Does he know everything?"

"You'll have to ask your mother. I would think so, that's his job, to listen to people's problems. But there's one thing I'd like you to try not to do: don't mention Theo's name. I'm not trying to protect him, I'm trying to protect you and your mother. I don't want Amy to have to explain what she did to anyone. When you want to talk about him just say 'that man.'"

"I'm a little nervous."

"That's normal, everybody's nervous the first time they go to a psychiatrist. But you'll get over that. Everybody does."

"Does everybody have problems."

"How do you think psychiatrists live so well? Of course everybody has problems."

"What's your biggest problem?

"Seeing that you feel better. And that mommy comes around. And this," he held up the play. "This sonuvabitch play is a big problem at the moment. I've got to learn it by heart and then act as if I understand it."

"You can do it Daddy."

"I know I can baby. You can do it too."

* * *

With Amy waiting in the reception room, Leanne entered Dr Lugow's office alone. He motioned for her to come in, his hand moving in a circle. "Sit," he told her and she sat.

"Would you like some juice?"

Leanne shook her head.

"Some soda? Water? A beer?"

When she didn't smile he leaned forward, both arms on his desk, and asked conspiratorially, "What then would you like...if you could have anything at all?"

"To not have to be here," Leanne answered.

"That is no problem," Dr Lugow said. "What is more difficult is not feeling the need to be here. Am I not right?"

"I guess."

"Whose idea was it to come and see me?"

"Mine."

"Good. So it will be your idea to decide not to come too, okie-dokie?"

"You don't have to talk to me like I'm a child."

"You mean 'okie-dokie'? I always use okie-dokie. I'm an old man, old men should not say 'okay.' But okie-dokie, for you, no 'okie-dokie,' okay?"

"I'm sorry I didn't mean...."

"No apologies to me. In this office it is the doctor who must apologize to his patient. You know why? Because it is the patient who is paying the doctor. It's the least he can do."

Leanne looked at him and wondered if all psychiatrists seemed crazy. She had never talked to anyone like this man and she was having immediate doubts if he would really be able to put her mind at ease.

"Now," he said, "if at any time you change your mind and want something to drink or a stick of chewing gum or a hard candy, you tell me. So? Tell me, do you believe in God?"

"I'm not sure. My dad says God's a concept which exists inside you if you want that."

"Do you think God's here now?"

"Why? If there is a God He must have more important things to do than listen to my problems."

"Aha! Your problems are the reason for God's existence, did you know that?"

"Are you a priest?" Leanne asked.

"My child, do I look like a priest?"

"I don't know."

"Believe me, priests all have very narrow nostrils. Me, I've got a nose a horse would be proud of."

"Would it help if I believed in God?"

"Not necessarily. Then you'd only be mad at God for letting what happened to you happen to you."

"My mom and dad say it's not my fault what happened."

"And you don't believe them?"

"I think it's partially my fault."

"Did you receive any pleasure when it happened?"

"No."

"So how could it be your fault?"

"I was scared."

"Naturally. Sex like that is very frightening."

"My dad said it wasn't sex."

"Your father is right."

"Am I going to get better?"

"You're not sick. Your mind is just upset."

"Why do people call you a shrink?"

"Better than calling me a midget don't you think?"

"Do we have to talk about what happened?"

"Up to you. You don't want?"

Leanne shook her head. No, she didn't want. Not with Dr Lugow. At least not at the moment.

"O-kay then," Dr Lugow said. "We've got a half hour, want to play Parcheesi?"

"Yes," Leanne said, relieved. "Okie-dokie." She smiled at the old man with the large nose and hairy arms. He smiled back. Neither had played Parcheesi in years.

8

Dancing In The Dark

Although his home appeared smaller Andy was still glad to be back. Leanne told him she wasn't aware he had been away but he didn't believe her. Layton said he should have stayed longer but he knew his dad was kidding. Amy warned him not to make any noise because she had a headache and he felt like he had never left.

At dinner Layton asked him about his adventure at the estate of the famous Samantha Sanders. Before he could answer Amy accused Layton of never getting over Samantha, sinking so low as to pry information about her out of his own son. Andy felt bewildered but managed to shut them both up when he said, "Mark and I saw her working naked in her bedroom."

"Tell us about it," Amy said, suddenly leaning forward.

"I can't. I promised Mark."

"So why'd you bring it up?" Amy asked, disappointed.

"Because you guys were about to fight and I knew you'd stop if I told you that."

"Maybe Leanne should forget about Dr Lugow and just speak to her brother," Layton quipped. "He's got us all figured out."

"Samantha said she still likes you Dad, even if she doesn't ever agree with you about anything."

"Who does?" Amy said.

"Oh yeah? What else did she say when you weren't looking at her naked?" Layton asked.

"She said you could have been a great comedian if you didn't take life so seriously."

"She's talking!"

"And she said I'm right about sugarless bubblegum."

"So, that's it?" Amy said. "Your father the comedian and chewing gum? Some gossip you are."

"Oh yeah, I forgot, I'll be right back." He ran into his room and returned with an envelope. "She said I should give this to you."

Amy opened it: Samantha didn't want to intrude but if it was all right with Amy and Layton she'd like to invite Leanne to stay with her for a few days. Amy handed the note to Layton.

"Well?" Amy asked.

"It's not up to us," Layton said. "Leanne, Samantha wants to know if you'd like to stay with her for a few days."

"Why?"

"I don't know, perhaps she wants to get to know you."

"Now?"

"It takes her a while to warm up to people," Layton said.

"Ten years?"

"You don't have to," Amy said.

"Should I?"

"I would if I were you," Amy said.

"Why?"

"Well for one, Mark is your half-brother. And two, because it can't hurt being friends with someone like her."

"Why does she want to be my friend?"

"Maybe because she doesn't have any friends," Amy said. "It's not easy making friends when everyone wants to be your friend even if they don't particularly like you."

"What your mother is saying," Layton interjected, "is that Samantha is probably lonely and she only has Mark in the house and maybe she'd like to see what it would be like to have a girl like you to talk to, that's all. It's nice of her to offer."

"You should go," Andy added. "You won't believe the kinds of things you can get there for breakfast. And they've got every kind of ice cream in the world. And Mark's got some neat video games and they've got all the cable channels and even a forest in their backyard."

"Does Samantha know?" Leanne asked.

"Know what?" Andy asked.

"Yes," Amy said.

Leanne looked at the lamb chop on her plate. She touched the peas with her fork. She didn't want anyone to know. Not even her parents. It didn't feel good talking about it to a stranger like Dr Lugow. And she hardly knew Samantha Sanders even if she was once married to her father. "I don't know if I want to," she said.

"You don't have to," Layton said. "Why don't you call her after dinner and thank her and just say you'd rather not leave home for a while. She'll understand."

"Think it over before you call," Amy advised. "You might change your mind."

"What does Samantha know?" Andy asked.

"A lot more than you," Layton said. "Eat your peas."

It didn't take Samantha more than two minutes to change Leanne's mind. The conversation began with Leanne saying what her father suggested, but Samantha wasn't used to having an invitation turned down and was very direct. "I have something I want to talk to you about," she said. "You don't have to stay if you don't want to." Leanne didn't want to but didn't know how to say no.

"All right," she whispered. "I'll come."

■ ■ ■

"I was beginning to wonder what was going on," Barry Levine said on the phone. It was the first time Layton had called him and he was composing himself well. When a movie star starts calling, he thought, parking other people's Mercedes' will soon be history. "Arno wants us to stay in touch. We've lined up some writers."

"Tell Arno I want to talk to him."

"When?"

"Give me his number."

"Let me call him first."

"Give me the fucking number, carhop, or I'll drop this whole thing."

Levine gave the number and when they hung up he cursed Layton. "Fuck you, man! Star. Asshole. Don't you ever call me that, movie dick. I don't forget. Just remember *you* called me. One day I won't return your calls, fuckface."

While Levine fumed Layton called Arno and told him he wanted to talk some more about getting Samantha to drop her lawsuit.

"We talking talk or action?" Arno asked.

"Sometimes when talk makes sense action follows."

"You're sounding like a man who hears a clock ticking."

"The time is right," Layton said. "I need to know the details."

They agreed to meet later that night in the lounge of the Hotel Bel-Air. Layton was on time, finding a seat in a corner opposite the piano player. Arno and another man showed up a few minutes later.

"This is Mozart," Arno said. "You don't need to know his real name."

Mozart stuck out a calloused hand with a flower tattooed between his thumb and forefinger. "I like yer movies," he muttered.

"Which ones have you seen?"

Mozart looked at Arno for help. "Forget it," Arno said, "I told him to say that."

"You've got him programmed?"

"Mozart's reliable, that's what counts."

The piano player played "Stardust" as Layton told them of Leanne's approaching visit to Samantha's. He explained the rarity of his own visits there, mentioning the dog attack, the other security, and his very real concern for the safety of everyone involved. "We're talking of my children here."

"There's nothing to be nervous about, I've got it all figured," Arno said.

"The best laid plans still get fucked up," Layton cautioned. "I'm listening for foolproof."

Arno snapped his fingers and Mozart pulled out a bullet from his pocket. "Look at this," he said.

"I know what a bullet looks like."

"Only this isn't a real bullet, it's a dummy. It goes bang but it doesn't penetrate. If I shoot you with this from across the room the sound may scare you but you wouldn't bleed. So we've eliminated the danger of anyone getting hurt accidentally. Mozart won't be firing at anyone, but even if he was, it wouldn't matter. When one of these ricochets it's a cream puff. Your lady will know there's a sniper shooting at her but she won't know what's being shot. Which gives you the advantage of running out to capture Mozart while the shooting continues. Everyone else will be taking cover; you'll be out there acting like a hero.

"Now once you reach him you rough him up a bit–that understood Mozart?–and you bring him down. While everybody's still shaking you announce you're calling the police and call this number." He wrote a number inside a pack of hotel matches. "This will signal one of Mozart's friends to come and get him. He'll arrive in a cop car and be in uniform. He'll ask you a few questions, write some notes, and ask you for your phone number so he can contact you later. Then he'll handcuff Mozart, drive away, and you're home free. She don't drop that lawsuit we'll send Mozart back with real bullets."

As Arno talked Layton studied Mozart. What kind of guy was he to make himself available for such a thing? And could he be trusted? What if something unexpected happened? What if one of Samantha's dogs charged up the hill and attacked him? How would he defend himself? Did he carry a pistol for such what-ifs? Would he use it to protect himself? The plan sounded feasible but he had to be sure there could be no possibility of bloodshed or anyone–person or dog–getting hurt in any way. It was crazy for him to be sitting in the Bel-Air talking to these two about such a thing but the very craziness of it had some appeal. Samantha would never, not in two lifetimes, suspect he had anything to do with it. Not if everything went according to plan.

Then he remembered something.

"Tonya Harding," he said.

Arno didn't make the connection but Mozart did. "Amateurs," he said.

"Oh, the skater? Nothing like this," Arno added. "Those guys physically attacked the other girl. That was just stupid."

"But the principle's the same," Layton said. "The ex-husband wanted to win her back by eliminating her competition. He hired a goon and it backfired."

They couldn't remember Nancy Kerrigan's name but the incident had been widely publicized. That's all Layton needed, to get involved in some criminal scheme that could wind up making more headlines and land him in prison.

"If she ever finds out," Layton said, "that lawsuit will appear very small compared to the revenge she would exact."

"How's she going to find out?" Arno asked. "Unless you tell her."

"How do I know I can trust you—or him—to keep your mouths shut six months from now, when it might do you some good to make this known?"

"We'd be implicating ourselves wouldn't we? Do you think I'd want to be associated with anything like this? I'm breaking into the movie business not out of it. And Mozart—he makes too good a living to open his mouth. Besides, he knows he'd have his tongue cut out if he did. So it just isn't worth it."

"How can I be sure?"

"You can never be sure," Arno answered. "You can't be sure Mozart will even be there when you're there. But he will. You can't be sure I'm going to make this picture. But I will. About the only thing you can be sure of is if all goes the way I've outlined it, your former wife is going to have a whole new opinion of you. What that's worth only you know. But you can count on it."

"What's this going to cost?"

"Let me worry about that. It's my gift to you. Consider it a protection of my investment."

"Clever way to lock in an actor."

"I'm in the clever business," Arno smiled.

"Put your number on this too," Layton said, handing Mozart the matches.

They ordered another round of drinks and Arno told Layton about the two screenwriters he found who were interested in writing *Mr Sand Man*. Layton agreed to meet with them individually sometime next week, after this matter was closed and after he could put the Williams' play out of mind for short periods of time. Leanne would be going to Samantha's house in two days. Mozart said that would give him plenty of time to find the right spot where he could start shooting at them.

Driving Sunset Layton stuck a worn tape of Bob Dylan's *Infidels* in the cheap tape deck he had installed after his Alpine had been stolen a few months back. In the middle of "Neighborhood Bully" Dylan's voice became garbled, as if someone was pulling his tongue. Layton pressed the eject button and the cassette popped out, the tape stretching like a ribbon, caught by the cheap machine. Ruined.

He pulled another cassette from the glove compartment: Fred Astaire at the Philharmonic. But he decided not to make the insertion. The two cassettes of Astaire had cost him forty bucks and were hard to find.

Astaire had had a profound effect on Layton when he was a confused teenager. He knew he could never dance like the master but if he could act the way Astaire danced... that was a goal he could set for himself. Astaire's singing, like his dancing, seemed effortless. The year before he and Samantha divorced they actually met Astaire at his 80th birthday celebration and Layton asked him how hard he had to work to make what he did look so smooth. Astaire smiled pleasantly and said, "You've got to sweat like a bastard, practice until your feet are calloused, your socks soaked in blood, and everyone around you whispers dirty names whenever you pass. If you're prepared to be hated, sneered at and not invited to your own cast parties then perhaps you've chosen the right profession. If you're not, you'll melt into the celluloid and be forgotten ever after. Nice to meet you young man. And good luck."

Everyone was asleep when he got home. He went into the living room to turn off the VCR, which he had programmed to record *The Caine Mutiny*, one of his favorite pictures, especially the court martial scene when Bogart starts clicking those steel marbles as he begins losing his own, babbling defensively the way Richard Nixon would babble years later when everything was falling apart for him. He had always wondered if Nixon had seen that movie, sure that he had and that somewhere deep in his psyche the performance registered. But the only thing clicking in the living room was the VCR, going from RECORD to STOP over and over again. The tape hadn't unwound an inch. Something inside was fucked. What were the odds, he thought, of both his car stereo and Amy's VCR going blooey on the same night?

When he went to the bathroom to take a dump he saw there was no toilet paper. In the bedroom the tissue box was empty. In the kitchen, no paper towels. On the night table next to Amy the vial of Valium and a glass still brown with a gulp of Jack Daniel's. She was zonked in her zombie state.

He found the newspaper with his picture in it and took it to the toilet, tearing it neatly into quarters as he relieved himself.

The following day he began having second thoughts about both the play and Mozart. The rehearsals weren't going any better than the first day; his mind just wasn't on the material. Instead of clearing his head he had added a huge chunk of misery and confusion with this crazy scheme of Arno's. He couldn't get Mozart's flower tattoo out of his mind. Truman Capote had once told him at a party that the one thing all multiple murderers had in common was a tattoo. "Whenever you see someone with a tattoo," Capote had whined, "you'd better turn the other way."

The producers McCollough and Armen were patient men but their patience was beginning to wear as thin as a peel of white radish cut by a sushi chef. No one took theater in Los Angeles seriously; it was like bingo in Las Vegas. McCollough's dream was to change that; Armen felt the combination of Williams' last play and Layton Cross' notoriety would get them national exposure and a shot at Broadway. But Layton wasn't coming through. He was depending on prompters; he either didn't listen to stage directions or couldn't remember what he was told; his body was stiff, he walked clumsily on stage. "He's no Dustin Hoffman," Kevin McCollough said to his partner.

"Dustin Hoffman?" Malk Armen said. "I'd settle for a wounded Theo Soris."

That, of course, was out of the question. Theo was still in the hospital and would probably never regain the full use of his legs. And Layton had signed a contract. He was as committed to them as they were to him. That neither the actor nor the producers wanted to honor that commitment was irrelevant. In a week's time Layton Cross would bring back the critics and it would be theater as usual in Los Angeles. Bingo!

■ ■ ■

On Saturday, after Amy and Leanne went to see Dr Lugow, Amy drove her daughter to Samantha's house, hidden in a canyon, protected by hills, trees, guards, dogs, gates, fences, threatening signs, and poison sumac. Amy had been inside only once and that was a disaster. This time Samantha met them in the driveway. She was with Robert Mancino.

"Hey, Bob," Amy said. "How's the lasagna?"

"You two know each other?" Samantha asked.

"We're pasta friends," Mancino said, taking Amy's hand, kissing her cheek.

"Do you remember my daughter Leanne? She must have been seven when you last saw her."

Leanne smiled shyly. Mancino was her favorite actor. He had been in three movies that she had seen at least a half-dozen times. But she didn't remember meeting him before, not until her mother started explaining to Samantha how he had come to their house with a pasta machine and made this incredible lasagna. That was Robert Mancino? Leanne thought. The funny man who wore an apron and made such a mess in the kitchen? She had even helped, stuffing the dough through the machine, watching it come out as noodles. He had been her dad's friend. And it was one of her last memories of her family being together.

Mancino, darkly handsome, not much taller than Samantha, talked of that time as if it was last week. His career had risen dramatically the last few years. Now he was among the top five box-office attractions, up there with Cruise, Costner, Roberts. He hadn't seen Layton since that dinner and asked Amy how he was.

"He's living with us again," Amy said. "You should come by, he'd love to see you."

"Tell him I said go slow...and carry a wet wick," Mancino said with a smile. "There's nobody like that guy, you know."

"You don't have to tell me," Amy declared.

Mancino was visiting Samantha to discuss a movie project and said he'd come back the next day to continue their talks. He leaned over and kissed Leanne on the cheek, did the same to Amy, shook Samantha's hand and got into his Porshe Targa.

Samantha put her arm around Leanne and told Amy she'd be fine. "We'll call you in a few hours and see whether Leanne will be spending the night. Did you bring a toothbrush, just in case?"

"I forgot," Leanne said.

"No matter, I think we can find an extra one in the house."

Amy got back into her car and waved goodbye. Once outside the gate she pulled out a flask from under the seat and took a strong swallow.

Samantha asked Leanne if she had ever been in a sauna. Leanne said a Jacuzzi. "We've got that too," Samantha said. "What I thought is that we'd spend the day together. We can take a long walk, then come back and do some exercises if you like–if you don't you can hold my legs while I do sit-ups–and after we can take a sauna, a Jacuzzi, jump in the pool, then have lunch. How does that sound?"

"Okay, I guess."

"You guess? Listen kid, there are fat farms that charge a thousand dollars to do this kind of thing. We're going deluxe."

"Andy said your food's great."

Catch a Fallen Star

"Let me tell you something about your little brother—that kid made my kid look like an amateur at Dragon's Lair. And I thought Mark was some kind of genius because he could outscore me by a few thousand points. Mark's been so depressed since Andy wiped him out that he hasn't touched the joystick since."

"Andy likes you very much."

"Oh yeah? What else he tell you?"

"Not much. He's only seven."

"Seven going on seventeen if you ask me. You're going to have to watch your privacy with that kid, let me tell you."

"He's okay, he just gets excited easily."

"It's good he's got things to excite him. Wait'll he turns eight and finds out life's not so rosy."

"Yeah," Leanne said in a soft voice.

Samantha took a deep breath as they walked among the trees and down a narrow trail. She was never much for small talk. This was a delicate day. "Your father tells me you're seeing Dr Lugow. Funny man, isn't he?"

"Do you know him?"

"Know him? I practically paid for his house."

"He's not very good at Parcheesi."

"Fifteen years and I never even knew he played," Samantha joked.

"I don't think he really knows how to talk to me yet."

"How does one talk to you?"

Leanne shrugged. How many times could she say 'I don't know'?

They walked for an hour, stopping to pick some flowers, to look at a few of the wing-clipped exotic birds that lived in the trees, to listen to the burble of the stream that ran through the grounds. They climbed a large rock and closed their eyes to the sun. Samantha told stories of her childhood, of how shy and lonely she was growing up. But it wasn't until they were sitting and sweating in the sauna when Samantha got around to telling Leanne what it was she had wanted to tell her.

"This isn't easy for me," she said. "I've never told this to anyone. But when I heard about what happened to you I knew what you have had to deal with because it happened to me when I was about your age."

Leanne looked into Samantha's green eyes. The pungent smell of eucalyptus filled their nostrils. Both of them were wrapped in towels, their faces glistening with perspiration.

"Only it wasn't my father's friend who did it to me," Samantha continued, her eyes locking Leanne's. "It was my father."

Leanne shuddered. She didn't want to believe what Samantha was saying. What had happened to her was horrible enough. It had never occurred to her that there was something even worse.

"He kept telling me how much he loved me. And I would tell him back how much I loved him. He liked to tickle me a lot. And scratch my back. The scratching would turn into massaging. I was a kid, what did I know? It felt good. I liked when he touched me. Then one day he went too far. He touched my private part. I told him I didn't think he should do that. He said there was nothing wrong with a father holding his own daughter. No one else could ever do that, he said, but it was all right if he did. Just as long as I understood that it was out of love. He loved me so much he kept saying. And I was frightened. He was my father and I was scared to death of him. I didn't want to hurt him. I didn't know what to do. So I did nothing. I let him touch me. And then he asked me to touch him. I did. And I hated him for it ever since. It never happened again but it didn't matter. I've never forgotten it."

Tears rolled along with perspiration down Leanne's face. She didn't know what to say. She was embarrassed.

"It's good that you've been able to talk about it," Samantha said. "Even if it's painful. I kept it bottled up inside me all this time. I know I decided to tell you because I wanted to help you but I feel a great relief having told you. It's incredible how heavy it's been carrying it around for so many years. Believe me, honey, as bad as it probably was for you, you're lucky to have been able to share it. Even if it's only playing Parcheesi with Dr Lugow." She was holding Leanne now, hugging her closely. "And I want you to know that you can talk to me. I'm not always a big star, you know. Sometimes I'm just as lonely and frightened as you are. That's why I've built so many walls."

Leanne was openly sobbing as Samantha rocked her gently in her arms. It was the best she had felt since that awful night when her father left her alone in Theo's apartment. That awful, awful night.

Mark joined them for lunch that they ate by the pool. Samantha wanted to know what they thought of Robert Mancino. Leanne said he was her favorite. Mark thought he was pretty good.

"I'm thinking of making my next picture with him."

"That would be great," Leanne said.

"Why don't you make a picture with Layton?" Mark asked. It was a surprising comment.

"Layton Cross," Samantha said wryly. "What do you think of that, honey?"

"He'd like that," Leanne said.

"I bet he would. It's enough I'm not going to sue him for punching me in the face."

"He didn't really mean it," Mark said.

"Yes he did really mean it. He'd been storing it up for years."

"I think he felt very badly," Leanne said.

"How do you think I felt? He's a big palooka, your father."

"A movie with him would be really funny," Mark encouraged.

"Hysterical," Samantha said. She didn't want to say anything nasty about Layton in front of them. But the thought of acting with him was like taking a giant step backward. She had reached a point in her career where she could pick from among the very best actors in the world. None of them would turn down the opportunity. The finances were too big. Some may not like her but all understood the box-office. Samantha Sanders was box-office.

"So," she said, "what do you think–you want to spend the night with us? Maybe you can lure Mark back into the Dragon's Lair."

"Yeah, why don't you stay?" Mark added. "After Andy, I could use somebody to beat."

"What makes you think you can beat her?" Samantha asked.

"Aw, c'mon, Mom...."

"If you say because she's a girl I'll throttle you."

"Well...."

"Mark!"

"I'd like to stay," Leanne said, smiling now. "Really, I would."

Layton hesitated after speaking with his daughter. He had hoped she wanted to come home that day so he could call off the sniper. But he knew, as he told Leanne that he would swing by to pick her up around noon on Sunday, that his next call would be to Arno. He would allow Leanne's decision to influence his own.

Before he dialed Arno's number he made another call, to Sol Gordon. Perhaps Samantha had softened and playing Sunday's hero wouldn't be necessary. "So tell me, Sol, what are you doing home on the weekend? Why aren't you out on the golf course making money?"

"Saturday's my day to make money at home. You know how many studio lawyers I've talked with this morning?"

"Seven studios, seven lawyers," Layton said.

"Eleven," Gordon said. "Four of them had to do with your ex."

"Make that five," Layton said.

"If you want to know if she's available to make a picture, I don't know. But she's been meeting with Bob Mancino."

"I know. Bob's an old friend."

"He should be a new friend. Very hot potato."

"I haven't heard from you in a few days so I was wondering if the heat's off."

"Not that I know of," Gordon said. "She hasn't changed her mind since we last talked."

"Leanne's staying there for the night."

"That's nice."

"Andy stayed there for a few nights last week."

"You're trying to tell me something."

"We've been talking again."

"Anything I should know?"

"That's what I was calling you to find out."

"Sorry Layton. With Samantha I'm more an instrument than a counselor."

"Well Sol, keep that cash register humming."

When Layton got into his Jeep to drive over to Samantha's the next day he noticed a slight tremor in his hands. Not wanting to appear agitated he took a thin joint marked with a red dot from the glove compartment. He had a system of marking joints with red, green, or blue dots. He needed his wits about him so he knew whatever he smoked it shouldn't be too strong. But he wanted to feel calm. The red would do that.

Arno had told him that once shots were fired he should run in the direction opposite the house and up the hill. Halfway up he should look for snips of yellow cloth tied to branches that would lead him to Mozart.

When he pulled into the compound Leanne and Mark were outside. Mark had a video camera and was recording Leanne as she played with the dogs. He turned the camera on his father and Layton mugged. Leanne ran to him and gave him a big hug. She seemed genuinely glad to see him. She also seemed more like her old self than any time since the incident. Whatever Samantha had to tell her, it must have worked.

As Mark recorded his home movie, Samantha and Robert Mancino came out of the house, followed by Faye Collabella, Samantha's longtime secretary. Mark captured them as they walked to the circular island of grass in the middle of the driveway. There were two white iron benches and a fountain with a statue of a boy holding his wee-wee on the island. Layton went to shake hands with Mancino when the shots were fired.

Smiles turned to fear all around. Layton wasn't acting when he dropped flat on the gravel; for that split second he reacted as if the sniper was real. Leanne was screaming, standing frozen by the fountain. Mark ducked behind the fountain and aimed his camera into the hills. Faye Collabella crouched next to Mark hoping the statue would protect both of them. Layton crawled on his stomach to grab Leanne and bring her down. His first concern was to calm her.

Samantha had run into the house the moment the shooting began but now she was back holding a high-powered rifle with a large scope. The magnification was such that she could make out the glint of the sniper's rifle reflected by the sun. She stood erect and took aim. Her finger expertly flattened the trigger and the whiz-ping! of the bullet projected through the well-oiled barrel sounded almost like music. The sniper's scream was the next sound heard. One shot...and Samantha had proven her marksmanship.

By the time Layton realized what had happened it was too late. He stood up to run but Mancino was already there. He had bravely, instinctively, reacted to the shooting by running in the direction of the shots, Samantha's two Rottweilers behind him. Mancino was almost on the sniper when Samantha's bullet landed, knocking Mozart over. It was a clean shot through the shoulder. The dogs bit at Mozart's arms and legs but Mancino called them off. He lifted the sniper by the shirt and pushed him down the hill.

Layton seemed in shock standing next to his sobbing daughter on the grass island. Samantha's rifle remained pointed at Mozart. Mark was recording it all.

"The dogs would have chewed him to pieces," Mancino said as Samantha stood face to face with the wounded Mozart. Blood was pouring from his shoulder.

He felt weak and lowered his eyes, unable to hold Samantha's stare.

"I just want to see what kind of animal would do this," she said.

Suddenly Layton snapped out of whatever coma he had gone into and shouted that he would call the police. But Samantha, whose cool was almost eerie, told him to wait, she wanted to study this intruder. Shooting him wasn't enough. "Mark, bring the dogs over here," she commanded.

"Wait a minute," Mozart said, aware that his troubles may be just starting. "I didn't bargain for anything like this."

"YOU DIDN'T WHAT!?" Samantha screamed, releasing whatever tension she had been suppressing. Her scream reactivated Layton's adrenal glands that must have been numbed by the grass. If he didn't take matters into his own hands Mozart would start singing like a canary.

Screaming "MY CHILDREN! YOU ALMOST SHOT MY CHILDREN!" as he lunged at Mozart, he grabbed him by the shirt collar and, before Mancino could pull him away, managed to punch a mighty fist flush into Mozart's face, knocking him thankfully unconscious.

"What did you do that for?" Mancino asked. "He was already captured."

"That's some delayed reaction," Samantha said, standing over the fallen sniper. "Where were you when the shooting began?"

Layton looked at everyone, his nostrils flaring. He was working himself into a righteous anger. Samantha and Mancino may have been more in demand, but they weren't better actors. He knew what he had to do before Mozart came to.

"I'm going to call the police," he barked. "Any objections?" He stormed into the house and searched for the matchbook. It wasn't in either of his pants pockets and he began to panic. Then he found it in his shirt pocket, made the call, and got back out to keep an eye on things. If Mozart stirred he would have to kick him in the head.

Mark was sitting on a bench next to Leanne, his video camera between his legs. Samantha and Mancino were huddled together over Mozart. He was complimenting her marksmanship; she was praising his bravery. Layton looked at them with anger and envy. He felt both a fool and an intruder. Samantha proved more of a man than he; and Bob was a goddamn legitimate hero. He walked over to his children and asked how they were. Then he sat on the other bench next to Faye Collabella and waited for the second act to unravel.

"Where'd she learn to shoot like that?" he wondered. "She couldn't hit anything when we used to go out."

"Practice," her secretary said. "You know how obsessive she can be."

It didn't take long for the phony cop to arrive but for Layton it was an eternity. His nerves were shot. He felt dizzy, nauseous, disgusted. But when Mancino started talking to the cop Layton forced himself to stand and take charge.

"I'm the one who called," he said. "This asshole opened fire on us. We managed to shoot him down. The dogs had a turn with him, and then I knocked him out. You fill out your report and just deal with me. Keep these other people out of it."

Samantha and Mancino stood by as the cop scribbled some notes and asked, "You the one filing the complaint here?"

"That's right. The name's Cross. Layton Cross."

"Okay, Mr Cross. If you'll just help me with this guy I'll cuff him. I'll need your phone number—we'll be calling you for the details. I think now I better get this guy to a doctor."

"You don't bother anyone else but me, you understand?" Layton said.

"Don't worry, Mr Cross, we know when to keep something like this down." He tore off a copy of his report and handed it to Layton who carefully folded it and put it in his pocket.

"Well, Jesus Christ," Layton said after the cop and Mozart were gone. "Je-sus fucking Christ."

"Strange," Samantha observed, "he didn't call for an ambulance." She walked away from Mancino and held out her hand to Layton. "Come inside," she said, "I'll give you a tranquilizer."

Robert Mancino followed Layton to Amy's house making sure he made it without an accident. When Layton weakly invited him inside Mancino declined saying he promised Samantha he would return and stay with her.

"You really proved yourself today," Layton said.

"You did pretty well yourself."

"I'm good at hitting someone already down."

"I'd have done the same thing."

"You did more."

"You thought of your kid first."

"Some fucking world," Layton mumbled.

"You take it easy, Layt."

Amy came out as Mancino drove off. "What's going on?" she asked.

Leanne ran to embrace her tightly.

"We were shot at," Layton said.

"What? Where?"

"Everything's all right. Somebody opened up at Samantha's but we got him."

"Who was he shooting at?"

"Who do you think, me?"

"Why would anyone shoot at you?"

"What does it matter now, it's over, nobody got hurt except the sniper. Samantha shot him."

"Samantha!"

"And Bob caught him."

"And Daddy punched him," Leanne added.

"Daddy's good at that," Amy said. "Were you very frightened baby?"

"She was doing terrific until then, weren't you sweetheart?"

"Why did he shoot at us?" Leanne asked.

"Why'd they shoot John Lennon? Or Bobby Kennedy? When you shoot a star you become one," Layton said.

"Samantha wasn't even scared," Leanne said.

"Sure she was, she just didn't show it."

"I'd like to be like that."

"How the hell did a sniper get on that property?" Amy asked. "She's got more security than the Pope."

"They shot him too, remember?"

"You sure he was shooting at her?"

"Unless Mancino's got enemies we don't know about."

"Mancino's a heavy gambler, isn't he?"

"So?"

"So maybe it was him."

"Mancino's got more money than gambling debts."

"How do you know?"

"I don't know. But it wasn't him."

"What makes you so sure?"

"We were at Samantha's house. How would the sniper know Mancino was going to be there? I didn't know."

"Maybe he was being followed."

"What is this with you Amy? Samantha was the obvious target. She's the most famous."

"Did the police come?"

"It's all taken care of."

"I want you to follow this up," Amy said. "Somebody could have been killed."

"Don't worry about it."

But Amy did worry about it. She wanted to know every detail. When Leanne told her that Mark had recorded it all she insisted on seeing the tape. Layton said it wasn't a good idea to look at this as entertainment but Amy ignored him. They were shot at; she wanted to see what happened.

"Maybe we should invite the neighbors, have a party," Layton quipped.

Amy called Mark and asked if she could see the tape. Mark was watching it with his mother and Mancino at the moment but if she wanted to come by he would lend it to her.

"I don't think it's such a good idea," Layton said.

"Why not?"

"It'll just upset you."

"I'm already upset."

"It'll upset Leanne."

"She doesn't have to watch."

"It'll upset me."

"You don't have to watch."

"You're making too big a deal out of this."

"I'm going to look at that tape. I'm going over there right after dinner."

With the children in bed Amy and Layton sat in the living room screening Mark's first home movie. The camera work was shaky but Mark managed to get most of the action: Layton flat on his stomach in the driveway, Mancino climbing the hill with the dogs, Samantha aiming her rifle, Leanne and Layton behind the fountain, the wounded sniper coming down, Samantha jaw to jaw with him, Layton's punch, the cop's arrival.

"Wait a minute," Amy exclaimed as they watched the cop and Layton carry the sniper into the backseat of the police car. "I think I know that guy."

"Who?" Layton asked.

"That cop. Only he's not a cop, he's an actor who plays cops."

"What are you talking about?"

"I'm sure about it. Rewind the tape, I want to see it again."

"Amy, you don't know what you're talking about."

"You guys get shot at and then let some actor impersonating a cop take away the guy who tried to kill you? Call the police, see if they booked that guy."

"I'm not going to call the police. They'll be calling me about it tomorrow."

"Then I'll call."

"You're not going to call."

"Why not?"

"Because I was the one who called the police in the first place, that's why not."

"Why are you being so resistant? I just want to know if they got the guy, that's all."

"They won't tell you."

"How do you know?"

"Because we asked him to keep it quiet. There's no need for more publicity for Christ's sake."

"Layton, you're not hearing me. If that cop wasn't a cop, then that sniper might still be out there. You're all still in danger if he is."

"The cop was a cop."

"How can you be sure?"

"Trust me."

"Maybe he intercepted your call."

"He's a cop because I say he's a cop and you're not going to call the cops because I say you're not. Now enough! I don't want to continue this."

"Fuck you Layt, I'm calling."

"You're not calling because there's nothing to call about, it never happened. There was no sniper!"

Layton was standing and shouting now. Amy figured it had finally happened, he had flipped, gone off the deep end.

"Will you sit down and take a deep breath," she said. "I'll pour you a drink."

"I don't need a drink."

"You need something."

"I need you to listen to me, okay? I'm going to tell you something and I need you to just sit down and shut up and just listen. Can you do that?"

Amy poured herself a drink and sat down.

"Good. Now what you saw wasn't real, okay? It was a set-up. You were right, the cop wasn't a real cop. And the sniper wasn't a real sniper. He was shooting dummy bullets, fakes. What was supposed to happen didn't go according to plan. I was supposed to run up that hill, not Mancino.

Samantha wasn't supposed to shoot the guy, I didn't know she was that good a shot. I was going to capture him, rough him up, bring him down, call the cop who isn't a cop, and be the hero. Samantha would forget about the lawsuit and we could go on with our lives without a court battle that I would have lost. If she didn't put me into bankruptcy she would have taken Mark away from me altogether. I planned the whole thing. Okay? You understand now? It was me. No one was in danger. And it's over. Finished, do you hear?"

"Are you telling me the truth?"

"I swear it."

"On the lives of the children?"

"On their lives."

"Then you are a fucking lunatic."

"You would have never known..."

"I've always known."

"...if it wasn't for this goddamn tape."

"You wouldn't have told me?"

"Of course not."

"You would have let me believe someone was trying to kill all of you instead?"

"No one got hurt. Except Mozart."

"Who the fuck is Mozart?"

"The sniper."

"You hired a musician to terrorize your children?"

"Can we forget about it for tonight? Can we talk about it tomorrow?"

"What's there to talk about? How crazy you are? How you've probably destroyed what little was left in the way of faith in the world for your daughter? How you've turned into a liar? How I can never trust you again? What, Layton?"

"I don't want to talk about this anymore, okay?"

"You won't have to," Amy said. She finished her drink in a swallow and left the room. Layton followed her into the bedroom. The suitcases were out.

"Amy, don't start with me now. Please."

"Try finish, Layton. It's way too late to start."

"What are you doing?"

"I'm taking the kids and going to Michigan like I wanted to last week."

"I don't want you to do that."

"You're in no position to want anything. You try and stop me and I'll tell Samantha what you told me."

"Don't fucking blackmail me, you cunt!"

"You're a dangerous man, Layt. You don't realize it, but you are. You need help. Take my appointments with Lugow; maybe he can help you. I know I can't."

"I'm opening in the play next week, I want you and the kids there."

"Too late for that. You should never have taken on that play. That was Theo's play. Your best friend, remember? Remember what kind of friends you have?"

"You're not helping me."

"I can't help you. I'm the one you keep saying needs help. How can anyone help you? Just look at the mess you call your life."

"My life is not a mess, it's the people in my life who make it that way."

"There's your bed Layton. Sleep in it."

"I don't want to punch you, goddamn it."

"Then don't. Try and control yourself. Just a few more hours and tomorrow we'll be gone. You can stay here and wreck the house for all I care."

"This is not working out," Layton mumbled as he unscrewed the cap and chewed two of Amy's Valiums. "This isn't the way things should be."

The next morning Arno called wanting to know what had happened.

"What happened is your guy got shot and Amy recognized the cop you hired as an actor she somehow knows, that's what happened to your foolproof scheme," Layton growled.

"What was she doing there?" Arno asked.

"She wasn't there. My kid made a video of the whole fiasco. He could probably sell it to *Hard Copy* for a bundle."

"You've got the tape?"

"Why, you want to see it?"

"Destroy it," Arno commanded.

"It's not mine to destroy."

"Then buy it from your kid and then destroy it."

"It's his first documentary," Layton said, "he's not going to sell."

"That tape could wind up destroying you if you don't get rid of it. Don't pull a Nixon here."

"Amy's leaving," Layton said. "With the kids. Samantha's got a new hero. Who's going to pardon me?"

"Look, it didn't go according to plan but it went off without anyone but Mozart hurt and no police or media involved so it wasn't a disaster. Mozart lost a lot of blood but he'll be all right in case you're interested."

"I'm not."

"It would have been tricky if she killed him."

"He was lucky."

"Just for your information, this favor has cost me a bundle."

"Take a trip to Colombia."

"What is that supposed to mean?"

"Maybe you need a vacation."

"You can't blame me for what happened. I heard you ducked."

"I was being shot at."

"No you weren't."

"You're forgetting one thing—I'm an actor."

"So?"

"So I acted."

"What was the other guy, a stunt man?"

"The other guy was Robert Mancino."

"Robert Mancino? What was he doing there?"

"Securing his next part."

"The guy's got guts."

"Tell me about it. Why the fuck did you hire an actor?"

"Who better to play a part? Would you have preferred an amateur?"

"I would have preferred a crooked cop."

"They're not as easy to control."

"How do you know your actor won't sing when he gets hard up?"

"Don't worry about that. You just worry about making that tape disappear."

Andy didn't want to go to Michigan. He refused to do any packing until he saw how serious his mother was and then he reluctantly gathered his sticker books, Game Boy, Elmo doll and a few more of his valuables and stuffed them into his knapsack.

Before the shooting Leanne also didn't want to go away but now she was glad. Glad to be away from movie stars who get shot at; from a psychiatrist who can't even win at Parcheesi; from answering any more calls from Theo Soris. She also couldn't stop thinking about what had happened to Samantha when she was a girl. Her grandmother was a bit eccentric, but compared to the people in L.A. she would be a relief.

Amy had made all the arrangements while Layton slept. The plane tickets were reserved, her mother was expecting them, a taxi was coming to pick them up. She had resolved never to depend on Layton again—not even for a ride to the airport.

When Andy asked how long they were going for, Layton told him it was up to his mother. Amy wouldn't commit. "Maybe a month, maybe six months, it depends," was as far as she would go.

"Depends on what?" Layton asked.

"On how I feel."

"You've got to think about the kids. They've got friends, school..."

"There are schools in Michigan. They'll make friends. Don't worry about them."

"How can you tell me that? They're my kids too."

"So you'll call them whenever you remember."

Layton went into Leanne's room to see how she felt about this. "Don't worry daddy, it's probably for the best."

"I'm going to miss you."

"We'll come back, I promise."

"You'd better. I want you to convince your mother."

"Nobody can convince her about anything," Leanne said.

"Give it a shot, okay baby? I'm counting on you."

Leanne hugged him. Then she remembered what Samantha had said before the sniper incident. "I forgot to tell you about her suing you."

"She talked about that?"

"She just said she wasn't going to."

"When did she tell you?"

"At lunch on Saturday. Mark was there."

Layton felt chilled, though he began to perspire. Had she called him that night none of this would now be happening. He wouldn't be losing his family. Mozart wouldn't have gotten shot. The charade was for nothing. He didn't want to lose it in front of Leanne but he couldn't help it.

"Daddy, don't cry, you're scaring me."

He didn't mean to scare her. He didn't mean to lose her. He didn't mean to have so fucked up. But he couldn't stop the tears from falling or his heart from aching.

9

Who's That Knocking...?

Alone, Layton walked through the house with great sadness. He had never lived there by himself. He was the one who had returned to be with his family and now they had walked out on him.

He couldn't understand Amy–just because he refused to leave them was no reason for her to take off that way. How responsible was that? How could she so abruptly abandon her work? True, she was in-between editing jobs, but still, she wasn't that secure to take an indefinite leave of absence.

He looked outside at the homes across the street. Everything seemed so calm, so normal. Were people in those houses just as crazed and emotional and scarred as he and his family?

Ava Gardner had once lived in this canyon. So had Frank Zappa, David Hockney, Richard Dreyfuss, Bruce Willis, Rob Lowe, Molly Ringwald. Someone had mistakenly told him that Henry Miller had lived out his last years in the neighborhood and before Layton found out Miller had lived in the Santa Monica mountains and not the Hollywood Hills he and Amy used to try to guess which was Miller's house, trying to imagine seeing the grand old man riding up the steep hill on his bicycle. Layton had fantasized running into Miller, who died in 1980, a few years before he and Amy discovered the canyon. He was sure he would have liked the writer, who had as many problems with women as Layton had. They could have talked for hours about the silly cunts who so dominated their lives, and how an artist deals with fame. Miller believed an artist didn't want fame—just room enough to move around in and do what he likes. Layton was still searching for the room.

Towards the end of Miller's life he had grown disgusted with his readers, who were mostly interested in the sensational aspects of their salty hero's life. Miller thought he had given much more. Layton understood that.

He went into the living room and picked up Mark's tape. Watching it a second time was just as painful and embarrassing as before. He couldn't erase the whole thing. Instead, he stopped it as the cop was pulling into the driveway and erased it from there. He felt like a shit doing it. His son's first film and he ruined the ending.

When Alex Briar called a few days later Layton was in no mood to talk to him. "The problem with journalists," he said, "is that they're all looking to make friends with actors. You lose perspective after a while."

"The problem with actors," Briar countered, "is that they think they're superior to journalists. Talk about cockeyed perspectives."

"You're the guys who are coming to us."

"And when you were first starting out it was the reverse. We use each other."

"Well, you've certainly had your share of me."

"The *TV Guide* piece is finished. I was calling because someone I know saw your wife and kids at the airport a few days ago and the rumors are beginning to circulate."

Why did these reporters, these so-called fact-keepers, continue to refer to Amy as his wife? Why couldn't they even get that minor detail straight?

"And you're calling for a scoop?"

"I'll keep it in perspective."

"They've gone to India to join an ashram. It's a three-month package deal guaranteeing enlightenment or their money back. I couldn't join them due to prior commitments."

"What you're going to read is that you split up."

"Well now you know differently. We were never together."

"Do you care how it's reported?"

"Fuck you and your reported. I don't give a shit. If the press started getting things right I'd start reading the papers again."

"There's something else floating around about you," Briar said.

"Let it sink."

"Some kind of bizarre assassination attempt at Samantha Sanders'. You know anything about that?"

"Where'd you hear that one?"

"You know what kind of town this is."

"What I know is that this town sucks. Beginning with the likes of you."

"Hey, I'm telling you stuff you should know, true or false. I'm doing you a favor."

"You want to do me a real favor? Find another subject to leech onto."

"When you're hot you're hot."

"Even when you're not. That's what this town's really about."

So, Layton thought, it's already out. Who talked? Certainly not Samantha. Mark? He wouldn't. Mancino? He would if he thought it was in his interest. Samantha's secretary? The maids? Butler? Gardeners? Chauffeur? Sure, for a buck. That's how these things usually get out–always someone willing to pay and someone willing to talk. No wonder news of Brando dried up after he let all his help go. Smart man, that Marlon.

The next call was truly unexpected. Charles Greenbloom's secretary announcing Mr Greenbloom's imminent arrival on the line. "Please hold for Mr Greenbloom." These self-inflated fucks, Layton thought. They can't even dial a number any more.

When Greenbloom finally came on Layton reproached him. "I was just trying to count the years since your last call Charlie. What's the matter, you've got a part only I can play? You got some need for me Charlie?"

Greenbloom had become a man who didn't appreciate this kind of ribbing. He never liked Layton, not even when he represented him. And he always regretted introducing him to Samantha. But Greenbloom had heard about what had happened at Samantha's house and wanted the low down. He'd already spoken to her and to Mark, now he was calling to hear it from Layton. When someone starts shooting at the most expensive piece of property in Hollywood, especially one that directly concerns Quickstart Studios and Charles Greenbloom's lifestyle, Charlie Greenbloom gets concerned. He wants to know. He wants to hear every friggin' detail.

"Where did the police say they were taking him?" Greenbloom asked.

"I never asked. I was more concerned about my kids."

"I spoke with Mark, he sounded okay. Is he? How did he behave?"

"It was Leanne who got freaked, Charlie. Remember her? She's the one I had without Samantha's help."

"I called the Beverly Hills police and they said they know nothing about this."

"We asked the cop to keep it quiet, they're just being respectful."

"Not to me, Layton. I'm talking about me—I called them. I talked to the chief. He knows who I am and he said no such incident was reported. Now what the hell do you make of that?"

"I don't know Charlie. I must have punched a phantom."

"Samantha said she shot him."

"Annie Oakley," Layton said. Charlie Greenbloom was not going to get to the bottom of this one, not at Layton's expense.

"I'm going to find out what happened to that sonuvabitch."

"And when you do Charlie, think of me for a small walk-on."

Greenbloom practically snarled off, pissed that he couldn't get any more from Layton than he could from anyone else who had been there. What the hell was happening in this town when even Charles Greenbloom couldn't get answers to something as extraordinary as this?

■ ■ ■

At the Coronet Layton did all he could to put everything out of mind and just concentrate on the play. But some of the other actors began asking him if it was true about Amy leaving him and his getting shot at. It didn't matter that he had stopped reading papers, the papers didn't stop writing about him. McCollough and Armen were optimistic about it: such news could only bring in the curious. Even if Layton didn't understand his role the people would come. Tickets for the following weeks' performances were already in demand.

Al Low sounded excited when he called to say that Freddie Franklin wanted to book him for his radio talk show on Wednesday, two days before Layton opened at the Coronet. Layton never listened to Franklin but knew he had a popular show. "I don't want to be asked embarrassing questions by some local Stern wanna-be," Layton said.

"He doesn't want to get into your personal life," Low said. "He'll just talk about the play and the TV movie."

"You got that guaranteed?"

"You know they don't do that."

"Then how do you know what he just wants to talk about? You know what's going to happen. When have I ever come out of these things without adding to the confusion already around me?"

"If you just answer his questions without ad-libbing your unusual array of asides you'll do okay."

"Trying to take away my substance, eh?"

"I think you should do it."

"You willing to put your dick on the block if I get fucked?"

"Then it's a yes?"

"I'm not a yes man."

"I am," Low affirmed. "Yes?"

"No."

"No what?"

"Know yourself."

"You see, that's what I mean. That's what you've got to avoid."

"I thought you weren't working for me until I paid you."

"The only way you'll ever pay me is if you start making money. Publicity helps."

"I've got plenty of that thank you."
"Say yes, Layton."
"Why?"
"Because I already booked you."

■ ■ ■

Because it was lonely eating by himself at night Layton agreed to meet for dinner on consecutive nights with the two screenwriters Arno and Barry Levine had found for *Mr Sand Man*. The first night he met with a woman named Alice Wonders at Barney's Beanery in West Hollywood.

"With a name like that you should relate to the material," Layton remarked after they were seated in a booth. Wonders was in her late twenties and had been a child actress before deciding she was really a writer.

"My head's full of stories," she said enthusiastically. "I think *Mr Sand Man* is a wonderful fable. It could be the Nineties' *Wizard of Oz*.

"No small cult classic for you then," Layton chided.

"I've got ideas. It's a great story."

"Just between us, and no offense meant, but you know you're full of shit about this, right?"

"You mean it's not really movie material?"

"What do you think? Forget about sucking up to an actor for the job."

"I think it's a children's book," Wonders demurred. "My childhood is all I've got. Twenty years ago I did what you do, then I grew tits, my face broke out, and suddenly I was a has-been. I've written four scripts in the last three years and have been living off option money, which means I'm up to these tits in debt. I understand *Mr Sand Man* because it's about dreams and hopes and imagination. I've got a surplus of all three. So maybe it's not *The Wizard of Oz*. At least it's not *Death Wish 6*."

The next night at Chin Chin's on Sunset Layton met with the second writer, Harold Fjord III. There was no second Fjord, Fjord III told him, he just thought the number three more distinguished. Especially in Roman. *Mr Sand Man*, according to Mr Fjord III, was really a parable of our economic and social times, expertly crafted to reveal through a child's dreams what the country wanted, set up against the oppressiveness of poverty and the decline of the American Dream. The child, of course, must be changed to a middle-aged actor for Layton to do the part, but that should pose no problem once the overall theme was established.

Alice Wonders got the assignment.

■ ■ ■

"Hello, I'm Freddie Franklin, this is talk radio. My guest for this next hour is the well-known actor whose name has been in the news lately for all sorts of strange goings-on in his life, star of stage and screen, Mr Layton Cross. Good morning Layton."

"Hello Freddie." Layton could almost smell the odor of high ambition and ratings in the room. Franklin was young, fat, aggressive. His hair looked as false as his smile. His was a local show but what he wanted was national syndication, then an MTV talk show, then a shot at late night. Layton was the perfect kind of guest for Franklin if he could get him to open up.

Layton's reputation of being unpredictable didn't unnerve Franklin because he didn't care about his guests' reputations. Once they were on the air live anything was fair game, good talk happened unexpectedly.

"So what is it with you, a big big star what seven, eight years ago? The world is your oyster, then you sink out of sight–how does that happen?"

"I don't know Freddie, you tell me." Layton gave him an icy stare. The play and the TV movie, Al Low guaranteed. Nothing else.

"Was it drugs? I mean, you had the talent."

"I'd like to think the living deserve the present tense."

"Well how do we know if you've still got it if we haven't seen it lately?"

His instinct was to walk and leave this asshole with an empty hour to fill but that would make a shit like Franklin the winner, and Layton felt he should be able to handle no-talents like him without having to flee.

"You want to see it, come to the Coronet Theatre on Friday, I'll be there performing just for you."

"That's a play a friend of yours was in until recently when someone attacked him and put him in the hospital. Let's get to that after a break, maybe you can tell us what you know."

Franklin shuffled through his notes during the commercial break, not looking at Layton or attempting any small talk to put him at ease. Layton looked at the overhead mikes, the electronic equipment, and thought about who might be listening to them: commuters in their cars, people who worked at home, housewives taking care of their children, joggers and those in gyms working out listening on headsets. How would his personal troubles benefit any of them? What would be the point of unraveling over the airwaves?

"Hey, scumbag," Layton said while they were still off the air. Freddie Franklin looked up and saw the anger in Layton's face. He held up a finger to indicate one moment then slyly switched them back on the air without letting Layton know. When he looked up again at his guest, Layton laid it out for him. "There are things I'd prefer not to discuss which I thought was made clear with you before I came here."

"Nothing was said," Franklin told him.

"Then let me say it. I don't want to talk about my private life with you. I don't want to talk about Theo Soris and why my former wife stabbed him. I don't want to talk about my children; Amy's leaving; why I punched Samantha Sanders; or the shooting incident at her house. I'm not interested in analyzing my own fall, which is a very old and tired story. What I will talk about is the play and the TV movie. If you've got any callers, let them call and we'll see what's on their minds."

"I'd think they'd want to know what I want to know," Franklin said, speaking into his mike. Layton turned his head and saw the bright red ON THE AIR light and realized that Franklin had duped him. "And what I want to know is all those things you just said you don't want to talk about. What are you afraid of? Your career's been in the toilet and you're still young enough to rescue it, why not tell it like it is? People appreciate honesty."

"We're on the air aren't we?"

"I'm afraid we are. Now maybe we can make this an interesting hour, if you want to explain why you're so reluctant to talk about all the things that have put you in the news recently."

"Because none of it has anything to do with me as an actor."

"But beyond that doesn't it have everything to do with you as a person? And isn't your acting an extension of your person?"

"What's been going on in my life is an extension of the manner in which Tennessee Williams died."

"Which was an absurdity."

"You've got it Frankie. And to talk about it over the radio doesn't seem to make any more sense than to have lived through it."

"I wonder if our listeners would agree. The switchboard's lit up, let's take our first call."

"Hi this is Marie from Tarzana. I just wanted to know why you and Samantha Sanders broke up. She's my favorite star."

Christ, how did he get himself into this? Fucking Al Low and his nose for publicity. "We were very young when we got married," Layton said. "As we got older we both felt a need to experience more of life. It happens all the time."

The next caller brought up the big punch at the Bel Air garage sale and challenged Layton for being a tough guy.

"Were you there?" Layton asked.

"No, but I read about it," the caller responded.

"If you weren't there then you don't know what happened. And if you had been there then maybe you could tell me what happened because I still don't know."

The third caller wanted to know about Mark, how old he was and what did he want to be?

"He's fifteen and lives with his mother and he would like to be sixteen." Why were all the calls about Samantha? What was it about her that interested so many of these people?

Another caller wanted an answer to the question Freddie Franklin had asked: what happened to his career?

"You stopped coming to my pictures," Layton said. "It all has to do with money. That's what runs this town, that's what runs the country."

"I read that it had to do with your behavior and had nothing to do with money since your films didn't do that badly."

"You may be right," Layton said. "But I really can't speak to that because I don't know."

"I can speak to that," the next caller said. Layton recognized Theo's voice immediately. The drama of his life was about to continue, on the air, as listeners throughout Los Angeles stayed tuned. "Layton Cross has always been a brave, no-nonsense actor, and because he's never been able to put up with the b.s. that goes on here he's been denied the roles he deserves to play. If you want to see how good he can be the Williams play is the perfect opportunity. I know because I was in it until my accident."

Freddie Franklin wasn't about to let this conversation slip by without interjecting. "Now that we've got Theo Soris on the line perhaps we can finally clear up what happened to him. Theo, the rumor is that you were stabbed by an old family friend, Layton Cross's former wife Amy,

which he's already confirmed for us. Can you explain how that happened and why?"

"She didn't do nothing," Theo said. "I've read those rumors, it's ridiculous. Why on earth would she do something like that? I was mugged outside my apartment, someone stabbed me and then ran me over, but it wasn't Amy Cross, it wasn't a woman. Layton agreed to go on for me in this play that was a courageous decision on his part because he had little time to rehearse. And from what I'm hearing, he's going to be terrific in it."

Freddie Franklin watched Layton as they both listened to Theo. Franklin had no doubt that Soris was covering up and pressed Layton about it. "Theo Soris says she didn't do it, you've said she did but you don't want to talk about it. Can you help us out here Layton?"

Layton looked at Franklin as if he were staring into a diseased face full of maggots. "I was referring to the rumors. I'm sorry about what happened to Theo and I think our sympathies should be with him. He was the one who was attacked, he should know who did and did not attack him."

"Theo, while we have you on the line, is there anything more you can say about this?"

"I just called to wish my friend good luck on Friday. He's a special guy who deserves some credit for taking over the play. People should go see it."

Layton resisted thanking Theo. He was pissed having to endure so much bullshit on the air and he wasn't ready to accept Theo's attempt at making up to him. What Theo had done could never, not ever, be forgiven. Still, his call changed the tone of the Franklin show and made it easier for Layton to get through the last half hour.

The next night Theo called Layton to wish him luck again. He was still in the hospital and would probably be stuck in a wheelchair for the rest of his life but he missed not having Layton to talk to. Layton blamed Theo for his empty house and his missing children whom he would have liked in the audience on Friday night.

"I'd like to see you again Layt. In spite of everything, you're my best friend."

"Get it through your sick head Theo, friends don't do what you did. I don't want to talk to you. You need professional help."

"I'm going to," Theo said. "I just need time."

Layton, too, needed time. Time to understand the play he was about to do. Time to sort out what had gone wrong between him and Amy. Time to rethink his career and priorities. Time to be accountable for his actions. Time to grow up.

He smoked a mild joint to get to sleep and listened to a tape he had made of the Williams' play. Instead of counting sheep he kept telling himself that acting was fun. "That's why I do it, acting is fun." But just before the Sand Man arrived he mumbled, "Like hell it is." He fell asleep with the twisted grimace of truth distorting his face.

The following day was a blur until the time came to drive to the theater. He had tried calling Amy but couldn't reach her. It annoyed him that she hadn't been thoughtful enough to call and wish him a broken leg. Knowing her, if she had, she would have meant it literally.

Kevin McCollough and Malk Armen had placed an ad in the trades with Layton's picture. Layton would have preferred to open quietly, get the bugs worked out, before trumpeting to the industry his latest try at a comeback.

On top of that Arno and Macky had chosen this day to also take an ad out announcing the signing of Layton Cross for their company's first picture, *The Sand Man*. With the way things were going, Layton thought, they should rename the film *The Phoenix*.

There was an air of excitement in the audience that night but not backstage, where the actors knew what kind of disaster to expect. Layton hadn't had a single decent rehearsal in ten days and the most anyone could hope for was that he at least remember his lines. Any actual acting would be a bonus.

With such low expectations Layton didn't disappoint. He walked through the play like a somnambulist. He didn't flub a single line but it was plain to all who bravely sat through it that his heart was elsewhere.

There were no parties that night and the reviews the next morning were less than kind. The *Times* suggested an early closing might be the most respectful tribute to the late playwright's memory. The *Daily News* told their readers that when scanning the entertainment pages for something to see to put a big cross through Layton Cross.

Nonetheless the reviews didn't hurt the box-office that had sold out for the length of the run because of Layton's name. And no one had called for a refund after the panning. Layton didn't bother to read the reviews. When he finally reached Amy on Saturday she said she had seen him being interviewed on *Entertainment Tonight* and thought he came off well.

"Did the kids see me?"

"No, they were already in bed. My mother thought you looked a little pale."

"They talked to me an hour before the show, I felt a little pale."

"So? Did you fuck up?"

"Let's say on a scale of one to ten I did a half."

"It's good that I left then, it could have been a minus."

"I'm saving that for next week."

"If you were really that bad how much worse can it get? You'll find your rhythm, don't worry."

"How are the children?"

"They both say they miss you but they don't act like they do, so I don't know."

"You're so encouraging."

"What do you want me to say, they're crying for daddy? They're not. They've had plenty of practice living without you. They've made some friends, the air is fresh, Leanne almost seems happy."

"Did you tell your mother?"

"Are you crazy?"

"Good. Is she sleeping okay?"

"The nightmares have stopped, yes."

"I miss them."

"You should."

"I don't think I miss you."

"Why should you? I make you miserable."

"Don't give yourself so much credit."

"Planning any more murders lately?"

"Just keep looking over your shoulder when you go out."

"Have you started seeing Lugow yet?"

"I'm saving my money to send you a snake. A king cobra."

"Just make sure you spell my name right. I'm using my single name here."

"You hitting the bars? Leaving the kids with crazy grandma?"

"Crazy grandma happens to love her grandchildren and I wouldn't worry about them. Worry about yourself and who you might hire to do your acting for you."

'It's very easy to hang up, you know."

"Good idea," Amy said, leaving Layton holding a dead phone.

■ ■ ■

By the second week the rest of the cast stopped going out of their way to avoid the star. Layton had actually improved. He was no longer simply enunciating his lines but adding emotions as well. When the *TV Guide* cover story appeared he didn't have to feel embarrassed by the attention. He was more than just a household name. He was an Actor.

Alex Briar's story hinted at Layton's darker side but didn't go into the kind of lurid details that Briar was capable of. The piece had gone to press before the sniper incident and his family's departure but enough was written of his having belted Samantha and Amy having carved up Theo to let the readers know that Hollywood Babylon was alive and kicking. The one thing the article did for sure was guarantee a large TV audience for his ghost story movie.

The critics hated the movie but the publicity surrounding Layton made it the highest rated program of the week, above *Home Improvement, Roseanne*, and *60 Minutes*. Few people who watched it actually liked it but the Nielsens don't poll reactions and television executives don't question the ratings. All four networks were suddenly ready to talk to Layton's agent...but none of them knew whom to call.

"Come on now Layton, it's different now, you're in demand," Perce Dent was saying on the phone.

"It's fleeting Perce, like your hair. Where were you a few months ago when the phones were dead and I was discussed in the past tense?"

"Nobody wanted you months ago. An agent can only negotiate with those who want to deal."

"An agent can help his clients find work."

"Those kind of agents stopped agenting years ago and became managers."

"There's gotta be some out there who are still hungry," Layton said.

"I'm starved," Perce Dent said. "Shall we do lunch?"

"Perce honey, don't go around town saying you represent me because you do not. I want you to refer all calls directly to me. No ten percent into your sweaty palms."

"I beg your pardon. I'm famous for my dry hands."

"Exactly."

"Hey Dad, you looked great on *TV Guide*," Andy said when Layton called.

"Did you see the movie?"

"Yeah, mom let us stay up. It wasn't very scary."

"Did you like it anyway?"

"I liked the part where you were yelling, it reminded me of you and mom."

"You doing okay there partner?"

"Hold on, Leanne wants to talk."

"Hi Daddy."

"Hi sweetheart, how you doing?"

"Fine."

"What did you think of the movie?"

"It was okay. I'm sorry what happened to Farrell Lee."

"What happened?"

"He had a stroke and is in a coma. It was on the radio just now."

Layton paused. Farrell had never made it out of the hospital and now he probably wouldn't. Judith must be a wreck. He'd go there immediately.

She was holding his limp hands; her face blotched from makeup ruined by crying and eyes swollen red. A plastic mask around his nose and mouth pumped pure oxygen to Farrell's brain. His arms were purple from the IV's that had been stuck into them. His face had hollowed since Layton last saw him. No other family members were there. Farrell's oldest son lived in Europe and hadn't spoken with his father in eleven years. His other son had been killed in Vietnam. His daughter by his second wife lived somewhere in Brazil and could not be contacted. When Layton came in Judith stood up and told him to talk to Farrell. Layton sat on the bed and took the old man's hand but said nothing. What could he say? What could Farrell hear?

"If you can understand me squeeze my hand," he finally whispered. Farrell didn't respond. "If you don't want to die in the hospital squeeze my hand." This time he felt faint pressure, not exactly a squeeze but enough to make Layton believe he could understand.

"When did it happen?" he asked Judith.

"Yesterday. I was feeding him his lunch and suddenly his eyes just rolled back. The doctor said it isn't a full stroke but that the next 48 hours are the most critical."

"Has he said anything?"

"Just 'tired.' When he's not sleeping he says that."

"Is he sleeping now?"

"I don't know. He can't open his eyes."

Layton stayed with Judith through the afternoon but had to leave for the theater at dusk. He promised to return after the performance and before midnight he was back with some Chinese take-out for her. The doctors had put a tube into Farrell's nostril down to his stomach so he could be fed. They had a catheter in his penis to remove the liquids. Bowel movements couldn't be helped, when they happened a nurse came in to wipe him clean.

"This isn't what he wanted," Judith said.

"This isn't what anybody wants," Layton responded.

"The doctor said he'd never get much better, that if he came out of it he'd need constant attention; he wouldn't be able to do anything for himself."

"They're not always right."

But sometime that night Farrell suffered a second stroke and when the neurologist came the next morning with the CAT-scan pictures taken over the last three days there was no question of hope remaining. The first set of pictures of Farrell's brain were normal, gray. The second showed the result of the first stroke: a quarter of his brain on the right side was white, where blood had gone. The last picture was obscene: the entire left side of his brain was black from the loss of oxygen. Farrell was definitely going to die...or remain in a vegetative state for as long as he lived.

Layton convinced Judith to go home, take a shower, and get some rest while he stayed with Farrell. He would read to him he said. Judith didn't want to leave but he insisted, just three or four hours. When she left Layton spoke with the neurologist who said there was no chance for any meaningful recovery, half the brain was gone and it couldn't be replenished, but with intravenous feeding, drugs, and careful monitoring it was possible for Farrell to remain alive indefinitely. Eventually he would get bedsores, pneumonia, maybe another stroke. A heart attack wasn't likely because when his heartbeat got too low his pacemaker would kick in. Modern medicine and technology could keep a dead man alive even if it couldn't get him to open his eyes to watch the World Series.

"Why?" Layton asked.

"Because that's our job, to preserve life."

"He may be alive but you can't call that living."

"We don't play God," the doctor said.

Layton remembered the deer he suffocated and thought about horses that are shot if their ankles get broken. After a nurse came in to change Farrell's diaper and wipe him clean Layton stared at his withered face with the dry, parched lips and the heavy breathing. There should be more dignity to dying that this he thought.

When Judith returned Layton left to get some sleep before the night's performance. He stretched out flat on Amy's bed, crossed his feet, and shut his eyes, imagining what it would be like not to be able to open them again, to have a tube in his nose, another up his penis, his hands tied so he couldn't remove them, his lips and mouth desert dry, an annoying itch somewhere he couldn't get to, voices being shouted and whispered which he couldn't decipher. Alone on his back with no one to turn to, no one to help, knowing you won't get any better...or not knowing, not able to think because half your brain has been blown out like a burned-out light bulb. Imprisoned in darkness, tied and tubed, exposed and uncaring, washed and wiped by strange nurses who call you 'Sweetheart.'

The horror was not just that death was approaching but that death might not come fast enough. Knowing all the organs inside your body are working except for the brain. Not being able to take even the simplest pleasures: the smell of your wife's perfume, the taste of chocolate, the sound of a golf ball well hit, the beauty of a line well spoken, the touch of a dog's fur. What's the purpose of sustaining the body if the mind can no longer function? If the senses can't appreciate anything?

Judith, too, had reached the same conclusion and the next day she asked Layton to help her end Farrell's life. Because the hospital had begun their life-sustaining efforts no doctor or nurse could order the feeding and monitoring stopped, but one nurse told Judith that if she pulled out the tube going into his stomach and requested that the intravenous liquids be stopped when the nurse came in to change it, then Farrell would be allowed to starve to death before any insertions were made to feed him directly through his stomach or through his neck. Judith said she couldn't do it herself but asked Layton to pull out the tube from his nose. "It's what he would want," she said.

Without too much hesitation Layton slowly brought the tube out as if he was pulling up an anchor. The nurse came in a few minutes later and removed the needle in Farrell's arm and said she was going to change the liquid. Judith asked her not to and the nurse left the room. Now it was a matter of days but it wouldn't be easy. Even a near brain dead man would suffer from thirst and dehydration.

Over the next three days Farrell's skin got looser, his mouth and tongue drier, his nose cracked and bloody, his hair sticky. A doctor came and pinched his skin and got no reaction, satisfying himself that he was in no pain. On the last day he began to moan and his breathing became hard. His tongue seemed to have begun to peel, it looked as if some dental work had broken in his mouth but it was his tongue, black and shriveled. Judith wiped his mouth with a wet cheesecloth and a part of his brittle lip broke off. His breath was foul with the smell of decay. And then, suddenly, his eyes that had seemed permanently bonded closed opened wide. His body shuddered, his mouth remained opened, and he died. Judith was right there. Layton was behind her. Farrell Lee was finally at rest.

Going against his wishes for a small, private burial Judith spared no expense. It was a funeral in the grand Hollywood tradition of years past. Farrell deserved to go out with a bang, Judith felt. Let the Industry come to a halt for a few hours and pay tribute to a man who devoted his life to enriching the culture of his country. The man's plays and films made millions for his producers and the studios. He saw little of that, never being paid anything near what the stars of today received. He never complained because he was happy to be paid at all for doing what he loved. It was Judith who had to juggle their finances to keep them living in the manner befitting a legendary actor. Now, along with the actors who worked with him and the fans who loved him, she wanted to see the faces of the high and mighty, those who ran the town behind the scenes, whose faces were not immediately recognizable but whose last names were–Wasserman, Sheinberg, Greenbloom, Eisner, Katzenberg, Wells, Tanen, Jaffe, Calley, Canton, Guber, Davis, Diller, Kerkorian, Korshak, Roth, Stark, Zanuck, Ovitz, Meyer, Berg, Brokaw, Baum, Benedek, Feldman, Fields, Geffen, Gallin, Solters, Kingsley. She wanted to be consoled by them all.

Cars were backed up for miles from the entrance to Forest Lawn as attendants removed one sticker and put on another. The Los Angeles police department assigned ten cars to assist in keeping the traffic flowing and to keep away troublemakers. Stars and celebrities by the hundreds had their own security around them. The media was roped off near the front gates, so crammed together that the inevitable shouting of names occurred as people like Robert Mancino, Gregory Peck, Robert Mitchum, Katharine Hepburn, and Samantha Sanders passed through.

Judith had considered Hollywood Memorial, where Lee's old friend and drinking partner John Huston was buried, but thought it was too run-down and decided on Forest Lawn in Burbank because of its convenience to the studios where Farrell Lee did most of his work–Warner Bros., Universal and Disney. It also wasn't too far from Paramount and Raleigh on the Hollywood side, where Lee also found work in the Seventies and Eighties. Forest Lawn had been satirized by the English writer Evelyn Waugh and his *The Loved One* was turned into an equally scathing movie by another English writer, Christopher Isherwood. It was still the preferred place of burial for those whose wishes didn't include heavy marble or granite tombstones or ostentatious mausoleums. The pretentiousness was in the sculptural replicas of Michelangelo's David (with fig leaf) in Burbank or the "world's largest painting" of the life of Christ in Glendale.

Layton thought he would arrive early but found himself stuck between Diane Keaton's ice cream white Range Rover and Elliott Gould's red Honda Accord, two hundred cars from the entrance, slowly inching forward. Judith had asked him to say a few words but he hadn't bothered to prepare because he felt he was best when he was spontaneous. He also felt woefully inadequate as a writer and had no one to ask on such short notice. Sitting in his Jeep he began to fathom the proportion of this tribute. He doubted if there had been such a concentration of Hollywood power in recent memory outside the Academy Awards, Al Pacino's 50th birthday party, and Barbra Streisand's two nights at the MGM Grand in Las Vegas. Judith had asked him to speak because he was the only one who cared about Farrell when he was no longer of use to those who wrote, directed, hired and fired. He was the only one who treated her like a woman and not just a caretaker.

The eleven o'clock services had to be delayed three hours to accommodate everyone. Those who were there on time found themselves looking at their watches and wondering how they'd ever get their cars out before dark. By one it became apparent that any business to be done that day would have to be done on the cemetery grounds. One could only pay respect to the departed for so long. Deals must go on.

When Layton finally saw Judith she was being hugged by Lew Wasserman. Charles Greenbloom was next, then Bruce Willis, who never knew Farrell but once met Judith at one of Demi Moore's parties. Layton stood next to Hugh Hefner waiting to pay his respects. Hefner was wearing a conservative brown suit with a black silk shirt opened at the neck, a blonde at his side.

"Haven't seen you at the Mansion in a while," Hefner said.

"Haven't been invited lately," Layton said.

"We'll have to see to that," Hefner smiled.

"Nice to be back in favor. Have you seen my play yet?"

"No, I'm sorry, we missed it."

"It's still running, I'll put you on the comp list."

"That would be nice," Hefner said politely. He didn't like making social commitments because he rarely left his five-acre estate in Holmby Hills.

"So how's the empire?"

"Still going strong."

"The cable stuff, I've seen some of it, it's kind of soft porn isn't it?"

"We like to think it's tasteful."

"Should be more hard core don't you think? Probably pull a bigger audience showing stiff dicks being sucked in new ways," Layton said.

Hefner was uncomfortable with such talk. In spite of what people might have thought he was really a prudish man with a morality forged out of the Fifties. "This isn't the appropriate place for discussing business," he said abruptly.

"I wasn't talking business," Layton said. "Just chit-chat. I was trying to make you feel comfortable."

When Layton embraced Judith he felt her body press against his in what seemed to be relief. She was exhausted and was glad to see a friend. "Thank you for what you did," she whispered, "and for speaking today. He'd be pleased it was you."

Layton doubted that. It should have been one of his cronies. Peck, Richard Harris, George Burns, Walter Matthau, Hepburn. They would have prepared for such an event, would have memorized their lines. CNN would have sent their eulogies around the world, touching the hearts of millions. But they hadn't been asked. The limelight was Layton's. All because he had the audacity to squeeze Judith's breast while her husband was still alive and pull out his feeding tube to speed his demise.

"Layton, I heard you were speaking," Harry Sales, the Century City flower vendor said. He had done a beautiful job arranging all the flowers that had been sent.

"You take gigs where you find them," Layton joked. "How's business, Harry?"

"Look around you. Wait until you go inside, it smells better than Kauai."

"Been to the play yet?"

"Caught it last week. I figure it's better now."

"I'm not very good am I?"

"Williams takes years."

"Were you embarrassed?"

"Hey, it wasn't me up there. You need guts to do that. You should be proud."

"It's better this week."

"I don't doubt it."

"Why don't you come again, I'll leave a pair of tickets for you."

"What are you two hams conspiring about?" Sol Gordon interrupted. He had seen Layton with Judith and waited for a more appropriate moment to catch him.

"Sol, you know Harry Sales? Used to be a terrific actor until he decided he couldn't afford lawyers."

"Of course I remember Harry. Flower business. This your work here? Smells like paradise."

"Sol represents Samantha," Layton said. "I have a feeling he's coming to take my wallet."

"On the contrary, I've come to tell you you can keep it. She's changed her mind."

Leanne was right. Gordon was making it official. "Good news comes in strange places," Layton said.

"She thinks you've suffered enough. Is it true Amy took the kids?"

"Just a vacation, they'll be back."

"Glad to hear it," Gordon said and walked on.

"What was that about?" Harry Sales asked.

"She gave me a free punch. I better go thank her. Samantha's not big on freebies."

Layton found Samantha inside, sitting quietly next to Charlie Greenbloom, waiting for the service to begin. She looked beautiful, dressed in dark blue, a wide-brimmed hat partially concealing her face. He kneeled near her. "I don't know what you told Leanne," he whispered, "but whatever it was, it helped."

"I told her my father raped me when I was her age," Samantha said softly. She was a master of compression, creating tidal waves or tremblers with a few chosen words.

"I never knew that," Layton said, genuinely surprised. "Is it true?"

"Does it matter?"

"You mean you told her what you thought she needed to hear?" Layton was just trying to regain his balance.

"I didn't say that." Samantha kept him teetering.

Layton didn't press. Whether it was true or not really didn't matter for Leanne's sake; but it would explain so much about Samantha. He'd have to replay their entire relationship with that in mind. Greenbloom slightly nodded his way as he stood. He still had the missing cop and sniper on his mind but didn't like bringing up assassination attempts at funerals.

When the time came for Layton to speak he thought of Farrell's final tortuous days starving in this land of plenty. "Work" was his message. Let others fuck around. Actors should work. He stood before the most powerful captive audience in the entertainment business and began to ad-lib what he thought Farrell Lee, twice his age, might appreciate. He was only off by all that he would say.

"Farrell Lee—King of Players—was a tough, no-nonsense, rugged son of a bitch," Layton began, adjusting the microphone when it hummed. All talking had ceased on the word "bitch" and he had their full attention. "He was a worker who took pride in his profession. Each of us has died a little with his passing for he was a small part of us all. Who among us hasn't been touched in some way by Farrell Lee's performances? He showed us what it was like to be a hero, to stand up against adversity and ignorance and prejudice. He faced down evil in all its forms—whether staring down the barrel of a gun or saving the world from tyranny and oppression. He showed us what truth and courage and goodness were. And the few times he played the bad guy he played it so convincingly that he showed us that as well.

"As he got older he appeared on the screen less and on the stage more. There was a reason for that. On the stage he could get back to his roots, he could dig deeper into a character. And there were more offers to do plays. The studios didn't call as often–there aren't as many parts for aging actors–even when the name was Farrell Lee. Like women over 45, old actors aren't in demand for the action-adventure sci-fi robo-techno special-effects rock-'em/sock-'em big budget go-for-the-blockbuster films of today.

"We're all here now, a big happy family, paying last respects. But where were you last year? Or two years before when Farrell was waiting for the phone to ring; for the scripts to arrive?

"We honor our dead because they are dead, but it was when he was alive when you should have honored him. With parts. He played old men the same way he did young men when he was younger: with dignity, integrity, truth. He had the gift to hold a mirror to his age. But like Lear, he was not exactly welcomed in any of your houses. He was respected, yes. Awarded, certainly. And forgotten–to all of our misfortunes.

"So when the Sand Man came knocking for the last time Farrell Lee heard the footsteps, he knew it was the final scene. The curtain was ready to fall...and that's what our being here today is all about. We are his standing ovation. Because there are no encores, no fourth act. And Farrell wasn't about to hang on as a prop, attached to some life-extension machine. His brave wife Judith made sure of that.

"So...we're here to pay tribute...and to get out of the parking lot before the sun sets. If there is justice in Heaven then a new star was born when Farrell Lee died. A star who also burned long and brightly when he was here on earth. Remember him well–we truly won't see the likes of him again."

A priest led the congregation outside where Lee was laid to rest. Layton stood back, watching everyone as the coffin was automatically lowered. He congratulated himself on a pretty good extemporaneous speech. But no one else did. For Layton spoke fiction, not facts. He eulogized his own failing career more than the man they had come to bury. Farrell Lee had never waited for the phone to ring–it was constantly ringing. He turned down more parts in the last years of his life than he had played all together. He was never a Lear outcast but a sought-after and welcomed guest wherever he went, including the executive suites of the major and independent studios. Farrell Lee had never been forgotten. Layton Cross had spoken at the wrong funeral.

10

Target Practice

Two weeks after the funeral Layton found himself in Farrell Lee's king size bed trying to console his widow as she screamed deliriously, "Fuck me, pleeeease fuuuuck meeee!"

Farrell may have been a great actor but it took more than acting to get Judith Lee to come. Her body shivered when Layton touched her, her back arched when he mounted her, her nails scratched his flesh, her lips smothered his face, her ass bounced and liquid dripped from her in anticipation. Layton hadn't been with a woman this much in need since he was nineteen and went to the apartment of a sales girl from the men's department at Macy's in Astoria. The girl had false upper teeth that she removed before going down on him and a glass eye that popped out during her orgasm. She loved sex and picked up strangers because no one ever returned. The gummy blowjob was an incredible turn-on but that eye bit was too much. Layton thought he had fucked her so hard her real eye had popped out.

Judith Lee was eager, aggressive, and hungry for sex. It had been a long time and she had dreamed about making it with Layton since the kiss in her car. She had fantasies about the size of his organ. She imagined doing it in the shower, in the garden, in the hallway leading to the bedroom. After the funeral she waited two long weeks, an eternity, before calling to invite him for dinner. She knew Amy and the kids were gone and he was probably lonely too.

The dinner went uneaten. Judith was so anxious she over-excited Layton from the start. He almost came in her mouth but managed to pull her away so he could go down on her and compose himself. That's when she started screaming. No one had ever said please before. Please. Please. Pleeeeease ease my pain.

Layton did the best he could, getting his hand covered with discharge before she pulled it away, grabbing his cock.

"Pleeeease fuck meee!"

Her pelvis rose to meet his as he thrust in once, twice, oh God, he wanted to hold on but he couldn't. "I'm sorry," he said, feeling drained.

"We'll do it again," she huffed.

Layton didn't know he had it in him but Judith brought it out. It was work keeping him hard, especially the third time. And when he left the next morning she gave him a present: a pearl handled derringer that Duke Wayne had given to her husband after they had worked together. It was inscribed: "From a not-so-tough guy to a real one."

"I can't take this," Layton protested, the small gun no bigger than a flower in his palm.

"Of course you can," Judith insisted. "It was one of Farrell's prized possessions."

"You never know when you might need something like this."

"I've got a real gun, that thing's just a toy; it can only fire one bullet. Please, put it in your pocket and don't say another word. Let it remind you of last night."

"Then you'd better give me the revolver."

"That shoots six times. You're only halfway."

■ ■ ■

He drove that morning to Pasadena, near the Huntington Library, to visit with the author of *Mr Sand Man*. She was an old black woman named Abby Sigmund who had lived in Southern California for over seventy years. *Mr Sand Man* was the story of her childhood and was the most popular of her nineteen books for young people.

Layton felt her strength the moment they met. When he made an attempt at explaining the movie business she cut him short with a laugh that rumbled deep in her chest.

"I know all about the movie business," she said. "It's a bullshit business. My husband was an assistant director for more than twenty years, worked up from the editing room but never any higher if you know what I mean. He did the work and never got the credit. Pour soul met his Maker unrecognized by the people in your business who sent him there, Mr Cross. He was bitter the last years but I never was because I always knew what kind of business he was in. Not a pretty business. Too much money to expect that. Look at you, coming here to talk to me about making a picture out of *Mr Sand Man*. Why, there's nothing there for you other than the Man himself and that's a small part. It's a story about a young girl but it won't be when Hollywood gets done with it. It'll be something completely different, but that's okay, just as long as you keep me out of it. To me it's nothin' but found money and I'm grateful, thank you very much. But don't go worrying yourself about keeping faithful to my book because you and I, we both know that's not going to be."

"Have you ever seen any of my films?" Layton wondered.

"All of them. When my husband was alive I never missed a picture made in this town. I still get invitations to all the screenings. You used to be a good actor, then something must have troubled you deeply because you lost your confidence and it showed. Up there on that screen everything shows. Can't hide when your nose is as big as a baby's head. And once you started to lose it they didn't let you forget, did they? Just look at some of those pictures you made. And then that TV thing—now a man of your former talents shouldn't have to be wasting his time doing such shinola on television. But a man's gotta eat, I know that. You also gotta get back in shape; find the confidence to make the magic up there on the screen. May already be too late, they don't like to give second chances in your business. But you've been so much in the news of late maybe you got a fist around their balls and you don't know it."

Layton just sat and listened. He thought of asking her to manage him but let it pass. She was probably in her eighties. He wondered if she read palms.

Before leaving she gave him copies of some of her other books plus a watercolor she had done of her street. It was a fabulous picture. "What can I give you in return?" he asked.

"You make a good picture and we'll call it even," Abby Sigmund said.

On the drive back Layton pondered when it was he began losing his confidence. Probably around the time Samantha left. But did she leave because he had already lost it or was her leaving the cause? Were the drugs he started taking then an attempt to regain his confidence or to help him self-destruct? This little old lady from Pasadena was a far cry from the old ladies he knew, like his mother, Samantha's, and Amy's.

Whatever he thought of Amy's mother it wasn't enough. Dolly Hinton was a woman Abby Sigmund would have trouble imagining—and from appearances Abby Sigmund had no trouble imagining. Dolly painted life with sweeping brush strokes. Her friends included derelicts, dope dealers, carnival people and local politicians. Her enemy was the Internal Revenue Service, which she refused to acknowledge. The only reason she wasn't serving time in jail for nonpayment of her taxes was because her friends sent all IRS correspondence to Amy in California who took care of things on the sly. Dolly fully believed she had fought the IRS to a standstill.

She also believed–and with good reason–that she led a charmed life and could get away with anything. To Dolly there was no such word as illegal. If she had a need there was always a means to fulfill it. At different times in her life a house, car, money in the bank were all needs. When her husband died under mysterious circumstances the insurance paid for their heavily indebted home. The car was a present from her lover, who had to hightail it out of Michigan hidden in its trunk as Dolly deposited the dope in Calgary, Canada. Amy and the kids arrived in the middle of her money scheme and Leanne and Andy were soon put to work kneading the hard black bricks of hashish into soft flat rectangles the size of a loose leaf page. These pages where put in plastic and sold three-to-a-binder for twenty to fifty times what she paid when she brought the bricks back from Nepal. Her friends had warned her of the improbabilities of getting such a score past U.S. Customs but Dolly never worried about it. She was a practitioner of positive thinking. She was also in partnership with one of her best friend's son who was a customs agent. Going to Nepal was his idea. Splitting it 70-30 was Dolly's.

Layton always suspected his mother-in-law of being crazy. Andy thought she was a neat old lady who didn't act like a grandma. Leanne wondered what Dr Lugow would think of her. Amy never got along with her mother but that was because they were so much alike.

She didn't mind her kids softening the hashish, which they were told was black clay, but she resented her mother insisting she pay for samples.

"This is a business, dearie. Can't have you smoking up the profits now can I?" her mother said the first time Amy pinched a pipeful.

"You've got enough of this shit to finance a movie," Amy retorted. "A fingernail's worth isn't going to be missed, let alone send you into the red."

"But I do notice, Amy my darling. And before long fingernails add up to fingers, then hands, feet...in a month's time you'll smoke your body's worth. I know you sweetheart, you're my daughter."

"You're such a selfish bitch," Amy rasped.

"Not in front of the children now," Dolly hushed.

"The children are sleeping."

"You only think so. They're probably listening through the wall."

"My children are not snoops."

"You used to do it all the time when you were a child."

"How would you know?"

"That naive side of you–it's from your father. He was such a simple soul."

"Is that why you did him in?"

"Nonsense, what are you talking about? The poor man drowned in the lake, you know that."

"After you poisoned him."

"That's ridiculous, why would I ever do such a thing?"

"Because he was worth more to you dead than alive."

"You have a very strange imagination for a Hinton. It must be living in Hollywood."

"I live in Los Angeles."

"It's all Hollywood my dear. That's why you've come back, this is the real world."

"Dealing dope is the real world? What do you think they do in Hollywood?"

"Why, I thought they made movies."

"Do you have any idea how impossible you are?"

"Please darling, don't upset yourself thinking about me. You're the one with family problems. I'm glad to have a room for you."

■ ■ ■

Alex Briar was waiting for Layton when he arrived home. He had come to tell of the book offer he received based on the *TV Guide* piece. A publisher in New York was interested in doing a quick biography of Layton Cross.

"Not interested," Layton said.

"They are, authorized or unauthorized."

"Hardback?"

"Paper."

"Fuck that, I'm worth more."

"I agree," Briar said. "If you work with me on it I'm sure I can get a hardback deal."

"I'm not old enough for a book," Layton said. "Wait fifteen years, then we'll see."

"It's an offer I'm not ready to pass up."

"Good, then call me in fifteen."

"I mean the paperback. There are lots of them out now; they're like extended magazine articles."

"Is that what you want to be, a schlockmeister?"

"It's possible to do a good book."

"You're becoming a pain in the ass, you know that? First it's a piece for *The Star*, then *TV Guide*, now a book. I don't like other people making their living off my life. Go find a life of your own to live off of."

"I'm a journalist," Briar said. "I write about people. No one's interested in my life."

"Because you don't have a life. You're like a carrion bird. I'm not dead yet."

"A biography keeps you alive."

"My pictures do that for me."

"This is another medium. How can it hurt you?"

"I'm sure you'll find a way." He tried to recall something Alec Baldwin had said in *Movieline*, that most celebrity journalists were really fifth-rate sideline observer dick-in-their-hands scumbags whose lives were not really happening for them, their lives were about other people's lives and that made them bitter. Baldwin was right. Guys like Alex Briar were just sideline observers. But no more so than actors who weren't being bad-mouthed by Disney, replaced by Harrison Ford, hosting *Saturday Night Live*.

The difference was Briar never gave it much thought, whereas it was all Layton thought about.

"Seriously," Briar said, "I'm not a bad writer; you've seen my work. I'll do a good job whether you agree to it or not. But I'll do a better one if you're cooperative."

"Forget it."

"Don't authorize it then, just deal with me off the record. Point me in directions, I'll do the rest."

Layton put his hand in his jacket pocket and fingered the derringer Judith Lee had given him as they stood in the living room getting nowhere. Layton took out the small gun and looked at it.

"This was Farrell Lee's," he said. "John Wayne gave it to him."

"What has that to do with the price of bananas or your agreeing to cooperate with me?"

Layton pointed the gun at Briar. "You asked me to point you in the right direction. This is the right direction."

"Very funny," Briar said as Layton moved his hand up and down, the tiny barrel pointing at the writer's heart, stomach, crotch, thigh.

"How does it feel to be a target?" Layton asked. "To have the tables reversed?"

"Like shit," Briar said.

"Isn't this what you're always doing? Using people like me as target practice?"

"We build your myths."

"Well now, that's pretty high and mighty. You build so you can then destroy, isn't that the way it goes?" Layton liked the way the gun felt in his palm. His index finger barely fit on the trigger.

"Put it away," Briar said. "It could be loaded."

"Could be," Layton agreed, enjoying himself. Playing the role of trashed movie star getting his revenge. "Then again, maybe it isn't. What do you think?"

"I think you've made your point."

"Which is?"

"No authorization, no cooperation."

"And the book?"

"That's not your choice to make."

"My life, my choice. And I choose no."

"You're a movie star," Briar said. "You're public domain."

"That's not what this discussion is about. That's not what this little gun is about."

"Are you threatening me?"

"No book. Now, repeat after me: No...book."

"I'm not going to say that."

Layton's finger felt the trigger. He wondered how sensitive it was. He knew the gun wasn't loaded so he didn't want to pull the trigger and hear the empty click. He wanted to win this one in a showdown. Providing Alex Briar was an honorable man.

"I'm going to count to five," Layton said. "That's ample time to change your mind."

"You're being ridiculous. I'll say whatever you want me to say but it doesn't mean I mean it."

"One."

Briar looked straight into Layton's eyes. Layton had become a goddamn cowboy.

"Two."

Briar also didn't believe the gun was loaded. But he knew Layton was unpredictable.

"Three."

"All right, no fucking book."

"How good is your word?"

"You'll only know that a few months from now when you don't see your name on the best-selling paperback lists."

"Oh, it was a best-seller you were going to write, was it?"

"I think we had a shot."

"Well you wisely sacrificed it instead of being shot," Layton said, accidentally squeezing the trigger as he moved his hand down, sending a small bullet into Alex Briar's thigh.

"Jesus Christ!" Briar exclaimed. "You bastard!"

"Sonuvabitch," Layton said, stunned. "Fucking thing was loaded."

Briar fell to the floor holding his leg. "You shot me!"

"It was an accident."

"Like hell it was."

"Why would I shoot you after you agreed? Don't be stupid."

"You're the one who's stupid. This is going to cost you."

Just what he needed. Finally got Samantha off his back, now this. A lawsuit he could never win. Publicity that would do him no good. Further reason for Amy to keep the children from him. An increased reputation for being unpredictable–and uninsurable–among the studios.

"What do you want?" Layton asked, ready to deal.

"I'm not going to negotiate with you now. You must be really crazy."

"I'll give you the book."

"Authorized?"

"You're bleeding a lot."

"If I'm crippled I'm going to sue."

"Fair enough. Otherwise...?"

"Your authorization...and no compensation."

"I'll cooperate...that's as far as I'll go. No authorization."

"I need a doctor."

"Deal?" Layton asked.

"Deal."

Layton went to the desk and got a piece of paper. He wrote a few words and brought it to Briar who was holding his leg as blood poured from the wound.

"What's this?"

"Just an agreement. You won't sue if I don't stop you from writing a book about me."

"Give me the pen," Briar groaned.

Layton handed him an unsharpened pencil. "Use your blood," he said.

"What?"

"Dip it in your blood and sign."

"Come off it."

"Do it already so I can get you to a doctor before you pass out."

Briar scratched out his name in blood.

"Oh, one more thing," Layton added.

"Now what?"

"You can't write about this."

"Don't worry," Briar said. "No one would believe it."

It took two weeks before the cleaners finished with the small kilim that he had bought in Marmaris, Turkey years ago, when he and Samantha took the boat over from Rhodes. Alex Briar's blood had nicely blended in with the wine and red colors but evidence of the stain remained in the yellows and blues.

The same day he picked up the kilim Alice Wonders' first draft of *The Sand Man* arrived by messenger with a note from Arno. "Showed this to a few friends in the business," it said, "and they think we're onto something here. Levine loves it. Let me know what you think."

Layton moved the rocking chair outside and for the next two hours he sat and read on the patio. It was always a good idea to read a script in one sitting, visualizing as much as possible. Layton knew he was in for a rough read as soon as he opened to the title page and saw that Wonders had written: "Loosely based on the book *Mr Sand Man* by Abby Sigmund."

Just how loose became apparent on the very first page where Barry Levine's character was introduced. There was no "teenage delinquent who favored multicolored spiked hair and two sparkling earrings in his left ear" in the book. Nor were there any scenes of vandalism, shoplifting and general mayhem which lands this destructive punk in the county jail where he shares a cell with Lug Wallers, "a brooding hulk of a man who has spent more of his adult years in the can than out" and who was "the very persona of the hardened hood who left his conscience with his lost youth," "a man who was known by his fellow criminals as 'The Sand Man' because of his stature as a cold-blooded, merciless killer-for-hire who never lost a night's sleep after putting out the lights of those whom Fate had dealt a cruel contract against."

Lug Wallers made his appearance on page 25, near the end of the first half hour of this proposed film. Five pages later, approximately the end of the first act where tension and conflict should meet to propel the viewer on to the heart of the film, Lug Wallers gives Spiked Hairdo a lesson in twisted values, detailing some of his proudest hits, including his own brother who was singled out by his angry and vindictive partners after a bad business decision caused them to go bankrupt. Lug Wallers was the black sheep of his family and hardly knew his ten years younger brother or his family, so wiping him out had no more effect on him than any other assignment. But it definitely had an effect on Spiked Hairdo, whose eyes widened in horror and disbelief as he listened to Lug–for the man this "Sand Man" had eliminated was none other than Spiked Hairdo's father. Lug Wallers, the hired killer who shared his jail cell, was the punk's uncle!

Well, Layton thought as he read in disbelief, *Citizen Kane* this isn't.

It got worse. Spiked Hairdo cons Lug Wallers into telling him about each of his victims. When he's released from jail he changes his ways. Lets his hair return to its natural color and shape. Removes the jewelry from his ear. Becomes a new person—a young man with a mission: to do what he can to help the families of his bad uncle's victims. Lug Wallers—Layton's role—never appears again in the rest of the script but Barry Levine's reformed teenager is on every page as he anonymously good deeds his way towards redemption.

It wasn't a script one could take seriously. How could that nice, ambitious Alice Wonders, who "loved" and "understood" the book, who had visions of a modern-day *Wizard of Oz* dancing about in her head, create something so ludicrous and one-dimensional as this?

When Arno called later that afternoon Layton gave him credit as a practical joker, a quality he hadn't seen in this wanna-be producer.

"What do you mean?" Arno asked. "It's got some flaws, sure. You gotta have more pages, I know that. We'll straighten that out in the rewrite. Give you and the kid a scene at the end. But the potential's there, you can see that can't you?"

"Potential for what?" Layton snorted. "For making some future list as one of the most embarrassing films ever made? You've got to be joking Arno. This thing is more than just bad. It lacks even a glimpse, a hint, a paragraph of intelligence. The mind that conceived this left the body that actually typed it and stayed in Acapulco for the duration. You didn't actually pay that demented girl for this, did you?"

"You're way off here Layton. I'm not expert about such things but I've given it to some very established people—people who have made some pretty high-grossing pictures—and they don't agree with what you're saying. Read it again."

"I can only put so much shit inside my head before it starts leaking out my ears. This script has filled my personal quotient for about a month."

"You trying to tell me you don't want to do this picture?"

"Not trying Arno. There is no picture here to do."

"I'll give it to some more people," Arno assented. "But let me tell you something—if they agree with the others we're going ahead with it. And you're going to be there when we do. Your signature is on the contract."

"Give it to some intelligent readers. Producers don't read. Try a few directors."

"I already have. Two of them want to make this picture."

■ ■ ■

Layton had forgotten it was his birthday until Amy and the kids called to sing to him and Andy asked him how old he was.

"Five years away from being halfway to a hundred."

"Is that a joke?" Andy asked.

"No, it's a math problem. Figure it out."

"You're forty-five."

"Hey–not bad."

"Mom told me."

"Oh."

"I know a joke. Look up. Are you looking up Dad?"

"Right at the ceiling."

"Look down."

"I'm staring at the floor."

"Look at your thumb."

"Gotcha."

"You're dumb." He cracked up long distance.

"That's hysterical," Layton said dryly. "Is that what you're learning in Michigan?"

"Nah, I knew that one before we moved. I just forgot to tell you."

"Where does a nine-hundred pound gorilla sleep?" Layton asked him.

"Anywhere he wants to," Andy answered.

"How'd you know that?"

"You told me that one."

Amy got on the phone. "Did you get my card?"

"Not yet."

"Your present's inside."

"I'll look for it. When you coming back?"

"Not for a while. I like it here."

"Bullshit."

"It's the lack of that which I'm happy to be away from."
"Are you fucking around?"
"Are you?"
"I asked first."
"That's a guilt question Layt."
"Why is it I can never get a straight answer out of you?"
"Because you always ask the wrong questions."
"I take it you are then."
"No, you are. Don't shift your bad karma onto me, we're not married, remember?"
"How's Leanne?"
"Fine."
"What does fine mean?"
"She's got some friends, she goes out, she doesn't seem to be depressed."
"Where does she go?"
"How do I know? Want me to hire a detective to watch her?"
"What do you mean you don't know where she goes. She's ten years old."
"She goes with her friends to the mall. She sees movies. Roller skates. Eats ice cream."
"You don't go with her?"
"Not all the time, no. But there's always a mother around, don't worry."
"I worry."
"So worry."
"What are you doing there that you like so much?"
"It's not being here so much as it's not being there."

"This is your home."

"Not necessarily."

"What does that mean?"

"Just what I said."

"What about your work?"

"I'm being covered. I've never been that much in demand."

"I'm not having a very happy birthday."

"So do something that makes you happy."

"Like what?"

"Go to a massage parlor."

"I want happiness not gonorrhea."

"Take a rubber with you."

"You are fucking around, aren't you?"

"Layton?"

"What?"

"Does it really matter?"

Amy's card was the only mail. Inside she had taped a two-inch square of black hash. He dug out a small piece with his nail and smoked it. Then he called Judith Lee and invited her for dinner. When she arrived he ordered a large pizza with everything on it from Raffallo's on La Brea. "It'll be here in half an hour," he told her.

"That gives us time for a quick hors d'oeuvre," she said.

They went into the bedroom and he told her it was his birthday. She gave him a ten minute blowjob as a present.

During their pizza Samantha and Mark stopped by unexpectedly. Mark had bought him a present and had convinced his mother to drive him instead of sending the driver. Even though she'd never admit it Samantha was still a very curious person and it gave her some perverse pleasure to see how much better off she was than her former husband.

"Is it Halloween already?" Layton asked when he saw the gold BB in Mark's earlobe.

"Just an earring," Mark blushed. "A lot of guys have them."

"I see we're interrupting something," Samantha said.

"Not at all, sit down, have a slice."

"You know I don't like salami on pizza."

"That's right," Layton remembered. "How about a Coke?"

"How have things been for you?" Samantha asked Judith.

"Rough. Now that Farrell's gone people don't call as often. Layton's been a friend."

"I'm sure he has. I hear you're doing a movie," she said to him.

"The script's awful. How about you?"

"I signed to do that film with Mancino. I'm not crazy about the script either but there's something there."

"Ever wonder why there aren't as many good scripts as there are books?"

"Since when did you start reading books?" Samantha asked.

Catch a Fallen Star

"I don't read them, I smoke them."

"I thought I smelled something."

Judith Lee asked if anyone wanted coffee. Mark said he did. Samantha suggested they'd better go but Mark lingered.

"Dad, can I talk to you?"

Layton saw something different about his son, beside the earring; he had a look of suppressed pride and confusion. He knew Mark didn't want to talk in front of the women. "Why don't you leave him? I'll bring him back later."

"It's already late," Samantha protested.

"Just because the sun went down doesn't mean he can't be out."

"You want to stay?"

"Yeah," Mark said.

"You've got secrets?"

"Just man talk."

"Man talk? What's man talk? Who screwed who in the school parking lot?"

"C'mon Mom."

"Crude, Sam," Layton said.

"She staying?" Samantha asked.

"Up to her. You can stay too."

"I don't want to. Have him home before eleven."

"Thanks Ma."

"Nice seeing you," she said to Judith, who was making herself busy with the coffee.

"It's nice that we're both working at the same time," Layton said.

"If there were only some fucking writers in this town," Samantha asserted. She wished him a happy birthday and was gone.

Judith brought the coffee. It was obvious there'd be no more romping with Mark there so she too took her leave with Layton's promise to call the next day.

"I heard from Andy and Leanne today," Layton said once they were alone.

"Oh yeah? How they doing?"

"I couldn't tell."

"Why'd they leave?"

"I don't know."

"When they coming back?"

"You got me."

"You like living alone?"

"It's got its points."

"Don't you get lonely?"

"What do you know about that?"

"What's there to know?"

"You don't look like you're lonely."

"Dad?"

""""

"What I want to talk to you about is..."

""""

"Well, in a way mom was right."

"In the parking lot?"

"No, it was my room."

"First time?"

"Yeah."

"That accounts for the earring, huh? Congratulations."
"Thanks."
"So?"
"Well."
"How was it?"
"I'm not sure."
"All over before you knew it?"
"Sort of."
"That's the way it is the first time."
"I thought..."
"...it would be different. It will. Takes practice."
"It was pretty messy."
"A virgin?"
"I guess so."
"Blood on the sheets?"
"Is that normal?"
"Did she cry?"
"Only after. I didn't think I hurt her. It just...happened."
"Going to do it again?"
"I guess."
"You don't sound enthusiastic."
"Does it really get better?"
"Can it get much worse?"
"I don't know."
"That bad huh?"
"It's just...I thought it was something special. I thought I'd feel different. I mean, I do, in a way. But not..."
"She a nice girl?"
"She's in my class. Reya–you saw her picture."

"Did you use anything?"

"I...she said...no."

"And she, of course, isn't on the pill."

"It just happened. We didn't know we were going to do that."

"These things take some planning," Layton said.

"How can you plan something like that?"

"From now on, you'll see."

"What's going to happen?"

"Probably nothing. You could get AIDS if she's been with anyone else. She could get pregnant."

"We talked about it."

"And?"

"She started crying."

"Girls have more at stake."

"What if she does?"

"Then you've got a problem."

"Do I have to marry her?"

"Do you want to?"

"I don't think so. I mean, I'm still in high school."

"Tell that to what's dangling between your legs."

"Can't she have an abortion?"

"Let's not worry about that for another month, okay?"

"She said her parents would kill her if they found out."

"Understandable."

"You mean it?"

"Here," Layton said, carving another fingernail of hash from the square. "Let's smoke some of this."

Mark inhaled the first bowl, coughing out most of what he took in. Layton took a few short puffs. Mark watched and followed. Then they went into the backyard and sat in lounge chairs.

"Feels pretty good," Layton said.

"Is this hash?"

"I mean to get laid."

"Yeah," Mark said.

"It does get better you know."

"How?"

"After you get over the excitement of actually being able to do it you'll start thinking about how you can keep it going for more than a few seconds."

"How do you?"

"Think of Reya's parents."

"What?"

"While you're doing it think of what would happen if her father walked in on you."

"I don't understand."

"It'll cool you down a bit. Could make you lose it altogether but at your age I doubt it. Making love is a matter of balance. If you think about what you're doing it can become a blur, you come and it's over and Reya wonders what happened. So if you feel that starting to happen, think about things that don't excite you. Give yourself that balance."

"How long can you do that for?"

"At your age? You're lucky to get a minute."

Mark giggled. The hash was strong and had gone to his head. He forgot about the pregnant part of the experience and just remembered how incredible it was when Reya took off her clothes and he saw her naked body.

Layton too was lost in thought. Only he was thinking about Leanne and how different it was talking about sex with her. Sons and daughters. With Mark, it was technique and protection. With Leanne, it was love and caution. He remembered his own first time and how scared and wonderful he felt. Now he was balling a dead actor's widow while the mothers of his children wanted nothing to do with him. He was surely no authority on the matter but he knew that before he drove Mark home he'd stop at Thrifty's and buy him a box of condoms. It was the least a father could do.

* * *

Alice Wonders' second draft, like her first, arrived too soon. She couldn't have done much rewriting, Layton figured. Arno's note indicated they were going ahead as scheduled and Layton was expected on the set in four to six weeks. That allowed very little time for preproduction; only a six-week shoot...it was being shot as if it was television. On the same Quickstart lot, no less, as Samantha's picture.

Layton was glad about that because with Mancino and Sanders getting together for the first time the media focus would all be on them, leaving Layton and *The Sand Man* mercifully unnoticed.

He didn't bother to read the script. He was being paid, it would be humiliating, but it would die a sudden death, like *Shakes the Clown* and *Going Crazy*, disappearing into the oblivion that pictures such as these deserved.

On the other hand, if Charlie Greenbloom bought the concept of *The Sand Man* then it stood to reason that he'd get behind the results. Layton was surprised that Arno and Macky were able to strike a deal at Quickstart, especially when Samantha's picture was there. But since both happened virtually overnight it seemed more of a coincidence than anything pre-scheduled. Layton was aware that Greenbloom was unhappy and frustrated over his inability to find out what happened to the sniper at Samantha's but he had also heard from Mark that Greenbloom was impressed with Layton's taking a swing at the guy, even if it was after Samantha had shot him and Mancino had brought him down.

To give Greenbloom credit, he figured that by getting into bed with Arno and Macky Greenbloom could control the project and, very directly, Layton's fate. If Samantha wanted to crush Layton then Greenbloom could bury the film and put out a press release that Layton Cross just couldn't cut it any more. If Layton didn't want to come through with more details about what had happened then Greenbloom could hold the picture over his head like a big club. In any event, Greenbloom agreed to the deal with the condition that Layton's role be supporting only.

He also wasn't putting up any studio money—Quickstart would sell Arno and Macky studio facilities and would distribute the film. The novice producers thought they got a good deal because it gave them instant credibility and, even though they weren't as protected as they thought, they weren't too worried about Charles Greenbloom fucking them over since they supplied him with the purest cocaine in Hollywood. That, ultimately, was how this deal went down. Layton Cross as Sand Man Lug Wallers was purely incidental.

When Barry Levine called and asked if they could get together Layton didn't see the point. "What's to talk about?"

"It's my first picture. We're in it together."

"I'm not in this picture," Layton said.

"What do you mean? Sure you are."

"This is your picture. I'm just a prop. Actors don't talk to props, they use them."

"Hey you're more than a prop. Jesus, you're Lug Wallers, the Sand Man. The straw that stirs the drink."

"Spare me please," Layton said, wincing at the unintentional allusion to Hall of Famer Reggie Jackson who, like himself, had kept swinging past his prime.

"I could use some pointers," Levine suggested.

"Don't worry, with this film there'll be nothing to point at."

"I've got a lot of ideas about your character I'd like to share with you."

"My character? Is that what Lug is? Could have fooled me."

"Listen, it's a picture, isn't it?"

"I can feel that golden statue firmly in my hand. Nicholson got one for *Terms of Endearment*, I'll have mine for this. I've got no problem."

"Okay, fine. Just don't fuck with my mind when the cameras are rolling," Levine said.

"To do that there's got to be a mind there to fuck with."

"You think an idiot could have landed the part I've got? Let's not start with whose mind got fucked."

Levine had a point. The kid had come from nowhere, convinced Layton to make this picture, then proceeded to steal it before there was even a director chosen to signal 'Action.'

"You really believe this is what it's all about, don't you?" Layton asked. "You're in the big time now. Made it in Hollywood. Your picture on the cover of *Sassy* magazine."

"No more kissing ass," Levine added.

"You've only just begun. What you've got to watch out for is getting your tongue stuck up some producer's asshole."

"As long as it's a she," Levine laughed.

"Shit tastes the same regardless of gender."

"Then I'll be careful not to step in any."

"It's not stepping you've got to be concerned with. It's swallowing."

"Are you talking now from experience? Or wishful thinking?"

Give the child a part and watch his balls turn brazen.

"I'll see you in jail," Layton said.

"That's a couple of weeks away. Shouldn't we oughta...?"

"Best we keep an edge." The kid was beginning to depress him.

11

If His Name Was De Niro

When the time came for Layton to go before the cameras he left strict instructions that neither Arno nor Macky could be on the set. Both men found this unreasonable but the director, a former martial arts instructor who once taught Elvis Presley how to finger tap dance off his opponent's eyelids, was able to act as peacemaker: the producers could be there, but must remain out of Layton's sight.

Barry Levine's acting was so far over the top the cinematographer could barely keep him in frame. His enthusiasm, though, never faltered. He even got off on the interminable waiting between shots as cameras and lighting positions changed. For Layton the excitement of making a movie existed only in his memory. In his dressing room, waiting to be called, he smoked the hash Amy had sent and watched soap operas on the two-inch Sony Watchman Judith Lee had given him. Although the movie would be shooting for six weeks he only had a week's work. A hundred thousand dollars was more than decent wages for a week. But was it worth the humiliation of appearing in a picture such as this?

If his name was De Niro perhaps not. And Brando had no problems as Superman's father Jor-El. Pay him enough money even he'd be Lug Wallers. What a business.

The first time Levine and Layton had a scene together Layton affected a heavy southern drawl. Levine could hardly make out the words. And the slowness of Layton's speech threw Levine's timing completely. He felt awkward, out of place, even a little scared.

The director loved it. Levine was supposed to be that way upon meeting his long-lost killer uncle. So what if Levine wasn't acting, the camera caught it perfectly. Layton's character played derisively but he brought out whatever was real in Barry Levine and the way the picture was structured, that's what counted.

On the second day Layton dropped the accent and played it straight Brooklyn tough guy. Again Levine was thrown into uncertainty; again the director loved it. The film began to take on a new dimension. Lug Wallers was obviously a mind fucker, possibly a lunatic.

When Layton played him as a Kennedy the third day Levine started to loosen up. Lug Wallers was a master of the unexpected, a man of a thousand faces. He was as menacing as some of the early Mitchum and around such a character it was best to act loose but always be on guard. Layton was putting Levine through acting school and both of them were surpassing expectations.

Arno and Macky didn't know what to make of the dailies. Initially they challenged the director, who had previously made mostly low-budget kung-fu movies. How could he let Layton fuck around each day like that? But after seeing it over three days they began to sense that something–they weren't quite sure what–was going on. Something different.

Midweek Layton received a call from overseas. A Japanese poet and essayist named Mariko Takeda was calling to invite him, all expenses paid, to attend a film festival in his honor. As many of his movies as they could obtain would be shown and if he would consent they would like to have him discuss these films in a formal question-and-answer session. An elegant catalog would be sold to the paying audience and the proceeds would go to support future film festivals.

Layton was flattered and immediately agreed. As an afterthought he asked if he could bring his family. Yes, of course, came the reply, though there was no room in the budget for that added expense. Hell, that didn't matter, Layton thought. Not with what he was being paid for *The Sand Man*. A Layton Cross Film Festival. Those Japs sure knew how to make one's day.

As soon as he finished with his scene he wandered across the lot to where Samantha and Mancino were filming. He felt like a school kid who had just won a Regent's scholarship and the person he most wanted to impress was his ex-wife. But when he got there the set was closed for an erotic love scene between the two stars; a scene which everyone had been anticipating since filming began. The woman who told him this spoke in a breathless whisper.

His enthusiasm tempered, he wandered back to his dressing room fighting feelings of jealousy. There was a time when those heavy, erotic love scenes were exclusively his.

He picked up the phone and called Amy in Michigan. He had to share the news with somebody.

"Japan?" Amy said. "Who wants to go to Japan?"

"I thought you might. They are honoring your children's father."

"Why not Europe? The French Riviera? The Cote D'Azur? Lucerne? Barcelona? London? When they dub you in Japanese your voice rises three pitches and you can't understand what they're saying. Those people have nothing in common with us."

"Since when did you become a social commentator? Where do you think everything we own that's worth anything comes from? You're being a real goofball on this. The kids'll love it."

"What are they going to do there? Who are they going to talk to?"

"What are they doing in Michigan? We're talking about the world here Amy; they've got to experience the world."

"They'll have plenty of time to experience the world; they don't need to go to Japan."

"Why the reluctance? You've got a boyfriend, right?"

"Here we go again."

"I'm offering a trip to Japan and you're acting like Pearl Harbor happened in your lifetime, which it didn't."

"I just don't feel like uprooting again."

"I'm not asking you to move there. It's a trip, an adventure, two weeks. If we like it we can go to Hong Kong, maybe China. It'll be good for you, for us. I want you to come."

"Let me think about it."

"Say you're coming."

"Don't you get it Layt? It's not Japan, it's you. I've got to think if I want to be with you."

"For the kids then. Let's do it for them."

"I don't know if that's best right now."

"Why not?"

"They're getting used to being away from you."

"Oh yeah? Well I'm not used to being away from them. I want them with me on this."

"Why's it so important to you?"

"When have I ever had a film festival before?"

"If it was such a big deal why isn't it in New York? Or L.A.?"

"Because they don't give festivals to actors like me in this country, okay? That what you want to hear? I don't want to talk any more about this. You're going with me Amy. And the kids. So prepare yourself."

"We'll talk more next week."

"No!" Layton shouted. "I'm through with the movie next week. I want to go to Japan next week."

"When is the festival?"

Layton paused. He didn't know. He had forgotten to ask. The poet said she'd send details. What was he getting so excited about? Maybe it wasn't for another month, or six months, or next year.

"All right, I'll talk to you in a few days when I know more."

"You don't even know when it is?"

"They're sending me the information."

"You sure it's for you? Maybe they got the wrong actor."

"Maybe you'd better start kissing your boyfriends goodbye."

"If we go—and that's still a big if—that doesn't mean we're coming back to live with you."

"You never know Amy, we might just get along."

"I'm not looking for temporary Layton. I'm looking for permanent."

"Nothing's permanent."

"I just want to be sure."

"No such thing as a sure thing."

"I want a relationship not a throw of the dice."

"Think of the kids."

"Why do you think I'm here?"

"They're gonna love Japan."

"Japan is no solution."

"Land of the rising sun, Amy. A new day. Together."

Silence on Amy's end. Reconsidering. "All right Layt, I'll go. But only Japan, not California."

"Let's leave that open."
"Call me with details."
"You'd better not be fucking around, Amy."
"Adios, mon amour."

That night, in spite of his better instincts, he called Samantha to let her know about Japan.

"Oh," she said, "they asked you too?"

Layton didn't want to know but she told him anyway. She was always being asked to attend festivals in her honor. So were people like Mancino, Hoffman, Eastwood. When any of these organizers found a celebrity who agreed they'd whip the thing together before the actor had second thoughts.

Suddenly Layton wasn't feeling so great. If they asked him then every major star had already said no thanks. He knew he should never have called Samantha.

"So how'd the scene go today?" he asked.
"What have you heard?"
"Cries and whispers."
"It was...intense."
"Creating a new image?"
"Expanding."
"Sounds hot."
"Let's hope so."
"Mark around?"
"Went to the movies."
"What's he seeing?"
"How should I know?"

"Oh, forgot, you're just his mother."
"What did he tell you on your birthday?"
"Man talk, remember?"
"Did he get laid?"
"How should I know?"
"He did, didn't he? Was it any good?"
"Don't you two talk?"
"Not about that. Think I should bring it up?"
"What for?"
"Are you sleeping with Judy Lee?"
"What have you heard?"
"It's what I saw."
"The woman's still in mourning."
"That makes a difference?"

Judith Lee was next. She was the only one who sounded excited. She invited herself over to celebrate. Why the hell not? Layton thought.

■ ■ ■

"You know," she told him, "Farrell's will left an endowment for a drama chair in his name at Washburn University. They've asked me to recommend someone."

"Where's that?" Layton asked.

"Topeka, Kansas. Where Farrell was born. I haven't a clue who to suggest."

"To teach in Kansas, that's a good one."

"If Amy comes back to you will it be over between us?"

"What do you want?"
"A little on the side."
"You've got it."
"You're a good man, Layton."
"You're the only one who thinks so."
"Nonsense. A lot of women would like to have you."
"I'm here to be had."
"Don't be a silly."
"Have me then," he said. "I like being had."

■ ■ ■

While Layton was sleeping with Judith Lee in Amy's bed, Amy was getting drunk with some old high school friends in a neighborhood bar on a rainy night in Ann Arbor. To these friends Amy's life in Los Angeles seemed nothing short of fantastic. They just couldn't get over that their little Amy set out on her own and wound up marrying, then divorcing, a movie star and getting to know along the way some of the biggest and most glamorous celebrities in the world. They were as interested in what Samantha Sanders thought of her as what she thought of the great actress. Just that someone like Samantha Sanders even knew that Amy existed was mind-blowing enough for these friends.

It wasn't with humility that Amy downplayed her life on the coast; it was more out of embarrassment and shame. Here she was, the focus of attention because of who she knew in the movie world when her feelings about those people were that they were a miserable, self-centered, thoughtless, uncaring, manipulative lot who used their celebrity status to get away with everything from adultery to child molestation. When she attempted in her drunkenness to detail the reason we call these people stars—because they truly do remain in the center of their own systems, with their managers and agents and lawyers and p.r. people and lovers all orbiting like planets around them, and with their groupies and hangers-on and the media and fans and detractors adding to their luster, attracted by the intensity of their glow, surrounding them like asteroids and meteors—her friends just laughed, enthralled at the mere mention of some of the names Amy so casually dropped.

When she showed them pictures of her kids, they argued over whether they looked more like Layton Cross, whom they only knew from the movies, or Amy. When she attempted to explain the problems she had with Layton, they insisted such problems were natural to everyone and that she should go back to him. "For our sakes if nothing else," one of her girlfriends blurted and they all laughed. All but Amy, who kept hoping the more she drank the less she'd feel.

But in her intoxicated state, as she drove recklessly back to her mother's house in the rain, she thought of the aspects of Layton that she had grown to love. He was a very lovable guy: handsome, tall, strong, vulnerable, sensitive, even caring in his own peculiar way. Sure, he needed to feel separate and alone, it was part of being a neurotic, fucked-up movie star–she didn't know a single one who didn't have some particular hang-up or tragedy weighing him down. Layton was no worse and far better than most actors she knew. And even if he would never be able to get over Samantha, he was a loving father who might turn out to be a good one if given the chance.

In this drunken reverie she almost managed to forgive him for his passiveness towards Theo Soris when she braked for what she thought was a stop sign crossing in front of her and lost control of the car as the wheels skidded across the slippery road. It smacked into a large oak tree folding the grill and hood like an accordion. Amy was lucky she wasn't wearing her seatbelt because she had neglected to close her door shut and upon impact it flew open and she was thrown onto the street, suffering only some painful bruises and a twisted ankle.

As she picked herself up and looked at the wreck she reached inside for her purse, took the keys from the ignition, and limped slowly home in the downpour, blaming thoughts of Theo Soris for her predicament.

With her mother and the children asleep and her head feeling like it was being axed into quarters Amy felt she needed to talk to someone and woke Layton with her call.

"What's wrong? What happened?" he wanted to know, sensing immediately that this was not a friendly late night call. Judith Lee stirred by his side but didn't wake up.

"Jush fel like talking," Amy slurred before blurting that she had had an accident and was almost killed.

Layton tried to calm her so he could find out exactly what kind of an accident but all he kept asking was, "Are the children all right? Were they with you? What about the children?"

"Fuck 'em," Amy sobbed, needing comfort for herself. "They're asleep, they don't know. It'sh me who was alone...the car's wrecked, gone. Wait'll mother sees it, she'll have a cow."

It took some doing but he managed to talk her into taking some aspirin and putting up some coffee. He was infuriated that she was out drinking and that she smashed up the car—just the thought of the kids being with her in such condition made him want to fly there and bring them back. But he tried not to upset her any more than she obviously was and when she told him that she actually missed him and wished she was back there Layton felt that they might have a chance after all, even though he knew that a good part of her reason for wanting to be with him was so she wouldn't have to face her mother in the morning. He stroked Judith's bare ass imagining it was Amy back in bed with him.

Before he left for work the next day he called to find out how she was. Dolly answered and told him Amy was sleeping. She didn't know about the accident yet and Layton wasn't going to tell her.

A fax came through from Japan informing him that the festival in his honor would be held the following month and listed the eight films they would be showing. There was nothing after 1985, which made him feel like a relic. It wasn't a very impressive body of work he realized and, along with Amy's drunken accident, it put him in a foul mood which wasn't helped when he arrived at makeup and listened to the director say to the makeup man that Layton looked too healthy, too tanned for a guy who's been in prison all these years. "Make him more sallow," the director instructed. "And those eyes, put some rings around them, give him pouches."

The two men discussed him as if he was a canvas: should his face be chalky? grimy? jowly? What about rings around the neck? spots on his hands? dirt under his nails? Not once did they bother to consult him. Even though this was standard behavior in the illusion business, today it irked Layton to be so ignored, to be talked about but not talked to. If these assholes wanted to change his appearance, what about the first three days of shooting? How unreal a look were they going for in this crappy movie?

On the set it got worse. Barry Levine told him he saw an old film on cable the night before, one of Layton's early pictures. "I figured it out, you were a year older than I am when you made it, I wasn't even born in 1971. Who'd a thought you'd be co-starring in my first movie?"

Then Arno came by and took Layton aside, whispering to him that Charlie Greenbloom hadn't forgotten about what happened at Samantha's and did Layton destroy his kid's tape?

"Don't talk to me about Greenbloom and don't you start talking to him."

"He's applying a lot of pressure," Arno warned. "It's a couple of months ago and he's still trying to figure it out."

"What are you trying to say?"

"He's a powerful guy."

"Yeah? So get your friend Mozart to shoot blanks at him. Powerful guys get just as scared as punks like you."

"I'm not scared Layton, just concerned."

Layton looked at Arno in disgust. If Greenbloom found out what really transpired it would get back to Samantha and if Layton thought his career was tottering before he might as well start hawking chili dogs at Tail-o'-the-Pup because all doors to the industry would shut like bank vaults at closing time. The very possibility of this happening capped off a lousy morning and Layton just snapped. He grabbed Arno by his shirt and seriously considered doing some damage to his face when, from behind, Barry Levine appeared and kicked him in the middle of his back. Layton dropped his grip on Arno and swung around. Levine was in his martial arts fighting stance and half a dozen crew members had gathered to see what would happen next. Layton quickly came to his senses enough to know that this was not going to be a working day for him and shouted "Fuck this!" as he pushed his way past the small crowd to the parking lot.

Driving back he fumed over the trap he was in as an actor. He didn't like how he was treated, he didn't like the people he had to deal with, he didn't trust anyone in the business, he resented feeling like a commodity on the meat market, he was pissed with himself for ever getting involved with someone like Arno, he saw the writing-on-the-wall with Levine. Instead of driving into the hills he decided to cool his anger by running on the beach, so he drove to Gladstone's at the west end of Sunset, parked in the lot, put on his New Balance sneakers and went out to the ocean's edge.

He ran for miles towards the Santa Monica pier, then turned back to the restaurant. Out of breath, soaking wet and thirsty, he found an empty table outside and ordered a beer. That's when he saw Theo.

He was sitting in a wheelchair at a corner table with a boy no older than Leanne. The boy was wolfing down a burger and fries and Theo sat next to him, his hand on the boy's bare knee. Layton stormed over to them.

"Just what the hell are you doing?" he demanded.

Theo looked up and his face flushed. He smiled weakly. "Layton! I just got out of the hospital this week, wanted to see the ocean. The legs don't work but I hired a driver. Good to see you."

"He your driver?" Layton asked looking at the kid. "Do you know what this man wants?" he shouted at the boy.

"A hamburger?" the boy guessed.

"Get the hell out of here," he yelled. "Now!"

The boy looked towards Theo for protection.

"Layton, take it easy..." Theo whispered, his eyes darting about to see if anyone was watching.

"I should have had you arrested," Layton said bending over, sticking his face inches from Theo's.

"It's not what you think."

"What is it then? Tell me."

"He was just hungry. I bought him lunch, that's all."

"Rubbing his knee while he eats? Will he wheel you down to the beach next?"

"Who is this guy?" the boy asked.

"Get out of here before you get into trouble," Layton said.

"You'd better go now Allen."

"Thanks for the burger," the boy said.

"You're a filthy, stinking, sick fucking man!" Layton shouted, lifting Theo by his T-shirt and slapping him across his face. "You dumb, perverse, lying asshole." He smacked him again.

Two waiters came to pull Layton away but they were no match for his rage. "I'm going to take you down to the beach and dump you in the ocean," he threatened, ripping Theo's T-shirt. The tear brought him to his senses. Theo was a helpless cripple; he couldn't fight back. Layton took a step and breathed deeply. "You said you were going to get help."

"I am," Theo said.

"Then what's this?"

"Nothing happened."

"Don't play innocent with me."

"Layton, come on, you can't get cured over night."

"It's been months."

"It hasn't been easy."

"I'm going to leave, but first I'm going to do something I should have done in the hospital."

"If it will make you feel better," Theo said.

"It won't," Layton said as he closed his fingers into a fist, "but I'm going to anyway." He pulled back his hand and hit Theo so hard across his jaw that he knocked him out of his wheelchair. The waiters who stood nearby couldn't believe the assault and rushed to help Theo. Layton took a five dollar bill from his wallet and threw it on the table. He didn't feel any better as he headed for the parking lot.

A woman in a Mustang convertible pulled up along side him and asked if he needed a lift. Layton said no without looking at her. "What's the matter, you too old to stare an old lover in the face?"

He raised his eyes and saw Amanda Rash, her lipstick matching her hair, her chest tightly compressed by an orange tank top. "My car's over there," he said.

"You look like you just fired your agent."

"I did that a while ago."

"I heard you're working on a picture."

"If you can call it that."

"Things that tough?"

"There are a lot of sick people in this town," he murmured.

"Tell me about it. I'm talking to one." She gave him a high sheen grin.

"You'll never forget will you?"

"Not until you give me a chance to get even."

"It was a lifetime ago. When we were stars."

"All the more reason." She asked him where he was going and he told her home. She asked if he was living with anyone and he said he was alone. She asked if he'd like to come to her condo on San Vicente and Ocean Avenue and he said he was upset and tired. She offered to fuck him and he said he would follow her.

All those years of smoldering humiliation and this was what she wanted all along, he thought. To get laid. It wasn't what he wanted, not with Amanda Rash who was the worst of old world Hollywood, a woman with a mouth as big as her boobs, and just as loose. But his nerves were on the verge of collapse. Theo, Barry Levine, Arno, Amy's accident, Alex Briar. Now Amanda was to become another piece in the absurd puzzle that was his life.

They went at it in her bedroom but he knew it couldn't be good. She wanted more than gentle stroking, quiet kissing, rhythmic fucking. She wanted to do battle, unleash what had been bottled up, work him into a lather and then deride his efforts. But she needed a willing warrior and Layton wasn't up to it. She used her teeth to bite, her nails to scratch, her cunt to grip his organ, tensing tightly as if to choke it, but Layton didn't fight back. He was there for her to do whatever she wanted. She wanted to fuck, not make love.

"Pull my hair," she demanded. "Pin my arms down. Push into me, let me feel what you've got."

So Layton pulled, pinned, pushed until their pelvic bones collided. If she was impressed she didn't show it. If she came he didn't know it. All he felt was pain. Fucking this prima donna washed-up movie star was painful.

Hitting Theo Soris was painful.

Hearing about drunken Amy was painful.

Thinking of his children was painful.

Losing Samantha was painful.

Being paid $100,000 to legitimize drug dealers and a teenage carhop was painful.

Not being able to say no was painful.

What he wanted, what he needed, was out.

What he got was more pain.

It happened on his last day of shooting. It was a scene written as a concession to Layton, a final touching moment when Barry Levine comes back to visit his Uncle Lug in prison. Levine has been redeemed; he has undone much of Lug's damage and made retribution to the families of those he put to sleep. Now he is returning to see the man who, ironically, set him straight. Lug was such a mean, nasty reprobate Levine's character just had to make one last attempt to break through. As written the scene would be emotional. It began with Levine sitting across a table being carefully watched by two guards as Lug Wallers was brought in. Lug sees the kid all cleaned up and looking like Joe College, spits, then laughs. He finds the kid pathetic, a cop-out. But the kid laughs along with Lug, then tries to shake his hand. Lug looks at it with distaste, eyes the kid slyly. The kid backs off, starts telling Lug what he's been up to, how he's gone and helped the people Lug made so miserable. Lug is appalled. He yells at the kid, demanding to know what right he had doing such a thing, interfering with Lug's business. The kid reminds him that his business is finished; he's in jail for life without a chance for parole. That makes no difference to Lug, who lunges at the kid. But the kid sidesteps him and Lug falls flat on his face. The two guards quickly restore order but Lug says he doesn't want to hear any more, as far as he's concerned the kid is hopeless, removed, dead. But the kid doesn't give up. He calls out a name—Lug's wife—then another, Lug's mother. He starts weaving an intricate story of what has happened to the people who once loved Lug. It's poignant, sad, tearjerking material. Lug begins to soften. He insists he has no regrets but in the end the kid approaches him and they embrace. Tears stream down the kid's face. Lug holds back but is obviously touched. The kid says goodbye as Lug is taken back to his cell. Outside the sun is shining, as the kid looks to the sky, ready for another day of freedom and good deeds.

That's how it was supposed to play but that's not the way Layton played it. All week Levine kept getting on his nerves. At first it was because Levine couldn't improvise and kept fucking up what Layton was going for. Then when Levine started to relax and catch on it was because he kept chewing the scenery, hogging the camera, acting like what he was: an amateur. And then when Levine started to roll he began to treat Layton like what he was: a bit player. And that kick in the back—the ass-licking little turd. So by the end of Layton's week Levine had become unbearable; he knew he was the star and he was doing all he could to act like a star—or like what he supposed a star acted like. He was obnoxious, condescending, arrogant, and he told bad jokes, expecting people to laugh.

With all that was happening in his own life Layton just couldn't put up with this pompous shitheel. So when he was brought in to see the cocky kid, as the cameras rolled, rather than spit on the floor in disgust Layton held his phlegm until Levine reached out his hand and unloaded in his palm. It was a far more powerful moment but it so took Levine by surprise that he recoiled in horror. It was a fair reaction and could have been used but Levine couldn't carry the moment and just fell apart, causing the director to stop the scene.

"Don't do that again!" Levine shouted at Layton.

But Layton answered as Lug by eyeing the kid with a sly sneer and chilling laugh.

Places were set, quiet was demanded, cameras rolled for take two. This time Lug didn't spit in the kid's hand, he tongued it right in Levine's face. Again Levine recoiled, but the cameras kept going and the scene continued–the kid now spitting out his good deeds defiantly, Lug threatening to take care of the kid once and for all. The tension on the set was electric. Layton may have been acting but Barry Levine wasn't. He didn't know how to act that good. He hated Layton, hated how he had mistreated him, how he put him down on the phone, hung up on him, treated him like a carhop. So when Lug lunged at him, instead of stepping away Levine hit him with a karate kick in the solar plexus. Lug didn't just go down, he fell hard. Levine stood over him daring Layton to get up as the two guards came to now hold the kid back. But Lug remained down, cursing the kid from the ground in a spooky low raspy voice. That's when Levine lost control and instead of talking of Lug's family the way it was written he started talking of Layton's inability to keep his women and how Amy was always searching for a real man.

The rest was all a blur to Layton, who remembered getting up to challenge this brash little prick only to be put down by another of those tricky, trained kicks. What he didn't remember was his lifting a chair over his head and swinging it at Levine, who was swift enough to duck and land a rabbit punch to Layton's chest. Layton then lunged at the kid and felt his jaw crack as Levine's fist landed like a lead pipe across his chin. As Layton went down the director signaled everyone to stay away as the cameras continued to capture this madness. He quickly scribbled onto a cue card the words: I TRIED UNCLE LUG...I'M SORRY, and held it up for Levine to read. The kid somehow managed to get back into character and the scene played. More than played–it had the look and feel of something gritty and real.

Layton, unfortunately, had the look and feel of someone grizzly and busted as he was rushed to a hospital for a minor concussion and a broken jaw that had to be set and wired. When he came to the next day he was told that it would be best if he tried not to talk for the next six to eight weeks.

■ ■ ■

Alex Briar sat in a corner of the Academy of Motion Pictures library on La Cienega south of Wilshire in Beverly Hills reading the files on Layton Cross when he spotted Faye Collabella, Samantha's secretary. She was standing at the counter in the back of the library writing a check for $1,500 to cover the outrageous cost of copying all the material in her boss' files. The library charged a quarter a page and didn't allow more than ten pages to be copied per day. The approximately four thousand pages, plus copies of all the stills that were on file, took two weeks of after hours work but for someone like Samantha they were there to please, hoping that when the time was appropriate she might leave her papers to them. Had they really wanted to please they wouldn't have charged her but that would have been too great an exception to their rules and budget.

Briar walked over and introduced himself as the writer who once wrote an article on her for a piece in *The Star* about heavy-duty secretaries to the stars. She remembered the article and the phone conversation they had.

"You even spelled my name right," she said.

Briar told her he was writing a book about Layton Cross with the actor's permission and he wondered if she'd be willing to have lunch with him.

"I'm afraid I'm in a hurry."

"Looks like you'll need a truck."

"I've arranged for someone to bring it down to the parking lot."

"Well how about another time? When are you free?"

"With Samantha there is no such thing as free time."

"What about a real date then? A late dinner maybe? A walk through the sculpture gardens at UCLA?"

"You asking me out so you can pick my brain about Layton Cross?"

"Yes. Unless you don't have anything to say about him, then we can talk about other things."

"I'll have to ask Samantha."

"You need permission to go out?"

"If it has to do with her, yes."

"We can keep it general."

"Like how many times did he hit her in a week rather than day-by-day?"

Briar smiled. Though still in her thirties, she had been around long enough to know every trick. She was too smart to fool and too efficient to beat around the bush.

"I've been talking to anyone who ever worked with, for or against Cross with the exception of his two wives, one of whom would never talk to me, the other is in hiding. You could provide insight into certain key years of his life that would be of tremendous help to me. I can't offer you money because I don't have much, but I can promise you anonymity. And I'd be willing to wine and dine you for however long it takes to loosen your tongue. You're not going to tell me any more than you want to, that's obvious. All I'm looking for is some honest insight and if I can ever return the favor I will."

Faye Collabella's social life had been at zero for so many months because of the exhausting nature of her job that she found Briar and the idea of being wined and dined attractive. "Give me your phone number," she said, "I'll see what I can do."

It was more than he had hoped for. She was capable of providing the inside behind-the-scenes story of the star-crossed volatile mismarriage between Layton and Samantha.

When he walked her down the stairs she noticed his limp.

"Accident?"

"I got shot."

"Mugging?"

"Layton Cross."

She was more than curious now. Samantha would love to hear about this one. "How?"

"Call me, we'll trade stories."

■ ■ ■

During the week that Layton was in the hospital he refused to see anyone. Arno and Macky, who were ecstatic with the publicity and the results captured on film, sent him huge bouquets of flowers and boxes of Godiva chocolates with promises of nose and head candy when he got out. Barry Levine tried calling to apologize but the calls weren't put through. Even Judith Lee was kept away, although she kept insisting that she had been through hospital-sitting with her late husband and knew how to make someone comfortable.

When Amy read about it in the papers she called and spoke with Layton's doctor who told her that he was doing fine and the best thing for him was complete rest. She offered to return immediately but the doctor persuaded her to give him some time to heal, suggesting a few weeks of solitude.

A nurse was hired to return with him but after a few days Layton felt strong enough to release her. He had disconnected the phone, discontinued the newspaper delivery, and kept the shades and blinds drawn. It gave him a lot of time to think.

He felt like he was slowly sinking in quicksand. Nothing was going right. He struggled to pull himself out of the funk he was in but with no support it seemed almost hopeless.

He knew this feeling. He would lie on the couch, turn on the TV and push buttons, staring. He would melt ice cream in the microwave and drink it through a straw or make a yogurt fruit shake. With each sip his aching jaw would remind him of how low he had sunk. He'd go outside and stare at the squirrels in the trees, the birds pecking at breadcrumbs on the lawn. He'd think of taking a drive but not know where to go. He'd remember how it was when he was busy and on top of things. Even the damn fiasco play was a good diversion. But the play was over, the TV movie was done, the lousy bit-part Sand Man was in the can along with, perhaps, his career. Nothing was being offered. He was getting older and his time had come and perhaps passed. What was there? Soaps? Infomercials?

Go behind the camera? Raise money for other actors to become stars? Run for governor? He wasn't a businessman or a politician but he was a gambler. Actors were all gamblers. If no one was willing to bet on him then perhaps he could bet on himself. He had bet on others over the years. Boxers, ballplayers, runners, horses, even the fate of hostages. Why not take the blood money earned from *The Sand Man* and invest in himself? It violated the cardinal rule of business—never use your own money, always use someone else's—but if he didn't believe he was still enough of a draw to reap a return then what the fuck was he doing with his life? He could start his own production company, direct, star, serve coffee and Danishes to the crew, keep the budget down by not paying for his services, have Amy do the editing...nothing to it!

Nothing, that is, but a script. A story. An idea.

There were thousands of story ideas floating around Hollywood but actors were always complaining that there were no scripts. Novels were being published all the time, surely there was something out there. Of course the good stories were quickly snatched up for loads of dough and long options. Maybe there was a favorite book of his that had never been done.

He walked over to the bookshelf in the living room and glanced at titles. Hell, he'd never read any of them. Like most actors Layton had a hard time concentrating for long periods unless it was for a specific part. The last book he read for pleasure all the way through was *The Catcher in the Rye* and Salinger wasn't talking to anyone. Besides, who could Layton play? Holden Caulfield's psychiatrist? 'Yes, of course I really want to know about it, just lie there and let it all come out...' And who would be Holden? Barry Levine?

He thought about Dr Lugow but didn't feel up to the intensity of verbal self-analysis. And what would the doctor tell him, that it would pass, this period of self-pity? That all creative people go through down times? That he's managed to survive into his mid-forties and that, alone, is a great accomplishment for an actor?

Well hell doctor, that may be encouragement to Nolan Ryan or George Foreman but not to him. It takes until forty to begin to understand the human heart. Why should he be forced to contemplate another line of work in a profession that cries out for experience, for soul exposure, for an accurate portrayal of the human condition?

Maybe because people didn't want to pay to see the actors they grew up with grow old like them. Wasn't the magic of the movies the promise of eternal youth? Stick in a videocassette and watch Olivier as Heathcliff, Dean in *Giant*, Clift in *Red River* every decade of your life and they never age. Henry Fonda gave a gutsy portrayal of old age in his last picture but wouldn't we rather see him so brave and defiant leaving Oklahoma and crossing the dustbowl west to California? It's one thing to fight death, quite another to wrestle life. Who wants to be reminded that your hands shake and your lips quiver just before you bite the big one? It's the young who still go to the movies—parade the marching technobots, cheer the one-dimensional Barry Levine's–listen to the tolling of the box-office bell as it tolls for thee, Layton Cross.

No, it wasn't Dr Lugow's sympathetic shoulder he needed. It was a good, breakthrough part. A surge of inspiration. A Purple Heart for living through the rejections and humiliations and broken jaws that were the essence of being an actor, a jester, a sad-eyed clown responding on cue to the crack of a cruel, fickle whip.

■ ■ ■

Alex Briar was the first person to see him when he arrived uninvited at Layton's door. He had come because he wanted information about this latest episode in Layton's life. His book was in better shape than its subject, he kidded, when he saw the wire brace holding the lower half of Layton's face together. Layton didn't find him amusing.

"Nice cane," he said squeezing the words between his teeth.

Briar had wondered if Layton would bring up the incident. It wasn't something he wanted to flog but if he could use it to get information for his book he was more than willing to work on whatever guilt feelings Layton might have. The doctor had told him the wound should heal completely and, besides a small scar, there would be no noticeable damage. But that's not what he told Layton. He hinted that he might need the cane for years or, if he was lucky, get away with a slight limp. He didn't feel comfortable lying but Layton was someone he had to deal with not someone who was going to become a friend. Briar fully believed that a good journalist must be willing to lie, cheat, and maneuver in whatever ways it took to get to the heart of a story.

Unfortunately for him Layton suspected Briar's deceptive nature and didn't succumb to his act for sympathy and disclosure. The shot had cost Layton an agreement he didn't want, as far as he was concerned they were even. Opening up about his beating at the hands of a nineteen-year-old ninja who had already stolen a movie from him was not conducive to a speedy recovery. Still, considering Briar as he sat across from him, it crossed his mind how that which goes around comes around. He had fired the first shot, now his jaw was wired. He wondered about how the movie business seems to bring out both the best and the worst in people and how it attracts those of like nature, be they actors, lawyers, writers or producers. Everyone smiled tiger smiles, everyone cried crocodile tears, everyone was willing to float their grandmothers down the river for their own personal advancement. No, he couldn't feel sorry if Alex Briar had to limp his way toward his own pot of gold–warriors on their way to celebrity couldn't expect to step into the limelight without at least a few battle scars to show for it. If Briar wrote a good book he could wear his limp proudly. If he didn't it would serve as a reminder that he had blown his chance.

When Samantha came to visit with Mark she told him that she had heard about the book some writer was doing on him. When Layton merely shrugged she told him how she had had to stop a dozen attempts by writers to write her story. It wasn't always easy–sometimes it took hints at future cooperation to a publisher who had contracted for the unauthorized version, other times veiled threats of a lawsuit if there was even the slightest distortion printed about her. She knew she couldn't stop what was written in the press but she was determined to keep anything from coming out between hard or soft covers. Books, to her, were permanent. They were put in libraries and would become part of her legacy. And since any biography of Layton would devote a few chapters to her she was trying to question his passivity toward such a project. She even had Sol Gordon check with the publisher to find out what sort of agreement was made and when she heard that Layton had given permission for such a book she wanted too know why. Even more, she wanted to talk him out of it.

At least, Layton thought, she hadn't heard about how the agreement had come about. And he didn't feel like revealing that she wasn't the only one who could shoot a gun. Thankfully Mark was there so the subject wasn't dwelt on. Mark at least had the good sense to ask how Layton was feeling.

"Not bad for a ventriloquist," Layton gritted.

"It'll do you good to keep your mouth shut for a while," Samantha said. "Probably lose some weight too."

Layton remembered when they used to sit in bed watching old movies on TV, eating Chinese food out of white paper containers. They had fun in bed together, before the world realized what a great actress she was. That's when it all changed. The whole world got between them. Everybody wanted a piece of her. Layton's touch wasn't enough. He'd have to pay for a ticket and get in line. But when the dust settled and the horizon cleared there was still Mark. You couldn't take Mark away from him. No matter how high she climbed there would always be that bond.

With Mark in the living room watching a space shuttle liftoff on CNN Samantha reflected on the different paths their lives had taken. Layton listened, thinking his replies but remaining silent, allowing her to go on uninterrupted.

"Had we stayed together I wonder where we'd be today?"

In your house watching your movies in your private screening room. Dealing with your manager and accountant over your money and your investments and looking for your next project.

"I've sometimes thought that your career would be farther along had we been together all these years."

No doubt, thanks to your power and your wishes. That's why my career took the turn it took, because you wanted it that way. How would it have looked if I had turned out an actor on his way up who continued to rise after you left him?

"But maybe it's impossible for two people in the same profession to support each other."

Oh yeah, what about Hawn and Russell? Newman and Woodward? Cronyn and Tandy? Bacall and Bogart? Tracy and Hepburn?

"And you wouldn't have had Leanne and Andy."

Don't forget the knife-wielding Amy, she deserves some consideration—after all, she's the only other woman in the world who shares the distinction of once having been married to me. But you're right, it's all worked out for the best. Even though my smile's locked behind wires at the moment.

"Mark thinks you still love me. Do you Layt?"

I'll always love you Sam. Just not as my wife. You're a part of me. We have Mark.

"For a long time I stopped loving you but maybe I've been fooling myself. I don't know–sometimes I think I never loved you, other times I begin to see that we once had something."

And now? What about now? Are you trying to say that there's some extra love in your heart put aside for the love of anyone beside yourself?

"When Amy came that night at first I thought she had gone crazy, then I realized she's a lot like me. She's a fighter."

God bless fighters.

"You know, she's probably good for you. Have you thought of getting back together?"

And here I thought you were going somewhere else.

"You were lucky to find her."

Yes, I'll nod to that.

"You were lucky to have had me."

Okay, I'll nod again.

"You're a lucky man."

Is she kidding or what? You call this lucky?

"It could have been worse."

How much?

"That little prick could have killed you."

Definitely worse.

"What should we do about him?"

We?

"The worm."

Weasel, rodent, rat....

"I hear the movie is going to make him a star."

Must be part of my continuing luck.

"But what he did to you is going to work against him. You're the one who'll get the sympathy."

And you, dear Sam, are the true Sand Man. So how are you going to bring me a dream?

"About that book, are you really going to let him write it without a fight?"

The fight's over. One shot, a bloody kilim and victory to the victim.

"Your life's all you've got, you should think more about protecting it."

Who's going to option my life? It's you they want Sam, you know that. To make me work they should cast you as me. Would make millions.

"If you want me to get involved I'll do it."

Boy does this woman run scared. You can't stop the world from knowing about you Sam, you're a commodity, face it. My value is invariably linked to your ever-rising stock. Nothing I can do about that. All I ever wanted was a space in your bed and a name of my own.

Samantha stood, kissed his brow, pet his cheek and told him to take care. The space shuttle had lifted without a hitch. Mark came and offered to stay with him if he wanted company but Layton shook his head. Amy was returning with the kids soon. He'd be fine.

He spent the next few days looking at Kurosawa movies and books about Japan. The poet Mariko Takeda had sent him a tentative itinerary along with a request from a Japanese beer company asking him to endorse their product for a television commercial for which they would pay him $20,000. Takeda had procured the offer hoping it would cover his family's expenses while in Japan. She also enclosed an English edition of one of her poetry books, *Masturbating at the Movies & Other Poems*. He opened the book to a poem called "The Defiant One."

> I see you
> Sidney Portier
> your black back
> sparkling like
> champagne
> Chained
> and struggling
> as I push quivering
> fingers into my
> body
> dripping hot discharge
> onto the cola sticky floor

He looked at her picture on the back cover. She had a classic Asian face with one very distinguishing exception: her long hair was fire-engine red. It made her look like a movie star.

■ ■ ■

When Faye Collabella finally called Alex Briar he was in the middle of entering this latest twist in Layton's career into his computer. She had free time that evening and Briar suggested they meet at Indigo on 3rd Street in West Hollywood.

Under a two wine dinner Briar told her the story of his life, including how he got wounded in action. Once he swore on his mother's life that he would keep her out of the book Collabella began to dish the dirt he had come to hear. Wine was her weakness. Too much loosened her normally sealed tongue.

She told him how Layton and Samantha never saw things the same way. They had disagreed about everything, from the color of their underwear to the quality of the movies they watched. When the arguments became too heated it often resulted in physical violence, with Layton wearing his share of welts and bruises. Samantha was a street fighter and didn't hesitate to pick up a bat, broom handle or fire poker to make her mark. Sometimes Collabella felt sorry for Layton and would comfort him. For a brief while when they separated before the divorce she even had an affair with him. Samantha never found out.

"And if she ever did she would fire me. And if I lost my job I'd...I don't know what I'd do. Get you."

"You could write a book."

"About Samantha?"

"Be worth a lot more than you're making."

"I make good money."

"Six figures?"

"I couldn't write a book."

"Do you keep a diary?"

"None of your business."

"You should. Or talk into a tape recorder."

"I'm not a spy."

"For insurance."

"I couldn't."

"Alice Marchak wrote a book about Brando and still worked for him."

"Six figures?"

"Easy."

"Jesus, you're making me confused. And I haven't even told you about the sniper who tried to kill Samantha or how Layton got fucked over by Charlie Greenbloom."

Briar ordered a third bottle of wine.

"I can't drink any more, I'll pass out."

"Sip. I'll drink." Collabella was the golden source every biographer dreams of finding. She knew everything and Briar was sitting there getting it all on tape. He was in research heaven.

The details of the sniper incident were fascinating and would have been more than enough to cap off the evening but the stuff about Greenbloom, that was so purely evil and cunning that Briar was beginning to think the book should be published as a hardcover first. It had to do with *Helix*, the uncompleted film Briar had tried asking Layton about. He had heard about Layton's taking a swing at Greenbloom and Greenbloom closing down the picture but Faye Collabella laid out what had really taken place, at least what Samantha had told her under sworn secrecy. Greenbloom apparently was nuts about Samantha and couldn't stand the fact that Layton was married to her. Layton was not in her class, he felt, and he wanted to destroy him before he became too big an actor. So during the production he slipped a tab of acid into Layton's drink and when Layton started to hallucinate Greenbloom called attention to his behavior. Layton didn't know what was happening to him but Greenbloom did and manipulated him to the point where Layton was flailing his arms helplessly and Greenbloom happened to step in front of Layton to catch one on the chin. It wasn't much of a shot but Greenbloom made the most of it, closing down the set, calling in some shrinks to declare Layton's behavior untenable. After that as far as any studio was concerned Layton was persona non grata. He wasn't wanted, he couldn't be insured, he would have to work for the most independent of independents. Greenbloom wanted Layton out of Samantha's life and proceeded to help drum him out of his career as well. And Faye Collabella's sworn secret was now recorded on Alex Briar's microcassette.

When she had finished with her expose Briar asked a diversionary question. "Was Layton good in the hay?"

"None of your goddamned business."

"That's what I thought."

"Are you?"

"I was hoping you'd ask."

"You'd better be good. I'm in no mood for a premature ejaculator."

For the information she just passed on Briar would do everything possible to see that the woman got some satisfaction that night.

* * *

Layton was so happy to see Amy and the children that he actually cried.

"Are those tears for real?" Amy asked, somewhat startled by his show of emotion.

Leanne looked very worried when she saw the misshape of his face and ran to hug him. Andy tried to squeeze between them but Leanne pushed him back.

"Hey, let me see Dad, it's my turn, don't hog him."

Layton made room for his son and held them both. Then came the questions. They wanted all the details—how did it happen? What did he do to Levine? How much did it hurt? How long would he be like this? What could he eat? What was he going to do to get even? Were they still going to go to Japan?

The quiet house suddenly took on life again. Andy ran to check out his room, Leanne talked about the friends she had made in Michigan, and Amy went to the liquor cabinet for a drink. When she caught Layton's look she told him she had no intentions of driving anywhere and had vowed never to drink and drive again. But when she looked in the kitchen cabinets and saw there was no food she volunteered to go down to the market.

"By foot?" Layton mumbled.

"Oh right. Well, get the keys, you drive."

"Do we have to go shopping" Andy complained. "We just got home."

"You and your sister unpack, I'll go with your father. And no fighting."

In the Jeep Layton asked about the fighting.

"Oh you know how it is," Amy said.

"Leanne is fighting?"

"She's a spunky kid, so what else is new?"

"That's a good sign. Means she's coming back."

That hadn't occurred to Amy. "You're right. I've been very concerned about her coming home. She seemed to be okay in Michigan but I wasn't sure if she'd start having nightmares again here."

Layton thought of telling her about his encounter with Theo but decided it was best not to bring him up.

She told him about her crazy mother's latest schemes and what she did in Michigan. "I must say my mother took the sight of her wrecked car very well, just passed it on to her insurance and said no more about it. I think she thought it a miracle I walked away from it and was relieved."

"So was I," Layton said.

"You don't have to talk, I know it must hurt. God, that bastard did some job on you." She lit a cigarette and took a deep drag, then pursed her lips to whistle out a thin stream of smoke. "So, you missed us, huh? That's good. Let me tell you, I did a lot of thinking. I've been trying hard to figure you out but you're too, I don't know...like smoke. Too amorphous. All these years I still don't know you. What you did at Samantha's, any way I look at it it's still wrong. Am I wrong? Okay, I figure it was the act of an irrational, out of control man. Maybe that was your way of reacting to what happened to Leanne. Maybe you really wanted to kill Samantha for leaving you and becoming such a big star. Maybe you felt cornered like a rat and were just trying to strike back, get out of it somehow. I don't know. But I came to the conclusion that just the fact that you did it shows you were sending out a signal for help. So maybe it was wrong of me to leave. But if I didn't leave I probably would have behaved just as crazily. I'm not exactly the rock of Gibraltar myself. But I've given all this some thought and I don't know what to expect this time. I don't know if you want to stay, if I want you to stay, if your staying will only lead to more problems, if it's best for you to keep out of our lives or become a part of them. It's all very confusing right now. I didn't expect you to cry, that was touching. Maybe that means something. I thought about suggesting we try counseling but that seems like we're throwing our problems into some outsider's hands and why not save the money and try it ourselves. We could have joint sessions, just the two of us, and talk out what's wrong between us, give each other enough space to get out what's inside us, try to cut down on the arguments and see how that goes. Does that make any sense? I don't even know what you're thinking. You don't have to say anything now."

Layton pulled into the Chalet Gourmet's small lot.

"You got some money?" Amy asked. "I left my bag in the kitchen."

"Amy...," Layton looked at her the way he did when they first met at another supermarket in another time, "you should stop smoking, it's turning your teeth yellow."

12

Clear Voiced Cuckoo

It was a difficult plane ride because Leanne kept grinding her teeth in her sleep. Andy, used to it by now, slept in the aisle seat, his ears stuffed with tissue. Layton sat between them unable to sleep, while Amy sat across the aisle reading *Lear, Elle, Vanity Fair* and *Mother Jones* as she enjoyed the miniature bottles of vodka she poured over the ice in her plastic cup.

She was thinking about the editing job she had turned down to join Layton on this excursion. The movie was one of those Steven Seagal/Jean Claude Van Damm blood-and-guts-with-a-moral exploitations—not the kind of picture one gets nominated for sound recognition but fun nonetheless, trying to come up with original ways to splat a body or create havoc in a slum alley or jungle village. With the way money went out faster than it came in it wasn't easy for Amy to say no but she had come down hard on Layton as an actor over the years and thought that she had contributed to his falling because of her own doubts about him. Actors were such vulnerable creatures who built their lives from the twig and straw of their own self-confidence; they needed support from those around them. And the children needed to believe in their father's importance. It was tough losing the recognition of his peers, which Layton had lost years ago, but that was nothing compared with having Leanne and Andy strain to come up with excuses for why he was no longer getting the parts in films that people stood in line to see. This festival, Amy reasoned, might help restore Layton's esteem. And after what happened with Barry Levine, Layton deserved some family support. Even if they were no longer family. With Layton's mouth still wired it was going to be embarrassing enough, the least she could do was bring along the blender and help prepare his liquid food.

Even before Sony bought the old M-G-M lot in Culver City and took over Columbia, TriStar, and Sony Pictures, Japan had become a major player in a big way. Universal boasted more 1993 Oscar nominations than any other company but in fact Sony Studios' three companies combined got more. Japan was impossible to ignore and Layton understood this. Being singled out there would garner attention back home. Mancino and Sanders and whoever-the-fuck-else might feel comfortable snubbing the Japanese but it just wasn't a smart business move. Layton ran his tongue along the wire in front of his mouth trying to remember when *konbanwa* turned into *konichewa*.

■ ■ ■

Mariko Takeda was waiting for them when they arrived. She was even more alluring than her picture: soft, delicate features and long striking blonde and red streaked hair. Layton had never seen anyone who looked remotely like her. From the way other people stared few Japanese had either.

"Did you have a good fright?" she asked.

"Wasn't scared at all," Layton said, but the remark passed without a facial twinkle of understanding.

"We are so looking forward, you are a favorite star."

Layton felt like a giant next to her. He was carrying Andy and holding Leanne's hand as he introduced them. Mariko was very polite but Amy didn't buy it, not by the way she looked.

"I am delighted to meet you. You must prease forgive my Engrish, I can speak but not so very well."

"Well enough," Layton said between his clenched teeth.

"I am so solly for your accident. I was afraid you might cancel coming. It is very noble to have arrived."

Outside Layton looked for his white horse but settled for the waiting Toyota. The taxi into the city took more than an hour. Andy was impressed with the way the doors opened automatically and that the driver wore white gloves. Leanne noticed that all the highway signs were in Japanese, which looked like chicken footprints to her. Amy sat quietly, looking for the black roots in Mariko's hair.

Mariko explained how they had arranged for eight of Layton's films to be shown over four nights. A press conference was set up three days in advance of the first night's screenings to help publicize the event. A slight problem had arisen in that another film festival honoring the late Federico Fellini had also been scheduled for the same four days. "But not to worry," Mariko said, "you are a movie star and he was only a director."

Only a director! Why on earth would anyone want to attend his films if they had the chance to see Fellini's? But maybe this poet knew something about the Japanese character and their need to be in the same proximity as a celebrity that he didn't know. Maybe there was room in Tokyo for Fellini *and* Layton Cross.

Mariko helped them check into their hotel and said she would be preased to be available as a guide. She politely excused herself and said she would come by in the afternoon after they had a chance to rest. She added that the hotel provided babysitting services if they wanted to go out in the evening. She bowed to Amy, then took Layton's hand and shook it. She was so preased he had come that she forgot to let go. When Layton finally let his hand go slack Mariko was smiling happily. Amy didn't seem preased at all.

Over the next few days they explored the city. In the Shinjuku area Andy was ecstatic playing video arcade games and learning pachinko, one of the Japanese workers' after-hours institutions. Leanne enjoyed shopping for dolls in the large department stores and trying different foods by pointing to them in restaurant windows. But what she didn't like was the subway.

Layton had heard about the incredible rush of underground traffic and thought it would be a good experience for them. Mariko joined them but it was upsetting for Leanne.

The crowds were so thick that uniformed men wearing white gloves stood behind people and pushed them forward when the train doors opened. One schoolgirl slipped between the train and the platform tearing her stocking and scraping her leg. Layton helped lift her before the doors closed on her foot.

Inside it was so crammed that people rubbed against each other. Layton had been in New York's subways at rush hour, in London's tube, in the Paris metro, but nothing compared to this. Andy thought it was amazing and held fast to his father's leg. Leanne felt dizzy. She didn't like being pressed in such a helpless way. Layton had a different perspective. He was so tall that he could see clearly from one packed end to the other. What impressed him was how the people seemed oblivious, receding into a world of their own, as if they had mastered the ability to leave their bodies and enter a place of calm and clarity. Amy had her own way of dealing with the crowd—she used her elbows, forearms and shoulders to push for some space. She, too, sought as much calm and clarity as the next person.

They were walking in the banking district one day when they noticed people making a wide arc off the sidewalk into the street. When they reached the place where people were stepping off the curb they saw why: a well-dressed man who had drunk too many beers with lunch was leaning against the bank wall and pissing into the street. It was a remarkable trajectory.

"That's really disgraceful," Amy exclaimed as she grabbed the camera from her purse. "My mother's gonna love this one."

Leanne tugged on her arm. She didn't want to watch this man relieve himself in public. It was the second time a neatly dressed man had behaved in a disturbing way. The night before they had gone for dinner and saw a man in a well-tailored raincoat scanning the back door garbage cans, picking out morsels with a pair of wooden chopsticks and delicately placing them into a plastic Ziploc bag.

As they walked on Layton stepped on a man who had fallen asleep in a taxi zone, his back against the curb. Hundreds of people ignored him as they crossed the street but Layton lifted the man onto the sidewalk. When he opened his eyes and saw it was a foreigner who had helped him the man jumped to his feet and bowed graciously, saying *Arrigato gozai mashita.* Layton returned the bow and then crossed the street, looking back to see the man returning to his prone position against the curb.

"I don't understand this place," Leanne said when they reached their hotel.

"It's another country," Layton said. "You don't have to understand, just observe."

"I don't like it."

"I think it's neat," Andy disagreed. "I've never seen people peeing in the street before."

"You're so gross," Leanne snapped.

"I know you are, but what am I?" Andy countered in that irritating singsong retort which drove Leanne up a wall; it was just so childish and stupid.

She pushed her brother in the chest, almost knocking him over. He charged her, wildly swinging his small arms and legs. She bopped him on the top of his head with her fist as Amy stepped in to break it up.

"What's the matter with you?" she blasted at Layton. "You're standing right there."

But Layton was too happy to see Leanne's return to the real world of brotherly hatred to think of interrupting. Amy had told him of their fights but this was the first time since the incident that Layton had seen it for himself.

That night after Andy fell asleep Leanne asked him if the Japanese were a little crazy.

"We're all crazy, darling. That's the price you pay for growing up. Life makes us crazy."

"That man by the bank, was he crazy?"

"Probably just drunk."

"And the man in the street?"

"Same thing."

"Why do people drink so much?"

"To forget."

"What are they forgetting?"

"Whatever it was that made them start drinking."

Leanne's nocturnal teeth grinding got worse each night. Layton bought ear plugs for Andy but it troubled him that she was chewing so strongly as she slept. A girl so young shouldn't be so tense. Fighting with her brother was only a beginning. They hadn't spoken about her dreams, her leaving L.A., Dr Lugow. He had hoped that coming to Japan would open her eyes to a new world, give her things to think about, make her adventurous. Instead she seemed to cling to him more tightly than ever and ground her teeth at night.

At his press conference Layton was struck by the number of reporters who showed up. Apparently they hadn't heard that he was no longer considered a star in his country. Their questions began politely but soon became cutting. He was asked about his life with Samantha, the reasons for their divorce, what he thought of her career, how he assessed his own. Then it got more intimate. They had read about his punching Samantha and wanted to know all about it. Why had his wife stabbed his friend? Why did his co-star break his jaw? How violent was America? Were prostitutes still available along Sunset between Crescent Heights and Fairfax?

He tried to answer the questions, no matter how bizarre. When it came to sex and violence he cracked jokes but the reporters didn't smile as they wrote notes or checked their tape recorders. When the conference was over he moved to another room where the photographers waited to take his picture.

The next day he saw the results in every newspaper in Tokyo. And when he walked on the street, crowds suddenly formed. The wonderful anonymity was gone. Layton Cross, the movie star, was on display, wired jaw and all.

It made the children miserable as they worried about disappearing in a crowd of amateur photographers and autograph hounds. When they went to the zoo Layton got into a scuffle with a young American transient who kept disturbing the crocodiles by throwing stones at them in an effort to make them move. The authorities came, recognized him, and called the press. The next day there were more pictures in the papers.

Mariko suggested that they take the bullet train to Kyoto but Layton didn't want to miss his festival. Leanne and Andy said they preferred staying in the hotel but Layton insisted they go out. "We didn't come all the way here to sit in a hotel room watching Japanese TV."

"It's not fun going out with you," Andy complained.

"You can go with your mother, I'll go out on my own."

"Like hell you will," Amy protested. "You're the one with an interpreter. I can't get around this place on my own, are you crazy?"

"I've got business here for Christ's sake. What's the matter with you all? You're in a foreign country—the Japanese will eventually own California—get used to it."

"Can we go home?" Leanne asked.

"We haven't even been here a week. We can go to Disneyland."

"We've been there," Andy said.

"It's probably different here."

"Too many people," Andy said. "We'd have to wait in lines all day."

"Yeah, you're right," Layton agreed. "But we can't go home yet, the festival starts tomorrow. Don't you want to see my pictures?"

"Haven't we seen them all on video?" Leanne asked.

"You've never seen them dubbed into Japanese."

"Who wants to?" Andy asked.

"We do," Amy said coming to his defense. "That's why we came here. Your father needs us."

"All right, look," Layton shouted through his wired jaw. "I promised Mariko I'd meet with the beer people about that commercial, so you guys do whatever you like, go out or stay here and bitch and moan about not having any fun. When I get back we'll try and figure out a way to get through another week, fair enough?"

Frustrated by their refusal to give Japan a chance Layton stopped in the lobby to mail a postcard to Mark, wondering if he would have appreciated this trip more than Andy and Leanne.

Wanting to prove that it was possible to get around Tokyo by himself Layton decided against a taxi and opted for the subway. How difficult could it be to get to the Ginza? He asked a uniformed attendant who stood by a turnstile if he was headed in the right direction but the man ignored him. "Ginza?" he tried again.

The attendant stared straight ahead. Layton thought he might be blind and passed his hand in front of the man's eyes. They blinked and Layton stuck his face directly in front of the man's face, practically touching noses. "Ginza?"

No response.

Maybe he was deaf. But then a woman asked him a question and he responded in rapid Japanese. Layton tried again, touching the man on his shoulder. "Ginza? Ginza?"

As far as this attendant was concerned Layton was invisible.

"Excuse me," someone said, tapping Layton on his shoulder. "He cannot speak Engrish so he doesn't answer. It is very embarrassing for him."

Layton turned to see a smiling man in a dark blue suit who offered to help. He led him through the turnstile and said that he, too, was going to Ginza and was he correct in assuming that he was speaking to the famous actor Rayton Closs?

Layton warmed immediately. "I have seen all your movies and rike them very much. I have read about your film festival. You are a fine actor. I am sorry..." his words trailed off and Layton never got to hear his regret because the train approached and they pushed their way in.

Ginza was only a few stops away. The ad company was on the twenty-seventh floor of the building opposite the subway entrance. Mariko was waiting for him, her red and gold makeup sparkled like her hair. "You look like Christmas," he said.

"That's how I rike to feel." She was beaming. She knew how excited these ad men were landing an American movie star to hype their client's product. There was great competition between these companies to see who could represent the most foreign celebrities, especially those like Woody Allen, Clint Eastwood, and Charlie Sheen who did commercials in Japan but wouldn't do them in their own country.

Layton thought their ideas were bland. Surely, they could come up with something more original than having him swallow a glass of beer in a crowded bar or hold up a bottle and talk about its pleasures after a hard day on location. Uninteresting, he told them. And with his mouth wired how could he drink the beer without a straw? He had a better idea.

He wanted to film it in the subway. Get the attendant who ignored him and have Layton approach him for directions, just the way it happened. Then have a woman come, ask a question and get an answer. Layton would return holding a bottle of the beer, offering it in return for a response. The attendant would bow and answer happily...in English!

The ad men and the beer executives held a conference and agreed to try it though they were careful to conceal their reluctance. Their concern was not to make the attendant appear foolish. Their purpose, after all, was to sell their beer to a very sensitive people.

He got back to the hotel in time for dinner but his family had already eaten–at McDonald's.

"What'd you have, a McSushi burger with squid McNuggets?"

Andy laughed and kept repeating it as Layton ordered fish soup from room service. He was in a better mood, having found transformers and gobots at a toy store that he'd never seen back home. Leanne got a porcelain doll dressed in a kimono. "You won't believe how much it cost," she said.

"Don't tell me, I want to like it."

"Wait'll you see what mommy got."

Amy came out dressed in leather: boots, skirt, suede shirt, jacket. "It cost a fortune," she said triumphantly. "Now we're all feeling better."

The next day, Saturday, was the opening of the film festival and they showed up at noon to meet the press, stand for photos, and thank the audience for coming. The theater was too large for the small crowd. Fellini must have captured the true movie buffs. Yet it was with much ceremony that Layton was introduced, and with some shame when he and his family left after the first twenty minutes.

"We've seen the picture," Layton explained to Mariko. "We just wanted to get an idea what it was like in Japanese."

"Maybe you would like to go to the public baths," she suggested. "It is very soothing."

An afternoon bath might be nice after watching himself talking Japanese in a three-quarter empty theater.

It was a new experience. Unlike the saunas and Jacuzzis of the ultra chic sports clubs in L.A. these were waters that tested one's spirit. There were no jets pumping bubbles like warm champagne, rather the appeal was the degree of the water itself. Like some of the pools at the Desert Hot Springs. Only hotter. So hot it was close to scalding, especially to skin that had never been in such water before. The steam from the shallow pool rose like smoke from a cauldron. Amy could make out figures of women soaking but couldn't see them clearly. There were mirrors on the walls but you needed a washcloth to wipe a circle clear enough to see yourself. Mariko led Amy and Leanne to low faucets where she demonstrated the Japanese way of bathing: washing with soap first, rinsing, then soaking in the hellish waters. As Mariko dropped her towel Amy noticed her perfectly formed large round breasts.

"Nice," she said, dropping her own towel, "where'd you have those done?"

Mariko smiled demurely. "You can tell?"

"God doesn't give such a pair to many women."

"Japanese women are not very big," Mariko said as she soaped herself. "I have always liked your Maliryn Monloe, she was so beautiful."

Leanne felt extremely self-conscious in a room with so many naked adult women but her mother encouraged her to follow Mariko's example and soap up. As Mariko rinsed Amy looked to see if her pubic hair was also dyed. It was.

"Japanese women all look the same down there," Mariko said when she caught Amy's glance. "I rike being different."

"What do the men think?"

"It makes them crazy. They become very macho."

They walked to the boiling pool and Mariko slid in quickly. Leanne held Amy's hand as they tested the water, pulling out instantly. "Mommy!" Leanne pleaded, not wanting to burn herself further.

"What the hell honey, it can't hurt that much if all these women are in there."

Bravely, they entered the water, their nerves screaming in pain from the shock. "Now I know how a lobster feels when we throw it into a pot," Amy said. She looked at Leanne's bright flushed face and felt her own. "I wonder how your father and Andy are handling this."

After undressing, and with no one offering instruction, Layton proceeded to embarrass himself and Andy by heading straight for the hot water, not understanding the old men who pointed behind him, waving their hands. They didn't want this big hairy *gaijin* and his young son to dirty their waters and were trying to get them to wash first. But there was so much steam that Layton couldn't make out what it was they were telling him so he just nodded, smiled and slid into the clean burning pool. Which didn't stay clean once Andy entered. The heat made him pee and since the water was so clear his urine marked a stringy path in front of him. This was too much for some of the men who got out yelling at these intruders. One small gentleman actually grabbed Layton by the arm and pulled him out of the water, walking him to the faucets. Layton watched as the man soaped himself and nodded understanding. He went back for Andy but didn't see him. Then, as the top of Andy's head bobbed to the surface, he ran in quickly to pull the boy out.

Andy had fainted from the heat and almost drowned. Layton squeezed him, then put him down and blew air into his mouth. The boy's eyes opened, he coughed, and Layton closed his eyes in thanks.

When Amy saw Layton holding Andy she knew what had happened and insisted they go back to the hotel for the rest of the evening. Layton reminded her that Mariko had arranged dinner for them but the children had had enough for the day.

"You go back," he said, "I'll meet you there later."

"Some festival," Amy muttered.

"Your wife is not happy," Mariko observed as they sat on tatami mats drinking saki.

"It's the children, they want to go home."

"And your wife?"

"We're not married any more."

"I forgot. You are together but not married, is that for the children?"

"No, it's for us."

"You are not sure."

"Amy's an extraordinary woman in some ways; she's got a certain spark. I like that. But she's also very emotional. It can be draining."

"I understand."

"You probably do. I read your poems."

"They did not embarrass you?"

"They're very explicit."

"I don't care much for symborism."

"If you want to know, I found them arousing. I was wondering how a woman as young as you could know so much about men."

"I am not as young as you think."

"Anyone younger than I am is still young."

"You are how old then? Forty?"

"Thank you."

"I am fifty-one."

"No one who looks like you can be fifty-one," he said incredulously.

"You fratter me."

"I can't believe it."

"It does not offend you being with an older woman?"

"Offend? You are one of the most beautiful women I've ever seen."

"Are you seducing me?"

Layton backed off. "Are your writings well known here?"

"My books sell well, yes. I think also because of the way I look. I was very infruenced by your movie stars. Maliryn Monloe, Jane Lussell, Jean Harrow, Madonna. I started giving poetry leadings in the sixties wearing very sexy outfits with my face all made up and my hair dyed different corors. People riked that."

"I can imagine."

"Today I perform less but still, sometimes."

"I'd love to see you perform."

"Maybe."

After dinner she took Layton to a karaoke bar where patrons sang into microphones that were passed around. It didn't matter if you couldn't sing, it was a chance to be in the spotlight and these bars were enormously popular.

They were also packed like the subways. People were mostly tipsy from drink and stood shoulder to shoulder, cheering on each singer, encouraging the shy ones, laughing at those whose voices cracked, crying over the occasional moving song. It didn't take long for Layton and Mariko to be noticed. He was the only *gaijin* and she the only redhead. A microphone was passed back to them and Layton took it, not knowing he was expected to sing. He began to thank everyone for being so kind and he said he hoped they would be attending the festival...but he was shouted down. No one wanted a speech.

"Stop talking, sing," Mariko said.

"I can't sing."

"You will offend everybody."

In a deep off-key voice Layton sang the first verse of "Time Is On My Side," followed by "Wake Up, Little Susie," and "Louie Louie." When he was through he handed the mike to Mariko who sang a beautiful Japanese lullaby. The laughter ceased and the crowd got quiet. Mariko had a way of taming the masses.

When she finished tall glasses of beer were passed to them. Drunken men slapped Layton on the back. One man said to him in English, "You rike fucky our women who won't fucky us."

"Your women are very nice," Layton shouted.

The man then spoke in Japanese and Layton asked Mariko to translate.

"He says he just came out of plison. He is a fool and should be ignored."

But the man kept talking and Layton, getting into the spirit of the bar, asked Mariko to keep translating.

"He says he has been rocked up for seven years and now he is cereblating his fleedom."

"Good for you. Let me buy you a drink."

The man continued talking as they drank. "He says that he has many tattoos and wants to know if you'd like to see them?"

"Love to."

"I don't think so," Mariko said.

By this time the man was rolling up his sleeves to reveal arms covered with snakes and flowers. As Layton nodded in admiration the man unbuttoned his shirt showing off the eagle on his chest, an airplane bomber on his back. There wasn't an inch of his skin that wasn't covered.

He unbuckled his belt and dropped his pants. Layton stared. The man was going to strip naked for him. Mariko told him to stop but he pushed her away.

"Don't do that," Layton said.

The man started talking very fast.

"What's he saying now?"

"He says he wants to know if you want to fight."

"Tell him no."

"He says he is a very good fighter and he would rike to go outside so he can show you."

"Not interested."

"He says he could beat you up in ress than a minute."

"How do we get rid of him?"

Mariko said some words and when he refused to listen she kicked him in the balls and he went down. "Let's go now," she said taking Layton's hand.

"I can't believe you did that. I never knew Japanese women were so tough."

"He wanted to hurt you."

"He was drunk."

"He was strong. And fearress."

"How could you tell?"

"His balls were very hard."

"I'd better get back and check on Amy and the kids," Layton said.

"Come one more prace with me. I think you will enjoy."

They walked a few blocks to a tall building and went inside. She paid a man four thousand yen and took Layton down a long hallway.

"What is this place?"

"This is capsule hotel."

She found the compartment she had paid for and opened the curtain. It resembled a sleeper in a train. There was a bed, a built-in TV and radio, kimonos to change into. Layton smiled.

"I thought we could make rove here before you go back," Mariko said.

"Is it big enough?"

"We can stay very crose."

There were compartments on each side and above; men were sleeping or watching TV in all of them. Layton felt awkward. Mariko was a very direct, experienced woman and he had no doubt he'd get an education if he took off his clothes, but something held him back. It didn't feel right, with Amy taking care of the kids at the hotel. He had drunk enough saki and beer to excuse himself for whatever he might do but he was also feeling guilty. It shouldn't matter, he argued with himself, he wasn't married, there were no promises, he'd certainly fucked around while they were married, this was Japan, he'd only be there another week, she was great-looking, her poems were hot, she was fifty-fucking-one, his festival was a disappointment, he was getting older, he trusted no one, he was owed half his money on a movie that had already cost him a working jaw, he was being offered a mighty tempting piece of ass, he had never made it with an Asian woman, his kids were safe, he wanted to do it. So?

So he was sure Amy would know. And although he wasn't certain it would even bother her, he reversed the situation and knew that it would bother him. If this meant that he was beginning to re-love Amy then why add guilt to his feelings just for the hell of it? Fucking Mariko might topple an already teetering trip. Better they should sit in the tiny compartment and watch the news. Talk of poetry. Pass meaningful glances.

"I don't think so," Layton finally whispered.

"I'm very good," she smiled.

"I'm trying to be."

"You were so funny when that man showed you his tattoo's," she giggled. "I wrote a haiku from what you said." She took out a small pad and translated her words:

> "I laughed
> when you wondered
> if the tattooed man
> had a snake on his
> plick."

"You know," she confessed, "I wanted this festival because I wanted to know you."

"I thought I was the only one available."

"No. I have always admired you. I wondered what it would be like to be with you like this."

"You write any other poems?"

"Small ones."

> "I go to the movies
> each time
> you look into my eyes."

Layton looked into her eyes. He wanted to kiss her but his mouth couldn't open. She read his thoughts, then read another haiku.

> "When we kiss
> call me Maliryn
> I'll call you Crark."

"Thanks a lot," he joked.

"It's just a poem. Crark Gable was a very romantic man. I rike his movies."

The subject had changed. In the taxi they made arrangements to meet at the ad agency the next morning and then she wrote another poem but said she wouldn't read it because it was just a fantasy, best to imagine than hear.

>   A short chirp
>   came from your mouth
>   as you came inside me.

By the time he knocked at their room Amy had decided that he had fucked that red-haired twat and not even a half bottle of Suntory whiskey was able to dull her rage. She had played out scenarios of her own and they all ended up with the humping of the two-backed beast. She saw it in Mariko's eyes when they bathed. She felt it in her gut when she arrived back at the hotel. And when Andy asked why his daddy had to go out with that lady she knew exactly why. The bastard brought her along to babysit! She could have been editing a movie, making money, feeling useful, not stuck in some goddamn Japanese hotel worrying about the effect 120 degree water had on seven and ten year-olds while their father was out doing the town with a whore cunt poet who masturbates at the movies.

"It's past midnight, you slime!" were the words which first poured from her mouth. "Don't deny what you've been doing, I don't want to hear your lies. Your practiced bullshit lines. I know. I KNOW!"

Layton also knew: that there was no way he was going to convince her that he had not slept with Mariko and that he should have done it since she wouldn't believe him, would always suspect him, and it didn't make him feel good being in the right knowing that she would be the one wearing the martyred look home.

"I had a great time," he teased inappropriately. "She was unbelievable."

Amy's eyes darted from side to side looking for something to throw. Layton was playing with her now; she knew this side of him. Here she was trying to put the pieces back together, to reason out another chance, and he was making her feel so low, so greasy. Smiling like that.

But she was misreading his smile. Her jealousy, like Leanne's fighting, was a positive sign, an act of recovery. There had been so much love lost; each had doubted whether there was anything to rekindle. Now Layton was resisting temptation and Amy was suffering from jealousy. There was still something between them. They had a chance.

"So okay, believe what you like, you drunken witch," Layton said resolutely, recalling something Fellini once said about marital relationships being based on fundamental misunderstandings. "Only if you think I fucked her wait till you see what I'm going to do to you."

"Stay away from me," she backed away.

"Not tonight. Tonight I want to stay as close to you as possible. I want to feel your insides."

Amy slapped at him but it was a submissive blow. He held her and felt her body almost crumble. She looked up and they kissed. It wasn't sloppy, open-mouthed, tongue-searching–that was impossible in his condition–but it was quietly passionate.

He led her to the bedroom and undressed her. Then they made the best love they had made in years. A short chirp came through Layton's clenched teeth as he came inside her.

Amy answered with a very large groan.

■ ■ ■

The role of subway attendant was too much for the real attendant to handle so the agency hired an actor. But it didn't feel right. He kept smiling at Layton rather than ignoring him. They shot the scene all morning and finally came up with one they all agreed might work. Then the crew and the executives applauded Layton and left him feeling he had mattered.

Mariko composed another short poem:

> You know so little
> of our customs–
> Yet you are game.

She said that if he stayed another week she'd probably write a small book. But at its heart, she told him, would be rejection. Unless he changed his mind about her.

And here Layton thought that Japanese women were shy, coy, subtle, mysterious. Mariko broke every stereotype. She was aggressive, straightforward, candid, and used to having her way. Seducing Layton had become a game for her. Now that her intentions were declared she had little doubt she'd emerge victorious.

Amy met them at the theater. If she was still concerned about Mariko she didn't show it. But she did slip her arm around Layton's and walked inside with him. The audience was the same as the first day and he offered to shake everyone's hand, figuring it would only take a few minutes. He posed for pictures with those who bought tickets, signed autographs, thanked them for coming, and then left when the lights went down. Mariko had got them tickets to a sumo wrestling match and they spent the rest of the afternoon eating packaged rice balls, watching giant naked men slam their bodies into each other as their hands searched frantically for a throwing grip. Leanne appeared to enjoy it almost as much as Andy. Layton held Amy's hand. They were actually having fun as a family.

On the third day of the festival Layton dutifully went to greet whatever audience was still interested only to discover that due to the small number of tickets sold the screening had been moved to a small theater in a nearby office building. Mariko was terribly embarrassed by this but Layton took it well. Hell, he thought, in another week he'd have the wires removed from his mouth and he'd be able to eat again.

She told him that she had arranged for a special closing night's party at the home of one of Japan's leading actors and that Kurosawa had indicated he would make every effort to attend. Layton didn't get his hopes up but he felt that if the great director appeared it would make a personally significant trip (Amy's jealous appreciation, their renewed feelings, Leanne's smiling face) memorable.

But an urgent fax waiting for him at the hotel kept him from ever finding out. Five brief words sent them packing and to the airport to catch a late-night flight back to Los Angeles.

                COME BACK. MARK'S MISSING.
                         Samantha

13

Holy Shit!

At the time when Layton sent the postcard to Mark wondering if he would have appreciated Japan more than Leanne and Andy, Mark was fumbling to remove Reya's bra as they probed each other's mouths with their tongues. Mark was enamored by her freshness, like the smell of clean laundry. Their sexual awakening had come at the same time and every touch tingled. They were at that age where nothing else could be as important as the exploration of each other's bodies. It was as if a whole new world had opened to them and their passion made them reckless. As soon as they got out of school they met at whose ever house was more available. Part of Reya's excitement was sneaking into Mark's house and up to his room. His mother was her favorite actress, even more than Winona Ryder, and that had a good deal to do with why she made herself so available to Mark. During their periods of calm she liked to explore the bathrooms, peek into Samantha's bedroom, scrutinize the paperweights, gilded birdcages, sculpted jade and coral; admire the Tiffany lamps, the priceless drawings and paintings, the Oriental rugs, the knick-knacks and gadgets of this very singular superstar.

She wanted Mark to introduce her to his mother but he was reluctant. He knew she would disapprove. Reya was too casual, too loose, too dripping with her new-found sexuality to be anything but disturbing to Samantha, who would recognize immediately that some of her attraction to Mark was his proximity to her. And Mark didn't want to have to compete with his mother for the attention he craved solely for himself. He certainly didn't want Samantha to dismiss Reya with a cutting remark or by ignoring her completely. Such behavior might cut off the sexual Pandora's Box that had been opened to him. Definitely, it was best to keep Reya away from Samantha.

But it wasn't easy. Once safely in his room she would ask if his mother was in the house. If Mark became uneasy she'd put her hand on his fly or take his hand and put it on hers. They'd touch each other, get excited, she'd pull away to prolong their lust and ask more questions about Samantha.

There is just so much restraint a fifteen-year-old can be expected to display before he agrees to make the object of his desire a partner in his private life. And so it was that when Reya discovered the intercom system Mark and Samantha used to contact each other she couldn't keep from suggesting that Mark press the HOLD button to the intercom in Samantha's study so that they could listen to her when she was there.

Such an invasion of his mother's privacy frightened Mark and he refused to consider it. But as Reya's passion waned and he began to feel the pangs of frustration due to his unwillingness to go along with her girlish curiosity, his nobility began to crumble. After all, it would be interesting to listen in on one of his mother's business meetings. And what the hell, it wouldn't hurt anybody. Reya could get off on eavesdropping and he could probe his fingers into her as they listened. He could even try out some of the mail-order sex toys he had sent away for.

So when Uncle Charlie Greenbloom came to the house Mark turned on the intercom and ran back to his bedroom where Reya waited naked under the covers.

Greenbloom had come to discuss their picture, which was nearing completion. Mancino had suggested a different ending and Samantha wasn't happy with it because it cut one of her dramatic scenes. Greenbloom felt there was room for a reasonable compromise but found Samantha in an irritable mood. When she was that way he knew not to attempt to ask her for anything, not even to listen to possible solutions. So they talked around the film, unaware that their words were not for their ears only.

"So what's on your mind Charlie?"

"Ah, a lot of aggravation. This business...."

"You didn't come to complain, I'm too busy for that."

"So, how do you feel so far?"

"You know how I feel. Like we're making a big mistake with this thing. I shouldn't have let you talk me into it. We should have waited until the script was right."

"I didn't talk you into it; you brought the project to me."

"And you jumped at it before you even read it. I know you Charlie, Just get the monkey to act, you'll sell the popcorn."

"Have I ever steered you wrong?"

"Don't let's get into that one."

"Name me once, one regret, name me."

"You're giving me a headache; I'll be back."

As the intercom hummed Reya bit into an apple and asked Mark if he had a joint.

"I don't keep anything in the house."

"Oh wait, I've got one." She jumped out of bed and found a joint in her pants pocket. "Wait'll you try this, it's like the best smoke."

"Where'd you get it?"

"One of the guys in school."

"Which guy?"

"Oh come on Mark, don't be a drag."

"I just want to know, that's all."

"You want to know if I'm balling him too, that's what you want to know."

"Are you?"

"None of your fucking beeswax. Do I ask you if you have other girls here? Huh, do I?"

"Do you care?"

"I know you don't, so I don't care." She lit up and passed it to him. He didn't like the way she could twist him into a knot so easily. Samantha's voice came back into the room.

"So I heard that *Sand Man* project is almost finished. How is it?"

"Piece 'a shit."

"Releasable?"

"Who knows? Could do business."

"Layton any good?"

"What do you think?"

"He hasn't been good in so long what can I think?"

"Let's put it this way, in this movie he's good. Only in it for ten, fifteen minutes, gets the crap knocked out of him, but compared, he's head and shoulders...."

"Mark thinks I should do a picture with him, can you imagine?"

"Sure, when you're ready to self-destruct. How is Mark?"

"He's got some girlfriend he's very secretive about."

Reya jabbed Mark in the arm. She was smiling so hard he thought her lips might split. He tried to get on top of her but she wanted to hear.

"You meet her?"

"Are you kidding? He won't bring her here."

"You should check it out. I'd hate to be a kid having sex today."

"You've got three of them, they got any diseases?"

"They've got their own families, think I see them? When they want to go to a movie they come over."

"Well, Mark's got a way to go."

"I wonder if he'll ever find out."

"You want him to know?"

447

"Probably too late, don't you think?"

Mark stopped trying to penetrate Reya and listened. What were they talking about? Find out what?

"I think I'd better turn this off," he said. Whatever it was he didn't want Reya to hear.

"Hey, don't be stupid, they're talking about you." She took his arm and pulled him back. He rested his head on her chest, touching one nipple with his index finger. Listening.

"Ever wonder what his father would do?"

"You mean Layton?"

"Yeah."

"Layton's a schmuck. I don't know what you ever saw in him."

"He provided you with a pretty good cover."

"I've never been comfortable with Mark thinking that's his father."

"What makes you such a prize? You're a glorified agent, just at another point in your pinwheel."

"I'm the boy's father."

"So, you got lucky that day."

"One day he's gonna find out."

"I hope not. For all our sakes."

"He's a...

"If you...

"Layton's not...

"Piece 'a shit...

They were talking, the words were coming in, but Mark wasn't hearing straight. What he had heard was so disorienting he forgot Reya was there. Other than an exclamation of "Holy shit!" she was almost as stunned as he. She just shared a stoned moment of an extremely personal revelation and didn't know how to handle it. And if she didn't, what about Mark? What was going through his head?

"You okay?" she whispered.

He didn't hear her. He was staring at the mirror, seeing himself in the distance sitting up in his bed. He stood, went to his desk, took the framed picture of him and his mother and flung it across the room, shattering it.

Reya slipped out of the bed and quietly put her clothes on. Mark was not taking what he had heard gently and she didn't want to be there if his mother came upstairs.

"Goddamn her!" he shouted. "Goddamn her!" His shouts released his tears. He stood in the center of his room naked, angry, shocked. His body jerked in spasms, he let out huge sorrowful sobs. His life had been a deceit. His mother was a whore. His father...his father...who the fuck was his father? Charlie Pompous Greenbloom? No fucking way. And who was Layton Cross? How could she do this? Why? GODDAMN HER!

"I'd better go," Reya said from across the room.

He looked at her as if she could reduce his anguish. Go? Right, he would go; he had to go. He couldn't stay in his mother's house any longer.

"Wait," he said, grabbing at his clothes. He dressed quickly, taking the skateboard by his door as they ran down the stairs and out of the house. Greenbloom's black

Ferrari was in the driveway and Mark swung his skateboard into the door.

Once in the street they walked in silence. Reya tried to thumb a ride from passing cars and eventually one stopped. They got in and she did the talking. Mark was lost in thought.

All those presents Greenbloom had given him. The interest he paid over the years. The offers he made. Anything you want, kid? Anything you need? You can always count on Uncle Charlie, kid. When you're ready I'll give you a job at the studio. One day, who knows, you'll take over; your mother will be making movies for you.

And his father? Those early years...his childhood... sitting on Layton's shoulders to see the Macy's parade. The games they used to watch as Layton stuffed him with ballpark franks, chocolate malts, souvenir pennants, hats, pins, stuffed animals. The Disney movies. The fights with his mother. The yelling, cursing, door slamming. His disappearing for days, weeks. And when he'd return, the hugs, the tears. Daddy, don't go away again; Daddy, I love you.

But Mommy didn't love Daddy. Mommy was too busy looking for love elsewhere. Finding it with "Uncle" Charlie. Who was always there. Especially when Daddy was gone. Charlie talking to Mom late at night. Go to sleep Mark, I want to talk to your Uncle Charlie. Talk? *Talk?*

"I've got an older cousin who lives in Burbank, I could call him," Reya offered when they got out of the car.

"What am I going to do in Burbank? It's the pits."

"Any place is the pits after your house."

"I just need some time by myself."

"Where will you go?"

"I don't know."

It was awkward for both of them as they stood facing each other on San Vicente Boulevard.

"You want to come back to my house?"

"No, my mom would find me there for sure."

"She doesn't even know me."

"You don't know her. She has her ways."

Reya kissed him on the cheek and he walked away, heading west towards the ocean. He had so few friends, no one he could really count on, no one to talk to.

At an intersection he waited for the right vehicle and when a truck approached he dropped his skateboard, stood on it, and held onto the back of the truck as it gunned its way down the boulevard. The wind in his face made him conscious of movement, the danger of letting go forced him to concentrate. When the truck slowed for a light Mark felt like the end man on crack-the-whip. He maneuvered the skateboard onto the grass divider before he came crashing to the ground.

"That's some trick," a young man in a Fiat convertible called out. "Do you practice that or are you just naturally into masochism?"

Mark brushed himself off without answering.

"I'm heading in the same direction as that truck," the young man offered, "you want a ride, hop in."

The guy looked harmless enough.

"So what are you, a street surfer?"

"That supposed to be a joke?" Mark said.

"Ooo, touchy. Sor-ry. Where you heading?"

"Just down a ways."

"Well I'm going to Santa Barbara so you just tell me when you want out."

Santa Barbara? Samantha would never think of looking for him there. The kids at school often talked about their weekends in Santa Barbara but he had never been there, even though it was only ninety miles away. If this guy was willing he'd go for the ride. What he'd do once there he had no idea.

Charlie Greenbloom was furious when he saw the dent in his Ferrari and came storming back into Samantha's house wanting to know who she had working on the premises. As it wasn't her car Samantha couldn't be bothered. "It's just a car Charlie, get it fixed."

After he departed Samantha went upstairs. Mark's door was open so she stuck her head in, noticing the messy bed. Then she saw the broken picture frame on the floor and stepped carefully into the room. The dent in the wall where her picture had been thrown indicated it was no accident. She shouted Mark's name. When he didn't respond she yelled for her secretary who came running.

Had she seen Mark? No? Was he in the house? Find out.

Faye Collabella ran down the stairs and began her search for the boy as Samantha picked up the shards of glass. What could have so upset him to do such a thing? His temper was usually contained; he rarely exploded in such fashion. Unless he was throwing it at somebody. It could be signs of a struggle; he could have been kidnapped like that Polly Klaas, right out of his own bedroom. That might explain Charlie's car as well, Mark might have kicked it in his struggle. Her greatest fear, besides losing her popularity as an actress, had always been that he might one day be kidnapped. He was such an obvious target. That's why she had been so protective. She didn't want to receive Mark's ear in the mail.

But then, she reasoned, how could anyone get through her security without the alarms going off or the dogs barking? More likely it was that girl he was seeing. He might have had an argument, got upset, and threw the first thing that came to hand.

She went to straighten his bed and noticed a strange flesh-colored plastic cylinder the size of a hair-roller near the pillow. She picked it up and examined the vein-like ridges on the outside. Was it part of one of Mark's transformers? she wondered.

His night table drawer was slightly opened and she pulled it further. That's when she found out that it was something to stick your penis through. The device was called a splint and the information in the booklet she found said that it was an erection aid for prolonging your staying power. But that was not all–there was another device called an ejaculator that was an inflatable sheath that went over a penis with an attached bulb that created a pulsating feeling when squeezed. Then there was something called a vibrating mouth that was another gadget to stick your penis into, connected to a multi-speed remote control. Samantha stuck two fingers into it and turned it on. The thing tightened and vibrated. She put it down and picked up a tube of sta-hard, which was a desensitizing lubricant to prevent premature ejaculation. And then she looked at the comic books he had hidden away: Young Lust, Tits 'n' Clits, Bizarre Sex, In Heat, Gang Bang, The Adventures of Luna.

Who was this stranger living in this room? Why didn't he come to her if he had problems with premature ejaculation? What did he need a plastic splint for? Was this stuff normal for a fifteen-year-old?

Mark's private sexual world gave her the creeps. She wanted to empty this drawer of personal toys in the trash but that might be over-reacting. If he was getting himself jerked-off with these things, wasn't that safer than actual sex? But that didn't explain away the tube of sta-hard or the plastic splint. You didn't use those things unless you were getting laid. So, it was true. Her boy, her baby, was no longer a virgin. Okay, she could live with that. But did he have to be so perverted?

Her secretary returned saying she couldn't find Mark and no one saw him leave.

"Probably needed some pussy," Samantha cracked. Collabella, never having heard Samantha talk like that about Mark, figured she meant he was out looking for a cat.

■ ■ ■

"You look kind of young to be going to Santa Barbara on your own, you have friends there?"

His name was Etan. He was twenty-four, gay, a native Californian who sold bagels from a factory in Santa Barbara to outlets in L.A., Malibu, and Ventura County. He had moved out of his house at seventeen when his parents could no longer deal with his sexual persuasion and he'd been on his own ever since, living with different men who treated him as a son, lover, boy-toy, or meanly. But he had managed to survive, liked his life, and was willing to show Mark a few tricks if he was so disposed.

That's what Mark had learned by the time they had passed Pepperdine University and lost sight of the Pacific. Mark's silence encouraged Etan to go on, detailing his experiences in the rough trade that led him, finally, to seek out a partner closer to his own age. "But with AIDS and what-have-you it's practically impossible to find someone unless he's a virgin, you know what I mean? You aren't a virgin by any chance? Are there any left after puberty? You're not, heaven forbid, straight, are you? Would be my luck to pick up a straight virgin and take him all the way to Santa Barbara without so much as a kiss to be expected in return."

"I'm not a virgin," Mark said.

"Well that's half of it, isn't it?"

"And I'm not a fag."

"No need to be so hostile."

"Sorry."

"I could show you ways to make your prick get harder and thicker that you wouldn't believe was possible. But

I'm not going to force myself on you or anything, just idle conversation to pass the time."

My mother should see me now, Mark thought. Listen to what this guy's talking about. Jesus.

"You running away? I'm only asking because you seem to have a lot on your mind, you're so pensive."

"When did you know you were gay?" Mark asked.

"When I pushed away my mother's tit when I was three months old. Just had no interest, right from the start."

Mark didn't have to say another word all the way to Oxnard as Etan proceeded to relate his childhood history, including graphic descriptions of all the little penises he fondled and what the sight of his dad's big hairy dick did to his impressionable mind. He was actually quite funny but Mark couldn't appreciate such twisted humor. He kept thinking about how Layton was going to react when he found out the truth. Could it really be that his dad was no longer his dad? And would it change their feelings towards each other? Layton was the only father he ever knew. He loved him. Charlie Greenbloom was just an asshole, had always been one. He could never call Charlie father, even if that was who he really was. It was all his mother's fault. He would like to strangle her.

When it got dark Samantha began to worry. Layton had always said she was overprotective; that she should leave the boy alone, let him develop independently. Well she hadn't raised him to be independent and now she discovered he had a secret life, her picture was cracked and he was missing. He had so few friends; he must have gone to see that girl. What was her name? Where did she live?

"Faye! I want you to find him. Call his friends, his teachers, find out who the girl is and see if he's there."

"I'm sure he'll be back soon," Collabella volunteered.

"I'm not paying you to be sure about the whereabouts of my son. Just get him on the phone and tell him to get his ass back here immediately. Tell him if he's not back in an hour there'll be no dinner for him."

Dinner, she thought. What did he care about dinner when he probably had his head buried in some teenage hair pie? She looked in the mirror examining her face for wrinkles, white hairs, skin discolorations. She looked terrific, not like the mother of a boy who was old enough to use mechanical ejaculators and rubber cocksuckers. What was really disturbing her was that Mark had apparently grown up overnight. She hadn't prepared herself for that.

■ ■ ■

Santa Barbara was the second home for the Hollywood rich. It was also the Beverly Hills for the illegal aliens who managed to make it out of Los Angeles. It was a beautiful place to retire and walk the few streets of a meticulously kept downtown or stop along the coast and watch the sun go down. And for the entrepreneur with a poet's heart it was a place to start a small business as the children grew up in a sheltered, nonconfrontational environment.

As Etan drove down State Street Mark looked at the tiled sidewalks and low-rise buildings. Etan parked behind the Brooklyn Bagel Factory and they entered by the back door. Stacks of freshly baked bagels were piled along the walls. The place smelled from cinnamon, onion and whole wheat. Mark stood by the conveyor belt as it carried soft bagels and wondered if his prick would fit through a bagel hole.

A middle-aged Santa with sparkling eyes and a red beard stood watching as the ovens were unloaded, as the bagels were picked off the belt and placed on trays, as they were cooled and hand wrapped in plastic sleeves that held six. When he noticed Mark a smile that approached a tease appeared as he asked him if he was with Etan.

"He gave me a ride," Mark answered.

The man looked him over and was sure this kid had a face he had seen before.

"Jacob," Etan said. "I was looking for you in your office."

"I saw you come in. How was L.A.?"

"Wrote up 7-11, you're going to make a fortune. And I'll take my bonus in cash not bagels, thank you."

Mark didn't know what he was doing there. The way this Jacob looked at him made him feel vaguely uncomfortable. It was only then, when he put his hand in his pocket, that he realized he had forgotten his wallet. He had no money.

Jacob Asher owned the Brooklyn Bagel Factory but he wasn't just a baker. Bagels were the idea he and his wife

Manya had when they moved to Santa Barbara. Before that he had worked for a local think tank and before that he was an assistant dean of men at USC. He had published two volumes of poetry and kept in close touch with his screenwriter and journalist friends in L.A. He had an enormous appetite for magazines and read dozens of them each week. His mind worked like a computer, restlessly sifting through facts and images until arriving at points of understanding through association. Ten minutes after studying Mark's features he recognized the face. He had to be the son of Samantha Sanders.

"You look hungry," Asher said, "eat one of these, they're new." He gave him a jalapeno chocolate sour dough bagel.

"Jake, can we talk, I want to get back to L.A. before midnight," Etan interrupted. "You're going to have to schedule the truck."

"Go across the street to the deli," Asher told Mark. "Ask for the cheese blintzes, tell the waitress I sent you, my treat."

"Why?" Mark asked. He was used to people being nice to him because of his mother but here, on his own, it was unexpected.

"Because you look like you just lost your dog. There's a space in your heart the size of a bagel hole. What's your name?"

Mark told him, then walked to the deli thinking the man was off only by degree. It wasn't a dog he'd lost.

"Let me make a call, then we'll take care of business," Asher said as he went to his office. He wanted to check in with his old college roommate Alex Briar, who he knew was working against a deadline to finish his first book. If this kid really was who he thought he was that meant he was Layton Cross' son and Briar should be very interested in that.

"What's Samantha Sanders' son's name?" he asked Briar, lighting a cigarette and smiling at the answer. "Well, I don't know if this means anything to you but the kid is eating blintzes at my deli right now, looks about as glum as you must have felt when Cross shot you."

Briar didn't know what it meant but from all he had gathered in his research the kid was hardly ever out of his mother's sight. If Asher could find out what he was doing there it would be worth knowing.

"What are friends for?" Asher said.

He went across the street to join Mark, who apologized that he had forgotten his wallet and didn't even have money for a tip.

"Forget it," Asher said. "Next time you see a hungry kid with his hands in his pockets buy him a sandwich."

It was dark as Mark sipped coffee and wondered about this friendly bagel man who told him about his past lives and how he wound up in Santa Barbara. Asher was so giving and open Mark almost reciprocated, but what could he say? He was never comfortable telling people who his parents were; it always created a distance that was difficult to bridge. And with the current turmoil in his life he wasn't able to focus on anything else. Like his mother, he wasn't good at small talk.

"You need some part-time work?" Asher offered. Mark shrugged. "Where're you staying?"

"I don't know."

"Well, seeing as you're broke, it's not a bad idea to give it some thought."

"I could sleep on the beach."

"Gets pretty cold. I've got a small guesthouse that's vacant; it's yours for the night if you want it. I'll make you a deal–I've got a four-year-old who loves books. If you read to him for an hour and if he trusts you, then maybe my wife and I will take in a movie and let you babysit. We'll throw in breakfast and call it even."

On the drive to Asher's home in Carpentaria Mark wondered about what it would be like working at the bagel factory. He had never worked in his life. Once he applied for a job at Baskin-Robbins and was accepted but his mother wouldn't let him take it. "It'll just wind up in the papers and who needs that?" she said.

When Faye Collabella wasn't able to locate Mark Samantha told her to call the police, Sol Gordon, and her publicists. She called Charles Greenbloom herself.

"I'm going to release his picture to the media before it's too late," she said. "I don't want him to end up a face on a milk carton six months from now."

Greenbloom was equally upset but he thought it premature to bring in the media, it hadn't been a full day yet. That's what Gordon and her publicists told her as well but it didn't deter Samantha. When a detective arrived she showed him Mark's picture and said that her instinct was that something had happened to him. The detective promised an all-points alert and told her that if the boy was kidnapped the chances of finding him were greater during the first twenty-four hours than at any time afterwards. That was all she needed to hear. She immediately told Collabella to get on the phone to all the local news stations and find out if it was still possible to get Mark's picture on the eleven o'clock news.

"And find Layton," she instructed. "Tell him to get back at once!"

It was too late to make that evening's news, much to everyone but Samantha's relief. Mark would just be Mark through the night, before all of Southern California knew of his mother's concern.

As for Layton, Collabella had to make several calls to Japan before she could locate the hotel where he was staying. When she couldn't reach him by phone she sent a fax. Asking him to return from a festival in his honor made her feel that something out of the ordinary had better have happened to the boy.

■ ■ ■

It wasn't until after they returned from the movies when Asher was able to find out what Mark was doing in Santa Barbara. It was Asher's wife Manya who found out.

She was a quirky, understanding woman who gave an impression of complete sincerity and yet was capable of sneaking onto an airplane going to New York without being noticed. And if she was caught she could charm her way out of any embarrassment by convincing the authorities the mistake was theirs but all would be forgiven. It was just such a story that got Mark to trust her enough to open up as they talked in the kitchen while Asher smoked a joint and went over his accounts in his study.

"I knew it was something," Asher said after Mark had gone to sleep, "but I didn't expect that. What do you think it's worth to Alex?"

"Do you think you should?" Manya asked. "He's your friend but you know what he does with such information. It doesn't seem fair."

"It's too good not to tell him. Besides, we owe him for getting us into *Buzz's* Best Bets. I'll call him and let you tell him what you want."

Manya's news hit Alex Briar like a jolt of lightning. If it was true it would have to rank among the most sensational stories of the year, above what Faye Collabella had told him about how Greenbloom had basically destroyed Layton's career. With a caffeine-injected burst of energy he had finished the manuscript and sent it to his publisher but he figured they would hold off printing anything when they heard about this. Unless there was another way to handle it. But first he had to check it out and there were only two people in the world that could verify the story.

And there was no way he was ever going to get near Samantha Sanders to confront her.

● ● ●

Getting up with Asher before the sun had risen was not Mark's idea of a lifestyle to emulate but the physical labor of a baker was enough to take his mind off his predicament. After loading and unloading trays of hot bagels in and out of a 500-degree oven all morning and packaging them in the afternoon he felt a pride of accomplishment similar to his not coming for nearly a minute the last time he and Reya did it.

But when he returned to Asher's home and saw his picture on the six o'clock news he knew it was only a matter of time before he'd be back in his room listening to his mother's orders over the intercom. Gone one day and already on TV.

The Ashers were supportive, telling him that he was welcome to stay until he felt he could deal with his emotions, but Mark knew he'd be found if he remained and they'd only get into trouble. He went to bed early and decided not to return to the bagel factory where he might be recognized. If they'd let him he'd just stay in Carpentaria until he thought of what to do.

● ● ●

Alex Briar had no trouble getting to see Charles Greenbloom once the message was conveyed that it had to do with Mark Cross Sanders.

"I know where your son is," he said getting right to the point, watching Greenbloom's reaction for a clue. But the mogul was a tough character who didn't get to where he was without an ability to take matters into his own hands.

"Which son are you referring to, I have two."

"The third one no one knows about, the one who's missing."

Greenbloom studied Briar. If this wasn't a bluff he was staring into the face of trouble.

"What is it you want?"

"To verify the facts. I've got a book coming out about Layton Cross and I'd hate to be inaccurate about something like this."

"I don't know what you're talking about. Like what?"

"Like the fact that Mark Sanders or Mark Cross is really Mark Greenbloom and that's why he's disappeared."

"If you know where that boy is I'd suggest you contact the police."

"He overheard a conversation between you and his mother. Apparently one of you revealed your secret and he found it hard to believe. I'm sure Layton Cross will as well."

Greenbloom's steel gray eyes narrowed and he looked the way Briar supposed David Begelman must have when he was told of Cliff Robertson's accusation that he had forged the actor's name on a $10,000 check.

"I've got nothing to say to you," Greenbloom said with some anger.

"I think you've said all I need to know," Briar bluffed.

"Where's the boy?"

"You can read about it."

"You know anything about libel? You'd better if you think you're going to report that story because your next ten books won't cover the lawsuit I'll slap you with."

"I'm familiar with the laws, that goes with my territory. I'm sorry you're being uncooperative, I thought we could talk like men."

"I'm going to have to report you to the police."

"Fine. And I'm going to have to tell them what I've told you. It should make for some attractive gossip on the morning talk shows."

Greenbloom felt cornered and didn't like the feeling. He couldn't just let Briar walk out now. If he really knew where Mark was and if he was telling the truth about what Mark overheard then he would have to deal with Briar. He was a practical man and this was a practical matter.

"All right, let's begin again. What is it you really want? Confirmation? I can't give you that. What else?"

Now it was Briar's turn to think on his feet. The story was true, that much he knew. He could put it in his book but what was that worth compared with how much more was it worth having the head of Quickstart Studios in the palm of his hand? What could he offer Charles Greenbloom?

His book. Of course!

"What's the going rate on buying the film rights to a book these days?" he asked.

"Depends on whether your name's Crichton or Grisham or what'd you say your name was?"

"I always thought Layton Cross' life would make a good movie." Briar held his breath. He was bordering on blackmail and he knew it.

"You're a scumbag, you know that kid?"

"Let's say the feeling's mutual and go from there." Briar had the man by the balls and, knowing all he knew about him, was willing to squeeze.

"If the book's any good, we can consider it."

"It's good. You know Cross' story. Hell, you're a pretty important part of it."

Alex Briar was going to cost Greenbloom; there was no getting around that. It was now down to a negotiation. He threw out standard option figures, $5,000 for a year, another five for eighteen months, but Briar wasn't interested in options, he was thinking in six figures. He wanted to sell the book outright.

Greenbloom wanted to know what assurances he had that Briar's unconfirmed allegations regarding Mark were part of any deal. Briar said he'd put his silence in writing if they could come to an agreement. And he'd throw in Mark's whereabouts in the bargain.

Greenbloom offered $50,000. Briar said he'd heard $200,000 was more in line. "Not in any line I'm going to stand," Greenbloom said.

"You can throw in a screenwriter's fee as part of the deal," Briar offered.

"Now you're a screenwriter? I like that. From a scumbag extortionist to a film writer. What about directing, you want to direct too?"

"I've worked with dialogue and story structure all my professional life, what's to know? I've got ideas, Mr Greenbloom. Just like you."

Greenbloom wanted to get rid of this arrogant pest. "You're nothing like me, kid. $75,000 for the book, $50,000 for a script if we think there's a movie in it." He figured there were enough cut-offs in a script's development that he could kill it after a first draft and no more than $20,000.

"Double that and you've got a deal," Briar said. "Otherwise I'll have to turn this over to my agent."

"Seventy-five for the book, seventy-five for the script, that's as high as I'll go, take it or leave it."

Briar was tempted to leave it, figuring there was no way Greenbloom was going to let him walk. But why be greedy? $150,000 and entry into the insulated movie world was a whole new life for a phone call's worth of information.

The deal was struck. Greenbloom brought in his secretary and dictated the terms, then called Briar's literary agent to make the offer formal. "After today I don't ever want to see you again," he warned the writer. "You breach this contract, you won't have a life. I'm not threatening, just letting you know where you stand. Now where's Mark?"

"He's working at a bagel factory on State Street in Santa Barbara."

Greenbloom looked like he had been hit in the face with a pie. Briar shrugged but wrote down the name of Asher's company and left it on the desk. Greenbloom believed it but couldn't rid himself of the feeling that he'd been had.

When Briar called Asher to inform him that Greenbloom knew where Mark was, Asher felt compelled to tell Mark. Briar didn't tell his friend what had transpired in Greenbloom's office—such information would be too costly. Asher might expect more than the big screen television Briar was going to send him.

Mark decided to return to Los Angeles in one of Asher's trucks. He had the driver drop him at the corner of Laurel Canyon and Ventura Boulevard in Studio City, then hitched a ride up to Mulholland, and walked the two miles to Amy's house. She once told him where she hid an extra key and he figured he could stay there without anyone knowing.

14

Just Me And You

Like Marlon Brando reaching out to the media to put the best face on his son Christian's killing of his daughter Cheyenne's Tahitian boyfriend, Samantha had also sucked in her aversion to the press and tried to open herself as much as possible so they would get Mark into the national consciousness. But Charlie Greenbloom disagreed with her tactics. He wanted her to call off the newshounds because the story they might discover wasn't a story any of the involved would want to make public. What he had to tell her was almost as dreadful as the thought of Mark's being kidnapped, and in some ways worse. This was something no amount of money could resolve.

"Was he there?" she demanded. "Did you find him?"

"He was there all right but he left. The owner said he came back to L.A. after seeing himself on the news. There's no sense further traumatizing him by having the police out looking for him. He'll be back after he's had some time to think."

"Think what? That I've lied to him all his life? That I pretended Layton was his father and you were good ol' Uncle Charlie? What's he going to think? He hates me. What am I going to do to change that?"

"Deny it."

"I'm not going to lie to him anymore."

"We'll talk to him."

"What makes you think he'll want to talk to us? What would you do if it was you?" Samantha's anxiety was approaching Valium level but when Greenbloom suggested it she began to rant at him.

"I'd give my mother a chance to explain," he finally said. "Then I'd think of the opportunities that suddenly opened up to me. How many kids find out their father's the head of a movie studio?"

"There's nothing you can offer him that he doesn't already have through me," Samantha screamed. "If he wanted a goddamn studio I could fucking buy him one!"

The real issue was Mark's relationship with Layton but Greenbloom's ego was too encompassing to understand that. As far as he was concerned Layton had always been a front. A loser. He refused to consider that Mark might actually love Layton. Hell, he was practically out of the boy's life for two-thirds of it.

"You're a fool," Samantha told him. "Now leave me alone and let me think how I'm going to handle this."

■ ■ ■

On the Japan Airlines flight back Layton's thoughts were divided between what might have happened to Mark and seeing the doctor immediately to get his mouth unwired. He had grown proficient at finding the small spaces between his teeth where he could push spoonfuls of baby food but he was so sick of mashed and blended fruits and vegetables that thoughts of eating real food had become an obsession. The only positive thing that came out of being unable to chew for six weeks was that he had lost twenty pounds. He was looking good but he knew it wouldn't last. He'd probably gain back ten the first day he was free to chomp.

Amy and the children weren't sorry their trip was cut short by three days although they felt badly that Layton wasn't able to attend the party after the festival. Layton was relieved because the way it had been going the last day might have wound up in Mariko's living room with the films shown on videocassette.

Amy was convinced that nothing had happened to Mark–he was probably late for dinner and Samantha freaked out. Layton suspected it could be more dramatic than that but not much more. Neither of them were prepared to find Mark asleep in her editing room when they arrived home. From the way he was sleeping–fully clothed, his arm touching the floor, his mouth open—-he appeared exhausted.

"Might as well call Samantha and let her know he's safe," Amy suggested. But Layton disagreed. If the boy was here there must be a reason. If he had run away Layton wanted to give him a chance to tell his side before facing his mother.

The next morning Mark seemed strangely remote, surprised to find the house full. Andy had been the first to wake him, bouncing a Nerf soccer ball off his head. He couldn't wait to give Mark the present they got him—a computer watch that stored ninety phone numbers and had an alarm that voiced the time.

At breakfast he didn't seem interested in their trip and hardly listened, keeping his face buried in his Cheerios. When Layton asked if he wanted to talk he shrugged and looked embarrassed. Amy shuffled the kids into the living room and left the two of them alone.

"Does it have to do with your girlfriend?"

Mark shook his head.

"She in trouble?"

"It's not that."

"School?"

"No."

"Something you did?"

"No."

"Your mother?"

Mark didn't answer. Layton suggested they go for a ride and they drove to Will Rogers State Park. Layton used to jog around the polo field when he and Amy were first married and sometimes he'd walk the two-mile path up to Inspiration Point. After being cooped up in an airplane for so many hours he felt like walking.

"You don't have to tell me if you don't want to," he said as they headed up the mountain.

"It's not that," Mark stammered. "I don't know how to tell you."

"That bad, huh?"

"It's pretty serious."

"Is it something we can work out together?"

"I don't know."

"Is it a color? A food? Something living?" His attempt at 20 Questions humor sank like a rock thrown in mud. They walked among the pines and eucalyptus in silence for half a mile in the morning chill. Then Mark told him.

He started from the beginning with how Reya convinced him to eavesdrop and when he got to the part about Uncle Charlie being his real father he started to sob, gulping breaths of air as he bravely went on.

As Layton listened he felt his body go numb. It began in his hands, which he had clenched into fists as tight as his teeth. The pain in his jaw was soft as a down pillow compared to this. His head and heart began to pound, his legs went wobbly, he had to stop walking and lean against a boulder for support. Once again one of his children had raised his anxiety to a point of near-collapse and had rendered him speechless.

The betrayal Mark had revealed went beyond anything he could possibly have imagined. Life could be cruel, hard, depressing, but one learned to cope, to accept whatever fate had dealt. But this? Was God trying to test him? First there was Abraham, then Job, and now Layton

Cross? Could his life have been such a charade? Was anything real?

Mark was crying as he leaned against Layton, who hugged and cried with him. Both had been hit with the same sledgehammer and their anger mixed with their confusion and their love. Layton never felt more Mark's father and Mark more Layton's son then on this path halfway up the mountain where Will Rogers once trod for inspiration.

"You're my son," Layton cried, hugging the boy.

"I know it dad," Mark sobbed. "I know it."

The walk to the top became important to them as they gathered their strength to continue. Layton put his arm around Mark and squeezed his shoulder to let him know they were one. Mark felt greatly relieved and told Layton of his Santa Barbara adventure. He also said that he'd never go back to live with Samantha again and would never see Charlie. He wanted to live with Layton, who felt Mark was old enough to make such a decision and was willing to do battle with the ogress Sanders and her lizard lawyer Sol Gordon.

They stood at the top of Inspiration Point and looked towards the ocean, then at the city. It was easy to feel small and humble before such a vast panorama; just as easy to feel tall and on top of the world as they got lost in their thoughts. Then they headed down to confront their fears head on.

Although he wanted to go directly to Samantha's, Layton knew he'd be at an insurmountable disadvantage having to yell through clenched teeth so he drove with Mark to his doctor and insisted the wires be removed.

After an examination and x-rays the doctor agreed that he was ready but warned him that he wouldn't be able to open his mouth wide enough for a spoon to fit in for a few weeks and it would be another month before he could chew solid foods.

"As long as I can talk," Layton mumbled.

So, for the second time, he was given a general anesthetic and put out as the doctor removed the wires from his mouth.

While under, Layton kept seeing a young Charlie Greenbloom slipping it to Samantha as Layton watched through a keyhole. He heard them laughing and saw the baby Mark between them. Try as he did he couldn't turn away. It was as if his eye had been stuck to the keyhole with an impermeable bond.

Mark waited patiently for two hours, then helped a groggy Layton to his Jeep and drove back to Amy's.

In the morning when Layton awoke he heard his jaw click. Oh Christ, he worried; I cracked it again. He jumped from bed, found his doctor's home number and called, only to be reassured that the clicking was the cartilage slipping into place and would continue for months. It would disorient him but was part of the healing process.

After breakfast he called Faye Collabella and said that he'd be coming to see Samantha in an hour if she was there. Collabella said Samantha usually slept until eleven. "Then wake her," Layton said.

Mark was apprehensive but Layton told him that he had not said anything to Amy and promised not to go crazy at Samantha's. He had thought it through and felt confident that she would have to accept that Mark would be staying with him for as long as he liked. He had also decided not to let on that he knew why Mark had run away–at least not before she had a chance to present her own theories. He knew what Mark had overheard but what he didn't know was that Samantha and Charlie knew as well.

On the drive over he thought that this could turn into the worst day of his life if he wasn't careful. He had contained himself when first confronting Theo, had provoked Barry Levine, now he was going to face the toughest cookie of them all and the thought passed briefly that if enraged he could do far more damage than a punch to her jaw. He might very possibly kill her.

She was waiting for him on the patio. As soon as she saw him she put down her coffee and Layton heard the cup rattle onto the saucer. He had never seen her so nervous.

"We've got to talk," she said.

"I know." He stretched his mouth too wide and heard his jawbone click.

"This isn't going to be easy."

Layton had assumed she was going to go on about Mark's disappearance but from the look on her face and the way her hands slightly trembled he stood stiffly, awaiting a full frontal assault. It would be kind for him to say he already knew what she was about to say and spare her the details, but he was not in a kind mood. He wanted to hear of her deception from her own lips. He wanted her to squirm.

But Samantha was, above all, a great actress and she used her talent to maneuver onto the highest ground. It was an admirable performance: how Layton was often cruel and unsupportive of her rising career; how he made her cower during arguments; how she needed a sympathetic figure, someone to lean on, to be there for support, to encourage her and boost her confidence. She went on...and on...and Layton marveled at her incredible ability to defend what was an indefensible action, a blatant betrayal of trust and marriage, a continuing carrying out of a deception that had already lasted fifteen years. He listened as she relived her suffering, cried real tears, got lost in her own memories of anger and insults. Finally, she came to Charlie, who was around when she needed someone, who was there to lend the support after Layton had disappeared for days working out his own position in their marriage. Charlie, whom she never loved, but who comforted her. Charlie, who had his own family, but who believed enough in her to be there when Layton was gone. Charlie, who showed his emotions when she was vulnerable. She didn't mention the Charlie who was the father of his kid but that was to be expected, she didn't have the guts, and that Charlie Layton would deal with when he was through listening to her bullshit.

As Samantha rattled on Layton began to feel as if he was having an out-of-body experience. Here was this woman whom he had never stopped loving, telling him she never had enough respect for him to be honest, and suddenly he was feeling as if he was riding a wave, freefalling from the sky. Samantha was talking and he stood there outside himself empty of emotion and feeling for her. What was happening to him was a sudden loss of love. He was unburdening himself from the unrequited love he had had for her all these years. He felt light, buoyant, the way he got when the dentist filled his head with nitrous oxide.

Instead of screaming his hurt, he let her finish. And then he said, slowly, deliberately, like Dirty Harry talking to some vermin, "Mark's with me. He doesn't want to live with you any longer. So fuck you and Charlie Greenbloom."

Samantha's owl eyes widened in disbelief. "You knew?" she said between her own clenched teeth. "You had me go on when you knew?"

"Just leave the boy alone," he warned. "He doesn't need to be the centerpiece of any scandal."

"It's not true you know." She was sounding desperate. "He's not going to live with you. He's my son."

"Let's let him decide."

"He's not old enough! I'm still his mother."

"Yeah, and as far as we're concerned, I'm still his father."

"I'd think you'd have enough on your hands with Leanne."

"Sam, he feels you've deceived him. Like he's been living a lie his whole life. I have a hard time believing it myself. Charlie is such a weasel."

"You tell him I want to see him."

"Give him some time."

Samantha was too stunned by Layton's self-determination to do any more than fume. Even when he turned his back and walked away.

■ ■ ■

Charles Greenbloom had just finished screening a rough print of *The Sand Man* with Arno and Macky when Faye Collabella called to say that Samantha was on her way to his office. He wasn't thrilled with the movie, especially with Layton, who happened to be good, but figured it would do kid and drive-in business and advised Arno to cut ten minutes to pick up the pace. Arno then slipped him his weekly vial of coke and Greenbloom instructed his secretary to write out a personal check.

"How long I know you Arno, five years? Now you're a wheeler and a dealer."

"A man's gotta move up."

"Soon you'll be financing other people's pictures, and then you'll own a studio."

"Takes a lot of rock candy to afford that, Mr Greenbloom."

"In this town that's not so hard. So let me give you some advice: keep your budgets under $3 million, presell to cable and the foreign markets, keep your distributor happy, and you'll never lose money. That excludes using big-name talent but there's plenty of business without them."

"Sounds good to me."

"So with all I'm doing for you, how come you still charge me top dollar?"

"If I didn't you'd suspect I was cutting it with impurities. Someone like you, I want you to feel that you get what you pay for. You don't need a bargain when it comes to what's going into your brain."

"Let me make another suggestion, about the movie. I know it's your baby but I wouldn't put Layton Cross' name up there as big as your title. He doesn't have the drawing power anymore."

"He's the only name we've got. I paid a bundle for that name."

"Think about it."

■ ■ ■

"Layton's got him," Samantha blurted as she stormed into Greenbloom's office, passing Arno and Macky on their way out. She had only one thing on her mind and Greenbloom was the only person she felt she could talk to.

"Have you talked to him?"

"He came to tell me Mark's not coming back."

"That's preposterous, he can't stay there."

"So what are we going to do?"

"You go and get him, talk to him, you're his mother for God's sake."

"And if he won't see me?"

"How can he not see you? That house isn't big enough for him to hide." Greenbloom noticed the vial of coke on his desk and quickly stuck it in his pocket. Samantha didn't approve of drugs. "How'd Layton take it?"

"He thinks he's Mark's father."

"Always said the man had shit for brains. But good, it's better that way. At least he's not out punching."

"He knows it's you, he's just being protective."

"I don't think it's a good idea for the boy to live there. Layton's too unstable; he's not even married to that woman, what kind of environment is that? Look what happened to that girl of theirs."

"He's not going to live there; I just want some way to get him back."

"Let me think about it."

"The longer he stays there the harder it's going to be. If I lose him you can forget about me making any pictures for you, Charlie. So you do something."

"Samantha, don't. I've just paid a king's ransom to keep this out of print. I've got my family to protect."

"Fuck you and your family Charlie. Mark's all the family I've got. He's mine and I want him!"

Greenbloom wasn't used to seeing Samantha so vulnerable and out of control. She was bordering on hysteria. At first she told him she would handle it, now she was appealing for help. He didn't know what to do. Layton surely wouldn't be receptive to him. The only thing he had over Layton was his movie that he could keep from being released. That might be a bargaining chip, though Layton's part was so small he probably wouldn't care. Still, it was something.

The one thing they all agreed on was that they didn't want the media to get hold of this. Greenbloom had his family to consider; Layton his honor; Samantha her reputation; and Mark his life. Wife swapping and love triangles had always been grist for the paper and video mills, look at what was made of Layton, Amy, and Theo, and that wasn't even close to the truth. When Eddie Fisher left Debbie Reynolds for Elizabeth Taylor it was a bigger media event than the My Lai massacre. When Robin Williams left his wife for their nanny, reporters had a field day, as they did when Sharon Stone broke up Bill McDonald's marriage and his wife went over to Joe Ezterhas. That one was like Peter Fonda and Tom McGuane exchanging wives. And what would the early Nineties have been like without Donald Trump's seesawing with Marla Maples? Eastern European and Middle Eastern politics were too complicated to grasp for most people, but dish up a celebrity break-up or rebound marriage and people would buy magazines and endure commercials to hear all about it.

Greenbloom knew that although he had paid Alex Briar off, once someone like him knew about it public disclosure was inevitable. Samantha would generate the most copy. Her face would be plastered across every tab-

Catch a Fallen Star

loid and gossip rag. And Layton would have to again suffer through the humiliation of being the wronged man. His career–what was left of it–was the most in jeopardy.

■ ■ ■

When word got back to Arno that Greenbloom had decided to hold the release of *The Sand Man* indefinitely he went to find out why. It was his money that paid for the film, how could Greenbloom suddenly make such a decision?

"I'm not sure we're going to get a return," Greenbloom told him, but that wasn't good enough. Arno sensed it was something more. Something that had to do with Samantha Sanders. And Layton Cross.

"Didn't you just tell me that it would play well in the South?"

"Tell me something Arno. Did you ever find out for me who was sniping at Samantha Sanders?"

"That what this is about?"

"You know, don't you?"

"You'll release the picture if you know?"

Greenbloom nodded.

"It was a set-up. Layton couldn't do the film because she was suing him. Blanks were fired, he was supposed to capture the sniper and turn him over to a fake cop; she would drop her suit, he'd make my picture. No one was supposed to get hurt. Who knew she was a marksman?"

"So it was you Arno? And Layton agreed to this?"

"I had nothing to do with it. It's what I heard."

"And it just happened to be your picture. Think you might hear about a way to get her kid back from him?"

"I get it now. She's holding you up, so you're holding me. It's the kid."

"He wants to stay with Layton. I don't like Layton; Mark doesn't belong there. I don't want to make a big deal of this but I don't want any part in distributing that asshole's performance. Not while he's blackmailing my star. I've got a far more important investment in her."

"So what we're looking at is a situation where Cross needs some nudging to convince the kid to go home."

Greenbloom sat behind his solid oak desk fingering the vial in his pocket. It had come to this: waiting for his coke supplier's thoughts on how to solve a personal problem dealing with his secret son, the country's biggest star, and a man who might soon walk into his office intending to beat him to a pulp.

"Why not set him up? Bust him on some phony charge, bail him out for the kid."

"You're a sinister man, Arno."

"It's my business. You've got to make it so the kid wants to go back, to help his old man." Arno was back in his element, scheming to get things to work out his way. That's how he was able to get his movie made; now he was going to double-cross Cross to get it released. He liked the symmetry of it. "Here's how: me and Macky visit Layton. I go to take a leak and hide a packet of coke behind the toilet. Half hour later two phony cops arrive with a phony warrant, find the coke, and bust him. While he's screaming for his rights, you call on some movie business. He tells you what's going down, you tell him not to worry, your friend's the chief of police, you can fix it for a price: the kid goes back to his mother. What's he gonna do, refuse?"

"Too crazy. I can't get involved with drugs."

"You won't be involved."

"If there's coke there's trouble. Forget it."

"So we make it sugar, who's to know? Nobody gets hurt."

"Sugar huh?" Suddenly it didn't sound so crazy.

"It sounds crazy," Samantha said when Greenbloom called. "I don't want Mark back as a prisoner; he'll only run away again."

"Yeah, that's what I thought. Except it might work. It's fast, it's clean, nobody's who they say they are so it's not going to get out, you get Mark, Layton becomes more cautious, life goes on. And Layton did this to you first with that sniper."

"You really believe he did that?"

"Without a doubt. We can forget about this and let Mark end up with him or we can act out this charade and move towards a resolution. If Mark knows he can't stay with Layton, where else is he going to go?"

"You think Layton will talk to you, even in the middle of a bust?"

"Probably not. But he'd talk to you."

"I'm not calling, forget it. Keep me out of this."

"How can you keep out of it when this is all being done for you?"

"What about you? You want Mark living with Layton?"

"Definitely not."

"I don't like any of it, it's not honest."

"I know it stinks. There is no way you're going to come out smelling of lilacs. But once Mark is back you'll work things out with him."

"I'm not calling."

How could Greenbloom get Layton to take his call and confide about the bust? He'd have to say up front that he knows about what's going down because his friend, the police chief, told him. So he could be calling to warn him. Layton would then say it's too late and he could say that he knows Layton has every right to want his ass but maybe if he could get the charges dropped it would be a way of saying he was sorry. Provided he gave up Mark. Sure it was nuts. But it just might work.

■ ■ ■

Amy was finding the right sound bites for a Wesley Snipes cop movie when Layton suggested she take a lunch break. She wasn't hungry and neither was he, but he didn't have food on his mind. They went into her bedroom and took advantage of working at home. But the phone interrupted their lovemaking. It was Arno saying he'd like to come by to discuss some business. Layton hoped it had to do with the $50,000 final payment he was owed.

When Amy went to shower Layton followed. "We're not finished," he said taking the soap to wash her body.

"I don't know what it is, but you've become a different person."

"It's the family. Being all together. I feel like a burden's been lifted."

"A burden named Samantha."

"She means nothing to me," Layton said, playfully inserting the soap between her legs.

"Only took fifteen years."

He hadn't told her what Mark had overheard. It was still too raw. But he had become more affectionate, less riddled with anxiety. She was liking him more.

Arno and Macky arrived at two. Layton inquired about the film's progress and Macky told him it was pretty good. "You came out okay."

"That should make my accountant happy," Layton said.

"It's about that we came to see you," Arno said, unlocking his eel skin attaché case. "We've got a problem regarding the money you think we owe you."

"I don't think. Half up front, half upon completion. Your payment's late but I'm forgiving, I won't charge interest."

"According to your contract, you were to receive the final payment upon completion of your work."

"That's right."

"And according to what happened that last day, your hospitalization prevented you from actually completing your role. We had to work around what we had."

"What the fuck are you talking about?"

"There was another page of script you never got to because of what happened."

"Are you going to make me lose that money to lawyers?" Layton winced as his jaw clicked. "Because they'll get it from you."

"We figure maybe we can work something out."

"You want to bargain, go to Morocco, don't come to me."

"Let's not get emotional about this, we've come in good faith to talk to you." Before Layton answered Arno stood and asked where the bathroom was. He excused himself as Amy came into the room.

"Anybody want a drink?" she asked.

"We're not serving these assholes anything until I know what's going on."

Macky smiled. He liked Layton. Under different circumstances they could have been friends. It was just too bad it had to be Hollywood, where friendship was impossible.

Arno relieved himself and found a place in the cabinet below the sink to hide the cocaine he had under his sport jacket. It wasn't sugar because if Layton tested it in front of the "cops" he'd know the difference. Greenbloom would never have to know. This one was much simpler than using Mozart at Samantha's.

"Here's my offer," Arno said when he returned. "If you help publicize the picture we'll pay you twenty-five grand—which is twenty-five more than we're obligated contractually to pay you and more than you'd get if you did sue and spent a few years in court fighting for it."

"You want to break the contract, it's in the hands of lawyers," Layton said. "If they tell me I can hold up your movie, that's what I'll do. If you think I'm going to say anything good about the piece of shit you're calling a film, you're already in the wrong business."

"Fine with us," Arno said closing his case. "Talk to your lawyers, see what they say."

"Count on it. And fuck you both."

The hired "cops" were waiting at Blockbuster Video at Sunset and N. Orangegrove when Arno pulled in and told them where he'd placed the dope. They waited fifteen minutes and then drove up the canyon to Amy's house.

She answered the door and before she could protest they were in, flashing the fake warrant and heading to the bathroom. Layton was in the kitchen when he heard the commotion and came out to find these two guys in police uniforms waiting for him. One was holding the cocaine. "Recognize this?" he asked.

"What the hell is this?" Layton asked back. "Who are you guys?"

"You have the right to remain silent," one of them began. When he was through Layton looked at him and said, "You work for Arno? That stuff's probably not even real."

He took the foiled packet, opened it, stuck a finger in the powder and put it to his lips. Fucking Arno wasn't shooting blanks this time. "So what are we going to do about this?" he asked. The "cops" were stalling, waiting for the phone to ring.

As they stood there Amy went back to her editing room where she rifled through a box of sound effects she had been working with. She, too, was suspicious. The way they went right to the bathroom. They were as phony as the cop who came to pick up Mozart. But to be sure she found the reel she wanted and looped it in her machine, then turned the volume up and blasted police sirens through the loudspeakers in the living room. It sounded very real...and closing in.

The two "cops" looked at each other and panicked. If real police were on the way they didn't want to be there when they arrived. Impersonating a police officer was a serious charge, especially considering they were also driving a police car. And they certainly wanted no part of the dope that they left behind as they rushed out the door when the phone rang.

It was Greenbloom calling to warn him about an impending bust. Good old Uncle Charlie.

"You're late," Layton said. "The boys just left. Probably running to tell Arno how they botched the bust."

"I don't get your drift," Greenbloom said.

"Well maybe you'll get this. When it comes to Mark, Charlie, you're not even a contender."

He hung up and went to the editing room where Amy was stopping the tape. "That was brilliant," he said.

"Those guys were so phony even I could tell."

"You want to know what's going on, right?" She nodded. "It's got to do with Mark."

Amy listened incredulously as he told the story. It sounded like something her mother used to read to her from old *True Confessions*. It wasn't real, it was Hollywood. That poor kid, she thought. What a way to find out. And Layton—the hold that bitch has had on him and all these years she was wearing a mask. How treacherous and despicable and...ugly. When he was through he asked what she thought.

"How can you ever let him go back to her? He belongs with you."

Layton hugged her. "The next question is do we belong here with you?"

"All I know is none of us belong in a place like this," she said, glancing at the dope on the table. "This is a very unhealthy place to live."

■ ■ ■

Samantha was fed up with relying on Charlie to accomplish anything. Charlie was a jerk, she'd always known it; how could she have allowed such a harebrained scheme to go down? The only way to deal with Mark was in person and she wasn't going to let Layton or anyone else keep that from happening. She called and suggested they meet for dinner. Layton asked Mark and he agreed to the following night on the condition that he be allowed to make his own decision about where he wanted to live. Samantha argued that since he had already made his decision the dice were loaded, but Layton convinced her she had little choice if she wanted to meet at all, since the purpose was to avoid a scandal and work out what was in Mark's best interest. If she could convince him to return to her, Layton wouldn't stand in the way. She was a great actress, he said. This seemed a good time to prove it.

Before they left to meet at Olive on Fairfax Barry Levine appeared to see Layton.

"I know this doesn't seem appropriate," he said awkwardly, "but Arno asked me to come and collect a package that was dropped here by mistake."

"You've got to be kidding," Layton said, the click in his jaw coinciding with a nervous twitch in his face.

"I've got nothing to do with it. It's between you and Arno. I didn't want to come here."

"So why did you? You doing his dirty work now?"

"Look, Layton, these guys can play rough. Why don't you just give it to me and forget about it."

"Yeah, maybe you're right, wait here." He told Mark to wait in the Jeep as he went back into the house to the kitchen where he took down the sugar bowl and poured a fair amount into some tin foil. He then carefully folded the foil, put it in a paper bag, and brought it out to Levine. "Give this to Arno and tell him I hope it brings sweet dreams."

"No hard feelings then?"

"None whatsoever. You just keep doing what you're doing Barry. You'll fit right into this business."

In the Jeep Mark wondered if he was causing too many problems. "Maybe I should go back."

"That what you want?" Layton asked.

"No."

"So tell her. That's what this is about. You're in control here. Your mom's not used to taking a back seat. She's strong, so you've got to be stronger. Just talk from the heart, make her understand. It's your decision."

Mark looked worried when they walked into the small dark restaurant. Samantha wasn't there yet but they ordered anyway.

"I learned long ago not to let her lateness affect my life. If she's not here by the time we finish, we're gone."

She arrived just as they were being served, wearing a large felt hat, thick sunglasses, a turtleneck sweater, black leather pants, and knee-high purple boots.

"If you're going for incognito you're failing miserably," Layton said as people turned to stare at her.

It was impossible to see her eyes through the glasses but Mark could feel them penetrating his. She would have preferred a more private meeting.

"I see you've ordered," she said, sliding a chair from the table.

"We said six," Layton shrugged between chews. "You're late."

"You can have mine," Mark said, offering his pasta. Layton wasn't pleased with the boy's weakness in front of his mother. She had wronged him but he was acting like the one seeking forgiveness.

"I didn't come to eat," she said abruptly. "I came for you. If you're angry, so am I. You want to have it out, let's do it face-to-face. You want to be a man act like one." She was coming at him hard. Direct confrontation, she knew, was not his strength. She hadn't come to plead but to demand.

"Face-to-face would be a lot easier without those glasses," Layton suggested.

"I don't have anything to say to you," she said removing the sunglasses. "I know about the sniper. You're out of your mind if you think I'm going to let Mark live with a psychopath."

"I did it because you left me no choice. You wanted me to give up all rights to him. I couldn't do that."

"And the money had nothing to do with it I suppose?"

"What money?"

"The money you would have lost if I sued you."

"There was that too. You were threatening to take away the last remnants of my life. The sniper was a set-up. He was firing blanks."

"I don't care if he was firing malt balls! We didn't know that. You were playing on our fears. It was a criminal act."

"Let's just call it desperate."

"Desperate's no excuse. You've been desperate since I've known you."

"Oh yeah? And what about Charlie sending Arno to plant cocaine in my house? That's rational?"

"It wasn't cocaine, it was sugar."

"It was cocaine, I tasted it. At least my guy shot blanks."

They had almost forgotten about Mark, who sat there wondering what they were talking about and why there was so much hatred between them. "What about Uncle Charlie?" he interjected. "How could you keep something like that from me?"

"Keep what?" Samantha asked.

"That he's my father."

"Because he's not your father. Layton's your father. And believe me, I'm not proud of that."

"Why are you lying to me? I heard you."

"You heard me tell Charlie what he thinks is true. He thinks you're his son. I let him think it all these years because it was a good career move when I was first starting out. But it's not true."

Layton seemed as dumbfounded as Mark. Samantha had thrown a knuckleball that was dancing all over the plate. "Just what are you trying to say here?"

"Just what I said. When our marriage began to crack, Charlie was there to comfort me. He didn't know I was already pregnant then, and I wanted the lead in *Lady Do Right*. So I told him he was going to be the father of my child. He already had a family and didn't need another so it worked out very conveniently. He'd look after me, I'd look after the child, no one would ever know."

"And *I'm* desperate?" Layton exclaimed.

"I was never desperate," Samantha said quietly. "I always knew where I was going. This was a way to make it happen faster. Once Mark was born I realized I'd always have a studio as long as Charlie believed Mark was his. I used him Layton. I never told you about it because there was nothing to tell."

"You used me too," said Mark.

"You've never wanted for anything."

"I was just there for you to get ahead."

"You're my son, Mark. That's what this is all about. You're all I've got. I don't want to lose you."

"You don't even understand."

"So Uncle Charlie still doesn't know?" Layton asked.

"No."

"Somebody's got to tell him."

"You tell him," Mark said. "You tell him I'm not his kid."

"If that's what you want. If you'll come home."

"I don't want to come back."

"I'll tell him," Layton said.

"He won't believe you."

"You deceived me all these years."

"I didn't deceive you, I deceived Charlie."

"But you slept with him."

"We're not talking infidelities here, we're talking fatherhood. Mark's your kid. Look at him. You see any Charlie?"

Layton turned to Mark and they both smiled, satisfied and relieved that they were really father and son. Samantha put her dark glasses back on as she looked at them. Whatever she was thinking was now as carefully hidden as her eyes.

"Well, are we in agreement here?" Layton asked. "Mark stays with me until he's ready to go back to you?"

"You do this," Samantha threatened Mark, "and you're cutting yourself off from everything that should be yours. He's not going to provide for you the way I can."

"I can live without stuff," Mark said.

"He doesn't have to grow up the son of privilege," Layton added.

"Don't come to me for his college, his cars, his clothes. If he's out of my house, he's out of my life. You understand that?"

Mark nodded but Layton protested. "You talking disinheritance here because he's taking a stand for the first time in his life? You trying to beat him down with a material stick? What kind of a woman are you? You can't have your way, you pick up your equipment and go home? He's not asking you to stop being his mother. He wants some time away from you. He wants a change. We're not talking about ownership here. Nobody owns Mark. Can't you even see that?"

"All I see is he's making a mistake...and it's going to cost him."

"No," Layton said, "you're the one making the mistake. Some things aren't measured in costs."

She was about to speak but Layton held up his hand. "Don't say any more now you might regret later."

"That it then?" she asked Mark.

"I think so."

"Then there's nothing further to discuss." She stood and walked out without saying goodbye to either of them.

While they were gone Amy kept thinking about the phony cops and the planted cocaine. If people like Arno and Greenbloom would do something like that, there was no telling what they'd think up next to get their coke back and to blacken Layton's future. If they could get into her house so easily it just didn't seem very safe to live there any longer. And if Mark was going to live with them he'd need a room of his own and the only place to put him was her office.

Maybe it was time to move. She firmly believed that things didn't happen arbitrarily but that there was an overall design, a grand scheme to things. Layton's career had been sinking for years. Now he was back in their lives and it had become chaotic. Bad things had happened to Leanne, Mark, herself, Layton. Only Andy seemed spared and he could be next. She had rationalized the novelty of living in the Hollywood Hills, but the truth was it had worn off long ago. Cars sped too fast up the canyon, new construction and remodeling obstructed scenic views, destroyed the wildlife, and made it a noisy place to live; graffiti began to appear on outside walls, pot holes opened by the earthquake and storms were slow to be fixed, the sanitation department had yet to get around to picking up recyclable glass and plastics, car and home security alarms were constantly going off but it didn't prevent thieves from taking what they wanted. She'd be just as happy leaving it all behind. But what about Layton? What else was he capable of doing?

She didn't ask him when they returned but she was curious to hear what happened. "She threatened to take away all his toys," Layton told her. "Then she got flustered when he said he didn't want them anymore. She couldn't handle the fact that he's growing up and has a mind of his own."

"What'd she say about...you know?" Amy asked.

"She said she lied to Charlie," Mark said. "He's not my dad but she told him he was so she could get a movie."

"No, get out of here!"

"That's what she said," Layton affirmed. "Knowing Samantha, she's perfectly capable of such deception."

Amy shouldn't have been surprised, since she viewed the entire movie industry as diseased, but this was right up there with Layton's sniper and Greenbloom's planted coke bust. These three people belonged in a separate category, the Terminally Ambitious. At least Layton was beginning to open his eyes to other realities.

"Tomorrow I'm going to see Sol Gordon and Greenbloom," Layton said. "Take care of some business."

"There's no school tomorrow," Amy said, "why don't we do something together?" They had never been to the Gene Autry Museum in Griffith Park and agreed to meet there at noon.

Samantha's lawyer assumed Layton was coming to talk about Mark but Layton said that had been settled and was there to see him about his contract with Arno. "They're withholding a final payment of fifty grand and I'd like you to collect it." He showed Gordon the contract, explained the problem, and was given a choice: he could hire Gordon by the hour, which at $250 could mount significantly, or the firm would take it on a contingency basis for 30% of the money collected. By the hour was a gamble. Gordon could write a strong letter, charge for two hours, and Arno might cave in. But if Arno chose to fight it could easily run to a week's work, maybe more. Arno might count on such a tactic to break Layton. Best to go the contingency route. If Gordon didn't think he'd win he wouldn't have offered it and Layton was determined not to be screwed. If it cost him fifteen grand to get back thirty-five, then at least he was back in the game. It wasn't fair and it wasn't fun but that's how it was played and he was a player.

But Arno was bush compared to a major leaguer like Greenbloom, especially behind closed doors. He was standing behind his desk, his face blotted in unsuppressed anger, wishing he could reduce Layton to dust. "You've got every right to be angry," he said, "but the bottom line here is Mark's not your kid and I don't want you fucking him up."

"You may have done some fucking, Charlie, but you're the one who's been fucked." Layton liked being in control, knowing something Greenbloom didn't.

"You're a germ," Greenbloom countered with as much tact as a wrecking ball impacting on a damaged building. "I've watched you for twenty years and you're nothing but a washed-up movie star, a bit player. You've got no self-worth, no values, nothing to pass on to any kid of your own, let alone to a sensitive boy who is nothing to you. You're stoned half the time and depressed when you're not; you're in the news not for your work but for your reckless behavior. I don't care what you think of me but you're in no position to raise Mark. He belongs with Samantha."

"You think you can get away with anything because you control people's fantasies," Layton said, not about to crumble before Greenbloom's diatribe. "Well, Uncle Charlie, I've got a few fantasies left in me and they're way beyond your control. You ever try to set me up again, or go anywhere near any of my children, then the next time we meet like this you'd better have a bodyguard because a weapon won't be enough."

Layton sounded like every cowboy/cop cliché he had ever seen or played. Greenbloom had heard it all before. He approved that kind of dialogue regularly. What was Layton really trying to say?

"You can't come in here and talk to me like this!" he shouted.

"There's nothing more to talk about. You want to talk some more, speak to Samantha. Ask her to tell you the truth about whose kid Mark is."

He was on the phone as soon as Layton was out the door. "What's he talking about?" he demanded of Samantha.

"Nothing, as usual," she said calmly. "I just told them you're not really Mark's father, that I made it up as a career move."

"That's not true...is it?"

"You know better than that, Charlie. Just look at Mark. Do you see any of Layton in him?"

When it came to players, she was the master. Stilts above the men who thought they could manipulate her. Layton and Charlie were maneuvering for position. She was playing to win. And to win you couldn't lose, even if it meant playing it both ways.

On the drive to Griffith Park Layton kept imagining the conversation between the pig Greenbloom and the lying Samantha. He was under no illusions that anything she said was true, though if the waters were left muddy he could accept the final outcome, which was that Mark was out from under her.

They were waiting for him in front of the museum, which was dedicated to a time when disputes like the one between him and Greenbloom would have been settled by duel. Same with him and Arno. How much more direct to take care of matters of pride and affairs of business by walking out into the street, standing ten paces apart, and opening fire. The gangs in L.A. obviously understood this. Courts and lawyers were a waste of precious time.

After three hours of such daydreaming, checking out guns and holsters, saddles and spurs, they came upon an exhibit honoring Farrell Lee and the westerns he made. Andy asked if Layton knew him and Layton said he did but that he had recently died and was buried at Forest Lawn that they would pass on the way home. Andy wanted to see where Lee was buried.

"It's just a marker in the ground," Layton said.

"Is he under there?" Andy asked.

"Most dead people are."

"I want to see it."

So they drove their two cars to the cemetery and Andy kept asking questions about being dead. He didn't quite get it. When you die you go to heaven or hell, so how could you still be under the ground? How can a soul leave a body? What was the soul? How about people who say you come back to life? What about the body snatchers? Were mummies dead? Ghosts? What did it feel like being dead? If it felt like sleeping then being dead meant you could still dream. What if you dreamed you were dead? What if everybody was already dead and was just dreaming being alive?

Thankfully it was a short drive. As they parked the cars they ran into Judith Lee who had come to talk to Farrell and was just leaving. She felt awkward with Amy there but Layton made it easy for her and Amy never suspected anything between them.

"What have you been doing since his death?" Amy asked.

"I've been busy," she answered. "Mostly about him. I'm still trying to find someone to fill the position at Washburn. I think it should be an actor but I don't know who'd want to go there."

"You mean to teach? Where's Washburn?" Amy's wheels were turning. Kansas was not bad. Only four states away from Michigan. It was flat but the earth didn't quake underneath your feet and she had not read any reports of gang violence or drive-by shootings. There was that sensational murder of a family that Truman Capote wrote about. And Dorothy got lifted by a twister into Oz. Kansas. Something to think about.

Because they drove in separate cars she had time to mull it over before discussing it with Layton. But when they got home and found the house had been ransacked any thoughts of looking for the Wizard were transferred to figuring out if they had been randomly vandalized or specifically targeted.

Drawers and closets had been emptied, furniture upturned, bags and suitcases ripped open, TVs and radios smashed, the kitchen stripped, even the refrigerator door was torn from its hinges and on the floor.

The looters had destroyed everything but apparently had taken nothing, indicating to Layton that it wasn't a robbery but a search. Which meant it had to have been Arno's men looking for the coke, which he had buried in a shoebox in the garden.

"I knew they'd be back," Amy said, unable to pull herself together enough to shield the kids from this intrusion.

Leanne stood in the living room afraid to go into her room. Andy ran into his and came out crying after he saw that his toys had been broken, his computer wrecked, even his stuffed animals unstuffed. Mark had never seen anything like this–his mother's house was so well protected the thought of being robbed never occurred to him. Shot at—another story.

But it was Layton who felt the most violated and the most guilt, for he had brought this on and now he was torn between seeking revenge or giving up altogether.

The electricity was off because someone had taken a hammer to the fuse box so any attempts to clean up would have to be put off. Amy found two flashlights and some candles and they did what they could to throw mattresses and sleeping bags on the floor so they'd be able to huddle together that night.

As Amy went through her things, Layton went out back to see if they had found what they had been searching for. It was still there. Leanne and Andy went into their rooms holding candles. Andy put his down on his small rocking chair as he began picking up his ruined toys. In the dim light his foot bumped the chair and the candle rolled down under the bed igniting the bedspread. Within seconds the bed was on fire, then the curtains. Andy was trapped in a corner and began to scream.

With Layton outside and Mark helping Amy at the other end of the house only Leanne heard him and came running. Andy was yelling and wouldn't listen to her so she jumped through the flames to get him. The fire had taken control of the room and the children were in danger but Leanne acted swiftly. She pulled his shirt over his head to protect his face and did the same for herself, grabbed him by the waist and forced him to run through the blaze. Once out Mark appeared and he ran to get Layton.

"Is there a fire extinguisher?" he shouted at Amy. She went to the kitchen and found one under the sink. "Call the fire department," he commanded as he took the device, pulled the ring pin and aimed the nozzle at Andy's bed. But the extinguisher was old and in need of a charge. Nothing came out. The fire continued to spread. Amy got the outside hose but it wasn't long enough. All they could do was get out of the house and wait for the fire trucks as the fire jumped to Leanne's room.

The fire department on Mulholland responded in time to save most of the house. But it was enough to break down any resistance Layton had. When the five of them went to spend the night at his one-bedroom apartment in Los Feliz he didn't have to think about it when Amy suggested they move. It was only a matter of where.

"Out of here," she said. "I'm no longer impressed with the business you've chosen to beat your head against until you're knocked senseless. What's here for you, Layt? Bit parts? Commercials? Television? Is that what's going to make you happy, to wind up on that rotten box?"

"I'm not exactly trained to wear a suit and be a stock broker," he said. "There's not a whole lot out there I'm qualified for."

"There are a lot of people in your position who change careers in the middle of their lives. Show business is only glamorous from the outside. You've been inside long enough to know what it's all about. And that fucking drug dealer isn't going to be satisfied until he's got what he wants and breaks your legs for putting him through the trouble."

"Time to fold the tent then?"

"Call Judith, tell her you're interested in that teaching position."

"You're ready to move to Kansas?"

"Think of it as an adventure into the unknown. We can live on a farm, raise animals, the kids'll love it."

"Just one condition, Amy."

"Don't create obstacles Layton. It's time to move on."

"That you marry me again."

Her house had been trashed and burned. Her children had survived the earthquake, a molestation, near death by fire. Leanne had saved her brother's life. She'd gained another son in Mark. Such a family needed to be together. She started to cry.

"If we do try again," she sobbed, "I want you to know it's for the children. I think they need you."

"The children will survive either way. We get back, it's because we want to, not because the children need a model family. There are no model families left, Amy. Kids grow up in broken homes and some of them actually make it. You want me back, tell me you want me—don't tell me children. They already got me."

"Do you want me?"

"What is this, Amy? You've got to make your own decision."

"Do you?"

"I wouldn't be talking like this if I didn't."

"You love me Layt?"

"If I didn't would you run me over?"

"I had to do something."

"I know."

"Leanne was so brave saving Andy."

"She's going to be fine."

"What about us?"

"There's only us, Amy."

"You really didn't do it with that Jap poet?"

"You're something, you know that?"

"The kids will be happy."

"Fuck the kids."

"C'mon, Layt, don't talk like that."

"I love them, you know that. But I want you to see me Amy. Me."

"I see you, Layt."

"And?"

"Okay already."

"You're my only, Amy. Just me and you."

15

Rest, Erection

It took a few weeks before they could move back into the canyon and during that time they made their plans to move out. There were insurance people and realtors to deal with, Arno's return-my-coke threats, Samantha's silence, Mark's adjustment to living small. Sol Gordon had advised Quickstart that he could legally hold up any projected release of *The Sand Man* until Layton was paid the money due him and Charles Greenbloom had no problem with that, though Arno wanted the movie out and would eventually capitulate. And then there was Alex Briar's paperback book, which had been rushed into print to capitalize on all the adverse publicity Layton had generated since that ungallant punch in Bel Air. *Variety* was the only paper to review it, in the same issue, ironically, as a front-page item it printed on the shoplifting arrest of Theo Soris, a third-time offense that denied him bail and guaranteed the invalid jail time. When Amy read about it she thought he was caught in the wrong act and had lucked out, but perhaps an anonymous letter might steer the police in another, more serious direction.

The inside review of *The Resurrection of Layton Cross* gave a column of attention to "not just another Hollywood biography, but the story of Lotus Land itself, where hype takes precedent over substance and careers rise and fall and rise again like pork bellies on the Commodities Market."

Had she not been so personally involved she wouldn't have read on but until she had the book in her hands the review would at least highlight what they could expect.

"This is the story of a man who fails upward: a private look at the Belushi-like fast-paced life of an actor who achieved stardom after marrying Samantha Sanders. His career began to unravel once she began to outshine him. His downward spiral touched all bases: drugs, divorce, violence, megalomania. Briar describes in tabloid detail the sordid events that were yesterday's news and the reason for this book's existence: how Cross publicly slugged Sanders, how he drove his second wife to drink, divorce, and an affair with his best friend (whom she later attempts to murder by stabbing and then running him over), and how Quickstart chief Charles Greenbloom spiked the actor's punch and turned him into a zombie, costing him his rising career. There's enough bed hopping with starlets, actresses, secretaries and wives of actors to put Cross in the same league as Charlie Sheen, Johnny Depp and Woody Allen.

"Journalist Briar portrays Cross as an avid 'stick' man; a selfish, wife-beating, publicity hound whose career sinks as an artist–from bad films to worse TV and an embarrassing stint in the theater–yet whose fame and popularity steadily rises. Not surprising in these times of the glorification of serial cannibal killers, pop singer child molesters, and Olympic hit women figure skaters.

"The tone of the book is set by the foreword, where the author describes how he came to seek the actor's permission to write his biography and was shot in the leg as a result. After reading this book, one can understand why."

Layton expressed no interest in reading the review or the book itself but Amy was so upset with the reference to her having had an affair with Theo that she went immediately to Chatterton's Bookshop on Vermont, then sat in the House of Pies to read all about Layton's resurrection and see whether it was worth suing this bastard.

But a lawsuit would bring out the truth behind the stabbing and that could only be damaging to Leanne, who had seemed to put it all behind her. And if he was so off about that, how accurate was he about all the women Layton supposedly had had?

It was a hatchet job, quoting only the bad or sensational things people said. While Perce Dent may have considered Layton "a washed-up actor who couldn't face reality," she knew he also thought Layton received a raw deal and was a far better actor than any of his later work showed. Layton had been caught in the crunch when fewer major pictures were being made and only a handful of box-office attractions were getting the parts. Dent had told her that himself.

And Sol Gordon always liked Layton. Surely his saying that "the man has had severe psychological problems" was taken out of context. What actor hasn't had severe psychological problems? But how unprofessional for a lawyer, currently his lawyer, to say something like that.

Why would Spider Ray tell this Briar that, "Layton came to me seeking representation but I didn't know how to handle him. There was a time when he could name his price, but that was years ago. Careers change rapidly in this town. Layton just made too many mistakes." Spider Ray! Who came and ate bagels and lox at their breakfast table. Right along with Dent and Gordon and Al Low.

Low, at least, didn't bad-mouth Layton. "What can I say about a man who still owes me money? The publicity he generated on his own far exceeded anything I was able to do for him. I guess we're even."

Amanda Rash remained true to her cunt self. If she felt that Layton "wasn't much of a lover," it was probably because she didn't appreciate water sports.

But what galled Amy most was Theo Soris' telling what a wonderful guy Layton really was, that no one truly understood his complex nature. Soris was quoted for pages. He had nothing but good things to say about his friend, about Amy, about the children. How dare he! The one solid endorsement from the man she still regretted not having killed.

As the time of their departure drew near Layton suggested to Mark that he call his mother to let her know. Mark felt it would be better to see her instead. Layton drove him but waited in the Jeep as Mark went inside.

At first, Samantha thought he had decided to return and looked wickedly triumphant. But her face fell when he said he was moving with Amy and Layton to Topeka. She was still scheming to get him back, now he was going thousands of miles away.

When she looked at him she noticed the change. He wasn't a boy any longer. He had a slight stubble and his eyes looked weary. He had grown up in just a few weeks and was making decisions that were affecting them both. She knew, as she looked into his pale blue eyes, that if she was to ever get him back she'd have to let him go.

"You know I love you," she whispered and he came into her arms.

"I love you too, Mom."

"You sure you know what you're doing?"

"I want to go."

"It gets cold in Kansas."

"It'll be good for me, I've never been cold."

"Why Topeka?"

"Dad's got a teaching position."

"Layton's going to teach?"

"He's an actor, he'll pretend."

They smiled. "I can't believe this is happening," she said.

"I'll write. We'll get to know each other again."

"What about that girlfriend of yours?"
"I'll write her too."

When Samantha called to inform Charlie Greenbloom of Mark's imminent departure, the potentate's reaction was to get the boy away from Layton immediately. He had been skimming through Briar's book and was livid with the way he was portrayed. But he calmed down when Samantha said she had accepted the move and thought it might be for the best. Once Mark got a taste of life in Kansas, he would better appreciate what he was giving up.

"Yeah, but what if he likes it there?"
"Come on Charlie, nobody likes Kansas."

The contract Greenbloom made with Alex Briar would keep Layton's story from ever being made into a Quickstart production. There would be no script ordered because he wanted no movie made. Let the book, like *The Sand Man* when it would finally be released, run its course and disappear like its protagonist. But with Mark in tow, Greenbloom felt obligated to make a gesture. He signed over the contract and sent it to Layton by messenger along with a note: "Heard you were getting married again, so I thought a present was in order. Take back your life and live it well. You've got some precious cargo with you." In return, Layton dug up the shoebox from the garden and mailed it to Uncle Charlie.

It was Andy who kept asking what they were going to do in Kansas and whether or not they'd pass through Dodge City. When Layton said he could join a 4-H club and raise prize pigs, Andy asked him what the four H's stood for?

"Health, happiness, Hanukkah, and hot dogs," Layton said.

There was one route out of the city, the Santa Monica Freeway to the 15 to Barstow, and then they had to decide which way they wanted to go: west on 40 through Flagstaff, Albuquerque, Amarillo to Oklahoma City and then north into Kansas or continue on 15 through Las Vegas, up into Utah to 70 and then west through Grand Junction and Denver. The southwest seemed more appealing, especially as it avoided the circus that was Las Vegas, but at the Arizona border at Needles, between the Sacramento and Mohave mountains, they came upon a Mexican traveling troupe called Circo Cortez, consisting of three small animal acts (dogs, ponies, and parrots), four trapeze artists who were also the clowns, a juggler, a contortionist, and a Zacchini cannon. It was the cannon outside the tricolor tent that caught Layton's eye. The children were all for stopping. Only Amy had her doubts. "Isn't that what you were shot out of?" she wondered.

"Looks just like it."

"I want to see a human cannonball!" Andy shouted.

They parked the van and walked over to the tent. A man named Enrique Cortez said they were in time for the afternoon show but when Andy asked about the cannon he told them that unfortunately it wouldn't be used because the contortionist twisted his ankle and no one else was willing to get into it.

"That's a Zacchini isn't it?" Layton asked.

Oh yes, Cortez said. "You know about this?"

"Don't even think about it," Amy warned.

"My dad's done it," Andy said.

"You are a circus man?" Cortez asked.

"It was for charity," Layton said. "But yes, I've been a circus man all my life."

Leanne asked him what he was talking about. Layton looked at her and said something about being a trained monkey but she didn't get it.

"Can he do it?" Andy asked.

"The cannon?" Cortez said. "Oh no, you have to know what you are doing."

The taped circus music blasting out of two speakers began to attract an audience and Layton paid for four tickets to see the performers. It was a good way to leave California he thought. Watching a dog-and-pony show right on the border.

But once inside the tent he could hear the disappointment of other children when it was announced that there would be no cannon shot that afternoon. The cannon was always the big attraction and if anyone wanted to come back another day they would refund their money. But Circo Cortez would only be in Needles for four other performances and there was no guarantee that the contortionist's ankle would heal in time.

"I'll be right back," Layton said.

"Layt, don't," Amy said.

"What? Just seeing if there's any cotton candy, some caramel popcorn..." and whether Enrique could get him a protective mask and a helmet that fit.

It was crazy, of course, but it had also been exhilarating the first time. He had made just one mistake, easily correctable, the half-somersault into the net. The force of the piston slingshotting him out of the chamber would momentarily shut down his brain but the recovery was quick and it was a chance to redeem himself, to get it right, without the added pressure of a television camera or media publicity. That was all behind him now. They were in Needles headed for Kansas. No more celebrity bullshit, a scholar's life and a house in the suburbs was waiting for him out there in the great heartland, right smack in the middle of America. But this was irresistible. Had it not been a Zacchini he'd never have gone back to convince Cortez that his show must not only go on, but not disappoint. He would go into the cannon, sign whatever insurance waivers, put smiles on the faces of the children.

"Don't worry," he assured the circus owner, "I know what I'm doing. Just make sure it's facing east."

And with much static fanfare the cannon was driven into the arena as the 21 x 50 foot net was set up 140 feet away. "Ladies and gentlemen," the announcement came, "it is with great pleasure that we can bring you the human cannonball after all." Andy and Leanne turned their heads hoping that Layton would get back in time to see it but

Amy knew he wouldn't be sitting with them. She felt a large hollowness in the pit of her stomach when she saw the 6'2" man with the helmet on his head raise his hands to the sparse crowd as they applauded his entry into the mouth of the cannon. There were no drummers to send him off with a proper drum roll, but a pony whinnied and a dog barked as the small bomb exploded at the rear of the cannon and the compression pump forced air into the chamber which then drove the piston and sent Layton Cross hurdling through the air traversing the border out of California.

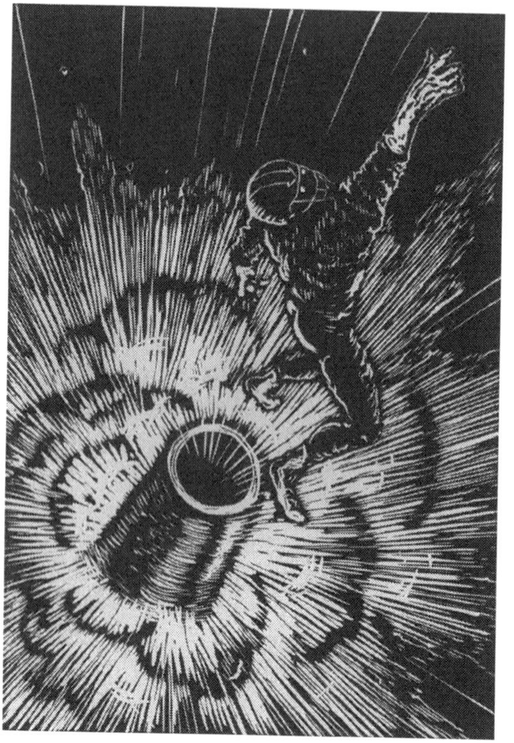

Lawrence Grobel (www.lawrencegrobel.com) is a novelist, journalist, biographer, poet and teacher. Four of his 22 books have been singled out as Best Books of the Year by *Publisher's Weekly* and many have appeared on Best Seller lists. He is the recipient of a National Endowment for the Arts Fellowship for his fiction. PEN gave his *Conversations with Capote* a Special Achievement Award. The French Society of Film Critics awarded his *Al Pacino* their Prix Litteraire as the Best International Book of 2008. His *The Art of the Interview* is used as a text in many journalism schools. *Writer's Digest* called him "a legend among journalists." He has written for dozens of magazines and has been a Contributing Editor for *Playboy, Movieline, World (*New Zealand), and *Trendy* (Poland). He served in the Peace Corps, teaching at the Ghana Institute of Journalism; created the M.F.A. in Professional Writing for Antioch University; and taught in the English Department at UCLA for ten years. He has appeared on CNN, *The Today Show, Good Morning America, The Charlie Rose Show* and in two documentaries, *Salinger* and Al Pacino's *Wilde Salome*. He is married to the artist Hiromi Oda and they have two daughters. His books are available on Amazon.com and other retailers.

Begin Again Finnegan

■ ■ ■

Lawrence Grobel
An excerpt

1

When Devin Hunter woke up Thursday morning he had no idea that he wouldn't go back to sleep until Friday night and that over the next 20 hours he would be confronted with two life-altering decisions.

He was doing a piece on singer Amanda Donald, and as he prepared for a meeting with her personal manager, Hayden Channing, he turned on NPR. He had a moment of amused irony when the lead story was about the actor who had recently told him for *Spotlight* magazine that God was a fraud and a prop for feeble-minded people. Now, having been fired from his popular evening sitcom, the actor had decided to run for governor of California.

Though he didn't have much time, Hunter couldn't help himself. He turned on his laptop, opened a new document, and quickly wrote:

I have a confession to make. For the last two decades I have earned my living writing about celebrities. Much like actors who feel somehow diminished by their profession, as if being highly paid to play make-believe is not quite like becoming a doctor or scientist or tree surgeon, celebrity journalists aren't quite putting their lives on the line as reporters do who cover wars, riots and natural disasters. Sometimes, though, a celebrity encounter can be life threatening. You don't want to piss off a drug-snorting or booze imbibing celebrity by asking questions too close to the bone, because in their drug-induced or alcoholic rage they might forget that they're fair game when they signed up for being in the public eye and it can result in bodily or psychological harm. Sometimes a celebrity forgets what he says as he's being recorded; sometimes a celebrity is too wasted to remember; sometimes a celebrity needs to be protected from himself. And sometimes a journalist makes the mistake of being seduced into thinking he has found a friend in the celebrity he is covering. When a certain celebrated actor got fired from his hugely popular sitcom, the reason given was something he had said to me, which appeared in print because neither of us thought it would cause such outrage and commotion. He took the high road, owning the remark and throwing his fedora in the ring to become the next governor of the great and singular state of California. If it weren't for George Murphy, Shirley Temple Black, Ronald Reagan, and Arnold Schwarzenegger, this might seem an absurd act of supreme egotism. But his remark, which could lead to his actually becoming governor, and, who knows, a future president, is something he didn't quite say. It was something I put together from one rambling paragraph, which I smoothed over and wrote as one sentence because his half-sentences, full of stuttered starts and stops, made little sense. He could just as easily have meant to say that God is a needed crutch who protected the weak, or that God is all-knowing and all-loving who embraces those who shun him. What our actor really said was "God, how did we get onto this topic? I feel so feeble-minded right now. It's like I need a prop—a crutch or a hydraulic jack–to lift me to a different height. I feel like such a fraud. God! Why have you forsaken me? I can't get my mind around any of this. People out there, can you dig it?" I tried to make sense of this nonsense. He was trying to answer a question I asked about God. Did he believe in God? I took the words "prop" and "fraud" and "feeble-minded" and "people" and concocted a sentence that at least gave our lazy-minded actor an opinion: "God is a fraud and a prop for feeble-minded people." A silly celebrity remark for a silly celebrity magazine. Only the results are not so silly. He lost his job because of it (and he hasn't even denied saying it, which just proves the jumbled state of his mind when we spoke). And now he might win a job where we would have to take such a "feeble-mind" seriously. And it's all my fault.

Funny stuff, Hunter thought, wondering if *The Onion* might be interested. He filed this quickie in one of his Story folders and closed his laptop. Satire appealed to him, and this was clearly a satirical opportunity. He wouldn't be surprised, if it got into print, that the actor would say that's what happened. He understood actors and knew this one was just having his Donald Trump moment. He would eventually come down off his high, apologize, and be thankful his show's ratings would allow him back into the fold. As Devin drove down his canyon his thoughts turned to where he was going. The NPR story reminded him of his own cardinal rule when meeting someone for the first time: Don't go in with preconceived expectations. Whoever you thought you were going to meet rarely turned out to be the one you did.

Hayden Channing was no exception.

Channing lived two miles above the Sunset Strip in a nine bedroom, seven bath, 18,000 square foot Gehry-styled modern house that he bought for $8.5 million in 1996. His backyard, with its oval swimming pool, occupied two prime real estate acres. When the butler let him in, Hunter made quick note of the paintings in the foyer and living room (a Matisse, a Picasso, a Klimt, a Chagall, and a Dali) and the Tiffany lamps on brass serpent bases. Left alone to browse the leather-bound books and finger the fabric covering the three couches and two massive chairs that might double as love seats, Hunter noticed a thin man who resembled a clean-shaven Manny Pacquiao in his underwear jumping rope on the patio. Thinking he was Channing's personal trainer, he went outside to make small talk and try to sniff out something about this suddenly intriguing man.

"I'm Hayden," the bare-chested rope jumper said. "Who are you?"

"Devin Hunter. We had an appointment to talk about Amanda for an article I'm writing."

"Amanda's terrific. She's like my best friend, and I'm her *manager*. She said she liked you."

"I'm glad to hear. I like her."

"She also said you're good friends with Adrian Kiel."

"We talked about him. She's a fan."

"How'd you become friends? How close are you? Gertrude and Alice close? Watson and Holmes? Shrek and Donkey?"

Devin wasn't expecting Channing to turn the tables and interview him. They hadn't even shook hands. But Channing was just jumping through Devin's universal rule to expect the unexpected. Devin thought of Oprah Winfrey when she put to rest the innuendos that her friendship with Gayle King was not sexual, telling Barbara Walters that King was "the mother I never had...The sister everybody would want...The friend that everybody deserves." That's how Devin felt about Kiel. The actor was seven years older and not a father figure, though he definitely was the brother he never had. As for the friend everybody deserved, that would depend on whether everybody deserved at least one high maintenance friendship. Something a guy like Hayden Channing would understand.

"Close," Devin said.

"Could you introduce me?" Channing asked.

The request made Devin uncomfortable. People were often trying to get to Kiel through him, but he always resisted. Channing, though, was in the business and could certainly get to anyone he wanted on his own. "He's shy," Devin said. "And he's suspicious of people who want to meet him."

"I can understand that," Channing said. "That's why I asked."

"I'll mention you to him, see what he says."

"No, don't bother," Channing said, sensing Devin's reluctance. "I'll get Dick Sinata to make the introductions." Sinata was Adrian's agent.

"Do you have a project for him?" Devin wondered.

"Not a project, a projection. I don't think he's being properly managed. Some of the choices he's made aren't up to his abilities. He's a great actor but he's not making great pictures lately. Look at what he did his first ten years and look at what he's done since. It doesn't make sense. Don Queeq's not the right guy for him."

"He's been with Queeq for years," Devin said. "And he's still winning awards." He didn't think it necessary to remind Channing of Kiel's two Oscars, three Tonys, and four Golden Globes.

"Because of his earlier work. They're awarding him for that, not for now. You know that."

"He says the scripts aren't as good as they used to be."

"Bullshit. There're plenty of good scripts out there, he's just not seeing them."

"Is that his manager's fault or his agent's?"

"Both. You're right, I shouldn't go to Dick."

"I didn't say that."

"Listen," Channing said, perking up, "how'd you like to work for me?"

"Excuse me?"

"Seriously. I'm always being asked to start a film division in my company—how'd you like to head it up? You're well read; you know how to deal with actors. You find the right projects, we'll produce them."

"Are you always this spontaneous?" This was an offer so out of left field that Devin didn't know what else to say. He wasn't looking for a job, especially one where he would have to answer to a mercurial boss like Channing. He liked his independence.

"I am," Channing said. "I'm making you a big offer here. I manage the careers of some of the biggest people in the music industry; some of them have successfully crossed over into theater and films—why shouldn't we produce them as well?"

"You probably should," Devin said. "It's just that I'm pretty set in my ways. I like the life I have."

"How much you make a year?" Channing asked. "Seventy-five? A hundred? Not much more than that, right?"

"You're in the ballpark," Devin said.

"You know how much you could make working for me? I'll start you at twice what you made last year and if you're still with me two years from now, I'll double that."

"And for this you'd like an introduction to Adrian Kiel?"

"No, he has nothing to do with what I'm offering. If we land Kiel, you'll get to find him projects worthy of his talent. Sounds like a win-win to me. You'd be helping your friend and earning enough to live a different lifestyle."

Devin had his doubts. It was pretty clear to him that Kiel was the real power behind this offer. It was yet another example of how that relationship opened a lot of doors that would otherwise be closed.

"It's flattering," Devin said, "but it's not for me."

"Why don't you think about it? You married?"

"I am."

"Talk it over with your wife. See what she thinks."

"I'll think about it," Devin said. "But I'm also thinking about Amanda Donald, my reason for being here. I'm on deadline and we haven't even discussed her."

"What's there to say? She's the best. She's got a movie coming out; she'll probably win a Golden Globe and maybe an Oscar for her song. And if you come on board you'll get to know her from a whole new perspective. You won't be outside looking in; you'll be on the inside."

On his drive back to his home in the Hollywood Hills, Devin tried to assess what had just happened. He was 45 years old, a freelance writer, easy going, untroubled, not overly ambitious, with one unusual celebrity friend. And because of that friend he was being offered a high-paying, high-powered, undoubtedly demanding job that would involve signing a contract, finding a lawyer, and working out of an office instead of his home. If he was twenty years younger he might have been tempted.

"You're kidding," his wife Jenna said when he told her about it. "How the hell can he make you such an offer when he doesn't even know you? He must be crazy."

"Like a fox," Devin said. "You should see how he lives. He didn't get where he is making bad decisions. He's just a quick study. And he's pretty savvy—I would be a good producer."

"Based on what? Your asking people in the business how they work? What do you know about producing? You're a writer."

"What do you think producers do? They put together talent with material. What do I do? I turn talent into material."

"Hey, I'm not going to stop you. We could use the money."

"That's OK, I'm not looking to change jobs. I like what I do."

Around midnight, Jenna drifted to sleep wondering if introducing business into Devin's friendship with Adrian kept him from seriously considering Hayden Channing's offer. She had been skeptical of their relationship in the beginning, but over the years she learned that Kiel was not a threat and so accepted the fact that her husband would have to be shared with a movie star. Devin adjusted his reading light so as not to disturb Jenna as he lost himself in a biography about Samuel Beckett, wondering if Beckett's early life, when he worked as an assistant to James Joyce in Paris, might make an interesting movie.

Beckett was 24 and Joyce's daughter, Lucia, was 23. She had fallen in love with the young Irish apprentice, making his work with the man he idolized awkward and, in the end, impossible. Lucia suffered from delusions and would eventually be treated at mental clinics in three countries. Her father had a hard time coming to grips with his daughter's illness and would wordplay her name as the heroine of *Finnegans Wake*, an incomprehensible novel that occupied the last two decades of his life. Beckett would go on to write experimental works of his own, leading to his being distinguished by the Swedish Academy in 1969 with their annual literary prize, saying that his new form of writing elevated the "destitution of modern man." James Joyce was never so richly awarded by any academy for the books he wrote but was, nonetheless, recognized by his former apprentice as the greatest Irish writer of them all. It was a story, Devin mused, that read like a fable. Just the kind of esoteric project that would keep Hayden Channing from doubling his salary if he decided to take that road not taken. But then the phone rang, at ten past two a.m., and Hayden Channing disappeared from his thoughts.

"I need to see you," Adrian Kiel said with a seriousness that bordered on melodramatic.

If one definition of a friend is someone you can call in the middle of the night, then this call came as no surprise to Devin who, speaking low so as not to wake Jenna, answered, "I'll come tomorrow, what time?"

"Not tomorrow, now. I'll come to you."

"You've got a driver working this late?"

"I'll drive myself."

"Something's happened."

Adrian hesitated. He didn't want to say anything more over the phone.

Theirs was an unusual, and to many an unlikely, friendship. Some would call it a friendship of convenience; others a friendship based on false assumptions. It was convenient for a movie star to have a working journalist in his corner. It was Hunter's assumption that when he saved Adrian Kiel from bodily harm during their first cable TV interview twenty years ago that Kiel would forever be in his debt. Kiel was sitting in the backyard of a Brentwood estate waiting for Hunter to resume their interview when the steel pole of the giant sunscreen began to fall in the direction of the actor's head. Hunter leaped forward, breaking his attached microphone, to catch the pole before it did its damage as Kiel crouched down, thinking the journalist had lost his mind and was about to attack him, and punched Hunter in the solar plexus. Miraculously Hunter managed to maintain his balance long enough to grab the pole just inches above Kiel's noggin, and though he could barely breathe as he accepted the crew's applause with reserve, it only further impressed the embarrassed star, who cautiously made him his friend-for-life.

Devin got dressed, boiled some water, and wondered what kind of emergency would bring Adrian Kiel to his door a few hours past midnight. Must be he finally hit a breaking point with Abby. He probably picked up one of the babies wrong. Or he didn't put them down to sleep when she wanted them down. She kicked him out. He didn't want to sneak into a hotel or drive up to the Santa Barbara house.

The dog, Brook, heard the car pull into the driveway and started to bark. Devin went outside to see his friend looking more disheveled than usual as he stepped out of the Range Rover.

"I'm sorry to do this to you," Kiel said before they walked into the house. His skin seemed jaundiced, his face swollen, his hair unkempt. This was what a sullen aging movie star looked like at 2:30 in the morning

"Do what? You know you can always come here."

"This time it's bad."

"She kicked you out?"

"You got coffee?"

"The water's boiled."

"Thanks. Jenna here?"

"Sleeping."

"I'm gonna need a favor. It's a big one."

"You don't have to ask."

They went to the kitchen. Devin poured the water through a filter. As the fresh coffee dripped into the cup, Adrian looked at Devin and said, "I killed her."

Devin didn't respond. He stared at Adrian to see if he was trying out a new character on him. But he could see in Kiel's eyes that he wasn't exaggerating for effect, he wasn't rehearsing for a role.

"It was an accident. She came at me, screaming the way she does, just that craziness."

"Oh God," Devin murmured. "Jesus."

"It was about the twins, but it was more than that. I turned my back on her; I tried to control my temper. The nannies were gone."

"Where are the kids now?"

"I left them there. I didn't know what to do. I was going to call Iona."

"You can't leave them alone."

"They usually sleep through the night. I figure we could talk for a while, then I'll go back before the nannies come."

"We've got to go there now, Adrian. What if they're awake? What if they're crying? Is Abby still there?"

"I didn't move her. She's in the kitchen. I slapped her. She fell backwards, hit her head on the counter."

"Are you sure she's dead? Not just unconscious?"

"She wasn't breathing."

"Still, you can't be sure."

"She's dead."

"You're in shock."

"I need to say I wasn't there. If I was here and you were interviewing me, then someone else did it. Or she fell."

What was Adrian saying? Was this for real? Lord knows, Adrian was capable of mind games, even at two o'clock in the morning. Was he testing just how far he could bend their relationship without breaking it? Devin's mind began to whirl with interlocking possibilities, aware that he faced, in this instant, one of those rare moments where his life—not just Adrian's—was balanced on a fulcrum. If Adrian had killed Abby then, accident or not, he was pulling Devin into a black hole that neither would survive unscathed. How much of Devin's love for Adrian was based on the real person and not just the star who had taken him in? And yet…he was flattered—flattered that one of the world's biggest stars was in his kitchen, asking him, Devin Hunter, to be an alibi for the most important moment of Kiel's life. It was twisted, but Devin was almost grateful. Was he up for it? It was such an audacious and unfair request.

Other Books By Lawrence Grobel

BEGIN AGAIN FINNEGAN (a novel)
How far would you go to help your best friend? That's the question journalist Devin Hunter faces when movie star Adrian Kiel asks him to be his alibi to cover a possible murder. Devin's decision starts a chain of events that spiral out of control as he tries to hold the pieces of his life together. This is a story about secret lives, psychiatric wards, celebrity "justice," buccal onanism, blackmail, betrayal and a modern day take on James Joyce in exile; but mostly it's about relationships and their consequences. It explores the loyalty of a friendship that increasingly appears one-sided and slowly implodes. The action is fast paced, with twists to the plot at every corner. The cast of characters runs the gamut of fawning fans to million-dollar lawyers and crooked accountants. It's set in Hollywood, and peels back the culture of celebrity to reveal the snake pit underneath.

THE BLACK EYES OF AKBAH (a novella)
After leaving Ghana, where they served for two years in the Peace Corps, Eric and Anika agree to travel together

to Kenya and India to get to know each other better and see if they want to spend the rest of their lives together. They agree to work their way across the Indian Ocean on a cargo ship ominously called The Black Eyes of Akbah. The crew is a melting pot of all the indigenous peoples of the region. They leave Mombasa for Mumbai, but the chilling terror that happens along the way will change the way they see each other and the world they thought they knew. Oliver Stone compared this story to a cross between *The African Queen* and *Midnight Express*.

COMMANDO EX (a novella)

Commando Ex is a wild Australian hedonist racing across Africa on his Motoguzzi motorcycle, chasing thrills and adventure, living life to the max and flaunting what you can be if you're absolutely free. "He's the cream of the freedom crop...nerve tingling the moments and bojangling experiences." This is nothing like any of Grobel's other books. It's wordplay on steroids. It's an uninhibited, uniquely styled story of a never lonely, one–and–only, who bites and grabs everything that comes his way. "So keep up, speed along, trip flip and skip through the one life worth living, the fully explored, high geared unfeared not scared life of the Commando. Sight...on!"

THE HUSTONS

When John Huston died at 81 on August 28, 1987, America lost a towering figure in movie history. The director of such classic films as *The Treasure of the Sierra Madre*, *The*

African Queen, The Maltese Falcon, Prizzi's Honor, and *The Dead*, John Huston evoked passionate responses from everyone he encountered. He was at the center of a dynasty, with three generations of Oscar winners (Walter, John and Anjelica). Now the complete story of this remarkable family is told in *The Hustons*. The book chronicles the family's history—from Walter's days on the vaudeville circuit and his later fame on Broadway, through John's meteoric rise, to Anjelica's and Danny's emergence as formidable actors in film today. Grobel interviewed John Huston for over 100 hours and conducted 200 interviews with John's four children, three of his five wives, many of his mistresses, producers, writers, technicians, and a number of celebrities who rarely grant interviews.

CONVERSATIONS WITH CAPOTE

Six months after Truman Capote died in 1984, *Conversations with Capote* was published and reached the top of best-seller lists in both New York and San Francisco. *The Philadelphia Inquirer* called it "A gossip's delight...full of scandalous comments about the rich and the famous." *Parade* called it "An engrossing read. Bitchy, high-camp opinions...from a tiny terror who wore brass knuckles on his tongue." *People* found it "Juicy stuff... provocative and entertaining...vintage Capote." Grobel talked to Capote over a period of two years and it remains an essential part of the Capote canon.

CONVERSATIONS WITH BRANDO

Playboy named Lawrence Grobel "The Interviewer's Interviewer" for his uncanny ability to get America's greatest and most reclusive actor, Marlon Brando, to speak openly for the first time. When Grobel expanded the interview into a book, *American Cinematographer* said it "penetrates the complex nature of a very private man, probing his feelings on women and sex, Native Americans, corporate America and the FBI." James A. Michener thought it "explained Brando accurately: the torment, the arrogance—almost willed towards self-destruction—but above all, the soaring talent."

CONVERSATIONS WITH MICHENER

After successfully publishing his book-length interviews with Truman Capote and Marlon Brando, Grobel approached author James A. Michener as his next subject, and wound up taping their discussions over a 17 year period, right up until the last week of Michener's life. The result is the most comprehensive of all Grobel's "Conversation" books. Michener, who didn't start writing novels until he was 40, was a true citizen of the world. He foresaw the future of countries as diverse as Afghanistan, Poland, Japan, Spain, Hungary, Mexico, Israel, and the U.S. His books—like *Hawaii, The Source, Iberia, Sayonara,* and *Tales of the South Pacific*—sold millions of copies and many were made into films or TV miniseries. *Conversations with Michener* is as relevant today as it was prescient when it first appeared in 1999.

CONVERSATIONS WITH AVA GARDNER

These conversations with the femme fatale of *The Killers, Mogambo, The Barefoot Contessa, Show Boat*, and *Night of the Iguana*, and one of the world's great beauties, are startlingly candid. Two years before she died, Ava Gardner asked Lawrence Grobel to work with her on her memoir. The reclusive actress opened up about her three volatile marriages to Mickey Rooney, Artie Shaw and Frank Sinatra. She tells about Howard Hughes' 15-year pursuit of her. She reveals how George C. Scott was so crazily in love with her that he beat her up on three occasions and once stuck a broken bottle in her face. She talks about her tomboy childhood as a tobacco farmer's daughter in North Carolina. She goes into detail about how she was "discovered" and became a contract player at MGM; her friendships with Hemingway, Dominguin, and Brando; and of working with her favorite director, John Huston. She admits to her struggles with alcohol. And she speaks intimately about the debilitating stroke she suffered toward the end of her life.

AL PACINO in Conversation with Lawrence Grobel

For more than a quarter century, Al Pacino has spoken freely and deeply with Lawrence Grobel on subjects as diverse as childhood, acting, and fatherhood.

Here are the complete conversations and shared observations between the actor and the writer; the result is an intimate and revealing look at one of the most accomplished, and private, artists in the world, as Grobel

Other Books

and Pacino leave few stones unturned. *Al Pacino* is an intensely personal window into the life of an artist concerned more with the process of his art than with the fruits of his labor—a creative genius at the peak of his artistic powers who, after all these years, still longs to grow and learn more about his craft.

"I WANT YOU IN MY MOVIE!"
My Acting Debut & Other Misadventures Filming Al Pacino's *Wilde Salome*

"Why *am* I doing this?" Al Pacino wondered a year into his personal movie about his obsession with *Salome*, Oscar Wilde's lyrical play, written in 1891. "No one saw *Looking for Richard*, who's going to want to see something about Oscar Wilde?"

In *"I Want You in My Movie!"* Grobel found the answer to that question and more when he joined the crew and followed the creative process of filmmaking from inception to completion. His meticulous journal is as close to being there as a reader can ever hope to get. This intimate peek behind the curtain, documenting the hopes, dreams, frustrations and complexities of Pacino and all the people who come in and out of his life, is a fitting sequel to Grobel's internationally acclaimed *AL PACINO in Conversation with Lawrence Grobel*, which was named the Best International Book of the Year by the Society of French Film Critics. *"I Want You in My Movie!"* takes you deeper into the mind and process of Al Pacino. Including exclusive photos Grobel took on the set and behind the scenes, it's a movie buff's delight, warts and all.

THE ART OF THE INTERVIEW: Lessons from a Master of the Craft

In *The Art of the Interview*, Grobel reveals the most memorable stories from his career, along with examples of the most candid moments from his long list of famous interviewees, from Oscar-winning actors and Nobel laureates to Pulitzer Prize-winning writers and sports figures. Taking us step-by-step through the interview process, from research and question writing to final editing, *The Art of the Interview* is a treat for journalists and culture vultures alike.

SIGNING IN: 50 Celebrity Profiles

From 2005—2010 Lawrence Grobel wrote over 50 magazine articles about his in-depth encounters with some of the most famous people in the world. Each piece had only one caveat: to include at least a paragraph about something the celebrity had signed. So Grobel built each portrait around a signed photo, poster, drawing, personal letter, or book inscription, many of which are shown in this engaging book. Among the entertainers and writers included are Barbra Streisand, Marlon Brando, Al Pacino, Farrah Fawcett, Henry Fonda, Madonna, Angelina Jolie, Robin Williams, Steve Martin, Luciano Pavarotti, Anthony Kiedis, Truman Capote, Monica Lewinsky, Norman Mailer, Elmore Leonard, and Saul Bellow.

Other Books

ICONS

When the editors of *Trendy* magazine in Poland asked celebrated journalist Lawrence Grobel to write detailed cover stories about some of the Hollywood icons he's known and written about over the years, Grobel took the opportunity to profile fifteen internationally beloved stars: Jack Nicholson, Angelina Jolie, Halle Berry, Anthony Hopkins, Kim Basinger, Anthony Kiedis, Jodie Foster, Nicole Kidman, Meryl Streep, Gwyneth Paltrow, Cameron Diaz, Tom Waits, Penelope Cruz, Sharon Stone, and Robert De Niro. Each profile is illustrated with the hip *Trendy* cover.

YOU SHOW ME YOURS: A Memoir

Lawrence Grobel's energetic memoir begins with him growing up on the streets of Brooklyn, where he was nearly kidnapped as an infant, and the suburbs of Long Island, where his sex education began at a very early age. By the age of 15, he was competing with his best friend over a modern day Lolita. In 1967 he marched with Dr. King in Mississippi under a hail of bullets, and came of age under the guidance of an enlightened Mexican Don Juan. After graduating from UCLA, he joined the Peace Corps, which afforded him the chance to communicate with a fetish high priestess in Ghana, pygmies in Uganda, and stoned-out hippies on the island of Lamu. In the '70s he became a New Journalist, covering stories like the Demolition Derby, Transcendental Meditation, Sky Diving, Sailplane Gliding, Archery, Karate and Performance Art.

When he left New York for California he turned his skills to celebrity interviews.

It's a journey through the Looking Glass of American Culture from the post-War '50s, the sexually liberated '60s, the Civil Rights movement, and the "Me Decade."

MADONNA PAINTS A MUSTACHE & Other Close Encounters

"Elliott Gould said to Elvis Presley/'I may be crazy, but/ What's that gun doing/ Sitting on your hip?'"

For 40 years Lawrence Grobel has interviewed some of the world's most talented and famous people and after each encounter he wrote a short poem crystallizing his insights and impressions. Tart, funny, sensitive, always succinct and sometimes downright scandalous, he filed them away. Until now. In this anthology of more than 150 poems, this jaunty dish on the rich and famous targets all these topics with attitude: Relationships, Mysticism, Paranoia, Bad Behavior, Race, Sex, Religion, and Gambling. These titles give a clue as to content: Madonna Paints a Mustache; James Franco was Pretty Crank-O; Dolly Parton at 3 A.M.; Drew Barrymore Keeps Her First Gray Hair; Saul Bellow Quite a Fellow; I'd Like to Say I Had a Ball Jake Gyllenhaal; Penelope Cruz Nothing to Lose; Ashley Judd Spits Tobacco; Nicole Kidman Brought Sushi; Bud Cort's His Harold Past; Zsa Zsa Ain't So Ga-Ga; Bruce Springsteen Gets Rejected; When Christian Slater Got Out of Jail; 14 Carat Goldie; I Kissed Farrah Fawcett; I'd Rather Be Alone, Sharon Stone.

Other Books

ABOVE THE LINE: Conversations About the Movies
Above the Line is a dazzling gathering of insights and anecdotes from all corners of the film industry—interviews that reveal the skills, intelligence, experiences, and emotions of eleven key players who produce, write, direct, act in, and review the movies: Oliver Stone, Anthony Hopkins, Jodie Foster, Robert Evans, Lily Tomlin, Jean-Claude Van Damme, Harrison Ford, Robert Towne, Sharon Stone, and Siskel and Ebert. Witty, scathing, gossipy, generous, the interviewees show just what make the movies work from "above the line"—from the perspective of those whose names go above the title. Each of these gifted individuals represents a piece of the puzzle that gives rise to some of the best in moviemaking today.

ENDANGERED SPECIES: Writers Talk about Their Craft, Their Visions, Their Lives
Norman Mailer once told Lawrence Grobel that writers may be an endangered species. And Saul Bellow told him, "The country has changed so, that what I do no longer signifies anything, as it did when I was young." But to judge from this collection, writers and writing aren't done for quite yet. Sometimes serious, sometimes funny, sometimes caustic, always passionate, the twelve writers in *Endangered Species* (Bellow, Mailer, Ray Bradbury, J.P. Donleavy, James Ellroy, Allen Ginsberg, Andrew Greeley, Alex Haley, Joseph Heller, Elmore Leonard, Joyce Carol Oates, and Neil Simon) memorably state their case for what they do and how they do it. And they even offer an

opinion or two about other writers and about the entire publishing food chain: from agents to publishers to booksellers to critics to readers.

CONVERSATIONS WITH ROBERT EVANS

"I don't want to have a slow death," Robert Evans told Lawrence Grobel. "That's my fear. I've had a gun put in my mouth, a gun put at my temple. I've had a gun put on me five different times to talk, and not once have I ever talked." But talk is what Evans does in his conversations with Grobel. As the head of Paramount Studios in the 1970s Evans produced some of the most iconic movies of that era, including *Love Story, The Odd Couple, Paper Moon, True Grit, Catch 22, Chinatown,* and *The Godfather*. But his life was much more than that of a movie producer and this book is eye-opening in its honesty and its finger-pointing.

CLIMBING HIGHER

A New York Times Bestseller, *Climbing Higher* is the story of Montel Williams' life and personal struggles with MS. In 1999, after almost 20 years of mysterious symptoms that he tried to ignore, Montel Williams, a decorated former naval intelligence officer and Emmy Award-winning talk show host, was finally diagnosed with multiple sclerosis. Like others suffering from the devastating and often disabling disease, which attacks the central nervous system, Montel was struck with denial, fear, depression, and anger. Yet somehow he emerged with a fierce determination not to be beaten down by MS, and to live the most vital and productive life possible while becoming a dedicated spokesperson and fundraiser for the disease. *Climbing Higher* is a penetrating and insightful look at a remarkable man, his extraordinary career, and the tumultuous life that graced him with hard-won courage and wisdom. In addition, with the help of a team of leading doctors, *Climbing Higher* offers up-to-the-minute information on new MS research and invaluable guidance for managing MS.

MARILYN & ME
In 1960 and 1962 Lawrence Schiller was asked by *Paris Match* and *Life* magazines to photograph Marilyn Monroe on the set of *Let's Make Love* and *Something's Got to Give*, which was never completed because of her controversial death. Schiller had befriended Monroe and he asked Lawrence Grobel to help him shape the story of that friendship into this memoir. It's a new addition to the Monroe saga from the perspective of an impressionistic young photographer and the iconic sex symbol.

YOGA? NO! SHMOGA!
Google "Yoga" and 103,000,000 items come up. One hundred and three *million*! Yet for everyone who practices yoga, there are dozens of others who just sit and watch. *Yoga? No! Shmoga!* is for those who sit and watch, as well as for those who actually do yoga and have a sense of humor. Best-selling author Lawrence Grobel has ventured into satire with this look at the lighter side of yoga.

Shmoga is the Lazy Man's Way to Inner Peace. It's like a non-diet book for ice cream lovers. In 43 short chapters it pokes fun at sports, religion, exercise, Wall Street, art, entertainment, and people looking for an excuse to not do anything more than lift a finger.